Pressing Matters

a novel by

Larry M. Tobin
www.larrymtobin.com

This novel is a work of fiction. Names, characters, places and incidents are either the product of the author's imagination or are used fictitiously. Any resemblance to actual events, locales or persons, living or dead, is entirely coincidental.

Cover design by Jamie Baumann

ISBN: 978-0-9795394-2-8

Father's Press
Lee's Summit, MO
(816) 600-6288
www.fatherspress.com

To Kathy – my inspiration, my best friend and the love of my life....

1

"Are you sure you're okay with this?" Press asked her as he drove them east toward the reservoir in the late summer heat. The sun was high, bright as the corn ripening in the passing fields. Three roses, wrapped lightly in thin green paper, rested on the seat next to Abby.

"I have to do it sometime," she replied as she cast an expressionless glance past him to the small embankment on the other side of the county highway. She had already cried three times long and hard this morning. The last was in the car as they began the drive. Abby's eyes rimmed red and her face lacked color.

Press eased the car to a stop at the side of the road. The rubber burns still had not been weathered from the pavement. After a long moment of silence, she gulped an extra breath of muggy air, picked up the flowers and opened the car door.

Press popped the release to open the trunk and got out. As Abby waited at the edge of the blacktop, he removed three white crosses and a hammer from the rear of the Buick. Slowly, the couple crossed the highway and walked down into the shallow ditch and up the other side. Dozens of bouquets of flowers, in as many varieties, lay scattered in the browning grass and weeds. Some of the bundles were flower shop bought; others freshly cut home garden contributions, as the dead teenagers' friends and families continued their remembrances.

Picking a spot among the scattering of flowers, Press laid two of the crosses down and began hammering the third into the dry ground.

"Are you sure we can do this?" Abby wondered through a hard snuffle. Already a trickle had begun to maneuver down each cheek.

"I'd like to see someone try to stop me," he replied grimly.

When he was finished with the three markers, Abby laid a single rose beneath each one and stepped back. In less than a moment she was trembling until hard sobs began to rack her body.

"Ouwaaaah, it hurts so much," she cried, throwing herself into Press' arms.

"It's so senseless...so stupid! How could it happen like this?" She pounded her fists on her husband's shoulders as her anguish vented in harsh, salty gasps. "Oh, God, why-y-y-y-y?"

For uncounted minutes they stood, bolted to each other in a tearful embrace. The wind sang quietly through the aging foxtails and seedpods that bowed in their own sad memorial on the tiny hillside, as in a rehearsed part of the small rite. Three cars, a couple of farm trucks, and a yellow county highway truck slowed respectfully as they passed the grieving parents.

When the tears began to dry at last and they turned to face the trio of crosses once more, Press noticed a slight tilt in one. He stepped forward and nudged it left, while tamping the ground against its right side to hold it upright. Turning when he was finished, he ushered Abby slowly back across the road to the car.

"I know I can come back again, now," she said when they were headed again toward Fremont. "I think I'll have to. Probably a lot."

"I know," Press said. He continued to look straight ahead, his jaw clenched in a struggle to keep from crying again. "I will, too."

That was everything said the rest of the way home.

2

Shenanigans were dancing at the cop shop and Press was bound to learn the steps. Backing away from the curb, he choked the steering wheel as though it had just defiled his daughter. He headed east toward the police station at the far end of Main Street under the high morning sun.

Preston "Press" Williams was not a man known to casually swear but he was on the edge now of being really pissed. The words punctuating his thoughts might blister the best latex wall paint that Delaney and Sons Hardware had to offer.

“Nordstrom's into something and I'm going to find out what the bastard's hiding,” Press raged. Derek Nordstrom was Fremont's long-time police chief and, for at least the third or fourth time in the last few months, Press had heard of some incident in town that didn't show up in the police blotter. Issues ranged from marijuana busts to indecent exposure to the cannery manager, Butler Devane, being hauled in for beating his wife. Just this morning Press had heard coffee shop chatter that Mayor Wes Hartley had been arrested again three nights earlier for drunk driving.

"Again," Press nearly barked to no one else in the car. He hadn't been aware of any first or other time. For more than a pair of decades Press had owned the local newspaper, the *Fremont Weekly Gazette*. It had always irked him that the common line on his small town paper was that everyone around knew what was going on first, they just bought the paper to see if the editor got it right. It wasn't that the city's highest ranking elected official getting nabbed for driving drunk was the stuff of Pulitzer Prizes; maybe not even front page material. But too many times Press was being surprised and embarrassed by undercurrents picked up on the town's neighbor-to-neighbor wire service that might have been the subject of news. Items the paper should have at least had the editorial license to decide if they were worth the mention in ink. Maddeningly, they were issues no one on the staff was even aware of. The paper was fresh on the stands and in the mail this Thursday morning with no announcement of any mayor's drunk driving arrest. Press knew his editor, Barry McGinn, had checked the police log the previous day.

Press screeched the car into one of the thirty-minute spaces in front of the limestone brick, three-story city hall. It was an old castle of a building that also housed the police station, the public entrance to its below-ground dungeon downstairs on the south side. Squad cars and ambulances entered and exited from the garage entry in the rear of the building. His gait took him down the steps two at a time and through the steel security door in barely the time it took to think about it.

"Mavis, let me see the blotter," he demanded as he lurched to a stop at the counter which restrained ordinary citizens from the official law enforcement premises.

"McGinn just checked it yesterday," the woman replied curtly, not getting up from her post at the police radio. Mavis Manheim was a stern woman of something more than fifty spinster years. She regarded anyone who entered the station not in uniform as apt to steal her valuables or her virtue or both. There was hardness in everything about her, from the thin brows that always seemed arced in annoyance over her eyes and the flat beak of a nose between them, to the sharp line of her jaw. There was even the square line of her shoulders that looked as if she'd ironed her sweater with the hanger still in it. She had a hammer for a tongue and she'd nailed half the county at one time or another. Mavis was the weekday police dispatcher and viewed herself as Chief Nordstrom's first in command whenever he was absent.

"I know that," Press said. "I want to see it again."

"What do you need to see it for? The next paper doesn't come out for another week?" Mavis still hadn't moved more than her fingers drumming on the desk. She hadn't yet looked at him or even past him. When she answered him she spoke into her computer screen. "What, does your boyfriend's name show up on it?" Press figured the last man who winked at Mavis was most assuredly a blind date.

Mavis glared at him, lips pursed so tightly they all but vanished. The quiver in her cheeks said she was working up to a suitable answer, but her silence said the response had obviously escaped her.

"The blotter's a public document, Mavis. You and I both know it," Press asserted. "Now, do you bring it over here or do I get a court order and have you held in contempt?" He knew the contempt matter was a bluff but it worked. In more time than it would have taken to carry an anvil to him if she'd had chronic arthritis, Mavis finally dislodged the blotter from the sergeant's desk and, without comment, deposited it onto the counter in front of the newspaperman.

Press flipped the pages back a week of days and started finger-scanning the names and transgressions listed. There were shopliftings, traffic violations, a dog running loose, loud music, two bar fights, a suspicious broken window, and a couple of domestic disputes. There were also three drunken driving arrests, but Press recognized all of the names and none belonged to the mayor.

"I'd like to see Derek," Press stated as he closed the log and slid it back across the counter.

"He's not in." Mavis had returned to her command desk and did not look up.

"When do you expect him?"

"Am I a mind reader?"

"Have him call me when he gets in...*pulleeeze!*" Press banged the steel door closed as he exited and bounded up the steps. Agitation erased the casual from his usual pace this morning. Even though he had lost nearly a hundred fifty pounds in the last couple of years and religiously jogged five miles every morning, his typical stride, born of bulk hauling in those previous years, was more steady and deliberate.

Moments later he pulled the car into Bernie Randazzo's Town and Country Convenience Centre and left the motor running as he went inside to buy a copy of *USA Today* and the *Avery Daily American*. On the other side of the lot he pulled onto Division Street, which was also the state highway that bisected town, and drove south three more blocks to the *Gazette* office.

Barry McGinn was at his desk in the newsroom, going through the paper when Press walked in from the back.

"How many typos are the readers going to find for us this week?" Press asked, his agitation slowed to a barely noticeable stir by now.

Barry looked up with a banana-wide grin.

"Haven't found any yet," he said with a single shake of his light brown-haired head.

"Come into my office for a bit," Press said as he shuffled out of his jacket. "We've gotta figure something out."

Barry was a long lank of timber, top to bottom, with boyish looks and an eternal grin tucked under his nose – a grin that softened even the harshest interview or critic and belied a dogged dedication to gathering and writing news. He had a curiosity in him that pumped like another set of lungs. Seven years past a graduation with honors from the University of Missouri School of Journalism, he could have probably made the staff of the *New York Times* or *Washington Post* by now if he'd wanted. But Barry McGinn was born and raised in Fremont, as was his wife, Angie, and neither imagined uprooting to any new frontier. He counted it his good fortune to land a job at the *Gazette* right out of college and Press counted his fortune even greater to land him. Within two years Press ceded the title of editor to Barry and had never given it a thought past the first.

Press sank down into one of the two, cushioned guest chairs in his office rather than taking a seat behind his desk and invited Barry to take the other. Without really passing on the notion, he considered his editor an equal when it came to the discussion of news matters. It just seemed more natural to talk at arms length rather than from opposite sides of the status division created by a desk.

"I was at Cruiser's this morning for coffee with the guys," Press began. "Lyman Dunnington wanted to know why we didn't have anything in the paper about Wes Hartley getting picked up for drunk driving *again* Monday night after the Lions Club meeting? You know anything about that?"

"It's the first I've heard," Barry noted as his eyebrows notched nearer the hairline at the top of his forehead. "Lyman's a bit full of himself at times, but I doubt he'll go to hell for lying."

Press nodded casually in agreement. "What especially irritates me is that Lyman said it's at least the third time that he's heard of. And it galls me even more because I hear other things sometimes that we should have known about and didn't."

He paused to hitch his right leg atop his left knee as if levering a fussy machine handle that seemed in need of a touch of oil.

"It's all stuff that should be in the police reports if there's any truth to it."

Barry sucked in a gush of air and let it escape slowly while pushing the sleeves of his cardigan farther toward his elbows.

"Yeah, I suppose we all hear things mentioned now and then," he acknowledged with a shrug of his hands. "I guess I just put most of it off to gossip or sour grapes of one sort or the other. Usually it involves school sports. The parent of a second-stringer complaining about their kid gettin' busted at a beer party. They claim some hot shot ballplayer was there, too, but didn't get pinched. Or, 'I got my name in the paper for speeding, so how come some prominent so-and-so didn't?'" Barry leaned on the chair arm and rested his chin on his thumb, his index finger pressed under his nose where a mustache might have been if he'd grown one.

"I know Nordstrom acts like the town commandant, but I always thought he did things mostly by the book," the young editor speculated.

"I've often wondered if he doesn't write his own book as he goes along, though," Press said, giving his jaw a speculative rub. "His uncle Silas was the police chief when I came here, but he retired within a couple of weeks. I never got to know the guy, but people told me he had his own *from the hip* ways of doing things. I've thought at times, maybe, that two apples might fall from different trees, but from the same orchard they can be just as tart."

"Then how do you figure in Bonner?" Barry posed, the grin again parting his nose and chin.

"You've got me there," Press smirked. The two were as different as Irish lace and canvas tarp.

Anson Bonner was the newest member of Fremont's police force and Derek Nordstrom's nephew on his wife's side of the family. The fact that they were related was discernable only through hospital records and their family's acknowledgement. Any other similarities ended there, much to Anson's genetic good fortune.

Bonner was tall and athletic. He handcuffed everyone, especially young ladies, with his good looks, curly brown hair, and easy grin. Even in his scant tenure on the force he had garnered respect, not fear, from those he dealt with on the opposite side of his badge. For instance, young speeders most often got off with a warning if it was their first offense. For second and other infractions, however, while other officers might lower the recorded speed to save the offender points off his driving record, Anson would not. One warning should have been enough, he'd point out.

His Uncle Derek, on the other hand, was better built for scaring crows, small children, and any manner of other timid creatures with his rail-boned frame, blond-turned-gray bristle of hair, and bushy, gray eyebrows that shadowed deep-set eyes and a hawkish beak of a nose. A local farmer had once described his appearance – quite appropriately Press thought – as like a weasel sired by a porcupine. And when Derek Nordstrom dealt from his side of the law, local lore would have recorded that leniency had not been yet invented.

That portrait of Nordstrom as a lawman was what so confounded Preston Williams now. Why were there persistent mumblings of modest miscreants avoiding the lash of justice?

"You know anybody on the force who might let something slip, off the record?" Press asked.

"Anson, maybe, if they weren't related. Even that might be a stretch. The cops have their own code and, besides, they're all afraid of Derek." Barry leaned forward. "He keeps them on a pretty short leash."

"Isn't Dick Flater a member of the Lions?" Press asked, cocking his head and squinting his right eye.

Barry nodded.

"Mr. City Council President and His Honor Lord Mayor don't particularly bask in each other's shine," Press noted. "Why don't you give him a call. See if he was at the meeting Monday night. Ask him if the mayor seemed to be in his cups by the time the meeting ended. Might ask him, too, if he's ever noticed Hartley drinking a bit too much on other occasions as well."

Barry thumbed up his agreement as he rose to leave.

"See if you can remember any other incidents that we haven't gotten anything on. Maybe you can dig into them a little further," Press continued. "I'll do the same."

Barry stopped at the door and leaned on the frame.

"I could just call Hartley and ask him flat out?"

Press shook his head as he moved to the chair behind his desk.

"Let's save that one for awhile. No sense in rattlin' his cage unless we've got a bone to play with. We might need him for something else."

"PRESSING MATTERS"
by Preston Williams
October 28

If William Shakespeare were alive today and sitting behind my desk, he might type something into his computer like, "Something is rotten in Fremont." And, in all likelihood, it would have hardly been worthy of critical acclaim in this day and age. Can you just imagine Siskel and Ebert playing with that scene? But old Will had an eye for intrigue and I suspect he might have found a measure of fascination in the hush-wire drama that plays in the alleys and backroads in and around Fremont. Somehow, there always seems to be a mystery playing about town that never quite makes it into the newsrooms of the cable networks...or the *Gazette,* for that matter. Strangely enough, such things don't even find their way into the police blotter....

3

Dusk was invading the evening as Press eased the Buick out of the company parking lot and headed down Division Street. The amber glow of the mercury vapor streetlights was already arcing its dome over the streets to keep the dark from overwhelming Fremont before dawn could fight back. It mildly irritated Press that the police chief hadn't called him yet. He put it off as Nordstrom's way of letting him know who held the higher rank in the local pecking order. When the mood struck him, the chief would call the newspaper publisher he thought of as a carpetbagger because he hailed from some anonymous place in Upper Michigan. The chief and a substantial flock of others in the small town always afforded lesser status to folks who weren't born, reared in and able to recite their lineage in Fremont starting at least three generations back.

Two blocks down the street a red Cavalier pulled out of the Dairy Queen lot and did its best to imitate a Corvette, leaving mild traces of Goodyear on the cement as the tail lights fled from whatever it was that might be chasing them. Or maybe it was dashing to whatever they might be trying to catch. Three blocks ahead the car careened around a corner and disappeared. Press recognized the Cavalier as the one he had purchased nearly two years earlier for his son, Jeremy.

The kid'll never change, Press sighed to himself. Even from the instant he had discovered that those things at the end of his legs could propel him anywhere, Jeremy's gait had been a hell-bent-for-leather run. By the time he was five he found that a bicycle could get him there even faster, even if it was only to the Starks' house next door.

The only place Jeremy had ever walked that Press could recall was to school, and then only grudgingly. Probably the only time even then that he walked in high spirits was when his teacher lined the students up and practice-marched them out of the building in case there was a fire. Jeremy could always hold on to the hope that it might someday be for real.

He was not quite a bad kid, just ever on the brink of being a really good one. He kept his grades manageable enough at least to get himself into college, but never quite good enough to make high honor roll or satisfy his parents. Good looking and gifted in the art of persuasion, Jeremy had used both to advance himself to such prominences as prom king and class president. Despite their several father-and-son conversations on the subject of sex, which included ample warnings on the consequences, Press was almost surprised that his son hadn't yet talked one or a few sweethearts out of their panties and himself into early fatherhood. The young man never put much effort into the pursuit of girls. Any chase would have likely ended in a head-on collision with a crowd. It seemed Jeremy had at one time or another been seen with three-fourths of the girls in his own class and the three grades behind him, as well as a few in a class or two since graduated. Jeremy worked two nights after school and on weekends at the Safeway on the north side of town in order to finance his romances, along with gas and insurance for his car.

The Cavalier was parked at the curb when Press pulled into the driveway and nudged the remote for the garage door opener.

Abby looked up from the stove where she was whittling a roast when Press walked in.

"Hi, Hon." She smiled as he paused to peck her cheek before hanging his jacket on a peg in the laundry room. "Anything new in town?" It was her every-Thursday habit at playing the wag, like she didn't know most of what was in the paper already.

"Chuckle, chuckle." Press grinned as he headed down the hall. "Be back in a minute."

He tapped on the door of Jeremy's room and let himself halfway in. The teenager, lying back down on his bed, shifted his history book to the side and smiled.

"Hi, Pop! What's up?" He had on that winning grin of a kid who expected to get the larger share of everything in life.

"You hiding a car magazine inside that school book?" Press teased.

"Dad, would I ever do anything like that?"

Press snorted and shook his head.

"If I had a dollar for every time a teacher told me about you doing that...."

"I know, you could probably retire," Jeremy interrupted, gleefully quirking a smile at his father.

"Anyway," Press noted, "you'd better tone it down some if you want to keep the keys to that car."

"What do you mean?" Jeremy asked with the injured innocence of a convicted felon.

"It was me you pulled out in front of at the Dairy Queen." Press gave his best imitation of a frown as Jeremy tried to hide behind the history book. "You get stopped and the cops won't do the *Gazette* publisher's son any favors. And neither will I!"

"Okay," Jeremy replied, grinning from beneath the book.

In the kitchen Press poured himself a cup of coffee and sat down at the dinette while Abby finished catering food to the table.

"How long till we eat?" Press quizzed.

"As soon as Kate gets home from cheerleading practice," his wife vowed. "Should be any minute. You look tired. Anything wrong?"

"Probably nothing, really." Press shrugged. "Lyman Dunnington asked me at coffee this morning why we didn't have anything in the paper about Wes Hartley getting picked up for drunk driving Monday night. I stopped at the police station and checked the blotter. There's nothing listed. It just irritates the heck out of me." He poured a long drink of coffee into his throat.

"It wouldn't bother me so much but Lyman said it's at least the third time that he's heard about," Press said, shaking his head. "I hear other things sometimes that don't show up on any official record."

"Oh, we all hear things once in awhile," Abby noted almost in a pooh-pooh sort of tone as she sat down next to him to await the arrival of their high school junior daughter. "I always put it off as small town talk or gossip."

"Like what?"

"Nothing that I can think of off hand, I guess," she replied. "Mostly just small stuff that women like to gossip about. You know…just *stuff*."

The front door opened and Press rocked back in his chair to see his daughter Kate bounce into the living room. He waved and she shook her pompoms at him.

"Dinner's ready, Katie," Abby called as she got up to pour three glasses of milk for her children. "Tell your brother and Cassie, please." Their daughter, Cassie, a seventh-grader, was in the basement rec room watching TV.

"Let me know if you think of anything, will you?" Press implored as he scooted his chair closer to the table.

Kate entered the kitchen and sat down, still in her gold and white cheerleading outfit, which was, according to her father, skimpier than any of the other high school cheerleading uniforms he'd seen, but a point that elicited little discussion and less change. She was followed shortly by Jeremy and Cassie.

All three of the Williams children were deliciously good looking. Jeremy's features favored his father's side of the family, although the resemblance wasn't an exact copy by any means. The son was already two inches taller than his father's two yards, and he rarely exhibited Press' serious side. And when he smiled his smile was all Abby. The girls replicated their mother's gentler features and ash blond hair. Behind the bubbly façade of a cheerleader, Kate was a dedicated student of school and her boyfriend of more than a year, Casey Delaney. Wherever she went, the boys' eyes followed the waist-length flow of blond hair and ideally sculpted female architecture. Cassie, on the other hand, was eminently more suited to "Cassie" and not the "Cassandra" her mother had hoped for. Bound for beauty in every way, with sprouting breasts offering an introduction to the geometry of the woman-to-be, she was yet more intimately acquainted with sneakers, jeans, and T-shirts than heels, blouses and skirts. Her ever presence in a group of boys was anything but flirtatious, her ambitions drawn more towards football, basketball, and baseball than any thought of romance. Abby cringed at the grass stains, scuffed knees, and scraped elbows but tried not to be excessively prompting in the direction of more feminine ways.

Abby offered a brief grace before any food could be touched. Press had heard the Lord thanked in places holy and unholy for food that both tempted and tortured the palate, but it always amused him that his wife found an entirely different way to state her appreciation for His blessings at every meal.

"Dear Lord, we thank You for the precious gift of this day, for the food that gladdens our bodies, and the family that gladdens our hearts. Amen."

"Amen. Becky Hartley's quitting cheerleading," Kate announced as she reached for a dinner roll. "She and her mother are moving to Minneapolis."

Abby's eyes saucered a startled look at her husband who was ratcheting his chin back up from the second button of his shirt. There was a noticeable protrusion of Jeremy's eyes as well.

"What's that all about?" Abby quizzed.

"Who's Becky Hartley?" Cassie asked as she was about to stoke a load of asparagus spears into her mouth. She was ignored.

"I guess her folks might be getting divorced," Kate mumbled through a mouthful of roll.

"Wasn't Becky one of your honeys for awhile?" Press jabbed at his son somewhere between curiosity and playfulness.

"D-a-a-a-d." Jeremy recoiled.

"Well, did you or didn't you go out with her?"

"A few times. Not for a couple of months, though."

"I heard she dumped you," Kate said, poking a wrinkled nose in her brother's direction.

The flush began to ignite in the boy's cheeks as he darted a varsity-sized glare at his sibling.

"WH-O-O-O is Becky Hartley?" Cassie insisted this time.

"What, are you an owl? She's a girl in my class," Kate replied with a quick frown that hinted any more questioning from the youngest Williams daughter would be fruitless.

"Did Becky ever say anything about problems between her parents to either of you?" Abby nosed.

"Not to me," Jeremy answered with a single shrug of his shoulders.

"Me neither," Kate replied. "I don't ever remember her talking about her parents at all, now that you mention it. Seems kind of funny I guess. Everybody says something about their folks once in awhile."

4

"I caught Dick Flater at his office this morning," Barry said as he leaned around the entrance to the publisher's office. "He was on his way out the door but he gave me a few minutes and some things to think about."

Press waved him to a chair beside his desk.

"Flater doesn't want to say much about the mayor outside of city business for professional reasons, I gather," McGinn said. "He doesn't want anyone to think he's knocking the guy for business purposes."

Dick Flater and Wes Hartley were more than antagonists in city government. Between them, they also owned the two largest real estate firms in Fremont. Though tenacious competitors, they still needed to work together occasionally on sales closings. Flater tried to keep business and politics separate as much as he could, although the two crossed purposes more than he cared for. If he could, however, he would keep personalities from affecting his business. The *Gazette* publisher and editor, as well as the mayor appreciated that. Wrangling on the city council floor, still, too often failed to conceal the dislike between the council president and the mayor.

"I may have been too up front the way I started out," Barry admitted. "First thing I asked him was if Hartley was drunk Monday night. Kind of startled Dick. Wanted to know why I was asking. I told him we'd heard a rumor about the mayor getting picked up on a possible DWI."

Press stopped opening envelopes and leaned over the stack of mail as Barry continued.

"Dick never would say anything direct, but when I pressed him on the matter he did say that Hartley might not have been able to pass a Breathalyzer when he left the Owl's Nest." Barry was tapping his pen on the arm of the chair. The Owl's Nest Restaurant and Lounge was the twice-monthly meeting place of the Fremont Lions Club. "I asked him if that was common for Wes and he'd only say that Hartley does like his Manhattans."

"Interesting," Press said, curling his mouth toward the squint of his left eye. He told Barry about the tidbit his daughter had laid out at dinner the night before concerning a possible divorce in the Hartley family.

"Maybe hizzonner is more of a lush than anyone suspected," McGinn surmised, arching his eyebrows farther up his forehead as he stretched back in the chair.

"Maybe," Press agreed. "But I still don't think that's the story we're after. Lots of folks can't wean themselves from the bottle, and lots of folks get divorced. I don't know about you, but I've never seen him appear to be even tipsy at any city function."

Barry shrugged in agreement.

"What I really want to know is why the log at the cop shop doesn't reflect him getting picked up?" Press wondered. He wove his fingers behind his head and rocked back in his swivel recliner to stare at the ceiling as if the answer might be written there in fine print. "I want to know what Nordstrom's hiding, along with the why and how he's doing it."

"Keep your ears open. Even the smallest thing." Press narrowed his eyes and chewed the tip of his tongue for a moment. "Don't make a big deal out of anything you come up with, though. I especially think we have to keep this out of the city loop. We don't know who's involved in what or even if there is anything. But I really do have an itch under my collar about Nordstrom. I think I'm going to have a talk with Galen Perry if I can catch him in."

"Why Perry and not Chuck Glorioso?" Barry questioned. Glorioso was the Fremont city attorney.

"Like I said," Press pointed out. "We just don't know at this point how big the loop is. Galen's sharp and honest, I suspect. He's too new in town to get himself caught in the loop yet. He might be able to direct us to a starting point."

Galen Perry was in court all morning but his secretary made an appointment for Press right after lunch. Perry ran his law practice from a suite in the old Delaney building on Main Street a short four blocks from the newspaper office. Like most of the buildings on Main Street, it was a red brick, 1920s vintage layered with several renovations on the first level. The lower floor amendments failed to make over the weathered years to the upper levels, the renovators thinking perhaps the human eye could inspect no higher than the sign above the door. It had originally housed a hardware store until Charlie Delaney had moved his operation to the north side of town some years back. Charlie Stilwell had tried selling major appliances in it for a couple of years. When his wife died, he began keeping too much company with the Jacks – Yukon and Daniels – and the Farmers and Merchants Bank eventually got the building and a bunch of used stoves and refrigerators. The manufacturers reclaimed all the new appliances.

The building had sat vacant for two years until Dick Flater and a couple of other investors bought it and remodeled the structure to house a half dozen small craft and hobby shops, a chiropractic clinic, the county annex, and a couple of law offices, one of them Galen Perry's.

Only three years out of law school, Perry had moved to town from Elmore, eighty-five miles away, and was still trying to get his practice established. He'd joined the Chamber of Commerce, the Tuesday noon Rotary Club, and the Wednesday afternoon golf league at the nine-hole course on Fremont's south side, and he was beginning to gather trust. Press figured that was an accomplishment in itself in a town slow to accept anyone who couldn't trace his roots to the first or second turn of sod when the community was planted.

Short and built like a fence post with arms, Press thought Galen looked more like the kids he saw bagging groceries if it weren't for the conservative, country barrister-type rumpled suits the young lawyer wore.

"What can I help you with?" Galen smiled as Press sat down on the opposite side of the attorney's desk.

"How much do you know about laws on open records and access to public information?" Press quizzed.

"Some, I guess, though it's not my normal area of practice." Galen looked mildly surprised. "Have you got a problem getting ahold of something?"

"I'm not sure," Press replied. He explained the questions arising from rumored incidents that never appeared in the police log. "I was sort of hoping you might point a direction for me."

"I'd be glad to if I could," Perry said, leaning back in his chair as he tested the tensile strength of his pencil between his thumbs and forefingers. "Tell, me. How come you're not talking to Chuck Glorioso instead of me?"

Press grinned as he scratched his jaw.

"Cause I don't know where any of this goes. This could just be the workings of a one-man gang in the chief's clothes, or he could be holding a lot of hands. Glorioso might be a saint or one of the sinners for all I know." Press nodded his head slightly. "I just don't know where to start to find out. I figured you've got the law background and haven't been in town long enough to get any local dirt under your nails."

Both men grinned.

"Just off the top of my head I do know that you can legally look at any record in the chief's possession," Galen noted, pointing the eraser end of the pencil toward the door. "That is unless it concerns work on a case in progress. And, while I doubt you could randomly check his mail, if you knew of a specific letter that he has, the law says he has to make it available to you."

The lawyer shook his head as he pursued a thought to latch onto.

"Without a specific point of reference, though…the law doesn’t allow fishing trips. You pretty much have to know what you’re after."

"Yeah, that's what we've been running into," Press said as he stood up to leave. He thanked the young attorney who followed him to the door.

"You might call the state attorney general's office," Galen offered. "Find out exactly what records the police are required to keep by law."

Press nodded his appreciation as they shook hands.

Back at the *Gazette* office, Press had a message waiting. While he was out the chief had finally called. He tossed his jacket over the back of a chair and sat down to dial the number.

"Tell me, Derek. I hear you picked up the mayor for a DWI the other night," Press stated after the chief's brusque 'hullo'.

"I wouldn't know about that," Nordstrom replied tersely.

"But I've got some folks who say it happened."

"Check the log. If it ain't there I don't know what else I can tell you," the chief stated flatly.

"Did that and don't see anything. That's why I can't make sense of it and figured maybe you could help," Press goaded.

"Listen. I told you, if it's not listed on the blotter, I can't help you. When you've got something else you want to talk about, call me back." He hung up. Derek Nordstrom was not noted for friendly or extended farewells.

Press sat for a long moment, elbows on his desk and chin tucked onto the weave of his fingers, staring as if to bolt his irritation to the wall.

5 Barry McGinn waved Press to his desk as the publisher headed to his office with the mail on Monday morning.

"Picked up something interesting over the weekend," Barry said with one of those 'bet-you'll-like-this' smiles. "Angie and I bowl in the Friday night couples' league at The Back Alleys. I don't even remember how it came up, but Wayne and Debbie Boginoski told us that the siren and flashing lights woke them up shortly after midnight a couple of weeks back. When they looked outside, Nordstrom had Wes Hartley stopped right in front of their house. It was right under a streetlight, so they could see faces and everything real plain."

"So Dunnington was right," Press said as he anchored the edge of the editor's desk. "I wonder why Wayne sat there at coffee, silent as a stump, when Lyman brought the whole thing up?"

Barry shrugged.

"Wayne said he saw the chief put Hartley in the squad and drive away. Hartley's car was still there when they got up at six that Tuesday morning."

"Nordstrom could have just given him a ride home instead of booking him," Press posed.

"Maybe," McGinn said with a knowing smile, "but Debbie said it was the chief who brought Hartley back in the squad to pick up his car about six-thirty."

"That is pretty expensive limo service. You have to wonder if the chief just took Hartley home, whether he'd make the personal effort to pick him up again and take him back to get his car." Press set the bundle of mail on Barry's desk and shifted the weight of his leaning to both feet.

"Something else puzzles me. Aren't the Lions Club meetings generally dinner sessions?" Press inquired.

"Far as I know," Barry replied. "Start about six."

"Yeah, and they're usually over by eight or so." He sandpapered a jaw with the palm of his hand. "If the needle tipped him to the drunk side when he left the Owl's Nest – and, if we assume he went someplace else to continue his toot – he likely would have been really sloshed by the time Nordstrom caught up with him."

Barry tilted his head to acknowledge the probability.

"We'll have to think about this one some," Press said as he picked up the pile of mail and headed to his office.

Later that morning Press called the state attorney general's regional office in Avery and spoke with a man named Jarred Kleinmeier. He asked Kleinmeier about what records a police department must keep.

"All arrest records, certainly," Kleinmeier stated. "They also have to log all incoming complaint or emergency calls as well…names, dates, times, nature of the business. Pretty much the stuff you would expect."

The assistant attorney general also told Press that, among other things, law enforcement agencies must keep all investigative records and evidence.

"In the case of on-going investigations, those records, of course, are not open to the press or the public, as I'm sure you know," Kleinmeier asserted. "Also files that might contain the names of informants or undercover police identities and things of that sort are closed. And, personnel records are not accessible to the public, of course."

"Whether or not he was actually arrested, what if you know, or are at least pretty sure that someone was picked up and taken to the station?" Press inquired. "Would there be a record?"

"By law, there's got to be an incident report somewhere. You've checked the blotter?"

"Yep. No listing that we can find."

"Man, I can't imagine any police department in the country not wanting to log something like that, even if for no other reason than to cover their own liability," Kleinmeier said.

"Liability for what?" Press asked, aiming his ear closer to the phone.

"Any manner of things," the state lawyer assured. "Some guy could claim he was roughed up in the station. He could say the cops stole his money while they were frisking him. He could say they falsified charges. You name it, the police need a paper trail to cover their butts."

"Is there any place a department could hide a record like that? Keep in another file or something?"

"Ah, years ago some departments liked to put things they didn't want the press to see in their case-in-progress files," Kleinmeier acknowledged. "A few lawsuits got them into so much trouble, though, that I can't imagine any lawman trying to pull that one now."

Press thanked him for his help and the conversation ended.

He spent a long several minutes rolling thoughts around inside his head. Finally Press got up and headed through the open newsroom to his editor's desk.

"You up for a bit of late night sleuthing?" he suggested.

"I don't know. What've you got in mind?" Barry replied quizzically.

"I'm thinking it might be time to try to shake something loose." He told Barry what he'd learned in his discussion with the assistant attorney general. "Can I pick you up a little after midnight. I've got an idea I'd like to try."

6 Barry had tugged back the drapes a bit and was watching for him from the living room window when Press pulled into the driveway.

"Angie thinks we're nuts," he said with a chuckle as he slid into the passenger seat. Even in the dim glow of the dash lights, Press could see the smile on him, the one always practiced like he might perhaps forget how. "As tired as I am, I might have to agree with her if this doesn't get us anything."

"It might not," Press confessed as he backed the car into the street. Except for the dim light filtering through the McGinns' living room window and the yellow puddles of the streetlights at either end of the block, the night was pierced only by the Buick's headlights. "But I think Pregler's our only hope for cracking something out of the police department."

Eldon Pregler was the graveyard shift dispatcher for the Fremont Police Department. A balding bachelor in his early thirties, Eldon loved police work but was too timid to dally with the notion of entering the law enforcement academy in Avery. Instead, he settled for sleuthing through the eyes and experiences of others, dispatching police, fire and ambulance calls, and always packing a mystery novel of some sort in either the brown paper bag that toted his lunch or in the hip pocket of his jeans. What excitement the night shift in Fremont generally lacked, Eldon made up for with his variety of detective magazines and whodunit books.

The newspapermen rode in silence until Press eased the car into a space in front of the municipal building. The age- and weather-worn structure loomed in darkness like something out of an Edgar Allen Poe tale, ever on the verge of crumbling into the nether world. A small, blue neon sign on the side of the city hall directed visitors as well as those with official business downward to the police department offices in the basement.

"What if Nordstrom's here tonight?" Barry questioned, his hand hesitating on the door handle. "Another Lion's Club meeting tonight, you know?"

"What if he is?" Press grinned. "We just confront him straight out."

Both men got out of the car and Press leaned across the roof of the Buick before closing the door.

"I really don't think he will be, though. I don't know what the deal was the other week, but Derek's normally not known for working nights except on weekends."

Press rattled the steel security door and found it locked. He banged the palm of his hand on the metal panel until Pregler recognized him through the door's wire meshed, glass window and hit the button to electronically release the lock.

"Hi, Barry. Mr. Williams," Eldon greeted with some surprise. The middle in his age was settling precisely there and he hitched his belt back in the direction of his chest as he waddled toward the counter. "What brings you fellas down here this time of night?"

"We'd like to see the blotter," Barry stated simply.

"Kind of an odd time for you guys to be checking that isn't it?" Pregler noted with the beginnings of a frown dimming his face.

"We just wanted to see if we've missed something," Press offered as the police log was plopped on the counter before them.

The two men paged through more than two week's worth of entries and, as they expected, found nothing that provoked a series of thoughts.

"How come there's no incident report on Wes Hartley being brought in awhile back?" Press asked abruptly.

The dispatcher's jaw tremored just above his collar as though words were being jostled behind his lips but nothing was tumbling out. He turned first toward the unlit hallway where the chief's office lurked, then toward the other hall leading to the police garage in hopes a SWAT team might respond to the alarm in his silent prayer. He turned back to face the publisher and editor, eyes darting fear and uncertainty first to one and then the other. The flush mounting in his face announced his mind was in a fever, even if his body wasn't, and tiny beads of sweat were beginning to boil above his extended forehead back to his hairline.

"I don't have access to…I mean we don't have anything like that," Pregler yammered when he finally found his voice.

Thoughts were echoing inside the bone of the man's head so fast, Press could almost hear Eldon's brain throb. "I gotta call the chief about this." Pregler started for the phone on the desk.

"Oh no you don't!" Barry's words stopped him quicker than if the dispatcher were wearing a leash.

"The law says any police record that isn't part of a case in progress and doesn't contain the name of informants and the like is open to the public," Barry demanded. "Since you're in control of the records at the moment, you have to produce it!"

"We don't want to get you in trouble," Press added. "But if you don't give us any record concerning the incident with Hartley two weeks ago, we can go to court for a writ of mandamus to force you to turn it over. And you can be held in contempt if you don't."

Barry looked quickly at Press but hid his surprise at the bluff. Press almost winked, catching himself in time to keep from giving it away. It had worked on Mavis. Press figured Eldon might be an even easier mark. Pregler was too uncertain of himself, however. Neither bluff nor bully seemed apt to persuade him.

"Nah, fellas. I gotta call the chief on this first." He hesitated as if waiting for his thoughts to be translated from Greek. He pawed the telephone at the desk, afraid it might bite him if he picked it up, certain it would if he didn't.

"Really, Eldon, there's no need. Wake him up at this hour for something you legally are required to do anyway, and all you'll do is piss him off."

Barry had anted into the bluff and Pregler backed away from the phone. The quandary wrestled him in every direction but inside-out as he slow-shuffled between the desk and counter and back again. Finally, Eldon reached for the receiver once more, this time picking it up and pointing a pudgy finger at the digits, ready to place the call.

"Nah, really guys. I gotta ask the chief about this."

"Let him sleep, Eldon," Press said. This time he did wink at Barry. "We'll haggle it out with him later."

The duo left the dispatcher stammering to himself like he'd just had his pants yanked down in the middle of the Fourth of July parade.

"Well, maybe we didn't get the file on Hartley," Press said as they walked through the darkness to the car, "but now we know there is one. One way or another, we'll find out what Nordstrom's up to. He'll either have to produce the incident report or face the court."

7

Police Chief Derek Nordstrom couldn't have exhibited more signs of anger if he'd had "I'm really pissed" stamped on his forehead. His face was as red as if taking the hat off his head might be the scratch that would cause him to ignite. His legs pistoned up and down with only a slight hint of limp caused by the long-barreled .44-magnum pistol that hung from his hip, the holster looking more like a saddle scabbard. He stormed past the startled receptionist, through the newsroom without his eyes shifting even a momentary visit to Barry McGinn or anyone else, directly to the publisher's office.

"Just what the hell do you think you're trying to pull?" Nordstrom bellowed when he stopped and leaned forward, his knuckles-down fists implanted on the top of Preston's desk.

Press looked up with every indication that he'd been expecting the chief to serve him soup, his calm exterior belying the tumble in his gut that always accompanied a confrontation.

"That's funny. I was going to ask you the same question," Press replied evenly as their eyes collided.

The response reined the cavalry charge of Nordstrom's thought process as he paused to sort his words with some care and glared coldly until he could regain his momentum. The scarlet rage in the back of his neck softened only one barely discernable tint.

"You've got no godammed right to try and buffalo my staff!" The chief's bellow lowered to a growl now, his eyes taking the measure, up and down and east and west, of the man facing him from across the desk as though he were deciding on hanging or merely flogging. His expression declared that he liked nothing much of what he saw. Hanging was the likely choice.

"And you've got no right to hide records," Press responded in his same even tone.

"I don't know what the hell you're talkin' about. I ain't hidin' nothing!"

"Then why doesn't the log reflect the fact that you picked up Wes Hartley for driving drunk again two weeks ago?" Press demanded.

"Because I didn't," the chief snapped back.

"I've got witnesses who say you did."

"Pregler didn't give you squat!" Nordstrom spoke the words like cubes of ice, his eyes narrowing to near closure.

Press rocked back in his chair, his mouth curling close to a smile.

"I didn't say anything about Eldon, did I?" he replied. "I *said* I have witnesses."

"Huh!" The chief expelled the grunt with a wind that could have blown a Stetson off Press' head. "Who?"

"Open the records the way you ought to and you don't need to know," Press said with a nod. "Keep hiding information and you'll find out who the witnesses are in a courtroom."

"You're bluffin'." If gall could smile, Nordstrom donned a smirk as he straightened and hitched his thumbs in his belt. "You don't have jack shit!"

"There's only one way you're going to find that out for sure," Press stated coolly as he leaned forward on his desk. "Don't turn over the information I want…the information the law says I'm entitled to."

The police chief hunched across the desk so that he was eyeball to eyeball with Press.

"Listen, you smart-assed sonofabitch, you're still an outsider here. ***I*** decide what the law is in Fremont!" He spat the words out like vinegar. "Don't you try an' intimidate me!"

"That's a rope that pulls both ways, Chief," Press said standing up, his temper rising to a pre-boil hiss as he looked down on the lawman. "I expect to see all the appropriate entries in the blotter when Barry and I come in to check them in the morning. Otherwise, I'll see you in court."

Nordstrom straightened and turned to leave. At the door he pivoted and gave a world record glower down the finger he aimed at Press.

"I'd be mighty careful just where I stepped if I were you, mister!"

"Don't strain yourself trying too hard to be me, Derek," the other suggested.

The chief of police said nothing more but it was a highly amplified word void as he stomped out with the same, heavy metal gait he had fumed in with.

Press returned to his swivel recliner as Barry appeared at the door.

"I guess we got his attention, huh?" McGinn grinned his utmost. "Acts like he's got a hot poker up his butt."

"You're a master of understatement, my man," Press replied with a smile that began to untangle his nerves. "You could probably sweep hell from end to end and not come up with a nastier SOB."

"What now?" Barry asked.

"Well, I guess we see if he makes any new entries in the log," Press said as he rocked sideways to turn on his computer. "Which I *don't* think he'll do. I suspect no one's ever banged on his cage like that before. So we're probably going to have to prove to him that we now have a bone to play with."

"Want me to get an open records-type editorial ready for this week's paper?" Barry wondered.

"No, I don't think we're quite ready for that, yet. I think we need to know specifically what he's got before we go public with this," Press said as he scratched under his chin. "I'll talk to the district attorney about getting a writ of mandamus if Nordstrom doesn't back down. That'll be something to report, but we'll save any editorial for later."

"PRESSING MATTERS"
November 18

Saw a cute poster at the Fremont Fitness Works the other day. It says "Blessed are they who hunger and thirst, for they are sticking to their diets." Something to think about as Thanksgiving Day approaches with all its belly ammunition. But if you do overindulge, for example, in the holiday spirits, maybe the Fremont police chief will give you a free ride. We hear he's prone to doing that on occasion....

8 Snow had delivered winter two days earlier and closed fall's open brown casket like a gravecloth. The highway was clear and dry now as Press maxed the speed limit at ten miles over legal in order to make it to Parsons in time for his one-thirty appointment with the district attorney, Del Schell. Two weeks and Thanksgiving had passed since the confrontation with Derek Nordstrom. It was the Monday after the holiday before Press could arrange an appointment with Schell.

Twenty or so miles to the south, Parsons was only a couple of Irish Catholic families larger than Fremont, but the fact that it was the county seat gave it a more cosmopolitan air. Shopping there was a diversion for Fremont's women, their hometown seemingly not holding many pastimes for them. A number of the Fremont men golfed at the eighteen-hole country club in Parsons rather than the shorter, nine-hole course in Fremont. They were the serious golfers or the ones who could afford more time away from their businesses (or chose it as an excuse to get away from prying eyes, for discretionary reasons). The course was being groomed now for cross-country skiing as Press entered the outskirts of Parsons and slowed for the final eight blocks to the county courthouse with five minutes to spare.

The district attorney's secretary showed Press to his office. Without getting up, Schell waved from behind a desk piled with stacks of files and papers to a chair for his visitor to sit. The waved hand held a cigarette pinched like a nit between his thumb and forefinger and the motion knocked a third of the smoke's ash onto some papers strewn about the desk. Carefully lifting the papers, Schell casually shook the ashes onto the floor as a matter of routine and mashed the cigarette butt into an already-filled ashtray on the corner of the desk. The room was heavy with the smell of stale smoke and dead tobacco.

Press wondered why people like Schell continued to smoke in an era when the dangerous effects were so well known. As a college student Press had smoked some and never really enjoyed it. He simply found no pleasure in pumping smoke into his lungs and wondered why people would move to get upwind of a trash burner or campfire and yet inhaled cigarette smoke. On their second date Abby had asked him why he smoked and, when he couldn't give her any kind of meaningful or intelligent answer, he quit on the spot.

The carefully trimmed black beard that bounded the lower shelf of Schell's face was the only neat thing about the man or his office. Around the other half-circle of his face was an also-black thatch of hair that looked blow-dried without the application of a comb or brush. Looking at the wrinkles in the prosecutor's shirt, Press wondered whether it doubled as a pajama top or if the man had hung it to dry on chicken wire. The sleeves were rolled three-quarters to the elbows and a well-used blue tie sagged from the open collar. Press could see nothing else of the man except the black shoes that pushed from beneath the desk. In wing-tip life expectancy, they were a generation or two in need of polish. Corners and walls of the small office were bordered with stacks of thickly papered legal folders.

"Excuse the mess," Schell said. He seemed preoccupied or edgy or something in between. "The one my predecessor left me was even worse."

Del Schell, who engaged his political career as a Young Democrat while in high school, was three-quarters through his first term as district attorney. His partisanship had stood toe to toe with the time constraints of his private law practice until he decided to combine the two interests by running for the county prosecutor post. He was expected to announce his candidacy for a second term at any time.

"What can I do for you, Mr. Williams?" Schell asked as he finished shuffling some papers into a file, which he then laid aside. He extended a hand over the desk to shake, an awkward gesture as though he held an ice cube in it.

Unzipping his gray and blue-trimmed winter coat and sitting down, Press recited the chapter on his recent dealings with Derek Nordstrom and the chief's refusal to provide an incident report on the matter of his detaining the mayor for drunken driving. He ended with a request that the district attorney seek a writ of mandamus ordering Nordstrom to produce any and all records pertaining to Hartley.

Schell pressed the tips of his fingers together and stretched back in his chair as he pondered carefully the political ramifications of the whethers and ifs, so as not to allow them to slip haphazardly out of his mouth.

"Hmmmm," he murmured at last, turning to the calendar on the wall behind him where he lifted several pages and stared at the scribbling there.

"I've never had any open records requests," Schell said as he swiveled back to face Press with a blinkless gaze. "The state bar is putting on some regional seminars on just that topic, though. I'm scheduled to attend the one in Avery in March. Maybe after that...."

"That's four months away!" Press' jaw elevatored up and down in astonishment. "I thought the end of the week would be more than enough time!"

The district attorney did some housecleaning on his vocal cords before he responded.

"Well, uh, it's not really my area of expertise," he stammered as he looked onto his desktop and shuffled a couple of files. "I really don't feel comfortable going into something like this without having all my ducks in a row."

"What ducks?" Press fumed, his eyebrows arched like battle flags. "Hell, man, this is a turkey shoot! The law's not that complicated! Even I understand it, but I'm not a lawyer and I can't argue it in court myself!" He waved his hands in amazement.

"Well, you could always hire your own attorney," Schell suggested with an octave of indignation rising in his voice.

"That's what the voters hired *you* to do," Press said, his eyes narrowing to glare across the stacks of files at Schell.

"I guess I have to say that I'm sorry. I don't think I can help you if you're in that much of a rush." Schell shrugged, swiveling his chair away from Press to avert the publisher's eyes.

"Then I guess I'll have to do my darndest to find a different district attorney come next election," Press growled as he got up to leave. "Most of us can't afford to be hiring private lawyers to do your job for you."

"I'm sorry you feel that way," the prosecutor said, his face pale as he came around the desk. "Perhaps I'll be able to help you more on something else." Politico that he was, it suddenly thundered into his mind like the first lightning bolt of spring that he might have just ticked off the publisher of the second largest of six newspapers in the county. He knew that could cloud his chances for a return to office at election time.

"Give me a week or two to look into the statutes on this," he called after Press. "If I can think of a way to deal with it, I'll call you."

Don't shift on that fence too much or you might catch your nuts, Press thought as he continued down the hall without replying.

Unpracticed as he was in the indelicate art of cussing, 'goddamned stupid sonofabitch' was the most vigorous turn of the tongue Press could deliver on the way back to Fremont. He figured Schell's lack of adequate response was deserving of his most elaborate and colorful subjection to profanity, so what he couldn't contribute in quality he made up for in repetition. By the time he stepped out of the car behind the *Gazette* office, however, the rpm speed had slowed to less than that of an old recording.

"You look like you're ready to lay a poached egg," Barry said with a hesitant grin as he followed Press into the publisher's office. "I take it the meeting with Schell didn't go well?"

"You could look up a horse's rear end and not see turds any more like the one he sees in the mirror every morning," Press grumped. "He said he'd have to wait until he attends a seminar on open records *in March* because that's not an area of his expertise. What he didn't say but *meant* is that he doesn't want to rock any boats this soon before the election."

"I guess I thought we could count on Schell to do right by us. It's such an obvious violation of the statutes," Barry offered smiling, though just barely for a change.

"One thing I've learned in this business is that the only things you can count on are the digits on both hands," Press said, plentifully vexed.

"So what next?"

"I'm calling Galen," Press answered, reaching for the phone. "Guess I've gotta spend the bucks myself."

Derek Nordstrom and Del Schell were the furthest from Press' mind that night as he and Abby sat on the gym bleachers at Fremont Middle School and cheered Cassie and her teammates on to victory over the visiting girls basketball team from Stillwater. Kate led impromptu cheers with a group of her girlfriends from the third row behind the home team's bench, and Jeremy patrolled the far end of the court where he divided his attention between the game and a pair of sophomore girls who also had sisters on the team. The Williams family pride was unanimously intense as Cassie led all scorers and grabbed a dozen rebounds as well.

After the game hugs were passed all around and Cassie even shyly accepted one from her older brother before he wandered off to continue charming the pair of sophomore coeds. Casey Delaney had arrived as the fourth quarter began and he and Kate excused themselves to the library to work on a chemistry project. Cassie was still chirping merrily more than an hour later when she and her parents left the Pizza Hut and headed home. The large pizza, slathered with every condiment available, had been a rare treat for Press – perhaps more so than for his daughter.

9 Galen Perry saw the judge Wednesday morning and was able to get the writ immediately. He and Press accompanied the sheriff's deputy into the police station later that day to see it served on Chief Nordstrom.

"I don't know who looked more surprised when the writ was served," Press chuckled to Barry later in the afternoon. "Mavis' face could have stopped a clock and if looks could kill, the one I got from Derek would have me at Mount Mariah six feet under right now."

"Well, if it's only looks, we don't have much to worry about," Barry said, the slightest touch of concern furrowing his brow. "So, what did you get on Hartley?"

"Nothing, yet." Press replied. "Nordstrom's still trying to hedge a way out, I suspect. He said he didn't know if they even had anything like that and, if they did, it would take him some time to find it. I told him to check the writ. It says he's got twenty-four hours."

"PRESSING MATTERS"
December 1

Something's apparently out of whack at the Fremont Police Department. I suppose it might be easier to figure out what it is if someone could explain to me first what a "whack" is that something can be out of. In recent months, however, we've been hearing rumors of things going on in town involving the department that don't seem to be showing up in the police reports....

Friday morning while Press was out having coffee with some friends at Cruiser's Cafe, a police sergeant dropped off a manila envelope for him at the *Gazette* office. It was waiting on his desk when he returned.

"Barry," he called across the newsroom. "Want to see what we got from Nordstrom?"

When McGinn had ambled in, the pair stood at the publisher's desk while Press opened the envelope and extracted the three photocopied pages.

"He's covered up or whited out everything but the incident reports on Hartley," Press chuckled. "Detained for possible driving while intoxicated March 17, July 4, and October 25. Blood alcohol content 1.4, 1.2, and 1.8. Released the next morning each time. No charges."

Barry let out something between a "whew" and a whistle.

"If that'd been you or me, we'd be pedestrians right now."

"No doubt," Press agreed.

"Ya know, it bugs me," Barry said, scratching his head and looking a new question at Press. "What files did Nordstrom dig these up from if they weren't entered in the log?"

"Good question. One we can start digging into," Press said as he eased around the desk to his chair. "We've also got a story here for next week's paper. Time to call Hartley for his story, too."

Barry agreed. Moments later he was back at Press' door, rapping his knuckles on the wall to get his boss' attention.

"I've got the mayor on the phone," he said, leaning against the door frame. "When I told him what was up, he said he wants to meet with us before he'll say anything. Wants to know if you're free yet this afternoon?"

"Set it up," Press said with a toss of his hand. "I'll make time. I'd like to hear what he has to say."

10 Barry followed the mayor into Press' office and closed the door behind them. Hartley shook hands with Press briefly and, without removing his long winter coat, filled one of the chairs in front of the newspaperman's desk. Barry took possession of the other.

Wes Hartley was maybe a couple of fingers short of six feet tall and didn't have far to push his age across the fifty mark. His most distinguishing feature was his hair, dark as the inside of a cow, and straight with a starched-and-ironed kind of stiffness to it. Some folks said he looked like he was in need of a new rug had it not been for the fact that the hair was his own, a feature belied by the small, polished bit of scalp that showed through in the back. Most thought the absence of gray was an ode to Grecian Formula, though some suggested more like shoe polish.

Missing today from the authoritative manner exuded in the grip of the city's executive gavel was the usual confidence and composure of one Wes Hartley. His fingers toyed with the buttons on his gray overcoat and his eyes were darting, unwilling to pay an extended visit to the faces of either Press or Barry.

"Look, guys. This, uh, this's all gotta be off the record." He sounded like he'd swallowed a tablespoon of sand with no tonic to wash it past his throat.

"We'll listen first, Wes." Press studied the uncomfortable real estate man and mayor. "You know, though, at some point it's got to be for print."

Hartley grimaced and shifted in the chair, reaching into his sport coat for a pack of cigarettes and scanning the room for an ashtray.

“Sorry, this is a no-smoking building,” Press said.

“Another of those vices I should give up,” the mayor said with a laugh that lacked humor. He slid the pack back into his pocket.

"The situation is two-fold for us," McGinn interjected. "One is the fact that the mayor got picked up – three times – for allegedly driving while drunk and nothing came of it. The other is that the police chief tried to bury the official account of it."

"I don't know anything about police records, but if I can just explain the rest of it, can't you keep it out of the paper?" Hartley scooted forward in the chair, nearly it seemed, about to drop to his knees with the plea.

"It's already gone too far for that," Press said coolly, "but like I said, we'll listen first. We'll tell you before anything has to go on the record."

The mayor slumped back deep into the chair, agitating his head from side to side and gnawing on his lower lip. Finally he began to unravel his story and his composure along with it.

"My life's pretty much in the toilet right now," Hartley said with a gush that neighbored on a sob. "I drink too much, I know that. But that's not all of it."

For nearly two years, Hartley related, he'd been having an affair with a woman named Susan Parker. She was in the process of getting a divorce when it started.

"I guess I sort've implied that I'd get one too. Kind of in the heat of passion. In all honesty though, I never really meant to," Hartley confessed. An eyebrow-raised glance passed between Press and Barry.

"Anyway, my wife, Sharon, started getting suspicious so I decided to break it off," the mayor continued. "Susan wouldn't hear of it and started getting pretty nasty. She's a very possessive woman. Over and over she told me she'd ruin my marriage and she'd see that I never got elected mayor again."

Hartley dragged a finger under his nose.

"I went to her place that night after the Lions' meeting. That was our regular time together. I'd have a few more drinks there and Sharon just thought I was out drinking with the guys. After the sex I told Susan it was the last time. She went ballistic. Said she was going to tell my wife. Tell you. She even said she was gonna catch Becky after school and tell her. While I was in the shower she sprayed perfume on my shirt – not much, but enough that Sharon was almost sure to catch it. All I could smell was the Manhattans on my own breath. I never noticed.

"She was still screaming what she was gonna do to me when I left. I didn't know what to do. I could just see everything falling apart. My marriage, my business, the mayor's office. It was all coming down around me. I couldn't go home, not then anyway. I just drove around for an hour or so. I finally just stopped the car in the middle of the street somewhere. I don't know. There were a bunch of houses around. I just broke down crying. After a bit I started to drive around some more. I guess I was weaving a lot. Anyway I hit a couple of trash cans at the curb. Turned out they were next door to Derek's."

The mayor waved his hand weakly and half-heartedly tried to muster a laugh, but didn't nearly make it.

A small smile slipped out of each of them as Press and Barry passed a glance across the desk.

"He heard the commotion and came after me in his squad car. The city lets him keep it at his house. When he stopped me several blocks later, I just sort of lost it. I told him everything. He took me to the station and told me to sleep it off there. Said he'd take care of everything."

Head bowed, Hartley peered under his eyebrows at Press, then sideways at Barry.

"He came back into the station in the morning and took me back to my car. He said he'd fixed things so Susan wouldn't bother me any more. He told her if she ever threatened me again or did go to my wife at all, he'd arrest her under the state stalking law. Told her I'd also have every right to sue her for breaking up my marriage. It didn't matter that I'd been having sex with her for almost two years. I guess it worked because I haven't heard from her since. She even ignored me when I saw her at the Fremont Stop and Shop getting gas. By then it was too late, though."

The mist that had been clouding Hartley's eyes turned to a full-blown downburst now.

"When I got home that Tuesday morning, Sharon had been up all night and was madder'n all hell. I told her I'd been stopped for drunk driving and spent the night in jail. She was giving it to me for that and then she smelled the perfume. Everything just went downhill from there," he was sobbing hard now. "That weekend she took Becky and went to Minneapolis to stay with her mother. I've been callin' her almost every night to try an' work things out, but I just don't know if I can. I don't think I can stand Christmas without her and Becky."

He was trying to palm the tears from his eyes between gasps, but his hands couldn't keep up with the flow. Press reached into a desk drawer and hauled out a box of tissues, which he pushed across the desk to Wes.

"God, if this hits the paper, Press, I know I'll never get her back!"

Press puffed his cheeks and leaked out a slow sigh.

"I guess the only story I see here is that you were picked up for drunk driving and the chief tried to cover it up. We do have to do that much," Press said, looking to Barry for confirmation. The editor nodded his agreement. "This isn't *The Inquirer.* We're not interested in who's screwing whom. But what the chief did goes further than that. It's pretty serious, we think."

"Do you know what Nordstrom did about recording the fact that you were picked up each time? Did you see him write anything down about it?" Barry asked as Hartley swabbed his eyes with tissues.

"No, I never really paid any attention," Wes snuffled. "I just figured he was letting me sleep it off each time. Didn't see the harm in that. Figured I'd have gotten a ticket or a summons or something if I was being charged."

"What about the first two times you were picked up?" Barry asked.

"I was drunk, no excuses. He got me for it."

"Why didn't he write you up?" Barry pressed.

"I honestly don't know," Wes shrugged. "But I was damned grateful."

"You didn't see anything wrong with that? Him letting you off so easy?"

Hartley shrugged weakly.

“Like I said, I never really gave it any thought.”

"On the record," Press initiated as he leaned forward on the desk, "did you ever ask him specifically not to cite you?"

"No, of course not!"

"Did you ever suggest or hint in any way that some favor might be returned?" Press grilled further.

Hartley dug his tongue into his cheek and rolled it around as though trying to taste the right words with which to answer and, after a mouthful of searching, came up with nothing more than the shake of his head. That rattled out a "No."

"Are you aware of the seriousness of a public official like the police chief hiding or falsifying record?" Barry offered.

"Yes, I suppose that's not right," Hartley allowed but quickly added, "Look, my life is shit enough right now without getting involved in anything like that. Whatever the chief did...I just thought it was a courtesy. I don't know anything about the way he runs his office."

Press rocked back and pawed his Adams apple a couple of times.

"We're going with the story, Wes. The drunk driving incidents and the cover-up," he said, swiveling to Barry for affirmation. "Send us your official response to that part of it by Monday and we'll go with that for your role in it."

"Unless, of course, we find you've cut a bigger piece of the puzzle than you're telling us," Barry injected quickly.

Hartley said he understood and struggled out of the chair. With a swipe of a coat sleeve across each eye, he turned and headed out the door, stooped and head down, trying to hide the pain that raked his face red like a hot poker. With their eyes, Press and Barry followed him through the newsroom and out the front door.

"I guess that's a twist in the rope that I didn't expect," Barry said as the two returned to their seats in Press' office. "I think you were as fair as you could be with him, though. Maybe more so than some would've been."

"It would appear that he's got enough other things messed up in his life right now," Press sighed. "Besides, I don't think it's important to the story." He chewed the inside of his cheeks for a long moment.

"Somehow I just can't help feeling that the pieces to the puzzle aren't all on the table yet, though," he offered finally.

"So what are you thinking?"

"I don't know. I can't put a finger on it. It's just like the picture's not all here yet. We've just gotta go with what we've got for now."

"How should we go about getting the file or files that Nordstrom hid Hartley's record in?" Barry asked.

"Why don't we wait until next Friday after we run the story," Press mused, stretching back, his hands entwined behind his head. "See if we can jack him up a bit. You know? Let him know that we mean business and then just go in and ask him point blank?"

"Sounds like a plan to me," Barry okayed, getting up to leave.

Press turned to his computer to begin work on his column for the next issue.

"PRESSING MATTERS"
December 8

Age doesn't always bring wisdom. Sometimes you have to coax it out of somebody with the help of a lawyer-type potion. That's precisely the insightful elixir that enticed Fremont Police Chief Derek Nordstrom last week, in a sage bit of recovery, to provide information to the *Gazette* that he was legally required to do in the first place. It's funny how doing the right thing isn't always the first option sought by some people who make laws and some who enforce them....

11

Hold a harmonica in the air and the wind off the plains would have played ragtime as Press drove through the four-way stop at Main Street and headed north on Saturday morning. Another two miles past the railroad overpass, the old boarded up red brick school, the Kmart, the shopping center, Delaney's Hardware, the Safeway, and two banks, he pulled into the lot at the new post office to pick up the mail for the *Gazette*. Six years in place, it was still the "new" post office to most folks in Fremont and still a minor burr in Press' shorts.

Yes, it was bigger and nicer, but Press still missed the old office downtown. It had been just a block from the *Gazette* building, an easy walk to pick up the mail. His circulation crew could also load the newspaper bundles onto a cart and haul them to the old post office on Wednesday afternoon. Now the papers had to be loaded into the company van and it took a couple of trips.

Still, he marveled at how the town was stitching the seams of its limits farther and farther, north and south.

Wasn't much north of the railroad overpass except a few houses and the old Jefferson School when I came here, Press recalled. Couple of gas stations, maybe.

Preston Williams had purchased the *Fremont Weekly Gazette* twenty-three years earlier from MacArthur "Mac" Burns for what was then the exorbitant sum of $54,000. Mac had outlived the final payment by only a month and three weeks and, in all honesty, Press didn't much miss him. Almost every week for ten years, one month and three weeks, Mac Burns had stopped into the office to critique the latest issue of the Williams franchise and offer an uninspiring monologue on why the Burns ways were better. For all the general crankiness that Mac Burns contributed to the atmosphere of the *Gazette* office in those years, however, he did also atone somewhat by providing fodder for Press' homespun weekly column, **Pressing Matters**. The fact that Mac was a better reference for local lore than the library, on the other hand, was largely offset by the ease with which one could get away from the library in less than an hour. And slip away while preserving a better than curmudgeonly state of mind.

Press had grown up in a place called Banning, a map dot with a post office and little more in Michigan's Upper Peninsula. It took him four years at the University of Wisconsin at Eau Claire, another move of nearly four hundred miles to Fremont, and three full years after that before he was able to shed himself of his "Yooper" accent along with the teasing that jigged to its less than melodious inflections.

For Press, growing up in Banning was not unlike passing the trials and rituals previous to adulthood experienced by other kids who were born and raised in the tiny town. It was just a time-biding until they could hitch a logging truck or a Greyhound someplace else. Press' father, Mick Williams, operated a small gas station and auto repair shop and his mother, Janie, did her best to operate his father. Neither garnered great success. Unfortunately for Press, about the only things that operated much around his father were gravity and his mother's tongue. The old man's notion of ambition was to dream that beer might someday flow from his kitchen tap – lager or pilsner, the vintage didn't so much matter. After a pile of years running the garage, all Mick Williams had to show for it was a stack of tool company calendars featuring pictures of well-equipped young women wearing minimal assortments of uniform.

His mother was forever spending whatever spare time she found in life waiting for one or the other of Banning's two taverns, the Iron Keg or the Copper Mug, to send her husband home. In later years when he would bifocal the past, Press figured it might as much have been the serrated edge of Janie Williams' tongue that chased the old man to beer as the draw of the malt taste awaiting. Somehow in the language of their wedding vows, the terms of existing together had been vague as a politician's promise.

Still, his father had his own tantrum to him, too, unique as a jagged spike of lightning. It was, perhaps, an added frustration that he didn't have enough fingers to point at all the reasons he could conjecture up that had caused him to be an unwealthy man. There were the Arabs with their oil price robbery. There was the government – everyone from the geezers on the town board, to the scoundrels in Washington, to the communists running the United Nations. There were the price-gouging Jews back East. There were the Indians and the Blacks who were getting all the welfare and idling away his tax dollars. And, when he couldn't think of anything or anyone else to blame, he offered a fine cussing to the weatherman. In his later years he had to orate about the misery of it all in self-inflicted isolation because no one else cared to listen any longer. He'd sit down at a crowded bar and, while he began aiming himself into the bottom of his first glass, people would gravitate to the jukebox or take up pool or find any other excuse to relocate. Still, you could see his lips moving as he practiced his outrage alone.

It hadn't taken Press long to figure that every tomorrow of his life in Banning looked just like a reintroduction of yesterday and today. Another lifestyle, better or otherwise, had to be waiting somewhere else. He'd bagged groceries all through high school and put himself through college with scholarships and part-time jobs. His mother died when he was a senior at the university in Eau Claire and, with the proceeds of the small insurance policy she'd hidden from his father, Press was able to make the down payments on a used Plymouth and on the *Gazette* after he graduated.

He'd only been back to Banning twice since finishing college. The last time was to see his father in the hospital in Ironwood five years ago. That was the week before the county placed Mick in a nursing home there. The old man's health had run out before Michigan's supply of beer had. His father suffered from alcohol poisoning and hadn't recognized his son. Press hadn't tried to speak to him since. He was too focused on making sure his own kids never wanted to recall their own father with any similar emptiness.

He still had an aunt and an uncle or two in Michigan and a few cousins he probably wouldn't recognize without posters diagramming names and relationships around their family tree. But a family tree was something Press never gave much thought to climbing for fun. The Upper Peninsula was just a place to him now, a bed and breakfast kind of place where he'd over-nighted a few years on his way to adulthood someplace else.

Michigan was farther from his thoughts than the mileage from Fremont this morning, however, as he headed toward the office with a pile of mail on the car seat beside him. He was thinking about Wes Hartley and Derek Nordstrom. What his nose told him wouldn't quite pass for rotten but he could sense the aroma of a fish out of water somewhere. He knew there was more, a lot more, to the story yet to unfold and he needed to catch wind of where to start looking.

12 The story of the mayor's drunk driving cover-up appeared in the *Gazette* the next week in a single column on the lower right hand side of page one. The news item matter-of-factly detailed Police Chief Derek Nordstrom's failure to comply with the *Gazette's* request for the incident records involving the mayor. It noted the decision of District Attorney Del Schell not to pursue the chief's public records violations promptly, and the police reports being turned over to the paper as a result of a writ of mandamus obtained on behalf of the *Gazette* by attorney Galen Perry. It also gave the mayor's official response to the matter:

> "I am deeply and profoundly embarrassed by the behavior which caused me to be detained by Fremont police three times in the past year. It is certainly unbefitting the type of mayor the people of Fremont deserve and have a right to demand. I have admitted that I have a drinking problem and am immediately entering the alcohol abuse program at Parsons General Hospital in hopes of saving my marriage and my career. City Council President Dick Flater will assume my responsibilities in my absence. I humbly ask the forgiveness of my wife, my daughter, and the people of Fremont. I want to state further that I had no knowledge of any improper record keeping or other allegations involving Police

> Chief Derek Nordstrom and his department. Again, I apologize for my improper behavior and ask the indulgence of the people of Fremont."

The response was immediate. The phone lines hissed the venom of at least a dozen callers to the *Gazette* office by Thursday afternoon, and Press and Barry each had ears lopped in uncharacteristic directions by a couple of more offended readers who called their homes that night. Most of the callers, all anonymous, blasted the paper, claiming it was nobody's business whether the mayor got picked up for drunk driving, and the police department shouldn't have to give out that kind of information anyway. Press pooh-poohed the calls, saying they were probably all from people who'd been nailed for DWIs and themselves been named in the paper.

Along with three subscription cancellations, two letters arrived in the *Gazette* mail on Friday morning. Ostensibly "to the editor", neither was suitable for print in a family paper due to their colorful references to ancestry and assorted body parts.

"If they'd had signatures, I'd have figured Derek for one and Mavis the other," Press smirked through a grin as he dropped the letters on Barry's desk. Concerning the cancelled subscriptions, he offered to bet with Barry that they'd probably see the 'former readers' buying the paper at the grocery store in a week or two.

"They get mad but they usually come back," he chuckled. "What do you say we go pay the chief a visit this morning?"

Mavis Manheim obviously still had her cranky coat on and looked purely furious. She returned to whatever she was scribbling as soon as she saw Press and Barry come through the door.

"Mornin', Mavis," Barry offered as cheerily sarcastic as he could muster and yet keep from expelling a full-blown laugh. Both men knew a genial greeting would be as lost on Mavis as a whistle in a March gale. "We'd like to see TC."

That did cause the woman to look up, though her expression dangled somewhere between inextricably befuddled and entirely hostile.

"You know there ain't no 'TC' working here," she said, her lips pursing as if she'd chewed them entirely off.

"Sure there is," Barry said with a grin wedging his cheeks apart. "You know...Derek Nordstrom? The Chief? Top Cop?"

Mavis harrrrumphed and went back to her scribbling on whatever form she'd been tending to when the men from the newspaper walked in.

"He don't wanta see you." It was no subtle snarl that issued from her.

"Maybe you ought to ask him first," Press suggested.

"He already told me yesterday afternoon," Mavis said as she inspected her scribbling before moving on to another form. "He ain't talkin' to either of you no more."

"Well, in that case, since you know everything that goes on in here anyway," Press suggested with a wink at Barry, "then that leaves you to give us whatever file the record on Mayor Hartley was kept in."

"I don't know what you're blabberin' about," Mavis retorted as she looked up from her scribbling.

"Sure you do, Mavis. The file on the mayor had to be kept somewhere. Everything on the pages was blanked out except the information on Hartley," Barry stated flatly. "That means there had to be more to the file. We want to see it."

"I can't give you that." Her voice muffled noticeably as she turned from the desk to her credenza so that her back was what she now offered the two men.

"Well, either you get it, or the chief gets it," Press demanded evenly, "or we go back to court."

Mavis got up and, without looking at either of them, marched stiffly to the hall that led to Chief Nordstrom's office.

"Mavis could give you the time of day and make you wonder why the heck you asked," Barry snickered when she was out of ear fetching.

Moments later the woman marched mechanically back to her desk and sat down, still not looking at Press or Barry. The chief, whose look matched Mavis' crankiness and appeared to have just been rousted from a nap, followed her.

"What the hell do you guys want now?" Nordstrom demanded in a tone that indicated he'd just been made a party to the conference without being let in on the details.

Press stated again that they wanted to see the file that contained the report on Mayor Hartley.

"You can't see that," the chief vowed. "It was *accidentally* written in the juvenile log."

"Three times!" Barry blurted incredulously.

Nordstrom shrugged to suggest it wasn't so hard to believe.

"And, what the heck is the juvenile log?" Press demanded with the cool stab of an ice pick.

"That's where we keep the reports on incidents involving anyone under the age of eighteen," the police chief asserted through the curled sneer on his lips. "The public's not allowed to see that."

Press rolled his eyes in disbelief and leaned sideways on the counter.

"So how long has this been going on?" he asked

"Since whenever the law was passed, I guess," Nordstrom answered, looking ever so much as though he'd just twisted a cat's tail without getting scratched in return.

"Look, Derek," Press began again after first inhaling a deep gush and then blowing it out through his cheeks. "We have every right to see the incident report on whatever the kids are involved in. We can even report that stuff in the paper. The law just says we can't publish their names."

"Well, I guess that's just why you also can't see the juvenile log," the chief replied with disdain. He glared at the pair while triggering his memory trying to recall if there was a bounty on idiots. "How'd I know you wouldn't print the names, elsewise?"

"You only have to worry about that if we do." The publisher's eyes narrowed as he returned Nordstrom's glare. "It's the law, Derek. You know, the civil code you're sworn to uphold?"

"Undoubtedly, the chief doesn't want us to see how many other incidents have *accidentally* been written into the juvenile log," Barry suggested with an elbow nudge to his boss.

Nordstrom waved his hands with elaborate indifference.

Press suggested that a writ of mandamus would be even easier to obtain on this matter than the first one was.

"You can try whatever you damned well feel like, but I'm not lettin' you see that log just on your say so," the chief assured with a growl that sent his Adam's apple ducking to hide behind the knot of his brown necktie. He gave the pair a punctuating glare, like it was an exclamation point to the last word of the sentence.

"Talking to him is like arguing with a parking meter," Press fumed as he and Barry left the station. "This one even Schell can't waiver on!"

But District Attorney Del Schell did waiver, or at least he wormed under the issue again without having offered any commitment.

"Sorry, Mr. Williams," Schell apologized into the phone when Press called him on Friday afternoon. "I'm just on my way out the door. Taking my wife to Vail for some holiday skiing. I'll be back in my office on January 3."

Ducking issues comes as naturally to that man as taking a morning dump, Press groused to himself. He had his hand on the telephone to call the attorney general's office once more when the receptionist informed him that Dick Flater was on the line for him.

"Mr. Mayor. How are things this afternoon?" Press greeted, honoring Flater's "acting" status in city hall while Wes Hartley was away at the hospital in Parsons being dried out. After exchanging a few pleasantries, Flater told Press he and the finance committee had been going over the mayor's proposed budget for the coming year.

"You got a copy of it?" the city council president inquired.

"I don't, but I'm sure Barry does if copies are available."

"I won't tell you what to look for, but get a copy and take a close look," Flater suggested. "Look particularly close at the police department budget."

"Do you think something's up?" Press asked, trying to keep his curiosity to a professional inquiry.

"I'm not going to say any more than that. Just take a good look."

Press hung up and sauntered into the newsroom.

"Barry, have you got a copy of the proposed city budget?"

"Sure do," Barry assured, turning to point to the volume on his credenza.

"Have you looked at any of it closely?" Press wondered.

"Not yet, really. I just got it from the city clerk's office Tuesday," McGinn offered. "About all I know for sure is that it's up about four percent over last year."

"Just got a call from Dick Flater," Press announced as he dropped into the chair beside Barry's desk. "Wouldn't tell me what it's all about, but he strongly suggested that we take a close look at the police department budget. How long is it?"

"I don't know, four or five pages probably," Barry said, reaching for the budget book and thumbing through the pages. "Five and a half to be exact."

"Why don't you photocopy those pages for me," Press suggested as he scratched deep into his left ear with the top off of a Bic pen. "Let's go over it tonight and we'll talk it over at breakfast at Cruiser's in the morning. I'll buy."

Back in his office Press dialed the number for Jarred Kleinmeier in the state attorney general's office. Kleinmeier had left for the day.

"Boy, lawyers on the public dole have sure got it rough," Press grumped sarcastically to himself. He had wanted to ask whether there wasn't something that the attorney general's office could do to jack up Del Schell in order to get him to pursue the open records issues in the Fremont Police Department. It would be even better, Press speculated, if Kleinmeier would even intercede on the *Gazette's* behalf and get Nordstrom to provide the records, either through intimidation or another writ of mandamus. Undoubtedly, it would shake up Nordstrom if the state guys got involved in the matter. Heck, even if Kleinmeier would just send the chief a letter telling him what records he's supposed to make available to the media might be enough to twist Nordstrom's tail in the right direction.

Press considered calling Galen Perry for another writ, but it *was* Friday afternoon, a week before Christmas Eve. He didn't want to spend the paper's money on a lawyer if he didn't have to and nothing was apt to come of it before Monday anyway, whether Galen handled getting the writ or the attorney general's office did.

Turning his back to his desk and lazing his head in the hammock weave of his fingers, Press stared out the window at the gray, snow-waiting-to-happen clouds that were billowing in low from the plains. The thought, too, was worrying other notions in his mind that, if there really were some newsy morsels cached in the juvenile files as he and Barry speculated, might not Nordstrom squirrel away the evidence once more or just trash it in order to keep it out of public sight?

As intriguing as it was irksome, Press enjoyed toying with conjecture over what other tidbits Nordstrom might have 'accidentally' forged into the juvenile police log. The gamut ran from a journal of who was screwing who, to the genealogical scaffolding of some local crime organization, such as one might be constructed in a town of fewer than five thousand potential felons and victims.

And, if the chief is so bent on covering up the mayor's driving drunk, Press contemplated, what else has he got to hide? I'd bet it would more than flavor the top of your Frosted Flakes, whatever this 'uppity side of up' lawman is into.

13 "You'd better go talk to Jeremy and get it over with," Abby told Press, aiming the side of her blond locks out of the kitchen as she half turned from the stove and whatever was about to become supper. "He's afraid you're really going to be upset with him," she added grimly.

"So, am I going to be?"

"You'd best let him explain," Abby opted.

Jeremy's head was anchored onto one hand, pinning his elbow to his desk as he pecked at the computer keyboard with his other hand. A frown worried his eyebrows together and, when he saw his father push the door ajar and poke into the room, a look of guilt wrestled its way onto his face.

"What's happening, Bud?" Press asked as he butted onto the corner of his son's bed.

"I got a speeding ticket," Jeremy replied dourly, looking back into the computer screen.

"Guess I warned you about that not long ago," Press noted with a hint of fatherly smugness. Still, he was mildly amused. Relieved, actually. At least it wasn't something that would keep him out of an institution of higher learning or herd him into a marital or penal institution.

"I don't really need to be reminded of that now," Jeremy said dryly.

"So how much is the ticket?"

"A hundred and forty-nine dollars," the boy responded meekly.

"That'll take a paycheck or two," Press surmised.

His son looked back, a tart response in the curl of his tongue, but judged better of it and said nothing.

"Where were you?" the father persisted.

"A block past Dairy Queen. Chief Nordstrom was sitting there with his radar on," Jeremy lamented.

The notion did trundle through Press' head that it seemed unusual for the police chief to be the one setting a radar trap on Friday afternoon. Retaliation, maybe? Press put the thought away, figuring he hadn't really buzzed Nordstrom's cranky button that hard yet.

"Well, the hundred and forty-nine dollars is the law's punishment, so we'll leave it at that," Press said as he stood and turned at the door. "Hopefully, that's enough to get you to tone it down now without me having to do anything more. Now you know that playing in traffic can be a might expensive if you don't play by the rules. Thankfully, this time, it's only costly to your wallet and not your life."

Jeremy nodded, grateful that his father hadn't amended the severity of the ticket, and Press measured his pace slowly back to the kitchen.

When Barry arrived at seven o'clock the next morning Press had already commandeered a square Formica top with accompanying chairs in the back at Cruiser's and was sipping coffee as he scanned the Saturday edition of the *Avery Daily American*. The editor offed his coat onto a rack and straddled the seat across the table from him. The restaurant chaired its usual weekend coziness of farmers in town to buy supplies, early shoppers waiting for the stores to open, and a couple of coffee klatches. There were also a few of those usual vagabonds who spent the night in one of the four local motels and now were soon to be bound for elsewhere down the road.

Stop in any small town and there is a Cruisers' Café, just with a different name. It's the kind of place noted more for its social lore than its haute cuisine. For the last decade or so, the place had been owned by Bernard 'Bud' Callahan. Bud was also the elected county coroner. Of course, that always added an extra flavor to the local humor and social commentary practiced daily over coffee at the lunch counter or the table squares fenced haphazardly by a mismatched cluster of chairs, some wooden, some metal framed with vinyl seats. Often Bud's elected position also allowed him to provide instant verification or insight into some of the area news, real or rumored. It was sort of the main office for the neighbor-to-neighbor wire service that served the small town and with which neither the newspaper nor the local radio station could compete. For that feedbag of information, Cruiser's patrons were willing to put up with Bud's mediocre food, sassy waitresses, and coffee stiff as the porcelain it was served in.

Naturally, Press and Barry took their turns in one group or another catching an earful for what was in the paper or what wasn't, or what might end up there. Most of what they gathered was banter more than news, generally good-natured, occasionally not. Once in awhile, the newsmen had to swallow a dish of criticism more acrid even than Cruiser's coffee.

"So? Did you come up with anything?" Barry asked as he laid his copy of the official budget volume on the corner of the table beside him.

Press folded up his newspaper and tucked it under the manila envelope that rested on the opposite corner of the table.

"What can I get you fellas this morning?" trilled the waitress as she splashed coffee into a cup for Barry. While his regular weekday presence for morning coffee and an occasional lunch acquainted him with most of the waitresses, at least by sight, this woman was unknown to Press. The plastic name plate she wore on the upward slope of her left breast introduced her as 'Hello I'm DOROTHY.' She was a jolly sort of beauty shop blond with an ampleness to her proportions that the pink uniform dress was stressed to contain. A red Santa cap sat starchly pointed atop her oval head, producing a color clash with the pink expanse of her uniform. Hello I'm DOROTHY produced a pencil from a tight cluster of curls above her right ear and applied it to a scratch pad cradled in her left hand in a manner that announced she was ready to take their orders and they'd better hurry up because she was busy.

"I guess I don't need a menu today," Barry chuckled. "I'll have two eggs over hard, some sausage, hash browns, and white toast with strawberry jelly. Oh, and a large orange juice, too, please."

"You do that just to irritate the heck out of me, don't you?" Press asserted, using the best imitation of seriousness that he could muster.

"Whaddya mean? Did I exceed the expense account?" Barry asked with a mild case of chagrin scrunching his eyebrows together.

"No, no, I can afford to buy your whole darned breakfast," Press said with a shake of his head as he turned to the waitress, who was waiting with her forehead furrowed like the first planting of spring. "I'll have half a grapefruit, a bowl of bran cereal, and two pieces of dry toast. And just coffee, de-caf." Turning back to Barry, he added with a wry grin, "If I ate like you do, I'd be back over three hundred pounds inside of six months."

"So, *did* you find anything in the cop shop budget proposal?" Barry inquired again, smiling, as he folded the pages over to the police department portion of the budget proposal and Press retrieved his photocopied sheets from his folder.

"I have to admit that I fell asleep on the couch looking at this stuff," Press acknowledged. "The only thing that jumped out at me is the fifteen percent increase in the dollar package. All other city departments are either getting cut or receiving pretty meager increases. What'd you say? Four percent or something?"

"Yeah, that's about right," Barry nodded in agreement. "And it's not like we've seen a major increase in drug traffic or gang violence. As if we have much of either. I can see the two new squad cars, but they rotate one or two of them every year."

The pair poured over the figures in concentrated silence, even as the waitress delivered their orders.

"You know, take a look once at the overtime allotment," Barry said, the words finding their way over and around half a pork sausage link. Pointing with a fork, he continued, "It's higher than last year's expenditure and last year's spending was more than double what was in the budget."

"I thought the city added Bonner's position just to cut down on all the overtime?" Press queried dryly through a bite of toast.

"That's right. That's what makes it so odd."

"Freshen your coffee, guys?" The pillowy, Hello I'm DOROTHY woman was back at the table wagging a pair of coffee pots latched handle-to-handle in her left hand, the one red-handled for de-caf. Press declined with a hand over his cup while Barry slid his aside for a refill.

"High octane, please."

"Gee, you boys look like you're workin'," Hello I'm DOROTHY conversed in a friendly stab at earning a bigger tip as she shifted the pot of regular coffee to her right hand and poured. "Dontcha know it's Saturday?"

"No rest for the wicked," Barry replied with an impish grin.

"Aw, Hon, you don't look too wicked to me," Hello I'm DOROTHY came back with, along with a pat, pat on his arm before largely whirling away to another table with the speed of a rumor.

Right hand on his hip, left elbow on the table, and his chin wedged into the vee of his thumb and forefinger, Press contemplated a long series of moments.

"Barry, I think you ought to spend some time over at the city clerk's office Monday morning," he offered finally. "Take a wander through the P.D. payroll files and see if you can't pick up on who's getting all the overtime and when. Then maybe we can figure out the 'why' of it."

"Too bad all of this is coming up just in time for the holidays," Barry mused. "As if there aren't enough other things going on right now."

"Yeah, I know," Press agreed. "Abby wants me to take her up to Avery Christmas shopping this afternoon. I can't for the life of me figure out what excitement women find in shopping, especially going all the way to Avery to do it. All I see there is a whole lot more of what we have between here and Parsons."

"I know," Barry agreed. "Angie's the same way. Thankfully, I think she had all of her Christmas gifts bought by August. I still haven't got a clue what to get her, though."

Hello I'm DOROTHY bustled by with a 'thank you' and the check.

"You gents have a Merry Christmas," she called as she swooshed away.

14 A bundle full of giggles and wiggles packaged in Abby's clothes sat beside Press in the Buick on the way to Avery an hour later. Shopping was her favorite pastime and Christmas was her favorite time of year. Combine those with a rare coaxing of her husband into an out of town spree and Abigail, nee Findstrom, Williams had found heaven without the inconvenience of dying. Any time she exuded such happiness, the glow soon duplicated on her spouse's face.

The pair had become what some considered an unlikely couple while students at the University of Wisconsin-Eau Claire, though they formally met, sort of, in Minneapolis. A year younger than Press, Abby was an education major and basketball cheerleader in college. Press worked two part-time jobs and wrote for the school newspaper, *The Spectator,* as he applied himself to the study of journalism. Her Swedish-blond hair, when not flowing down her back nearly to her waist, was slung fetchingly frontwise over a shoulder. Matching the yellow in her hair was a pair of eyebrows framed over a set of bunting-blue eyes. She had a wide-cut mouth where her usual expression was curled in a smile sometimes seductive, sometimes curious. The ample pleasures in the notice of her had snatched an extended visit from Press' eyes on a number of occasions. It began with a photo assignment at a Blugold basketball game, followed by an increasingly frequent series of coincidental visits to the library. Although Press caught her returning his glances with an accompanying smile on a number of occasions, shyness handcuffed any attempt at an introduction. The hours at work and study bridled his time and social aptitude. And, more to the point in Press' mind, he figured she was way out of his league anyway.

Ironically, they met while Christmas shopping, a circumstance that always made it harder for Press to decline when Abby beckoned at the front of the holidays.

His senior year, a roommate, Chris Carlson, had invited Press to spend the Thanksgiving break at his parents' home in Minneapolis. The two were wandering around the Mall of

America, proclaiming to be Christmas shopping the Friday after, when a voice cheered from the entrance of whatever shop they were passing, "Hey, don't you guys go to Eau Claire?"

Abby and her mom were up from Spring Valley, Minnesota, for a shopping tour before Mrs. Findstrom delivered her back to college on Saturday. Abby was cheering at a basketball game on Saturday night. After introductions, Abby's mother and Chris stood seemingly mute and idle as bookends for whatever lifetimes the other two could squeeze into a few brief moments. Within a matter of minutes – probably less than five – Press had determined to return to Eau Claire by bus on Saturday for a meeting after the game that night. When they had said their farewells, his eyes traveled after her as far as they could through the holiday shopping throngs and the pumpkin smile stuck on his face long after Abby and her mother vanished into another boutique.

Lord, how he'd wished that Greyhound had wings as it headed east along Interstate 94 the next morning. Even though their date wasn't until after the game that night, there was always the chance of glimpsing Abby around campus. For the rest of that term and all of the next he invented ways to squeeze her into his presence around the crush of classes and exams, and assorted part-time jobs, and work on the school paper. Even when she was not within view of his eyes, rarely was she far from sight in his mind.

The following summer Press had logged the five-hour drive to Spring Valley every Friday and back to Fremont again late on Sunday. It became an every-other-weekend ritual during the following school year as he drove eight hours each way from Fremont to Eau Claire and back again while Abby was completing her degree. The jokes and pranks and sass and love-making that danced away those hours together kept Press ever mindful of the next tune to come as he hurried the days along between weekends. They were married in a modest church ceremony in Spring Valley two weeks after Abby graduated the following June.

During their first three years together in Fremont, Abby taught sixth grade while Press waded headlong into the struggle to maintain and improve his weekly newspaper. Abby graduated to fulltime housewife and mom when Jeremy came along. While the notion of mothers working outside the home rocketed across America after World War II, that prospect had plodded through Fremont on a hay wagon. Abby never questioned the relegation from schoolrooms to homerooms.

"So, are we looking for anything specific or just browsing today?" Press grinned as the outskirts of Avery began to bump and shuffle with the farmland for space around the city.

"Kate has a dress picked out at Dillards that she wants and I thought we could look at a suit for you there too, since you still haven't said what you want for Christmas." A smile sneaked through the pout of her lips as she gave a playful jab at her husband's ribs.

"And did you give me some clue as to what *you* want or has it slipped my aging mind?" Press gave in return.

"Oh, you know I'm thrilled with whatever you give me," Abby giggled coyly. "Surprise me!"

"It may surprise me, too," Press said as an aside over the top of the outstretched right arm that directed the steering wheel.

"Jeremy wants some Play Station computer game or something, and a backpack at Eddie Bauer," Abby said, back now on the original question. "I'd kind of like to get some ideas for my folks, too. I've got to come up with something soon. And I don't have the foggiest idea what to get Cassie yet."

"How about a football and a set of boxing gloves?" Press suggested with a teasing smile.

Abby dug a *don't even go there* frown into him in return.

The return trip found Abby behind the wheel on her third wind while her exhausted husband dozed, a seriated chorus of *kct-kct-kct-kcts* escaping from the oval under his nose. The trunk of the Buick was amply Santa-fied with packages and bundles, mostly already gift-wrapped. A couple more rode in the rear seat. Before leaving Avery, Abby had called the kids and told them to eat one of the frozen pizzas in the freezer for dinner. Their parents were stopping at French's Restaurant on the north side of Fremont.

"PRESSING MATTERS"
December 22

...Final thought for the week...May the peace and joy of this Holiday Season find you and yours throughout the coming year....

15 "How was your week in Spring Valley?" Barry asked as he eased into a chair in the publisher's office.

"Really nice," Press replied. "Nice to get away from here for awhile and good to see Abby's folks. They're always thrilled to have time with the grandkids. Kate, of course, grumbled about not being able to see Casey on Christmas or New Years either. Kids in love, you know. Have you been able to come up with anything on the police overtime business?"

"It literally took me hours going through the records," Barry answered as he pushed a sheet of paper across the desk to Press. "I've pretty well listed the stuff there."

The puzzle wrinkled its way through several parts of Press' face.

"As you can see," Barry continued, "by far the majority of the overtime is for the chief."

"The chief!" Press echoed in astonishment. "How the heck can he claim overtime? He's a department head!"

"Yeah, and not only that, he hardly ever worked more than forty hours a week," Barry added, pointing to a couple of lines on the sheet in front of his boss. "But he did work every holiday and most Sundays…and collected *triple wages* for them, claiming holiday pay!"

"But he can't do that!" Press asserted in disbelief. "He's a salaried department administrator!"

"But he did just that, and expects to again this year if it clears the budget," Barry noted, his raised eyebrows keeping pace with the shake of his head. "Nordstrom's official salary is listed at eighty-seven thousand, one hundred dollars annually. Yet, last year he made almost a hundred thirty grand. And this year the finance committee's giving him a fifty-two hundred dollar raise on top of that!"

Eyes still worrying over the figures on the paper Barry had given him, Press laid his hands flat on the desk and snorted a puff through his cheeks.

"That's incredible! How the hell does Nordstrom get the council to go along with it?"

"Apparently he doesn't deal with the council directly," McGinn asserted. "I spent some time going over it with Dick Flater and he says the mayor went to every member of the finance committee and demanded that the overtime item be included in the budget."

"The mayor?" Press' amazement was intensifying with each new revelation. "Wes is usually so tight with the city's money, you'd think it came out of his own wallet. I always thought he'd rather open his own blood vessels than the city coffers."

"Flater said Hartley picked out items that each one of the committee members had an interest in and quietly threatened to veto them if the overtime wasn't included in the police department budget," Barry declared. "I talked to a couple of the committee members and they denied it. Said the expense was necessary to keep officers patrolling the streets."

"Did you point out that it was almost all going to Nordstrom?"

"Not yet," Barry replied, shifting back in his seat and shaking his head. "I figured I'd play dumb and see what they'd offer first. I guess they're either playing dumb, too, or it's just simple genetics."

"Looks like Hartley played us like a banjo," Press acknowledged through a grimace. "Appears pretty clear that he's paying off his debt to Nordstrom for not filing the drunk driving charges. Is Hizzoner out of the dryout program yet?"

"Another week, I think. I tried calling the alcohol and drug abuse unit in Parsons, but they wouldn't let anyone but immediate family talk to him," Barry answered. "I did call Nordstrom and asked him about the overtime point blank. His response was, *Do you think I should work for free?"*

"That sounds like Nordstrom all right. Did you ask him how he could justify overtime as a department head?"

"Yeah. He just said other people run their offices their way and he'd run the police department his. Said if the city council didn't like it, they could always find a new chief."

"I guess you've got a story now. Probably an editorial, too," Press said, turning to some other matters on his desk as the conversation ended.

"PRESSING MATTERS"
January 5

> They say that brain cells come and brain cells go but fat lives forever. We're still trying to decipher why all the fat abounds in the proposed city expenditure for the Fremont Police Department. Seems hiring a new patrolman wasn't the cure for excess overtime after all....

The story of the police chief's overtime wages appeared on the front page of Thursday's *Gazette,* the first edition of the new year. An accompanying editorial also noted that Nordstrom was a salaried department head and should not be permitted to draw overtime pay, since his compensation was sufficiently high to accommodate whatever hours he was required to supervise the department. Again, the response to the story was immediate and vitriolic, with only two of the callers to the office identifying themselves. None of those calling Press or Barry at home would give their names.

"You know, I'm thinking of having caller ID installed here and at home," Press grumbled as he passed Barry's desk on Friday morning.

"Yeah, I've thought about it for my house, too," Barry nodded a fraction. "The problem is, they can block it if they really want to. It's not too difficult. As stupid as some of these cranks are, though, I doubt they could figure it out. We'd at least know who a few of 'em are."

By press time the next week, a smattering of equally anonymous letters were followed by half a dozen signed and addressed to the editor for print. Two were from city council members defending inclusion of the overtime in the police budget as necessary for the safety of Fremont citizens. They ignored the fact that the extra wages were almost entirely for the top cop. The other correspondents railed against the newspaper for its alleged vendetta against the chief.

None of that was particularly troubling to Press. He'd been through controversial issues before, even losing a few subscribers at times. But the readers always returned in a few months, along with new subscribers to join them, as the increasing circulation figures for the *Gazette* had shown. What Charlotte McElroy conveyed to him on Wednesday morning, however, he did find especially troubling.

"Steve Anderson says he's thinking about going direct mail with the Kmart flyers," she announced across the publisher's desk when he'd returned from coffee. Charlotte was the *Gazette's* advertising manager for the past three years and the paper's top sales representative for four years before that. A failed marriage had forced Charlotte into the working class of mothers for the first time in her life and it turned out that she'd entered into a profession that she was really good at – selling advertising. Within two years she let it be known with no little pride that she was earning more money than her ex-husband who was still working at the cannery.

The surprise crinkled Press' eyes. "Why would he want to do that? Third class postal rates are more than triple what we charge."

"Ostensibly to try something different," Charlotte offered with a creative curl to her eyebrows and a pucker to her lipstick that suggested a lot more was lurking behind 'ostensibly.' Charlotte was meticulous about her appearance, beginning with the weekly beauty shop hairdo, to the Mary Kay Cosmetic face, to the designer clothes. She believed image was a major part of her job and she made sure she looked the part of a professional advertising consultant. And she was equally meticulous about her work. "But he did happen to mention also that he wasn't really pleased with what the paper's been writing about the police chief. Steve seems to think pretty highly of Mr. Nordstrom. He says he likes the way the chief handles bad checks and shoplifters and that we ought to lay off him."

"Well, maybe we ought to let him pay those postal bills for a month or two. He'll be back with us again." Press gave an offhand wave and started back at the stack of mail on his desk.

"Press, Kmart is a forty thousand dollar a year account," Charlotte gasped. The account also provided one of her bigger monthly commissions. "Do you really want to risk that?"

Press passed a hand over his face as if wiping on a new realization.

"I suppose not," he sighed. "I'll stop and have a talk with him."

Steven Anderson was engineering a train of shopping carts from the parking lot through the automatic doors back into the store when Press found him after lunch. The Kmart manager always had that look of a person never caught up with all his work. Though the air had the bite of a feisty dog, he hadn't gathered a coat when he went out to assemble the line of carts to deliver back inside. The sleeves of his dress shirt were rolled three turns, the tail was desperately trying to wriggle free over his belt buckle, the top button was undone, and his tie loosened to dangle in a fit that made him look like a child trying on his father's clothes. The thinning swatch of hair sat permanently windblown atop his head, and his nose seemed forever in danger of shedding the wire-rimmed spectacles that lodged loosely over its bridge.

"Got a minute, Steve?" Press asked as he followed through the electric door.

"Just," Anderson replied as he straightened the row of carts before leaning across them on his elbows, his eyes averting those of the publisher.

"I hear you're thinking of putting your advertising circulars in the mail," Press started.

"Considering it," Anderson said, running the glasses back up to his forehead while looking past Press.

The newspaperman started to offer some benefits to keeping the ads in the paper when Steve cut him short.

"Yeah, Charlotte went through all of that. She's really good. This is just something we're thinking of trying. Something different." He stood up and blew into his hands before snuggling them into his pockets.

"Anything wrong with our service or something?" Press posed tentatively.

The store manager let his eyes visit Press' briefly, then surveyed the floor. "Not your service, really. I just don't care for what you're trying to do to the police chief."

Press surrendered his attention to the man as Anderson vented his theory that Nordstrom was doing an outstanding job on behalf of the retail chain by going after shoplifters and bad check writers. Anderson pointed out that he'd worked at six stores in four states and Fremont had by far the most cooperative police department he'd encountered. When he was finished pointing out that, sometimes, creative ways are needed to compensate good people and that the news media shouldn't always be looking for dirt to throw on people, Press agreed with him.

"Wouldn't it be simpler to just get the city council to up his salary dramatically? Then it would all be up front and there wouldn't be any need to go sneaking about getting more money for the chief." Press suggested. Anderson supposed he agreed.

"But who cares if he didn't bust the mayor for drunk driving?" the store manager came back. "The police need to use a little discretion now and then. Besides, the mayor's not just any ordinary Joe."

"That's true," Press acknowledged with a hunch of his shoulders. "But would you rather find out about a drunk driver getting off now, or after he did it again and hit a little girl as she crossed the street? Maybe *your* little girl? And a drunk behind the wheel is still a drunk, no matter what his name or rank is."

Anderson supposed he agreed again.

"I certainly wouldn't mind reading in the police log that an officer gave a ride to someone who'd had too many," Press suggested. "We wouldn't bother printing that. But don't you think that should be recorded on the police blotter? Then, if something *is* amiss, like the mayor getting off on three different occasions, then people can find out about it. They can draw their own conclusions. Maybe do something about it if they want."

Still checking out the floor tiles with his eyes, Anderson nodded as if the publisher's words were the first dollars laid on a bet. Press left him with the suggestion that, if he ever had questions about something in the *Gazette* or any of its policies, he should call Press directly. "And if you want to live in a police state, why don't you move to Moscow?" he wanted to add but left it alone. Nothing more was mentioned about the advertising flyers in the following weeks, but Press wasn't sure he'd totally convinced the store manager. The possibility that the remaining smoke might rekindle into a full-fledge fire would gnaw at Press for a long time.

16 Industriously chewing her lower lip, Abby was waiting at the kitchen door with a grim look and a hug when Press stepped in from the garage on Monday evening.

"What? Did Jeremy get another ticket?" her husband asked almost jokingly.

"The manager of the nursing home in Michigan called," Abby said softly as she stepped back, her fingers still entwined at the back of Press' neck. "Your father's not doing well."

The smile dropped from Press' face more quickly than if Abby had sliced it with a bread knife.

"God, he hasn't done well for as far back as I can remember," Press said dryly, turning his head aside as he found what seemed to be a golf ball suddenly manufacturing itself in his throat.

"Press," Abby scolded gently. "The woman said he's probably going to die soon. The number's on the pad by the phone on your desk."

It wasn't totally unexpected news for Press. The surprise that climbed into his mind was only that it hadn't come sooner. Still, dread filled the gully in the pit of his stomach like river mud. He made the call.

"We're very sorry, Mr. Williams," the woman on the other end of the line consoled. "He's been declining ever since Christmas. We thought you should know that we feel his time is very short."

When he asked "how short?" he was told hours, maybe minutes. Death was, after all, a regular caller at the nursing home. Caretakers of the frail and dying soon grew to recognize the fade of life as soon as it attached itself like a second shadow to the occupant of any of the beds there. She said she'd let him know as soon as his father passed away.

The call he knew would come did so just before seven the next morning. Still, he felt ambushed, surprised by the feelings that tumbled inside him.

Press sat by the phone long after he'd replaced the receiver, staring out the window as if his father's portrait had just been hung there. The man in the picture was a younger one, smiling as though he'd just been handed a free beer; not at all like the father he'd last seen those five years earlier. That one with the commotion of gray hair and hollow cheeks; that one with dull, deep eyes that had lost any spark of knowing or recognition.

Thoughts ricocheted around his mind like fireflies trapped in a canning jar. His mother, dead these many years, and yet it was still hard to think of one and not the other. But it wasn't her picture that hung in the gallery of his notions now. Only his dad, Mick Williams, stood there. The man who had made beer drinking like a second job while his mother was alive had sought it out as a serious career when she was dead.

Seventy-one the old man was this day he died. On those rare occasions when the subject of his father came up, Press had joked that he was living so long because his body was always pickled in alcohol. After the death of one of the local celebrities in Fremont, Press had laughed with the guys during coffee at Cruiser's saying his father could never be cremated that way because the fire would go on for weeks. He wasn't laughing now.

Still tying the terrycloth belt of her bathrobe, Abby came into the den and saw the tears rivering down her husband's cheeks. She held his head and rocked gently as he buried his face into her robe, sobbing harder than any time since he was a kid, his body convulsing with the erratic rhythm of his gasps. When the storm had brawled itself out and was withering to a squall, Abby guided Press to the sofa and dug a handful of tissues out of a pocket of her robe. Press sopped up the remnants of the cloudburst with the tissues and was able to keep up with the remaining flow with fingers and palms.

"It's funny," he whispered at last. "I never thought I'd cry over the old man. Wasn't like we were really close or anything." He leaned an elbow on the back of the couch and quartered to face Abby.

"I guess so many emotions have been stored up in me over the years that they just all let loose at once." The words were beginning to flow now that the levee had been breached that had held back his thoughts as well as his tears.

"Growing up you have to figure your life's not all that much out of sorts from anyone else's. Maybe some kids had more money, some less, but that's all I saw of it. It used to upset me a lot when Dad would come home drunk and Mom was always yelling at him. But I never thought of it like I was having an unhappy childhood or anything. You just kind of put parents in a bag like you do teachers and figure they're all pretty much alike."

Press halted for a series of heartbeats, surfacing to gather air. He gave a soft snort and half a smile at Abby. It was a smile with an odd mix of sad and happy. A trickle of tears was realizing a route down Abby's cheeks now, too.

"Then I met you. And the kids came. Gradually I started to realize what a happy family life really could be, what a childhood should be like. Talk between parents doesn't have to be a verbal brawl and stink with beer breath. I realized that there is so much love in this family. I love you and the kids more than life itself. That's when I started to get really angry. I felt like I'd been cheated out of a family as a kid, like I'd been short-changed on my childhood. I wanted to grab the old man by the shirt and shake him and yell at him what a rotten father he'd been. But by then it was too late. The beer had pickled his brain so badly that he wouldn't have understood. I suppose the pickling process had taken a good measure of him even when I was still in grade school."

Press came up for air again.

"I've thought about it off and on for several years, now. I know it sounds awful, but I can't think of a single good memory of my father." His head moved side to side like a weather vane in a wind that couldn't make up its mind. "There were good times, sure enough. But they were a circumstance Dad's presence never played a part in. I didn't realize it at the time, but looking back I know that I tried to avoid him as often as not. Since I couldn't drink with him, he probably preferred it like that as much as I did."

The couple sat in silence for a time, Abby's hand resting on her husband's arm. At last he shook his head and continued.

"Do you know that my father never once told me he loved me? I assume he did. After all, he *was* my father and I was his only child. But he never once said it – at least not after I was old enough to hear it and know what it meant. I swore years ago that my children would never grow up not hearing their father say that he loved them. And the same for my wife."

Abby grabbed the shoulders of his T-shirt and pulled Press gently to her.

"I love you so much," he sobbed into the gold shawl of hair that draped her shoulders.

17

Even with the speed of air flight, the trip to Ironwood had overwhelmed all but the few hours left in Wednesday. Press and Abby had roused their children at three in the morning for the drive to the airport in Avery to catch the six-thirty flight to Minneapolis. After a long layover, which provided time for lunch, a browse through a variety of airport shops, and a wealth of waiting and napping at the gate, they boarded a connecting flight that would shuttle them to Ironwood with a stop in Duluth along the way. The five members of the Williams family occupied more than a third of the passenger seats available on the small commuter plane.

Press procured three-day ownership of a mini-van at the rental desk and loaded the family and their luggage for the drive to the Best Western. First they would stop, however, at the funeral home to go over any last minute details.

Ironwood had changed little since his last trip. Snow freighted in on northwinds off of Lake Superior – the Great one still some miles away – was heaped on everything that wasn't vertical or plowed clear for use by feet or wheels. The kids were in awe, noting that they'd never seen so much of the white stuff in their entire lives, even the relatively small glimpse of it that was now provided in the dark.

"I remember as a kid in Banning when it would snow four or five inches at a time and the sun would be shining," Press recalled whimsically.

"Aw, Dad, how can it snow without clouds?" Cassie wondered somewhere between disbelief and certainty that her father wouldn't make up a story like that.

"It's what they call *lake effect* snow," he assured her. "The wind gathers moisture off the lake, freezes it, and dumps it as snow on everything for miles inland."

With the daylight turned off for a couple of hours already, the temperature had dropped like a shattered icicle to a half dozen digits below zero. When they piled out of the mini-van in front of the funeral parlor, the wind was still swatting at them like invaders in its personal domain.

Inside the funeral home they stomped the remnants of sidewalk snow off their shoes and the circulation of warmth back into their veins as the family began unpiling their winter coats.

The sound of all the galloping announced the family's presence to Bailey Sorenson, the funeral director, who hurried out to greet them. Bailey was a friendly, gentle man in his late fifties, the next generation of his family to run the mortuary. He eased them through the finalities with no complications. There would be a one-hour visitation in the morning before a brief service to be held in the funeral parlor. A large gathering of mourners was not anticipated. Mick's body would be stored in the mortuary while awaiting spring thaw when he would be buried beside his wife. Sorenson then led Press and the rest of the family to a small sitting room where his father's casket waited.

"I assume you'd like some time alone with him," Sorenson offered quietly as he went to open the coffin. Press nodded and the man left the room. He stood there, peering into the opened casket, Abby at his side, while the dead man's three grandchildren bunched shyly behind their mother as if they were toddlers once more, first time meeting a stranger.

Press was surprised, wondering for a moment if someone else's body hadn't been placed in his father's suit by mistake. Mick's gray disarray of hair, what was left of it, had turned stark white. It was combed better than Press could remember seeing it as a kid, even in church on those rare Sundays when his mother could cajole him along. Though he was starvation thin – even lying on his final bed covers, the old suit sagging around him like something he hoped he might someday grow into – he looked relaxed and perhaps at ease with himself at last. It was almost a smug look, as though he'd finally won some argument that resulted in the payment of a free beer.

"It's amazing how they can make him look so peaceful," Abby said. She hadn't seen Mick since the day she and Press were married. Downing drinks as if they might otherwise get away from him, Mick had gotten rip roaring drunk at the reception and passed out in the men's room. It took two groomsmen and an usher from the wedding party to empty him into the bed in his motel room.

"I suppose life has its tensions," Press surmised. "We probably just get used to seeing it drawn in the everyday faces of people around us."

He glanced back at his children whose puzzled looks suggested they held no inkling of how they were supposed to act or feel. It suddenly woke him like a dash of ice water that this man, their grandfather, was a man they'd never met. It was an era in their family time that was opening and closing for the grandchildren at the same moment. Cassie was crying quietly and Press hugged her to him.

"How come we never got to know our Grandpa Williams?" she sniffled softly.

Press shepherded his family to a nearby couch and a couple of deep cushioned chairs while pleading a sideways 'help me' glance at Abby. She shrugged a 'what can I say?' reply. Press cleared his throat before beginning.

"Unfortunately," Press opened slowly, "we can't choose our relatives like we can our friends."

He glanced at his wife who was giving him an 'oh, that's a good start' lashing from the frown on her face.

"My father, your Grandpa Mick, wasn't a very good guy to be around. He loved beer much more than he ever loved me or my mother or anything else. Your Grandma Janie tried most of her life to get him to quit. The priest at our church tried. Social workers tried. He just wouldn't quit his drinking. He wasn't really a mean man, he just got more obnoxious and belligerent the more he drank."

Press paused to burrow the back of his lap deeper into the cushioned chair.

"After your mom and I were married we just never heard from him much again. I called him a few times, once to tell him about Jeremy being born. Even that didn’t seem to matter much to him. If he wasn't drunk he was always hung over. He never expressed any interest in seeing me or our family. He never asked about you kids when I'd call. So I guess we just let him be. The last time I saw him was five years ago, just before they put him in the nursing home, and he didn't even recognize me."

"Didn't he like kids?" Cassie asked.

"I really don't know, Sweetie. It was really hard to know much about him because he drank so much. Beyond that I guess I never really knew him much myself. He just never gave anyone or anything else much notice."

"He must have really liked to drink a lot," Cassie expressed.

"Honey, most times people who drink like that can't help it," Abby tried. "It's a sickness and they just can't help themselves."

"We tried to get him to recognize that," Press added. "But he just wouldn't admit he had a problem. He claimed he was a social drinker but no one would socialize with him because he drank so much. He just wouldn't be helped. Finally his health got so bad that he couldn't take care of himself any more. That's why he spent the last five years in a nursing home. He didn't know anybody. He just sort of vegetated away the last part of his life and never got to know how I turned out or what a great crop of grandkids he had."

"I guess we're pretty lucky," Kate broke in. "We're fortunate to have Mom and Dad, and Grandma and Grandpa Findstrom the way they are."

"Yes, we certainly are. All of us very lucky to have each other," Press cried as he leaned forward and squeezed his daughters to him. "I couldn't have done better if I'd picked you guys out personally."

He sat back and smiled thinly at Kate, Cassie, Abby and Jeremy in turn.

"Humanity isn't perfect," he said finally. "Mick Williams was a drunk who happened to be my father. Fortunately, I found your Mom and realized I didn't have to raise my family the same way I grew up."

Press looked across the four faces to see if any more discussion might be forthcoming. Seeing that it wasn't, he stood up in a way to suggest that it was time to go. As Abby and Cassie headed out the door, he tugged Kate and Jeremy back for another look into the casket.

"I'm not going to suggest that you always avoid alcohol. But when the kids at school or wherever want you to party, just use your heads," Press nodded at the remains of his father. "Think of where it can lead you. I don't want you to end up in one of these before your time, or after a wasted time like his."

The siblings shuddered their understanding and walked out arm in arm with their father.

Mick Williams' farewell service drew little notice beyond Press and his family. Those also attending included the nursing home manager and one of the attendants from Mick's ward, Bailey Sorenson, and Press' Aunt Eleanor from his mother's side. Condolences were brief and formal, even from the aunt who had always despised Mick. Eleanor did relate that she had two sons, one living in Chicago and one in Green Bay, but they couldn't get away from their jobs to attend. Press understood. They probably didn't know Mick anyway. Neither Mick nor Press would likely have known them either.

"It's too bad Mick ever got into that mess in the Navy," Eleanor told Press with a shake of her head as they stood before the open casket. "He wasn't a real heavy drinker till after all that happened. Until he came back from the war."

Press stared blankly at her and Eleanor caught the question marks in his eyes.

"You didn't know?"

"Sorry, but I don't have the foggiest."

"Apparently while aboard ship in the South Pacific during World War II your father saw some guys throw an officer overboard. A young guy, one of those 'ninety-day-wonders' they called him. Right out of officer candidate school." Eleanor shifted on her feet uneasily. "Some people said Mick was even involved, too. That his conscience just got to him. Anyway, he turned them in."

His aunt glanced at the man in the coffin and back at Press.

"From what we heard, the other sailors were going to kill Mick, too, but he got shipped home right away and was discharged early. Apparently the Navy just reported the dead officer as lost at sea. I don't really know much other than that except that for years he lived in constant fear that the other guys were going to show up here in Banning. He was sure they still wanted to kill him. He was drunk when he came home and I don't think he ever sobered up much after that. At least not until they put him in the nursing home."

Stunned, Press took half a step backward and turned to gape at the body of the man who had been his father, the man he wondered if he'd ever really known at all. He'd known his father was in the Navy during the war, in the South Pacific. That was all. No one had ever talked about it. But his aunt's story was plausible. At least he could see how something like that could drive a man like his father to be an alcoholic. It didn't make his younger years suddenly easier, but now he could see a possible reason for the way things were. Perhaps those times when Press was a boy that his father would wake up screaming in the night really were nightmares and not just drunken fits. Eleanor's story at least made some sense of it all. There may have been something more to his father than the alcoholic veneer.

"Maybe I shouldn't have told you. This day is hard enough already," Eleanor said, her fingers pressed to the side of her chin as she looked at the startled expression on her nephew's face.

"No, no, I...I'm glad you did," Press replied, trying to be assuring. "That might really explain a lot." His gaze drifted with his thoughts back over the casket.

Eleanor touched his arm and took a seat in the second row of folding chairs.

There was little other mention of his father's life. There was not much that anyone else could recall that might shed further light through the dark brown glass that had bottled his world.

The service, conducted by an enlisted minister whose denomination Press did not ask, lasted precisely fourteen minutes.

"Nobody should leave this world that alone," Press sighed to Abby as they followed their children out of the funeral home when the summation was over. He didn't mention the conversation with his Aunt Eleanor. He needed time, first, to tumble it around in his own mind, to make whatever sense of it he could and decide how this revelation about his past might tack a new look onto his present and future.

After a quiet lunch at a downtown café, Press piled the family in the tenure-limited mini-van and headed north for a tour of the town that he had grown up in. It was a lusterless gray day, the kind that offers little in terms of expectations. The pewter clouds were high and sanded smooth by the wind, not at all providing the expectation of snow. For its part, unless it fell in shovel lengths, more of the white stuff would have gathered little notice to the depths that already smothered the land. It seemed that tufts of evergreens sprouting from beneath steepled clusters of white along the roadside were the exception to this domain of white that separated towns. The ocean of snow seemed to part itself only to allow pavement to follow state highway plows from one community to the next.

"Well, I guess I can't show you the gas station Grandpa Mick ran," Press thinly chuckled half an hour later as they pulled into the parking lot of a convenience store with eight gas pumps on the south edge of Banning. "It used to be right here."

Press explained that his dad's station sold Sinclair gas from two pumps. It had a tiny service counter with two chairs for waiting repair customers, although his father put far more hours in one or the other of them than did any paying clients. There was a single garage bay where tune-ups and oil changes took place. Mufflers could be replaced or brakes repaired with a few days notice so he could order the parts. And tires were patched. The restroom around back was uni-sex.

Banning had labored hard at logging to survive after the mining boom fizzled to a pop, but it wasn't nearly enough. The town was scarred by the business exodus and, like wagon ruts, the scars hadn't healed. Buildings vacated when Press was a boy were still empty, gutted and broken like carcasses that had been stripped of their hides and left to rot. Joining them since was the IGA store where Press had bagged groceries while he was in high school.

Two blocks past the flashing red light that marked the intersection of two state highways, Press aimed the mini-van right for another block to a square, three story, rust brick building with a roof that rose from each of the four sides to a pointy top. The ground floor windows were weathered wood to keep the viewing from happening into the place as well as out. The windows on the top two floors were void of either glass or wood. A chain link fence surrounded the grounds and was posted with large, yellow 'keep out' signs. From the looks of the gaping sequences in the metal mesh, as well as the rock-shattered upper windows, neither the fence nor the signs had imposed much of a barrier.

"Well, kids, that's where your dad went to school for eight grades anyway. High school was in Ironwood," Press chuckled. "Lord, how I would have loved to have seen a fence with signs like those when I was a kid." The family joined in his amusement. At the far end of the street they could see the newer, one-level structure of copper-flavored brick that currently impounded elementary-aged school kids.

Press rounded the corner and headed the van back south, crossing the east-west highway and continuing another three blocks.

"At least the house is still here," Press sighed with some obvious relief. It was beginning, it occurred to him, to seem like every vestige of proof that he had once existed in a childhood here was gone. "It appears they did tear down the garage in back, though. It was a little, one-car shack that opened into the alley."

"Boy, Dad, it's not very big," Jeremy noted.

"No, it really isn't. I never noticed it as being particularly small when I was a kid, though." It was a neatly-kept, one-story frame house, entered by a front porch. Two small windows sided the front door. Press explained that the window on the right side was in the dining room. The kitchen was directly behind that, followed by a pantry and a small back porch. On the other side was the living room. In back of that was his parents' bedroom, then the bathroom, and then his bedroom. That was the house. No basement.

"We never had to cut grass in the front yard because two huge cedars used to take up everything on either side of the sidewalk. Every so often we'd have to trim back some branches so you could get into the house," Press reminisced. There might still not be any grass to cut, for all he now knew, with several feet of snow piled higher than the floor of the porch on everything but the narrowly shoveled walk. The engine idled through a long pause as Press contemplated the house as if the smell of beer breath and the echo of arguments still emanated from beneath the door and around the window panes. Added to it all now was the mental image of his father in a sailor's uniform and some men throwing someone over a ship's railing. He gave his forehead a rubbing like he was trying to erase the memory of it all before shifting the van's gears forward into the present.

Another quarter hour drive through the neighborhoods showed them that what little else had changed was hardly worth mention. Most of the changes were things that had disappeared. During the ride back to Ironwood they were quiet as strangers on a bus. It was a tangled web of emotions that Press was weaving through. He expected that nothing might ever wrench him back here and yet it was with some sadness that this portion of life written into his biography was now closed for good. He wouldn't miss it and still he wished he could.

Friday was spent replaying their airline hopscotch from Ironwood to Fremont. Everyone tried to sleep as best sleep can be achieved in airline chairs. Everyone except Press, who kept replaying his conversation with his Aunt Eleanor. He kept trying to determine how it could apply to each and any of the memories of his childhood, and the father whose image he could barely fetch back during the airborne interludes between terminals. It was an odd picture of his father, Mick Williams, that now played in his recollections. It was hard for Press to imagine the man as part of a group tossing another man overboard at sea. Despite all the shouting, the ranting and raving and verbal threats, he had never seen his father hit his mother even at his drunkest. Disciplining Press, the boy, had even been left largely to his mother. Press wondered if lies had been told to cover up the incident or whether it simply had never been brought up. What amazed him most, however, was that he had made a career of uncovering secrets and had spent a lifetime with a secret hiding in his father.

What other mysteries might lurk so close to home, he wondered?

18 Barry looked up from the tippity-tappiting on the keyboard of his Mac when Press walked by with the mail on Saturday morning.

Sorry to hear about your father, Press," he consoled.

"Yeah, thanks."

Press sacked himself into the chair beside Barry's desk and the two occupied several minutes with quiet talk about the funeral and a catching up on events in the newspaper office during the past few days.

"Anything new with the Nordstrom situation?" Press finally asked.

"Yes, I did finally get a hold of Schell Tuesday afternoon about getting Nordstrom to let us see the juvenile log. Boy, is he a piece of work," Barry said, working his head from side to side. "He won't touch it. Says his caseload is too big already."

"That horse's hinder," Press snorted and ran a hand over his face. "It wouldn't take him an hour! The work's all right under his stinkin' nose!"

"We know it and so does he," McGinn agreed. "But he won't even write a letter to Nordstrom telling him he should let loose of the juvenile log. I would have called the attorney general's office, but I couldn't remember who you had talked to. I figured it might be best if you did that anyway."

"It was Jarred Kleinmeier and you're probably right." Press threw up his hands in disbelief. "I'll try to get him first thing Monday morning. I'd bet we end up going through Galen again, though."

Two mornings later, in a telephone conversation with the assistant attorney general in Avery, Press explained the matter of the police department's juvenile log and the district attorney's refusal to get involved in the police records matter in Fremont.

"Listen, I understand your situation," Kleinmeier said. "Schell is playing politics, that's all. He's afraid that siding with you against the police chief might turn a simple feather into a new duster at election time. I can write a letter to the chief for you but that might not shape him up without a writ. I'm sorry I can't do more, but unless you've got pretty good evidence that he's covering up a murder or sex crimes or something, it's just not the heavy kind of crime to bring in the state criminal investigation guys."

"So, in other words, I'm stuck forking out the bucks for my own lawyer again," Press snorted.

"Hey," Kleinmeier responded. "The state open records law says the court can award you reasonable legal fees if you pursue a case like this and win. Didn't you know that?"

"Darn. I guess I'd forgotten that," Press whewed. "When you don't deal with this stuff all the time, you don't think of things like that. I doubt Perry did either."

Late Tuesday morning Press and Barry accompanied a sheriff's deputy once more to the Fremont police headquarters. Press couldn't help sensing a touch of smugness when the deputy handed Nordstrom the writ, along with a court-ordered notice of payment due from the police department to the *Gazette* for legal services incurred. The writ also demanded that all juvenile logs kept for the last three years be presented for inspection by representatives of the newspaper.

It was an Olympic-sized glare that Nordstrom sent the two newsmen before stomping to the sergeant's desk and returning with a large, blue three-ring binder that he retrieved from a lower drawer.

"I'll have to get the others from the vault," he snarled. Moments later he returned with five more binders stuffed with reports.

"I don't suppose you'll take my library card and let us check these out?" Barry grinned.

"You're a real smart sonofabitch, aren't ya?" The words rumbled off of Nordstrom's tongue like the departure of an armored tank.

"Mind if we use that desk?" Press asked, pointing his chin to a small, unoccupied bureau on the other side of the counter.

"Yes, I do," the chief said and stumped back to his office.

"The guy has 'asshole' written all over him like he's damned proud of it," Barry half laughed under his breath.

"Yeah, he's living proof that there's more bone in the head than anything else," Press added to the other's assessment of Derek Nordstrom.

Press and his editor skipped lunch as they each took a volume and spent the rest of the afternoon exploring the pages and taking notes. They didn't return on Wednesday, since the demands of getting out the week's issue of the *Gazette* took priority.

"PRESSING MATTERS"
January 19

As general wisdom says all of us are prone to sometime do, my father died last week. Through nearly my first two decades, he was the most dominant male figure in my life and, in later years, I grew to hate him. I don't...can't hate him anymore. He just left me angry. Although his body left the planet of his origin a week ago Tuesday, his mind departed years before that. There was no funeral for that first separation, though perhaps there should have been. I wish we could have talked once more, before that thinking part of him expired. There was a lot that needed to be said between us. Perhaps there were some things that could have been explained....

Press and Barry did return again to the police headquarters on Thursday morning, however, each carrying a barstool from the

Williams basement rec room, which they deposited next to the counter.

"Juvenile logs, Mavis," Press demanded, bellying up to the bar like he was requiring a shot of whiskey.

Mavis delivered the volumes singularly, as if she were carrying piecrust on a cement block and walking on thin ice, and that either haste or weight might cause the breakup of one or the other or both.

All morning the two men sat quietly as they leafed through page after page, occasionally ballpointing notes concerning items they found in the records of "juvenile" offenses. Once in awhile one or the other would hmmmph through his nose, shuffling a sideways grin at his partner before scribbling feverishly for a few moments.

At noon the pair announced to Mavis that they were going to lunch and would be back at one. Upon their return from cheeseburgers and sodas, they had to go through the whole routine again, with Mavis grudgingly handing over the police logs one at a time as she might ruefully deposited the diary of her own love life into the hands of the publishers of *Playboy Magazine.*

A few ticks before the clock tocked five, Press closed the binder he'd been perusing and slid it across the counter. Barry was still turning pages moments later when Mavis announced that it was quitting time and that she needed to put the files away so she could go home.

"Come on, Mavis. I've only got two pages left," Barry pleaded, not looking up from his investigation.

"IT'S QUITTING TIME, MR. MCGINN!" Mavis bugled in capital letters.

"Think about it, Mavis," Barry cooed as he looked up at her with his lips split in a smile that could have been seen from Parsons. "Two more minutes and you won't have to see me again till next week. Otherwise, I'll be back in the morning and you'll have to go to all the trouble of digging out this file again and making sure it's the right one and all."

Mavis cogitated on that for a short moment and finally snarled, "Make it snappy! The oven timer's set for my dinner and I don't want it to get cold!"

At four minutes after five, Press and Barry left the department office as the steel security door buzzed itself locked behind them.

"I don't know about you," Barry said as they scuffed to the car through the small shaker of snow that had spilled, "but all I have is about eight pages of notes concerning things that generally wouldn't cause jail time in nature. Just stuff that would embarrass the heck out of a few folks."

"Pretty much the same," Press replied, "except for two items."

They got into Press' Buick and he keyed the ignition before turning on the dome light and rolling some pages of his yellow tablet to show Barry.

"Remember Father Ennis, the assistant pastor at Saint James?" Press jogged McGinn's memory. "He was only there a few months, couple of years ago."

"Yeah, seems he got transferred kinda quick," Barry recalled.

"Well, the entry's not real precise, but it seems the good father got picked up for improprieties with a couple of young boys."

"Holeeeee shit!" Barry exclaimed in amazement, his eyes straining their sockets as they bugged forward.

"Then there is the matter of Bill Macek."

"The councilman who resigned in mid-term last year?"

"Yeah, that's the one. Claimed too much stress between the demands of the job and the city council," Press acknowledged. "Seems he really got stressed when he got caught with ten ounces of marijuana in his possession."

Press handed his notes to Barry and turned off the dome light.

"Looks like you've got some stories to write," Press smiled as he eased the car away from the curb.

19 It took three weeks of digging before the *Gazette* broke a major front page story on the police department cover-up of the priest's indiscretions with two juvenile boys and the ex-councilman's marijuana possession. The story made substantial notice of the fact that no charges had been filed in either case, despite the appearance of a preponderance of evidence noted in the police records. "Police Chief Derek Nordstrom refused comment on the matter, stating that the issues involved active investigations. When it was pointed out that Father Ennis had been transferred to a parish in Idaho nearly two years earlier, the chief simply added another 'no comment.' Both a spokesman for Bishop O'Brien in Avery and Saint James pastor, Father Roland Bellino, also declined comment. Chief Nordstrom and his wife are members of the parish. And the case of ex-Councilman Macek is now more than a year old, with no apparent further activity in the matter by Fremont police. Macek did issue a brief statement saying that he had made an error in judgment, that drugs were not a part of his life, and that he was now focusing on other matters."

A *Gazette* editorial that accompanied the story rebuked Nordstrom for concealing the items in the juvenile records, as well as for keeping two separate incident logs. The opinion piece also suggested that, having been required by the courts twice to make those records open to the media, he might be well advised to reduce the department's record keeping to a single source.

"PRESSING MATTERS"
February 9

We've been pretty smug, here in Fremont. We look at all the crime and loose morals and violence going on in other parts of America and think to ourselves, 'thank goodness that kind of stuff

> doesn't occur in our town.' Sadly, we are not that different, really, than other Americans. It is a terrible thing that persons involved in criminal activity, in at least two particular incidents, will likely go unpunished. Even more tragic, however, is that it now appears those activities were hushed up with the full knowledge and cooperation of the Fremont police chief....

The coffee crowd was mostly assembled and waiting for him when Press arrived at Cruiser's Friday morning. Bernie Randazzo, Lyman Dunnington, Gene Proctor, Blaine Peterson, Charlie Delaney, John Kershaw, and Wayne Boginoski had the two square tables nudged into a rectangle and eight chairs fenced around them. Delaney pushed the only vacant chair toward Press.

"The guys had me wire this one especially for you," Charlie said. The grin he fashioned was about the only thing that the man ever seemed to exercise on his portly frame. A shade over five and a half feet tall and something over two hundred pounds, Charlie looked like a heart attack waiting to happen in Press' view. For the sake of his daughter and her boyfriend, Casey Delaney, he hoped he was wrong.

"Well, unless you got the parts from the True Value Hardware store in Parsons, I guess it's safe enough," Press came back at the owner of local Delaney and Sons Hardware.

Of course, the major topic of discussion this morning, though the commentary was pretty jovial as usual, was the front page of the *Gazette.*

"So which part of the investigative team are you, Woodward or Bernstein?" Boginoski wanted to know. Wayne sold insurance of every variety and made a substantial impression in his success. He was always smartly dressed but there were two things he was most proud of. One was the thick head of black hair, which always looked sprayed into place atop his dome, and the other was the large Notre Dame ring he wore, with its equally large emerald that seemed to match the right fist that held it.

"I don't know," Press guessed. "Did one of them sign our employees' checks and shovel the snow off the front walk at the office?"

"Lots of things need shovelin' around the *Gazette* office," Petersen smirked wryly. Blaine Peterson was a wiry, retired farmer who could have bought and sold most of the folks in Fremont, but he never let his appearance give that notion away. He still dressed routinely in his blue and white-striped coveralls, red and black-checked flannel shirt and leather 'shit-kickers', as he called the boots. He added a John Deere-green cap, cocked sideways off his northeast corner. He had the callused, oversized hands of a man once accustomed to manually shucking corn, delivering milk from several dozen cows into stainless milk pails, and maneuvering every variety of large-handled tool as a matter of course. His manner dictated its own slow, easy pace that equaled his gait at storytelling and reminiscence, and camouflaged a devilish spark that ignited his grayish eyes at any opportunity to jab someone with an appropriately timed one-liner.

"Guess you got 'bout all the Catholics in town ready to hurry you off to hell," Randazzo tossed in. Bernie owned the Town and Country Convenience Centre at the four-way stop, as well as half a dozen rental properties around town. His slender frame and narrow face made him appear taller than he was. He sported a thatch of curly inkjet hair with eyebrows and mustache to match and skin that looked lightly stained in olive oil.

Press chuckled and shook his head.

"Must've been you were about the only one of 'em who didn't call me last night." The reply was a half snort, half smirk. "I guess it kind of surprised me how many people think that sort of stuff ought to be covered up unless it's some 'brand X' church down the street."

Ruddy-faced Gene Proctor, a jolly, retired postmaster who had fathered hard, co-producing eleven children, who in turn bore him and his wife forty-seven grandchildren and a dozen or so great-grandchildren, suggested that maybe a lot of folks didn't think everyone needed to know some things like that.

"You might think differently if a guy like Father Ennis was counseling one of your grandsons in private," Press suggested. Proctor lifted the eyebrows further up his face with an 'I-suppose-so' nod in reply.

"I think I'd be more worried about what kind of counseling Nordstrom might do if he catches you in an alley," Peterson noted. "Seems to me, you keep stickin' your pencil up his butt and eventually you're gonna get 'im *really* pissed."

"If you ask me, Derek never forgave the doctor for slappin' him the day he was born," Charlie Delaney interjected with a chuckle. "He's been pretty much pissed ever since."

The conversation rounded the table in several different directions before Dunnington finally produced the box and bar dice to determine who would pay for the group's coffee this morning. They were just about to begin when Galen Perry walked in sporting a fashionably new dark suit and a grin to match. He borrowed a chair from another table and squeezed himself in between Proctor and Delaney. Of course, the hoots chorused from the group immediately as if they'd each suffered the snatch of a fistful of feathers.

"Put the dice box away, boys. *Somebody* can obviously afford to buy us all coffee today."

"Must have sued them tobacco companies and won."

"Nah, I bet some old lady died and the estate paid his legal bill."

"What? Did you take over the funeral home?"

"If you ask me, it's like puttin' a forty-dollar saddle on a ten-dollar horse," came a smirk from under Blaine Peterson's John Deere cap.

Perry jugged his head up and down in feigned agreement to all of it.

"Actually, I think I paid for the new threads," Press insisted.

"No," Perry countered with a gleam deviled in the corner of his eye. "Actually, Derek Nordstrom did when the judge sent him your legal bill for not turning over those logs."

The laughs continued and an inadequate roll of the dice caused Perry to pick up the tab, even though the coffee he chugged barely had time to leave any taste on his tongue as it went in a hurry to his stomach.

Charlotte had a note taped to his door when Press returned to his office. "O'Leary's Pharmacy, Santori's Card and Gift, Case Insurance, and The Car Corner Used Cars have all cancelled their ads for next week as a result of this week's front page."

Another note from the receptionist announced twenty-two subscription cancellations so far this morning.

Press sat down at his desk and puffed a large sigh into his hands.

20 Press was just bookmarking *Angela's Ashes* for the night with the jack of hearts when he heard the Buick pull into the drive and the rattle of the garage door being machined open.

Folding her copy of *Good Housekeeping* shut, Abby edged forward on the sofa and was already rehearsing her lecture. "It's about time! She was supposed to be home before midnight!" Abby practiced her frown on Press, who took it as a command to remain stuffed in his recliner in case she needed backup.

Kate burst through the kitchen, her long blond hair bouncing from side to side and up and down at once with the heave of her chest as her sobs were gasped and expelled in a rush. The sixteen-year-old's face was flushed with tears.

"M-o-o-o-m-m-m, I *swear* I didn't do anything wrong," she wailed as she threw her arms around her now-standing mother. Abby guided her onto the sofa and brushed the streaks of tears and random strands of hair from her daughter's face.

"Settle down and tell us what happened," Press soothed as he eased in on the other side of Kate.

"A bunch of us went to Casey's house after the game," Kate explained through a series of shallow-breathed sniffles. "All we did was play pool and ping pong. We had pizza and sodas. I swear, Mom, all I had was Pepsi! None of us drank anything but pop."

"So?" Abby quizzed as she leaned around to look at Press. "What happened?"

"We left about a quarter to twelve and I took two other girls home," Kate's sobs were softer and more measured now. "I was almost ready to turn off of Division Street and a policeman drove up behind me with his lights flashing and the siren going. I thought he must be going some place else and I pulled off to the side like you're supposed to. But he pulled in behind me."

Abby managed to dig a tissue from the pocket of her sweater and handed it to her daughter.

"I asked him if I'd done something wrong," Kate continued as she pinched her nose into the tissue, "but he just asked me if

I'd been drinking. I said 'no,' and he wanted to know where I'd been. I explained to him about being at my boyfriend's house with some other kids, and he made me get out of the car. First he told me to walk a straight line along the edge of the sidewalk. Then I had to get into the police car and he took me to the police station."

Press took a long, deep breath and let it out slowly as he waited for his daughter to continue.

"When we got there, he made me take a Breathalyzer test. It proved I hadn't been drinking, but he said I was weaving all over the road. He said I crossed the yellow center line several times and gave me a ticket for inattentive driving. Mom, I didn't do anything like that." Kate was wailing again and buried her head into her mother's shoulder.

You could almost hear the grind of his teeth as Press' jaw jutted forward when he asked, "Was it Chief Nordstrom who stopped you?"

"Yes," came the reply muffled into Abby's sweater.

Lips pressed tightly inward, Press and his wife passed knowing head shakes between them as they tried to console their teenaged daughter.

“That sonofabitch,” Press growled softly, his hand resting gently on his daughter’s shoulder.

“Press…your language,” his wife shushed.

“He’s harassing us and there’s just no other way I can describe him.”

“Well, if you’d quit writing about him,” Kate barked through her sobs, “maybe he’d leave us alone!”

Press looked over at Abby, whose look said, “Now is not the time to argue.” He took a step back and hesitated for a moment before heading to their bedroom.

It was one of those crystal February mornings, the kind polished clean by a week's worth of wind that had rolled out of the Rockies and gathered momentum across the plains before buffing and sanding the face of Fremont as it headed east. Weeks like that made Press think that whoever named Chicago *The Windy City* had never experienced anything like the Great Plains, a Canada-to-Mexico stretch of America scoured largely void of trees and hills by the ever present bellows of the wind. Today, however, was crisp and clear as if encased in glass and his lungs burned with the infusion of frigid air when Press stepped from the car and proceeded into Delaney and Sons Hardware Store.

He found Charlie Delaney in his upstairs office at the back of the building.

"Charlotte picked up the ad yesterday," Charlie said as he swiveled a grin from his desk when Press mounted the last of the steps.

"I know, I know," Press defended with a laugh, holding both hands out as if to brace himself from any more assaults. "This one's personal."

"You want to buy some steel siding to protect your house from the Papist crusade against you?" Charlie dug gleefully. "Or how about a cattle prod to keep the police chief at a distance?"

"Be sure to keep plenty in stock. I may be back for the stuff later," Press countered as he eased himself into a corner of the old couch Delaney kept in his office. "Actually, I just wanted to confirm what the kids did at your place last night."

"Must have been eight or nine of 'em came over after the basketball game. Kate was one of them, of course," Charlie said through another set of grins. "I heard lots of squeals and giggles but not any heavy breathing, if that's what you're concerned about."

"No, no. Well, yeah, I'm concerned about it but not last night." Press laughed. "I just wanted to confirm that there wasn't any drinking."

"Hell, no," Charlie said with a force that jerked his head back. "At least not unless one of 'em was pretty damned good at sneaking it in. I know we didn't have anything there for them. Doc Cassidy and I took care of what beer was left in the rec room fridge the night before. All the hard stuff we keep in the upstairs cabinet. Why?"

"Kate got hauled in and Breathalyzed on her way home from your place last night," Press said as a frown dimmed his face. "She also got a ticket for inattentive driving."

"Sweet Katie?" Charlie's eyes bugged. "I can't believe that. Who…?"

"Nordstrom, naturally," Press confirmed with a nod.

"That sonofabitch!"

"Yeah, it appears he's getting back at me through my kids. He gave Jeremy a speeding ticket after the first story ran back before Christmas. Of course, I've seen Jeremy drive," Press puffed. "I'd have expected that one almost any time, but it sure was coincidental in the timing and just happened to be the chief with the radar gun. I wasn't sure he even knew how to use one."

As he backed out of the driveway to go to the office Monday morning, Press spotted the police chief's unmarked, white Chevy Caprice parked two houses away. Nordstrom was sitting in the car, the motor running. Press contemplated a long moment before easing the Buick into the street and slowly pulling forward. When the driver door paralleled the chief's, Press stopped and rolled down his window, hanging an elbow over the side of the car. When Nordstrom did nothing, Press pointed his chin to signal a word with the chief, who in turn lowered his window part way.

"You want to talk to me or are you looking for my kids?" Press asked through a glare that matched the police officer's.

Nordstrom *hmmphed* and slowly drove away, rolling his window back up as he left.

When he got to the office, Press immediately dialed Jarred Kleinmeier in the attorney general's office and then Galen Perry. The result of both conversations was along lines he had expected. He'd told the two lawyers about the tickets his kids had received and the fact that Nordstrom was parked two doors down from his house this morning, for no legitimate surveillance that he could surmise. But neither man offered much encouragement to put on his plate. Without a direct threat from Nordstrom or a bigger sampling of harassments, there wasn't much to pin a legal complaint on. Press would just have to chew on it for awhile and hope the police chief got tired of the games first. Either that or he needed to provide some more conclusive intimidation.

At dinner that night, Press relayed the morning events to his family.

"I know you're all good drivers," he said, shifting his eyes from Jeremy to Kate to Abby, "but you're all going to have to be extra careful until Nordstrom gets off his high horse. He's just out to get even with me and we're all going to have to watch it."

"No more jaywalking for you, either, Cassie," Jeremy teased. They all laughed but the quick return of Press' furrowed brow told them he was serious.

The next morning Nordstrom's white police car was again parked two houses from the Williams' driveway, the chief sitting behind the wheel as the motor idled. Press stopped the Buick before he got to the street and shifted the car into park. Reaching into a black bag on the seat beside him, he removed an Olympus digital camera that belonged to the *Gazette*. Stepping out of the car into the frigid morning, Press leaned across the top of the vehicle and aimed the camera at the police car.

The silhouetted lawman yanked the car in gear and hurried away.

As if it could be faxed, the incident repeated itself the next day.

Wednesday morning Press saw no sign of the chief until the white Chevy swung in behind him from a side street two blocks from his home. Press made sure he signaled at every turn and stayed two miles under the speed limit all the way until he turned into the office parking lot. Nordstrom's squad car continued on.

"PRESSING MATTERS"
February 16

It's certainly comforting knowing that my family and I will not be mugged or visited by some unlawful calamity these days. I guess that's the kind of service you can expect from a small town police force. Fremont Police Chief Derek Nordstrom has attached himself to the Williams bunch so tightly lately that even our shadows can't find a bit of

room to lengthen in the winter
sun....

Press leaned out his office door after the paper had gone to print on Wednesday afternoon and called across the newsroom.

"Barry, Sport, can you two come in here a minute?"

"What's up, Boss?" Sport Henry wondered as the pair entered the publisher's office. Reginald “Sport” Henry was the *Gazette's* sole sports reporter for more than forty years, the only job he had ever held. He had started writing sports for the paper while he was still in high school and was good enough at it that he simply gravitated into the position full-time upon graduation. He’d taught himself photography over the years and had turned himself into the *Gazette's* primary man with a camera in addition to covering all of Fremont High School’s athletic events. Between taking pictures, he filled his summers with fishing, golfing, and coaching senior league baseball for boys sixteen to eighteen.

Though it was a name that nettled both him and his father like blackberry briars, ‘Reginald’ was a concession to his mother who had demanded that their first child be named after her father. A daughter would have been ‘Regina’. ‘Sport’ was a label his father had tagged him with as a toddler and it stuck, appropriately as it turned out. His parents were long since dead, leaving his wife and purveyors of official documents like driver’s licenses and tax forms as the only ones who knew his true first name.

"Either of you have a video camera?" Press asked.

They both nodded.

Thursday morning Press backed out of the driveway as usual and headed for the office. In the next block he passed Barry's blue Mazda parked at the curb, the motor idling. Barry and Sport waved as he passed.

A block farther, Press checked the side street. Sure enough, the white squad car was at the stop sign and eased in behind him as he passed. Press grinned inside himself.

Stopping at the corner fronting onto Division Street, Press checked his rearview mirror before checking for traffic. He could see Nordstrom looking in his own mirror as well and knew the exact instant when the chief saw Barry behind the wheel and Sport, video camera in hand, in the vehicle in back of the squad car. The police car's turn signal immediately changed direction left to right and when Press turned toward the *Gazette* office, Nordstrom headed south toward the town's outskirts.

Barry and Sport were all smiles as the trio met at the back door of the newspaper building.

"I suppose I can erase *that* tape," Sport assumed out of a conspiratorial smirk.

"No, save it for sure," Press said. "That, along with the pictures I took of him sitting in the squad just down from the house the other day may add up to some useful supporting material some day."

Apparently Derek Nordstrom found other matters to occupy his morning hours in the days after that.

Nearly three weeks later, Barry leaned in the doorway of Press' office and executed a devilish grin under his nose.

"You look like you're just about to spit canary feathers," the publisher said, looking from under his eyebrows in expectation.

"The council voted on the budget last night," he winked. "Guess who's overtime perk got axed?"

"Serves him right." Press slapped the March on his desk calendar. "How'd it go?"

"Flater made the motion, passed unanimously with no discussion!"

"Was Nordstrom there?" Press questioned next.

"Yep," Barry reported. "After the vote he stomped out like fire and thunder intent on leaving some bruises in the vicinity."

"How about the mayor?"

"He looked like he'd have gone with Nordstrom if his presence wasn't required at the meeting," Barry replied.

"Makes you wonder if the council members' phones didn't ring more than ours did after we broke that story." Press folded his arms and wrapped his face in a pleased grin.

21

Press watched the busboy intently as the young man cleared the remnants of the previous customers' dinner so that Mr. and Mrs. Williams could also enjoy the cuisine at French's Family Restaurant this Saturday evening. It was like stepping outside of his body and watching himself while he pursued the temporary career of clearing tables and hopping to whatever bells were rung at a hotel and restaurant complex while a college student in Wisconsin those years back.

He had hated that particular job. It wasn't the work so much that agitated his goat as having to contend with J.D. Gonring. Press and J.D. had grown up as next-door neighbors in Banning and were 'friends' by way of proximity more than shared amiability toward each other. J.D., two years older than Press, sought him out whenever he wanted to do something. Press sought out J.D. whenever he wanted to do something and could find no one else within bicycle fetching in Banning.

J.D. had been a chubby kid who had a whiny and equally chubby, six-years-younger brother, Danny. He also had a mother pillowed in fat who demanded that the youngest Gonring be a party to whatever J.D. found to occupy his time. Mr. Gonring was a quiet, wiry man who looked forever like he was the last one to the dinner table and spoke about as often as he ate.

J.D. had managed to eke himself out of high school and into the U.S. Navy, from which time Press had lost track of him. That is, until the student aids office sent Press out for a part-time job interview. J.D. had extricated himself from the Navy at the end of two years with dubious distinction and was now catering manager at the hotel and restaurant complex where Press was applying. J.D. became his new boss.

J.D. Gonring had been sufferable in the circumstances of last resort in their youth. In the necessary demands of co-mingling careers, however – even temporarily – J.D. was an insufferable ass in the mind of Press. Similar and even less charitable notions were ascribed to him by the other laborers toiling under the direction of the catering manager. Though the position of catering manager at an upper Midwest motel and restaurant was not high up among the levels of the executive food chain in terms of remuneration or power, J.D. was as full of himself as a hot air balloon. The term 'manager' attached to catering was enough of a bellows to inflate his canvas brainbox to near bursting.

Press found there were two kinds of people working under the surveillance of the catering manager. There were those like himself who desperately needed any level of income available to support their college habit. And there were the single mothers, most of whom had married young and divorced young. Or they had pretended marriage in some bedroom or backseat of a car, and had come away with family consequences. They were single mothers either way, short of the skills and education that might better provide for themselves and their offspring. None of them could afford to be without that job and J.D. knew it.

When it came to work schedules, J.D. was marginally more tolerant of the college help, Press had assumed, because the catering boss was somewhat intimidated by the higher level of schooling or intelligence or both. If a waitress was sick (or if he fired one of them), J.D. would call one of the other single moms and demand that they be on the job in half an hour or whatever minimal time he granted. The women had to show up if they wanted to keep their jobs, whether it was their scheduled shift or not.

But when it came to being picky about job performance, J.D. reserved his particularly narrow construction of acceptable standards for the college students. Intimidated or not, he was out to prove that it only took a sheep turd to be a boss and not a sheepskin, as one of the other busboys had depicted J.D., much to the delight of Press and the rest of the crew. J.D. held Press' performance up to an especially harsh standard. Rarely did anything Press do escape some measure of critique from the catering manager. Tablecloths were left crooked, water glasses weren't filled quickly enough, he was too noisy as he cleared the dishes and silverware, or if nothing else could be immediately brought under scrutiny, Press was just standing around too much.

It was one such editorial comment too many that led Press to terminate his busboy and bellhop career. J.D. didn't like the way

Press was sweeping out the hotel entry one afternoon. The shoulders that bore the weight of two final exams that morning, an assignment for *The Spectator,* and a major term paper completion the night previous, and now a full shift at this job had left no room to spare for piddling arrogance.

Press dropped the broom on the floor and told J.D., "If you don't like the way I'm doing it, sweep it yourself." He headed toward the hotel dining room and called over his shoulder, "And stick the broom up your fat ass when you're done!"

"Come back here and pick that up or your fired," Gonring insisted with as much bluster as he could muster.

Press kept walking, right on through the dining room and out through the kitchen to the parking lot where he had deposited his roommate's Ford Fairlane. He did extract a bit of vengeance on his way out, however. He announced to the snickers and delight of the assembled catering staff that the 'J.D.' in their boss' name – a label the owner loathed in its unabridged state – stood for *Josiah Drayton!*

When the tableware was replaced and the menus in front of the couple, Press ordered glasses of wine for the two of them. Deciding quickly on the shrimp alfredo, he folded the menu back onto the table and let his eyes appraise the other patrons. Abby continued to assess her choices as if she were about to make a down payment on the whole of New Orleans' French Quarter or downtown Kansas City. French's was astir with the usual first night of the weekend bustle of mostly retired folks and a few families with young kids, all out for the Friday bargain fish fry. Still, it was only moderately crowded compared to Saturday nights when the area's working farmers knocked off their chores early and brought their wives to town for dinner and a few drinks. Later they might head for a movie or a couple of games of bowling if they had children along.

The waitress returned with the wine and Abby told Press to order while she finished deciding which part of the country to invite for supper, Cajun shrimp or Kansas City strip steak. At last she elected Cajun shrimp.

While they waited for dinner to be delivered the couple sipped white zinfandel and quietly deliberated the various sides of nothing consequential until two shadows hovered at their table.

Halted before them were two women of the silver haired, bifocaled, and black laced shoes with wide heels variety. One was plump and grandmotherly, the other thin and bent at the shoulder from the weight of years and osteoporosis. Neither was smiling. In fact, they both looked like they were assessing the odorous qualities of fertilizer.

"We don't want to interrupt your dinner, Mr. and Mrs. Williams," the grandmotherly one began. "We just want you to know that we think Chief Nordstrom is doing an excellent job and we think your paper shouldn't pick on him so much."

Press glanced at Abby and back to the two visitors, wondering why, if they didn't want to interrupt his dinner, they had.

"And how do you think we're picking on him?"

The thin and bent woman spoke now. "You keep suggesting he's done something wrong. Most older folks like us think he's doing a fine job and you should just let him alone. He looks out for us senior citizens and we need someone like that, especially when we live by ourselves."

"And you think it's all right to cover up the crimes that some people commit and get pay that he doesn't deserve?" Press smiled politely.

"I think he does deserve that pay," the plump one grumped and straightened a bit. "Why should he have to work holidays and not get paid extra?"

"Well, because he doesn't *have* to work holidays for one thing, and because he was hired at a salary that was meant to compensate him to do the job, no matter how many hours that takes him – just like other administrators are."

"But the police chief is different! His job is more important. He knows what he's doing and we think you should let him alone so he can do it!" The pair turned and indicated they were through with the conversation. "We just thought you ought to know."

"I appreciate that," Press nodded, but he didn't really.

He shook his head when they were out of sight.

"That's why I think we should go to Parsons when we go out to eat," he suggested to his wife. "It's hard to get through dinner without heartburn when people always want to editorialize on what's in the paper and mostly their versions don't agree with ours."

"PRESSING MATTERS"
March 23

Like mushrooms in a damp woods, criticisms are nuggets that will always be found sprouting in abundance around a newspaper office. When we're not dishing them out, we're getting them dumped on us. It's a part of journalistic life that requires thick skin and broad shoulders. Still, ask a newspaper publisher or editor how he feels about having his product or work critiqued and he'll tell you it's about the same as a fire hydrant's opinion of dogs. While in all honesty, it ruffles our feathers some, at least when people criticize us, we hope we've managed to get them thinking. That's always a positive step in the right direction. And at least we know they're reading the *Gazette*....

22 "I suppose my turn had to come!" Barry was without the usual banana grin on his face as he flagged the pink slip of paper in front of Press. "Nordstrom got me a block from my house this morning. Thirty-two in a twenty-five zone."

Press puffed his cheeks as he shook his head.

"He's out to be a pain in our necks, that's for sure," he came back. "But how can we prove he's harassing us?"

Barry stood in the office doorway, feet spread and arms woven across his chest.

"Well, for one thing, I'd assess the pain a little lower. And he's the only one giving the tickets. For another thing, it's my first ticket *ever* and today was the first time I've ever seen *any* cop on my street. It deadends at the end of the next block, for cryin' out loud!"

"I'll talk to Galen about it, but I suspect he's going to say our evidence is thin as barbed wire," was Press' answer. "You've gotten a ticket and so have my kids. Other than watching my house and following me a couple of times, he hasn't posed a direct threat to me, yet. It may take some more putting up with him before we have grounds to force him to back off." He tugged at his left ear as if looking for confirmation to his thinking.

"Plus, he's got radar to back up the speeding tickets. It's hard to develop that into a case file of harassment."

Later that morning Galen Perry confirmed the thinking Press had expressed to Barry concerning harassment from the police chief.

"I imagine most people would agree that he's out to make things hard on you and Barry," Galen admitted. "But proving that in court is awfully difficult with what you've got. The thing is, he can nail almost anybody for a traffic violation if he really wants to. How many people actually drive the speed limit in a twenty-five zone? I know my car idles faster than that." He cleared his throat before continuing.

"Probably the strongest evidence you have is the fact that he was watching your house and following you, but he's not doing that any more and you haven't got much else."

Press thanked him and the conversation was finished.

Two days later Sport Henry was the next victim of Derek Nordstrom's traffic assault. Sport had gone to the scene of a car fire to take pictures and was ticketed for parking too close to a fire hydrant. The fire hydrant was a block away from the car fire. As Sport expressed in thunderous terms in the newsroom, "It wasn't exactly like I was keeping the fire department from finding water to pump! They just used chemical extinguishers and didn't even need any hydrants."

Sport's tantrum over the ticket flared off and on all morning.

"You know, I even waved to that old turd after I grabbed my camera bag from the backseat and headed for the fire," Henry pronounced as he exited the composition room after processing the photos from the car fire. "He could have just told me to move the car right then instead of writing me up! Didn't even have the guts to give it to me face to face. He left it under my windshield wiper!"

It particularly irritated Press since media representatives were normally extended a bit of leeway at fire and accident scenes. Sport was even parked a block away, he noted again.

This morning was born spectacularly as Press jogged along the sidewalks and curbsides of residential Fremont. The sky was a cloudless, china-blue except for the golden globe that occupied a rising arc in the eastern sky. His daily jog was a long-practiced routine now and he had no problems with stamina, yet this day he could not haul in enough gulps of the fresh-scented air, buffed and washed new by the previous night's breezy rainfall.

The morning lope through the neighborhood – five miles worth – had not always been a part of Press' routine, nor was it endured so easily. Three years previous he had weighed more than three hundred twenty pounds and could barely have lumbered one of the quintet of miles at a slow walk, much less jogged it.

Press had known of a substantial weight gain from the return look he got in the mirror each morning, but he had not stepped on the bathroom scale in a couple of years. It was an avoidance born of fear of what he knew he would find there. The suspicions lurked in a dark corner of his mind and he wanted no light of confirmation shed upon them. Intimacy with Abby hadn't progressed past fondling and kisses in his memory since Cassie was born. Clothing purchases had become often and in expanded sizes, while his breathing came quick and shallow, and he didn't even smoke. Then Abby enlisted the support of Dr. Benton Cassidy at one New Year's Eve party and the duet backed him into a corner where they wouldn't relent until he promised to come to the doctor's office for a checkup that next week.

A couple of days passed and Press had not yet made the appointment when his curiosity at last conned him into stepping onto the bathroom scale. He was horrified when the digital total hit the three hundred pound maximum and nearly pleaded for him to get off since it could go no farther. The picture of obesity that he presented may have been an old, yellowed snapshot by now in the minds of everyone who saw him in recent years, but a whole new Polaroid flashed its awakening in his mind.

Two days later the scale at Benton Cassidy's office registered three hundred twenty-three pounds when Press had anchored himself onto it.

"There is a heart attack waiting to happen in you," Benton announced sternly. "It just hasn't occurred yet! How badly do you want to live to see your children graduate from high school?"

The message was not lost on Press, although he wasn't sure which might kill him first, a coronary or the Spartan diet and exercise regimen Cassidy had issued to him with a no-words-minced demand that it be followed strictly. But Press was determined to make it work.

Perhaps it was Benton's comment about seeing his kids graduate that hammered the notion into his head cavity the deepest. He had filled himself with years of anger over the fact that beer had built a bottle wall between his own father and himself, and Press had vowed that he would always maintain an active presence for his children. Now, here he was, nearly a sixth of a ton heap of cholesterol and fat too much aimed in the neighborhood of the mortuary. If he died it would make his absence precisely that kind of wedge between himself and his trio of youngsters. The reality of such a physical separation would be little different than the absence in spirit that he had grown up with.

Press purchased a three-month membership at the Fremont Fitness Works that same day and gave a treadmill a severe stomping for an hour that afternoon and each morning for the next ninety days. It was spring when the membership expired and he transferred the treadmill route to a more pleasant course around the streets of town where at least the scenery changed as the seasons passed and diminishing flab allowed his pace to quicken. By the end of summer his course was up to three miles and his weight down to two seventy-five.

The walking, it turned out, was the snap in the effort, Press quickly determined. The foods that he had savored so long had now become the enemy. As a child, with so much of his parents' budget delivered by his father to one or the other of Banning's taverns, Press' taste in the delicacies of dining had progressed little beyond a rare treat to an ice cream cone or slice of the even more occasional cake his mother baked. The latter was a delight generally restricted solely to birthdays and that meant only one a year, since she stubbornly refused to recognize her own or to reward her husband for having soused his way through another three hundred sixty-five days.

As Press grew more secure in the financial success of the *Gazette* and the comfort of family life that Abby's presence ensured in the Williams household, he had begun to experience the delights that desserts and junk food could offer. At first, Abby had provided a steady variety of pies and cakes and cookies for her children and spouse.

Lunch at home offered a nice break in the middle of the day for Press, along with a serving of dessert to anchor whatever Abby had cooked up for the two of them. Dinner was another substantial episode with food that ended with an ample assortment of pure calories. At bedtime, Press helped himself to a piece of cake or pie garnished with a couple of scoops of whatever ice cream was on hand in the freezer.

When Abby noticed that middle age was expanding noticeably more in the middle of her husband, she quietly cut back on her baking, hoping his appetite would slow itself. It didn't. Press simply introduced himself to Dolly Madison, along with virtually every maker of corn and potato chips, Dairy Queen, and about any other food that didn't require tamping in with a hammer. As effortlessly as his appetite for desserts had stepped into his life, Abby's desire for marital goodies had wandered away. At first Press didn't notice much. As it began to occur to him that the absences in their lovemaking were expanding, he just figured that was somewhat the natural course of things in women that he'd heard took over with child bearing. He was wrong.

Press found out just how wrong when he returned home from his walk that early September morning, some sixty pounds trimmer, and found the kids off to their first day of the new school year and everything off his wife but the smile her face was clad in. As the pounds found their way off of Press, so that particular smile found its way onto Abby's face more occasionally.

That encouragement furthered his determination to lighten the burden his body hauled wherever he went. It took two years, but Press managed to lose more than a hundred fifty pounds. With Benton Cassidy's declaration that he was now a healthy specimen and could at last eat *responsible* amounts of foods outside the prescribed diet, Press declared that he never wanted to see another salad. He said that he had eaten so much "cottontail cuisine," as he called it, that surely the rabbits of the world must now be starving. And he had quickened and lengthened the stride of his morning exercise ritual to the point that he could legitimately say he was running five miles daily. To be sure, it was not to be confused with Olympic time that he completed the course each morning, but neither was his routine any longer a walk. Without the continued fitness program, however, Doc Cassidy had assured him that the diet would be imposed indefinitely.

Press was jogging a block off Division Street on his return route when he noticed the white Chevy ease up along side of him. Derek Nordstrom was behind the wheel, the windows of the squad car rolled down.

"What, am I going too fast?" Press huffed.

"Neighbors have reported prowlers in this area lately," the chief announced flatly.

"After doing this every day for nearly three years," offered Press, "I think folks in the neighborhood all know me. I'm even on a first name basis with all of their dogs."

At the next corner, Press stopped. So did the police car. Press then looked both ways before trotting into the street to the curb on the other side.

"I suppose you'd ticket me for jaywalking now if I didn't interrupt my jogging for the stop signs," he said with more than a handful of sarcasm. The tremor of Nordstrom's chin pronounced that a surly reply was lurking somewhere within the chief's mouth, but apparently his mind couldn't assemble the phrases, so he remained silent.

Two blocks later the squad car was still stride for stride with Press. He couldn't resist saying, "If you're going to be my personal escort from now on, why don't you just park that thing and run with me. Maybe the exercise would reduce the grouch in you."

Without comment, Nordstrom eased the police car away and turned at the next corner.

"PRESSING MATTERS"
March 30

Running, as regular readers of this column certainly know, has become an important ritual to begin my day. When I started with a walk that later stretched distance and hurried in pace, I found myself pondering the great mysteries of life, like how the heck did I ever get myself into a shape that is more readily acquainted with helium inside and with "Goodyear" painted on the sides? Now, however, I sometimes find myself noticing that I've not pondered at all by the time I deposit myself back at my front doorstep after my jog. Maybe that's not such a bad thing. Perhaps there are times in all of us when we are not connecting with anything at all. There is a pleasure that we can extract from life by simply slipping out of our everyday world for awhile and refusing to participate with any but ourselves. Lately, however, reality has found its way back into my pace as Chief Nordstrom has determined to monitor my pace as if I were a participant in the Boston Marathon…or, perhaps, on the lam from the federal penitentiary in Leavenworth….

23

"Anna Mae Conroy would like to talk to you, Press," came the announcement over the telephone intercom at his desk. Press walked into the front office to greet the woman and discover what her business with the newspaper might be. She was a short, pleasant looking woman, perhaps a couple of years older than himself. Plumpish in general proportions that she tucked into a beige dress, and dark brown hair coaxed into a bun, Anna Mae gave the immediate impression of jovial countenance. Yet, standing on the customer side of the office counter, shifting her gaze furtively from the open newsroom beyond the receptionist's office to the closed entrance behind her, the jolly side was not the exterior she presented this morning.

"Hi, I'm Preston Williams," Press tried warmly. "How can I help you today, Mrs. Conroy?"

"Can I, uh…can I speak with you in private?"

"Sure. Come on back."

Press held back the swinging gate and directed her toward his office on the far side of the clutter of news and computer typesetting desks.

As he offered her a chair and started around the desk, he noticed the woman glance at the open door. Without expending words on the question, he quickly swung it shut and sat down behind the desk that warehoused stacks of paper.

Anna Mae was fidgeting with the small, paisley-printed canvas purse seated on her lap as she began softly.

"I don't really know how…or where to begin," she spoke quietly. "But this has to be just between us…off the record, I mean."

Just the exact words every newsman hates to hear. Invariably it seems someone has a story to tell on someone else and they don't want the someone else to know who spilled it. Or they've been caught at something and want the paper to know before it shows up on the police blotter so that it can maybe be kept out of print and public embarrassment. The request made Press instinctively wary, but it intrigued him now. What could this lady have been up to that she didn't want her neighbors to find out?

"Well, why don't you fill me in on what seems to be so troublesome and I'll let you know if we reach a point that it has to go on the record?"

He barely caught the nod she presented ever so slightly.

"Tubby Wilson died a couple of weeks ago," she began. Her voice spoke in little more than whispers.

"Yes, I remember the obituary."

"Tubby...Mr. Wilson, was our neighbor for more than thirty years. He was living there when we...my husband and I bought our home." Her eyes traveled little from her purse and when they did, it was sideways at the lower walls on either side of Press' desk.

Having coursed tales that began similarly in the past, the first inclination into the publisher's mind was that here was about to be announced a triangle and hushing from the husband would be requested. Gladly, Press was to learn that was not the direction of this matter.

"Tubby's wife died a lot of years back and he lived alone ever since. He had a couple of kids...one in Des Moines and one someplace near Kansas City. He didn't get to see them much. For the past several years, his health wasn't good." Anna Mae looked up briefly and then returned her stare to the purse. "Bernie...my husband...and I took care of him most of that time. Bernie mowed his lawn and shoveled the snow when it needed it. I helped Tubby with his laundry and cleaned his house...usually once a week. We never thought anything of it. Tubby was a sweet, old guy, always smiling. In all those years I never heard him complain or say a mean word about anything." There was a firmness in the way she announced those last words and Mrs. Conroy looked up at Press with a certainty in her eyes to confirm the matter. Press could see a dampness there that abutted a flood.

"He took care of our kids and our dogs for us at times over the years. When he could still manage a garden, he was always giving us things from it. Flowers, too."

"Sounds like he and you and your husband are the kind of neighbors we'd all like to have," Press comforted.

The woman swabbed a finger under each eye before continuing.

"I was the one who found him," she explained with a sniff.

"I'm sure that was very difficult," said Press. He was beginning to wonder if this story was headed in a direction or down a road he wanted to travel.

"I was going shopping that afternoon and stopped over to see if he needed anything. He didn't answer the doorbell so I opened it a bit and called inside. He didn't answer then either and I knew he should be home, so I went looking for him. He was still in bed. I knew as soon as I saw him."

The flood came. Mrs. Conroy was fumbling in her purse and sobbing quietly when Press handed her a box of tissues from his desk drawer. Several wipes and a couple of moments later she had recomposed herself enough to continue.

"I called the police. I didn't know, really, who I should call. So I just called the police. A few minutes later the police chief, Mr. Nordstrom, came. The ambulance guys were almost right behind him. They checked Tubby and confirmed that he had…that he was dead. Mr. Nordstrom told them they could head back to the hospital and he would call the coroner. Then he said I should go on home, that he would take care of things after that."

She was shaking her head slowly and twisting a tissue between her fingers.

"I left right after the two men from the ambulance. I didn't go to the store. I was too upset by that time. I just sat in the house, staring out the window at poor Tubby's place. That's what's so strange."

"What's that, Mrs. Conroy?"

"Shortly after I was back in my house, the police chief moved his car around in back by Tubby's garage and then went back inside. He was in there for a long time…I don't know…it must have been a couple of hours or more. After awhile he started taking things out to his car and putting them in the trunk. He made a lot of trips."

The woman's brow furrowed over her reddened eyes as she spoke. She now had the full extent of Press' attention, him leaning forward, elbows holding the top of his desk down.

"I don't think he should have been doing that," she declared, her head moving deliberately side to side now. "But I didn't know what to do. What could I say? He's the police chief. Who could I go to? That's why I came to you, Mr. Williams. But please don't put any of this in the paper. I don't know what he'd do. I just needed to talk to someone."

"Don't worry, Mrs. Conroy. I understand. What were some of the things Chief Nordstrom removed, do you know?"

"I couldn't see everything but some things I knew. Tubby had jars of coins. Probably a dozen of them or more. Not old ones or anything, just change. Any change he got, he'd throw it into a jar when he got home. I don't know what he ever intended to do with the money. I never asked. They were mostly mayonnaise and pickle jars, but a couple of them were really big, like the jars restaurants get stuff in."

"And you saw the chief taking those jars?"

"The two big ones, yes. And a box that you could tell was real heavy, the way he carried it. It was open at the top and I could see jar lids. He put everything in the trunk of his car."

Press could not have been more stunned if he'd just learned he was adopted, yet he was intrigued at the same time.

"Was there anything else that you could recognize?"

"He took several gun cases, too. The way he carried them, I assume there were guns in them. Rifles or shotguns, I don't know much about them. But when Tubby's son and daughter were going through the house after the funeral, I offered to help. Tubby's son...that would be Kevin...was asking about a gun Tubby had that his son had always kind of wanted. He thought he'd inherit it. They couldn't find any guns and Tubby's daughter, Marie, said he must have sold them. Tubby hadn't been able to go hunting for years. I didn't say anything and I guess Kevin accepted what Marie suggested. I didn't know what to say or what to do. Him being the police chief and all. Mr. Nordstrom, I mean. I don't know if Tubby's children ever knew about the coins. They didn't mention anything."

"How long did you say the chief was at Mr. Wilson's house?" asked Press.

"Probably a couple of hours after I left. Then Mr. Callahan came, the coroner, you know, he owns Cruiser's Café?"

Press nodded for her to proceed.

"He showed up. A few minutes later a hearse arrived. I saw them take Tubby out on a gurney after that and put him in the back of the hearse. It wasn't long then before everyone left," Anna Mae concluded.

"Do you know if Mr. Wilson had a will?" Press asked.

"I don't really know. He never mentioned it to me and his kids didn't mention anything about one."

"Were the jars of coins...and the guns...were they out in the open where anyone could see them or were they put away some place?"

"No, they were all in closets. Except the jar of coins he was working on filling at the time. That always sat on the dresser in his bedroom," she replied. "The rest of the coins were in his bedroom closet and another closet in the hall next to the bathroom. The guns were in a closet in the basement. I know. I saw them because I cleaned, you know?"

"Certainly." Press knuckled his chin, trying to massage another thought into his head. "Did Mr. Wilson ever talk about Chief Nordstrom? Mention that they were friends or anything?"

"Tubby did say that he liked Mr. Nordstrom, as I recall. Awhile back...maybe a year or so ago, he mentioned that the police chief had done some sort of survey in the house. He showed Tubby how he could make the place safer. Protect himself from burglars and that sort of thing. Showed him how he could make his house more secure, he said."

"So the chief might have reason to know what all Mr. Wilson had in his house, then," Press suggested aloud as if to himself.

"I suppose so," Anna Mae shrugged. "It was about that time that Tubby installed some deadbolt locks on his doors. He even planted rose bushes under all his windows except those facing onto the porch. He said the thorns were supposed to discourage anyone from trying to break in. I don't think Tubby ever used the deadbolts though. He never even locked his doors. Who locks their doors in Fremont anyway?"

Press shrugged his agreement.

"Mrs. Conroy, was there anything else that you saw the chief remove that you recognized?"

She shook her head, paused, then shook her head again when the thoughts came up negative.

"No, mostly he carried out boxes. Like I said, the two large jars of coins I saw, and the gun cases. And I'm pretty sure the one box had jars of coins. I could see the lids. But that was all," she finished.

"Can I call you later if I think of any other questions?" Press explored as he grabbed a pen and reached forward to his note pad. She agreed and Press jotted the digits of her telephone number as she counted them out.

"In all honesty, Mrs. Conroy, I don't know what we can do at this point." Press hunched forward, his elbow pinned to his desk to support the jaw that he buried in his left hand while his right drummed the pen on the note pad. "This is a bit more than we're used to digging into, but something's got to be done if what you say is true. This is a tough one because you're right, he is the police chief. I'll just have to make a few calls and see what we can come up with. But I really do appreciate you coming in with this."

"Like I said, I needed to tell someone. I didn't know who else to talk to." Anna Mae slid forward on the chair to get ready to leave. "Just don't say anything about where you heard this."

Press assured her that he would say nothing. "It may be that we will need you to confirm this to whoever ends up handling the case, though. I mean, at some point the authorities, I assume the state, will need to have witnesses in order to prove that the chief has done something wrong. That might take some time."

"I suppose, then maybe," she agreed with only marginally less reluctance than someone approaching the gallows.

Press thanked her again for coming in and ushered the woman through the newspaper office to the front door. On the way back he rapped his knuckles on Barry's desk and waved the editor into his office.

"Got a hot one out of that conversation," Press stated, shaking his head in near disbelief as the two men sat down. He then revisited the story in detail for Barry's benefit.

"H-o-l-e-e-e shit!" was Barry's offering when Press had finished. It was becoming Barry's favorite exclamation to define more than casual surprise. He leaned forward and braced his elbows on his knees, his head propped on the arch of his hands. "What do we do now?"

"Well, the mayor is Nordstrom's immediate boss, so we know we can't go there," Press said, his eyebrows tugged tight into his forehead as he scratched the back of his neck. "I don't think we'd dare go to the police and fire commission. We still don't know how far all this other stuff goes. Can't go to Glorioso for the same reason. And we know Schell wouldn't do a damned thing even if Nordstrom swiped the diploma off his wall while he stood there and watched."

The two men sat contemplating the top of Press' desk as though they might find a memo there that would provide the answer.

"I suppose I'll start with a call to Jarred Kleinmeier," Press posed at last. "I'm sure that's not his area, but he should at least be able to give me some advice on where to start."

He rocked back and swiveled side to side a couple of times while waiting for another thought to introduce itself.

"How many older folks do you know who live alone in their own home?" he queried.

A kink hitched in the corner of Barry's mouth as he gave a mystified wave of his hands. "Probably a bunch if I do some thinking on it."

"Let's do that," Press posed. "Approach it with the idea that we're doing a feature on how safe senior citizens feel in Fremont. Let's see if we can find out if Nordstrom has offered his services to any more older folks. Anything that might give him the opportunity to case their homes."

Barry agreed and anted his own addition to the probe. "I'll go back through the obits for a couple of years to see if I can pick out a sampling of names of people who may have lived alone. Maybe we can discretely ask some of their friends or relatives if anything was missing later."

"Good idea," Press concurred. "I think I'll wait until we've got something more, something more solid, before I call Kleinmeier. Let's see if we can't really give the state some reason to come down and get involved here."

24 The electronic ring of the telephone bolted Press upright from his sleep in the recliner as if an irate subscriber had yanked him up by the front of the shirt. In his awakening he found Abby gaping at him from her perch on the sofa with one of those 'should I get it or will you?' looks. The sound of the phone's second ring shuddered through Press with an ominous dread that said he really didn't want to answer the call.

"I'll get it," he told her as he hoisted himself out of the chair and glanced at the clock. Eleven thirty-five.

"Neither of the kids is home yet," she cried, covering her mouth with the tips of her fingers. She was at his elbow as he picked up the receiver on the third ring.

"Yes.

"What?

"I'll be right there!"

"Press, what happened?" The look frozen on Abby's face anticipated the worst.

"Jeremy's okay...he's at the police station," Press replied with no little irritation. "They busted a beer party at the reservoir."

"Blast it, Jeremy!" Abby's relief was expressed in instant irritation. "Do you want me to come with you?"

Press was already three-quarters into his windbreaker.

"Why don't you wait here for Kate? She might worry if we're both gone. I shouldn't be long."

Most of Fremont was still awake it seemed this warm Friday night in spring. The wind, that drifter that came into town off the plains having spent its winter pay, was bedded for the evening. There was still a bustle of traffic on the streets and few of the houses had gone dark, although some of the lights filtered through bedroom curtains and shades. Anger levered his foot on the gas pedal as Press drove toward the police station. Thoughts, all of them focused on Jeremy, pinballed back and forth in his head as he drove through town under a canopy of yellow umbrellas that were streetlights. One side of him excused the boy as testing his gallop and getting caught, while annoyance would bounce off the other side of him for going off drinking after what the kid had seen at his grandfather's funeral just a few months back. Juggled somewhere in the flock of notions was a sense of relief that the call hadn't been to tell him that his son had been hurt. Or worse.

Looks like you could call a PTA meeting here, Press smirked to himself as he approached the station and recognized a number of the cars parked outside. He turned left in front of the municipal building and drove nearly another block before finding a parking space. As Press found his way toward the entrance to the police department, terse greetings were offered as parents tried to smuggle their sons and daughters away from the building with as little recognition as possible.

In the station the scene was as crowded and hushed as the inside of a hotel elevator. Eyes mostly surveyed shoes and floor tiles as parents waited somewhere in the vicinity of anger and embarrassment.

"Damned kids!" A shy half-smile punctuated the remark like it was the last line of a book. Press didn't recognize the smile as it sidled out from under a downcast head. He just shook his head in reply.

One by one, parents were getting details from Deputy Sheriff Wayne Carter before signing the form to have their son or daughter released. Press could see Derek Nordstrom leaning against a desk behind him. Nordstrom was staring back at the newspaperman with an 'I told you not to mess with me' vinyl sneer stuck on his face.

Maybe for now, Press thought as the hair bristled on the back of his neck. But I'm not done yet, either, you turd.

"Jeremy Williams?" Carter pronounced nearly fifteen minutes later. The deputy was a portly man in his late thirties, with freckles spackled across his nose and cheeks, and strawberry hair that thatched like new-mowed hay from beneath his dark brown, department-issued baseball cap. He knew just about everyone in the county on a first name basis. It was his contention that if he could catch people in good situations as kids he might not have to deal with them through the legal system as adults. Whether it was through speaking to classroom groups or coaching Little League baseball or leading his Boy Scout troop or refereeing basketball or football games, Carter had gotten to know most of the kids and their parents from Fremont to Parsons. From his post in the dugout at Little League games, Wayne Carter had learned years back to recognize the voice of Jeremy Williams' father.

"I guess I didn't expect to ever see you here like this, Press," Carter said quietly.

"Couple of us in that crowd, I suppose," Press answered as he leaned over the counter on his elbows. "What've you got?"

"Underage consumption of alcohol, it appears. We're turning them all over to their parents," the deputy said as he pushed a release form across the counter for Press to ink his name to. "You'll be getting a notice of court date in the mail."

Press handed the form back as police officer Anson Bonner escorted Jeremy into the room from the jail area.

The boy darted quick glances at his father, trying to gauge the degree of trouble he was in. Press refused to look back. When Jeremy came around the counter, his father simply turned and headed out the door.

"If it means anything, I didn't drink at all," Jeremy said to his dad's back as they approached the top of the concrete stairwell.

Press whirled and grabbed his boy's sweatshirt in both hands, hauling their noses to a stop inches apart.

"Then why were you arrested?" he demanded.

"I don't know, Dad. Because I was there, I guess." Tears were welling in Jeremy's eyes. "I'd just gotten there when the cops showed up. I'd taken Cindy Zastrow to the movie and then we were just riding around. We'd heard about the party and decided to go see who was there."

"If you weren't drinking, Jeremy, why do I smell beer on you?" The anger in Press was welding his jaws tighter together as he vented through the clench of his teeth. "I grew up with the stuff. Don't you think I can smell it on you a block away?"

"Please let me explain, Dad. I didn't drink anything, honest!" The boy was crying now. "I was talking to this guy when the cops drove in with the lights going and all. Everybody went nuts. Kids were running everywhere. There must have been fifty or more people there. The kid threw his beer down and ran. It splashed all over me."

The two moved off the sidewalk to allow another father and son to pass as they talked.

"Cindy and I didn't even try to run because we didn't have anything to drink. The cops only caught about twenty or so of the kids. We didn't think they could arrest us just for being there."

"What did the test say your blood alcohol content was?" His anger had dropped a couple of degrees but still would boil water.

"I don't know. They never tested me."

"What?" Press was startled. "How can they arrest you for consumption and not test you?"

"I don't know but they did and they didn't," Jeremy shrugged his neck into his shoulders.

"Come on," Press said and they stumped back down the stairs.

Only a couple of fathers remained on the civilian side of the counter now, one with a son, the other with a daughter in tow as they were about to leave.

"What's up, Press?" Carter asked, his eyebrows quizzically arced above his freckles.

"Why didn't you test him for alcohol if underage drinking is what you're charging him with?" Press demanded.

"I dunno, I assumed we did," Carter said, turning toward Nordstrom. "The boy came in with you didn't he, Derek?"

"Must've missed that one," the chief replied with a shrug.

"Test him now," Press ordered.

"Sure thing." Carter waved Jeremy around the counter to follow Officer Bonner.

"The reservoir's six miles out of town," Press stated. "Why was *he* with you?" Press directed his chin in Nordstrom's direction.

"Mutual aid situation," the sheriff's deputy returned. "I'm sure you know we don't have the staff for instances like this. The departments help each other out."

An extended amount of loud silence filled the air until Bonner brought Jeremy back into the room.

"It's a zero, Wayne," Bonner reported.

"Change it to underage possession then," Nordstrom interjected quickly. "I saw him with a beer in his hand!"

"Dad, that's not true!" Jeremy's eyes pleaded to his father.

Deputy Carter's brows furrowed as he shifted from Press to Jeremy and back to Nordstrom.

"You're lying and you know it, Nordstrom!" Press charged.

"Take a whiff. You can smell it on him," the chief snarled back.

"Dad, I told you, the kid spilled it on me when he ran!" Jeremy flipped his plea to Carter and then briefly to Nordstrom and then back to Press.

"If he was drinking, then why didn't he run like the other kids?" Press was ignoring Nordstrom, fixing his stare directly on Carter. "And why wasn't he tested with the others?"

"Like I said, it was just an oversight," Nordstrom barked as he moved to the counter beside the sheriff's deputy.

"You seem to have a hell of a lot of *oversights* in this department," Press growled across the counter at the chief.

"All right, all right," announced Carter as he barricaded his arms atop the counter to further insure separation between the police chief and Press. "I'm sorry, Mr. Williams. I thought he'd been given the Breathalyzer. If I'd collared him I'd probably have let him go when it turned up negative. But I didn't so I have to go on the word of a fellow officer at this point. It's up to the court to decide from here."

Nordstrom straightened as if prepared to receive a victory medal.

Press stopped at the door and turned to glower at Nordstrom. "We're not through yet, so don't go getting your hopes up."

"Do what you think you can," Nordstrom smirked with words flung out of his mouth as though chiseled by an ice pick.

"I'll call Galen Perry and see what we can do about this," Press told his son when they were headed home. "But you probably shouldn't have been there anyway."

That night and the two that followed Press was able to impose sleep on himself only in a series of naps rather than extended rest. Thoughts of Derek Nordstrom stirred fits of temper in him like doses of pure caffeine. And he found it hard to loosen the rope of anger he had flung around his son. It wasn't so much that Jeremy had gone to the beer party when he shouldn't have. Kids will be young adults who will test their legs from time to time. What rankled Press more – and he knew he probably shouldn't hold it against the lad – was that Jeremy's presence at the beer party provided Nordstrom just one more opportunity to shovel some dirt on the newspaper publisher and his family. With all that had been going on, Kate's and Jeremy's own tickets dished out by the police chief himself, Press couldn't help but feel that his son should have known that Nordstrom was just looking for opportunities like this.

Still, that was really the point in the first place, wasn't it? Derek Nordstrom was out to harass Press in every way he could. Press found himself certain of the truth in it when Jeremy said he didn't drink. It wasn't that his son was any less prone than any other teenager to dancing with the devil on occasion. But the circumstances just lent themselves too greatly in favor of Jeremy's credibility. There was the likelihood that he had just arrived at the party, the idea of another kid throwing his beer and running, dousing Jeremy in the process, along with the fact that the police chief somehow conveniently neglected to give Jeremy a sobriety test. And the chief changing the charge from underage drinking to *possession,* suddenly claiming that he saw a beer in the youth's hand. All of it just didn't add up. It was all just too coincidental, too framed up in the mind of Jeremy's father. No, Nordstrom was looking for ways to get at Press, and Jeremy had lent the chief another opportunity.

With all that had been going on and all the things that he'd found out, Press found himself wanting the police chief's neck in a knotted rope. He didn't want to call Galen Perry at home but he found the hours until Monday morning dragged like they were being towed by a county highway department truck.

Press was still outing himself from his jacket when the phone rang in his office on Tuesday morning. It was Perry.

There wouldn't be any charges, Galen told him. Del Schell took no time in operating on that conclusion. The district attorney had told Perry that there was a lack of proof and corroborating witnesses to warrant prosecution, along with other uncertainties raised in his conversation with Deputy Sheriff Carter. What it really boiled down to, Galen admitted to Press as an aside, was that Schell figured he'd already gotten the publisher mad enough at him as it was, and there is an election coming up in November. Failure to prosecute this case wouldn't matter to Nordstrom one way or the other since he'd made his point. But if he pursued it, Schell would likely assure himself of no support from the Fremont newspaper in the fall.

Dinner was almost over when Press sprung the news.

"Oh, good," was Abby's acknowledgement of relief.

Jeremy's face brightened as if he'd just found the handful of years that had disappeared from his youth over the past four days. The smile quickly retreated, however, when he saw the absence of delight in his father's look.

"You were fortunate this time," Press warned after dousing his tonsils with the last from his coffee cup. "I'm sure you weren't drinking, but you have to exercise better judgment on things like this. You're just better off avoiding places where somebody's got alcohol. It's especially so when you know Nordstrom's out to get us any way he can."

"Yes, Sir," Jeremy said softly.

"Dad, kids like us just about can't go anywhere that somebody doesn't have beer," Kate sided. "You can only go bowling so much and we've all seen the movies that aren't rated 'R' at least three times."

"That doesn't mean you have to drink to have fun," Press countered sternly as he leaned over his plate.

"We don't, Dad." Jeremy was defending now. "It's just that there's not much to do in Fremont so someone's always having a party. Somebody's always bringing beer. Just because we go to a party where it's there doesn't mean we drink the stuff."

"I believe you and I understand," their father said as he settled back in his chair. "I guess what I'm really saying is that you have to be extra careful right now. Like I said, you know Chief Nordstrom is just looking for ways to use you guys to get even with me."

"Why can't you just back off of him so he'll leave us alone for a change?" Kate's eyes were on the hands she had folded in her lap. "Why do *we* always have to pay the price for what you put in the paper?"

Press glanced at his wife. Abby returned a shrug that said she wasn't so sure she didn't agree with her daughter.

"It's a point I've thought of a lot of times," Abby noted. "I know it's your job, but it puts a lot of stress on the rest of us, especially them." She nodded in general toward her kids. "More sometimes than you might think."

"Because, in this case for sure, Nordstrom's the one who's doing things wrong, not us. It's the newspaper's job to point out stuff like that," Press explained in his own defense.

"Why can't someone else do that? We're the ones who always have to suffer because of your job!" Kate cried as she butted her chair away from the table. "I wish you didn't own the stupid newspaper! I hate it!" She flung her head back and headed toward her room.

Surprise tugged his eyebrows nearer the top of his head as Press looked at Abby for an answer to Kate's sudden outburst. She reached across to lay her hand on his arm.

"They take a lot of abuse from the kids at school over things that are in the paper," she suggested quietly. "They always have."

"Is that true?" Press looked at his son.

"Sort of," Jeremy admitted. "Most of it I just try to laugh off or ignore. But Kate's more serious. She kind of takes stuff personally. There've been a lot of times when I wished you were a doctor or something, though. The comments do get pretty annoying after awhile."

"Do they bother you, Cassie?" Press pursued.

"Not much since I slugged a couple of 'em when I was in the fifth grade," Cassie smiled almost triumphantly.

Abby rolled her eyes across the ceiling and Press emitted half a laugh.

"I guess it just never occurred to me. I never considered…."

It was only logical, though. Press knew he received enough response from people who took exception to some of the news that was published in the *Gazette*. Children were seldom polite in their treatment of their peers. They could, in fact, be downright cruel to each other. Anything their parents said in the living room or over the kitchen table might be repeated in twofold helpings in the hallways and on the playgrounds of school. Statements made by a mother or father could be recited out of context far more assuredly than lessons taught from a school text or library book.

"PRESSING MATTERS"
April 6

We often speak of the innocence of youth and wonder why some of it can't be retained in adulthood. But innocence has its dark side. There is also a mean streak born of naiveté that can be brutally frank and cruel. Children embellish on each other's frailties, ridicule their flaws. Obesity, a new set of glasses, a 'different' way of talking or style of dress, the ways their parents earn their livelihood can be loathsome burdens that are endured a lifetime. And then we wonder why adults have lost their innocence. Sometimes, I think, rather, it's thrown away on purpose....

25

"Hi, Chief!" Barry chirped as he bounced into the publisher's office.

"That's not high on my list of endearing terms right now," Press noted with mock severity. He didn't turn or look up immediately. His mind had been off touring another county of his brain.

"Oops. Never even thought of that," McGinn flinched as he sat down across the desk. After exchanging perspectives on the first weekend of the major league baseball season and mutual grumbling about various spring yard chores, Barry told Press he'd come up with eleven names from the *Gazette's* obituary columns of people who'd died in the past two years who lived alone.

"I copied down everything I could in the obit that might tell us who relatives or friends were that we might contact," he explained. "Most of 'em had family right here in town, but some list kids living from coast to coast." He slid two photocopied pages of notes across the desk to his boss.

"I thought maybe we could split the list of calls to make. I'd take six," Barry suggested hopefully as he tilted his head to expose a sheepish grin.

The shake of his head couldn't dislodge the chuckle look from his face as Press picked up the copy of Barry's notes and scanned the names.

"Okay, but don't expect me to start covering council meetings on a *shared* basis for you or something," Press responded with a dry snicker. "Who knows when we'll be able to get hold of some of these people. From what I see here, just finding some of them may be a trick."

The first name on Press' list was Charlie Delaney's mother, Betty. He called Charlie at the hardware store. When Delaney answered Press explained that they'd been given information that items sometimes were missing from the homes of elderly folks who'd lived alone and died. If there was any truth to it, Press said, he was sure people should be warned so they could take necessary precautions. Who took care of his mother's estate and did everything seem to be in order?

"Nah, everything seemed okay," Charlie answered. "My brother and sister and I went through the house a few days after the funeral. Didn't notice anything in particular."

"Who made the call when your mother...how was she found?"

"My wife. She and my daughter were at the house cleaning for her when Mom collapsed. Why, what's up?" Delaney quizzed.

"Oh, nothing for sure. We're just checking things out to see if there might be something," Press replied. He thanked Charlie and went on to the next name on his list.

Eleanor Sweeney's two sisters lived in town. Her only daughter lived in Tampa. No one answered at any of the three numbers Press called.

Delbert Smith had a son, Carl, who lived in Avery. Press knew Carl. An easy going sort of guy as he recalled, the son owned Smitty's Speedy Print and Office Supply up there. Press dug out the Avery phone directory and dialed.

After Press explained the reason for the call, Carl acknowledged that there had been a couple of things that they couldn't account for.

"We just shrugged it off as probably something Dad broke," he said back to Press. "Dad's eyes were awful and his feet and knees were just as bad. He was always stumbling over or into something and breaking it. Luckily it wasn't his bones, most often."

"Do you recall what items? Any specific things you couldn't find?" Press inquired.

"Well, the clock my grandparents had given my folks as a wedding present, for one thing. I don't know if you could really call it an antique, but it had some sentimental value for me. My wife thought it was really ugly, but I still kind of wanted it just because it had belonged to my mom and dad." There was a pause while recollections visited the home of Carl's father. Then he resumed. "He had an old cavalry saber, too. Never got it out to show anyone much. I always thought it was in the same closet where he kept it when I was a kid. I guess I just assumed he gave it to one of his buddies or something."

"Was there a will that you know of?" Press wondered.

"No, I was Dad's only heir," Carl said back. "I asked him about it a couple of times, but he just said he didn't need one. Everything would go into his estate and I'd get it anyway."

"Did your father ever mention knowing any of the Fremont police officers or having one of them do a security inspection in his house for him?" asked Press.

"I don't recall him saying anything. I probably knew most of his friends. I did notice that Dad added deadbolt locks to the doors a year or two earlier, though. Don't know what good it did because I don't think he ever locked his doors in his life," the man replied.

"Carl, had your father been sick or...I guess the simplest thing is just to come right out and ask how he died?"

"He had a heart attack. One of his pals was supposed to drive him to bingo on a Wednesday night. When Dad didn't answer the knock, the guy opened the door and walked in. Dad was lying on the bathroom floor."

"Who was your father's friend? Do you recall?"

"Sure, it was Buzz Thompson," Carl supplied. "He still lives over on Ninth Avenue there in Fremont."

Press ended the call with his thanks and began thumbing through the Fremont telephone directory for Thompson's number. He found the listing under 'Beasley' Thompson. No wonder the guy goes by 'Buzz', Press snickered to himself.

Buzz apologized for the shortness in his breath when he answered. "I was out pullin' weeds in my garden when I heard the phone ring," he huffed to Press.

"No problem," Press grinned into the telephone. He explained that he was working on a piece about senior citizens who lived alone before he continued. "Carl Smith tells me you found his father, Delbert, the day he died?"

"Sure did," the other whewed. "That was something I wouldn't want to put anyone through. Walking in on a dead fella like that."

"Could I ask what you did when you found him? Who'd you call, I mean?"

"Oh, I could tell he was dead right off, gray as he was," Buzz related. "Soiled himself, too. I guess folks do that when they die. What a mess!"

Press wasn't really interested in that level of graphics in the detail, but he waited for the man to continue.

"Anyway, I didn't know who to call first, with Carl livin' up to Avery and all. So I called the police."

"Do you know who the officer was who showed up," Press asked, the interest intensifying the volume in his voice.

"First it was these two guys with the ambulance," Buzz specified. "But then Chief Nordstrom was pretty much right behind them."

"What happened while you were there?" Press could hardly spill out the questions and hurry along the answers fast enough. The excitement was jigging in him like a kid finding key pieces to one of those ten thousand-piece jigsaw puzzles.

"It wasn't much, really. The ambulance guys looked at Del and told the chief he was dead. I'd already told 'em that. Then Mr. Nordstrom told 'em he'd call the coroner and they left. He asked me if I knew who his relatives were and I told 'im about Carl up in Avery. He said he'd call the police up there and have one of them contact Carl. Then he told me that I could leave."

"So you did?"

"I did. Sure didn't feel much like playin' bingo that night, though."

"One last question," Press posed. "Did Mr. Smith ever mention having a security check done on his house or did he have a particular friend on the police force that you knew of?"

"Not to my knowledge," Buzz answered. "If he did, he never said anything about it to me."

Press made sure he could call on Buzz again if he had more questions before hanging up. A shiver worked its way down his spine as he finished jotting a rush of notes confirming his talk with Mr. Thompson. An urgency was working its way into the realization that a major story was forming.

The final two calls produced nothing. One man had collapsed in church, the other had died in the hospital after six months of fighting cancer.

Press had just scooted the chair back from the desk and was hefting the back of his lap off the seat when Barry burst into the office.

"Bingo!" Barry cried out of the banana-wide smile so common to the space between his ears.

"Bingo back atcha!" Press returned as he sat back into his swivel chair.

"You got something, too?" Barry's eyes widening over his already broad grin as he tugged a chair up to Press' desk and sat down.'

"Yeah, but go ahead," Press told him.

"Jerry Gruber died last August. His daughter, Anne, was in my graduating class in high school and his son, Don, was a couple of years older. She's married and lives in Phoenix now and the brother works for some oil company in Fort Worth. I talked to both of them!" He stopped to reassemble his breath. "Anne had called the police department after she'd tried to call her dad at various times of the day for two days and got no answer. The guy'd had open heart surgery less than two months earlier and she was worried when she couldn't reach him."

Barry passed a knowing look to his boss.

"Guess which cop found him dead," he urged.

"Nordstrom, of course!" Press answered back.

"You bet. And it gets even better." McGinn nested his backside into the chair as if preparing to deliver a tale of epic adventure.

"Mrs. Gruber had died several years ago. She was an avid antique collector according to both Anne and her brother, Don. The old man couldn't bear to part with any of the stuff, even to give a few things to his kids. Anne said everything appeared to be normal when she and her husband and Don and his wife stayed at their father's place earlier while he had his surgery. The spouses went home right after the surgery and she and her brother stayed on for two weeks to take care of their dad." Barry paused again to gather air.

"She called her father every day after she flew back to Phoenix. She said he seemed to be doing well and then all of a sudden she couldn't reach him for two days. Then she called the police. Anne said it was during her lunch hour when she called.

That would be between one and two here. Nordstrom called her at home that night about six-thirty and told her he'd found the old man dead."

"Makes you kind of wonder what went on all those hours between calls," Press mused. "The police log should confirm her call. I wonder how we can find out what took the chief so long in getting back to her?"

"I'm sure he'd try to cover his tracks, but this isn't over yet," Barry gushed. "When she and her brother got back to take care of the funeral arrangements, she said everything had changed in the house. Anne said they could tell it as soon as she and Don walked through the front door. Things were missing."

"Did they call the police?"

"Yeah. And Nordstrom showed up!" Barry answered back. "He told 'em the place must have been burglarized. They thought it seemed strange because they couldn't find any sign of forced entry, but they took Derek's word for it. The chief said he'd put his guys on it right away. After the funeral they went through the house and made a list of all the things they could verify that were missing and gave it to Derek. She said that since returning to Phoenix she's called at least once a month, but Nordstrom always tells her they're working on it and that they haven't come up with anything."

"When you check the blotter this week, sweet talk Mavis into digging out the log for last August," Press suggested with intended sarcasm toward the elderly Miss Manheim. "I'll bet you a piece of pie at Cruiser's that there isn't any entry concerning a burglary at Jerry Gruber's. Also see what time the call from Anne...Gruber?"

"Watson," Barry stated.

"See what time Mrs. Watson's call came in and see if there's a further entry that tells when Nordstrom went to the Gruber house."

"Got it. So what did you come up with?"

"In a second." Press held up a hand to keep from moving on too fast. "Before I forget, did you ask whether or not there was a will?"

"Oh, yeah, that's another thing," Barry recalled. "She and her brother went through the will with Galen Perry, in fact, before they left town. There were specific items intended to go to each of them, things that were missing from the house. Everything else was to be divided as the two saw fit or sold and the money split between them when the estate was settled."

"Nordstrom wasn't mentioned in it, though?" Press wanted to make sure and got a head shake reply from McGinn. "And Anne didn't mention anything...her father never said anything about Nordstrom doing him any favors or inspecting the house like he did for Tubby?"

Again, Barry shook his head.

Press leaned on his elbows and told his editor about the Delbert Smith death and the incident reported by Buzz Thompson. "Pretty much the same scenario Anna Mae Conroy told us. The chief shows up and sends the EMTs away, telling them he'll call the coroner. Then he sends Buzz away. I'd bet I can find out from Bud Callahan what time he received the call. And I'd also bet it'll be several hours after the call to the P.D. I intend to check it out in each of the three instances we've got so far."

Press swiveled sideways in his chair a couple of times before adding, "Oh, and Smith's son didn't remember his father mentioning Nordstrom, but he did notice deadbolt locks being installed in the house a year or so before he died. Pretty coincidental, don't you think?"

Barry nodded his raised eyebrows in agreement.

26 Abby could hardly get the 'amen' delivered quickly enough after the family was seated for dinner.

"Jeremy's got some news for you, Press," she announced, eyes beaming over her anticipating smile.

"Oh, yeah? What'd you get busted for this time," his father teased.

"D-a-a-a-d!" His eyes rolled around the ceiling as his mother frowned and gave Press a playful cuff on the shoulder.

"I've been accepted at the University of Missouri for next fall," he declared with a half-shy smile.

"Missouri!" Press echoed with more than a little surprise. "I thought you were going to apply to Drake or Creighton or Mankato State or someplace?"

"I did…and I was accepted at all three," the youth shrugged. "But I also applied to MU and when they accepted me too, I decided to go there. To study journalism!"

Press' jaw dropped to the second button of his shirt as he turned to his wife, who was giggling proudly over her meatloaf. He couldn't have been more astonished if Jeremy had announced that his career goals were to pump gas into cars and beer farts into bars like his Grandpa Mick.

"What happened to going to business sch…when did this all come about?" Press wondered aloud as he realigned his lower jaw to fit his upper row of molars.

"I've been considering it for quite awhile, I guess. I just wasn't sure. And besides," he grinned over a fork full of French-cut green beans, "running the *Gazette* is running a business isn't it? I'm planning a minor in business."

Press sensed a snugness in his shirt as his chest swelled in the same measure as his new-found pride. Not since demanding that his son sit at the kitchen table and read *Lord Jim* aloud to make sure he was completing a seventh grade homework assignment, had Press considered the possibility that Jeremy might follow him into a newspaper career. The boy was known to have a smooth way with vocabulary but Press had not seen much evidence of it on paper. Jeremy's way with words had caused his father to marvel at the potential in him for selling advertising. Could make a good lawyer, too, he thought. But Press just figured the lad would head off in his own direction, or two or several before he eventually settled into something. Yet this was a sudden twist in the family tie.

"Does this mean that Jeremy's going to write a column like Dad's?" Cassie wondered through a helping of meatloaf.

"Don't talk with your mouth full," her mother scolded.

"Yeah, but I'll probably win a Pulitzer Prize for mine," Jeremy noted with a hint of devil tucked into his grin.

"I'm surprised that you even know what a Pulitzer is," Press laughed with a shake of his head, still not certain whether to believe what he was hearing.

"I know lots of stuff, Dad. You just need more faith in me."

"I'd have more faith in you if the stuff you know showed up on your report card." The comment was delivered in a playful way that they each knew carried a cup of truth. Press couldn't help but think of how he'd always figured that, of his three offspring, Kate might be the next journalist in the Williams line of succession. Kate, with her seriousness, her thorough attention to detail, and her skilled essays and term papers had the makings of a journalist. Press knew she could write. Even Cassie had demonstrated a more studious dedication than Jeremy had shown. She could pursue her love of games with a camera and a pen in the ample tracks of Sport Henry, if she chose to.

But, Jeremy? Jeremy had always been an enigma to his father. Still the boy's smooth ways with words and people would make him a perfect advertising manager in Press' mind. With a journalism major and business minor, he could surely see the possibilities for Jeremy making the *Gazette* a family tradition. Press glowed inside himself at the thought.

"It's too bad you came up with this decision so late," Press pondered as Abby refilled his coffee cup. "We could have found all sorts of things for you to do at the *Gazette* that would have given you a leg up in school."

"A boy needs to have fun while he's still in high school, Press," his wife chided.

"Bagging groceries is fun?" the father asked. "If he was interested in newspapers, he could have had just as much fun helping Henry cover sports for us or something."

"It's not the same, Dad," Jeremy interjected. "When I get out of college I won't be covering the same kids I go to school with. There's a difference. Besides, like I said, I really didn't make up my mind until a few weeks ago."

Press accepted that with a settling shrug.

"So, you've been awfully quiet, Kate," he said, turning his view to his middle child. "Are there any surprises forthcoming from your perspective?"

"Not me," Kate issued, her eyes not leaving the plate where she was stabbing the last of the green beans with her fork. "I'm still going into accounting. I don't care if I *never* see the inside of the *Gazette* office again! Or Fremont, for that matter!"

She notched her chin in her brother's direction. "After all the newspaper business has put us through, I'm amazed that he would even dream of going in that direction."

Press shifted a look at Abby, who bucked her eyebrows to punctuate the last words of her daughter's sentence, meaning the start of a new paragraph was to begin elsewhere.

"Well, son, if you'd like to work for us this summer, we can always find things for you to do," Press offered, returning to Jeremy with a look of affection that all but ruffled the boy's hair. "You can start any time now, if you want."

"I think I'd like that," the lad affirmed with a warm smile.

27 Angie McGinn called Press Tuesday morning to say that Barry had been up all night with the flu and wouldn't be in this morning.

"He might make it in this afternoon if he feels better, but he was at the toilet most of the night getting rid of something one way or the other," Angie reported.

"That's more information than I need at this point," Press told her with a chuckle. "Tell him not to come in until he's better and not to bring it in here with him."

Press decided to do the checking on the police log entries himself. The itch was in him and he couldn't sit still until Barry could do the scratching around at the cop shop. He grabbed a note pad and headed out of the office.

"Morning, Mavis. Chief," Press said as he approached the counter at the station.

Derek Nordstrom was standing at the dispatcher's desk going over some papers with Mavis Manheim when Press walked in. He said nothing, simply daggered a look at the newspaper publisher and headed toward the hall and his office like a man walking in an ice storm. Mavis waited with a snarl curled in her lips as if she wanted to bark or growl but kept silent.

"I need the logs for this past March, and for July and August last year," Press stated.

"What for?" snapped the woman.

Press passed a hand over his mouth as if to wipe away the first words that might come out in favor of some better choices.

"DON'T start with me this morning, Mavis. Pulleeze. Just get me the logs – March of this year, and July and August of last."

Mavis finished scratching on a paper at her desk before slowly ambling to the sergeant's desk to look for the March log. When she had dispensed it on the counter in front of him, she turned toward the hall.

"The other two are in the vault," she declared with her back to him.

In no time Press found the entry for Anna May Conroy's call reporting Tubby Wilson's death. One thirty-five p.m. on March 12. Chief Nordstrom responding.

He was leaning sideways on the counter, tappy-tapping his pen on the note pad when Mavis finally approached with the two logs from the previous summer.

The incident notations were easy to find for the calls on Delbert Smith and Jerry Gruber as well. The call came in at six-twenty in the evening on July 14 when Smith was found dead, and the call for Gruber was reported at one-seventeen p.m. Derek Nordstrom was the respondent in both instances. Press searched the entire month of August for any report of a burglary at the Gruber home and none was entered.

"Mavis, I'd like the juvenile log for August of last year."

Mavis let out an exhaustive sigh like the request was yet another interruption keeping her from performing brain surgery. The volume was deposited on the counter with a thud when she returned from the vault with it minutes later.

Again, Press paid a mental call on every entry for the month and found no entry concerning a burglary at Jerry Gruber's home.

"Mavis, ask the chief," Press began, then thought better of it. As much as he wanted to ask the surly bastard why there wasn't any notation of the burglary investigation that Nordstrom kept stalling Gruber's son and daughter with, it dawned on Press that good judgment shouldn't tip the police chief off that someone might be on to him.

"Never mind," he finished with. He grabbed his notes and left.

"Is Bud still here?" Press asked the waitress who was filling the coffee cup in front of him.

"Yeah, but he's about ready to head out the door for the day," she replied. "I'll see if I can catch him."

Press managed to slurp some coffee and put a couple of bites of apple pie in him before the unaproned Bud Callahan ambled in and sat down on a stool at the counter beside him.

"Hey, Press. What's up?" asked the amiable café owner and county coroner.

Press tonsiled another slug of pie to his stomach and said, "You keep a log of all your calls as coroner, don't you? I mean what time you get the call and all?"

"Sure." Bud swiveled to get up, then waited to assure himself of the need. "I keep a double log, one here and one at home so that I've got a record no matter where I get the call. Why, what do you need?"

Press snitched a slip of paper from his shirt pocket and handed it to Bud.

"I'd like to know when the call came to you on these three deaths?" the publisher wondered through another mouthful of apples, cinnamon and crust. "The dates are listed next to the names."

"No problem," Callahan responded and departed for his office behind the kitchen. The pie was gone and Press was working on another cup of coffee when the man returned.

"I wrote the times on your paper for you," Bud declared as he held the sheet out to read at arms length.

"You're going to need longer arms if you don't get some new specs soon," Press advised with a laugh.

"Yeah, it's hell to get older. I've got a pair, I just don't like to wear 'em except on county business," Bud replied. "I got the call on Delbert Smith at five minutes to ten. The one on Gruber came in at eight-thirty in the evening, and the one on Wilson I received at four in the afternoon."

"EMTs call you each time?" Press knew the answer but didn't want to let on.

"Nah, Chief Nordstrom called me in all three cases as I recall. Why, whatcha after?"

"Nothing much, yet. Just piecing together some details on some rumors I've heard." Press dumped the rest of the coffee into his throat. "I'll let you know if there's anything to it."

Barry was at his desk scanning the stack of press releases and faxes that had arrived that morning and looking like the color had been sucked out of him with a syringe when Press returned to the office.

"I told Angie you weren't to bring anything with you when you came back and I meant it," Press smiled. "You look the color of a gravestone just waiting for the final date to be etched."

"I feel about as energetic as a rock, too." His face flickered a meek attempt at a grin that didn't stay long. "I'm sure whatever it was is gone now, along with everything else that I wasn't born with. I figured I'd go through this stuff and see what I can send to composing. I've got city council to cover tonight anyway."

Press rounded the corner of the desk and plopped into a chair at the side.

"My curiosity was itching a raw spot in me and I couldn't wait for you to get back," Press related, "so I checked the log entries for the three calls, both at the station and with Bud Callahan. Get a load of this." He hunched across the side of the editor's desk and slapped his notes for Barry to see where he was pointing with his other hand.

"Buzz Thompson's call about Smith was logged in at the police station at six-twenty that evening, but Callahan didn't get the call from Nordstrom until nine-fifty-five. The call for Gruber was entered at five-seventeen. But the chief didn't call Callahan until eight-thirty. And Mrs. Conroy's call about Tubby Wilson was listed at one-thirty-five in the afternoon and yet Callahan didn't get the call from Nordstrom until four o'clock."

Press sat back in the chair and passed a hand across his chin that couldn't coax the smug satisfaction from his look.

Barry's wide eyes gaped at his boss in amazement. "He had all sorts of time to pilfer anything he wanted in between, didn't he?"

"Yep. I think we've got plenty enough to get the state guys down here now," Press said, his head bobbing gently. "The guy's crooked as a dog's hind leg and it's time he gets his due."

"You have to wonder how things ever got to this point," Barry mused as he turned his look curiously.

"He may be a runt of a man but he's got the hat size of a nose tackle," Press posed. "He's been on the job so long that nobody's paid much attention any more. He thinks he's the king toad in this little pond called Fremont. Figures he can do whatever he wants and get away with it I suppose. He pretty much *is* the law here."

Press hoisted his arm for a look at his watch. "I'm going to try to reach Kleinmeier up in Avery," he said, getting up to leave.

But Jarred Kleinmeier was in a meeting with his boss, the state attorney general, all afternoon. Press left a message to have him return his call the next day.

Kleinmeier's call came just before lunch on Wednesday.

"We've got something big going on here and I'm hoping you'll know where to start," Press declared. He spent the next half an hour laying out the dirty laundry he and Barry had uncovered on the Fremont police chief. He delivered as many details as he could, from Mrs. Conroy's eyewitness account, to the items missing at Del Smith's and the coincidental installation of deadbolt locks, to the claimed but not recorded burglary at the Gruber house, to the unexplained lengthy intervals between the times of the emergency calls recorded at the police station and the time the coroner was called later.

When he was finished, there was a long contemplation on Kleinmeier's end of the line.

"This Nordstrom appears to be a piece of work, doesn't he?" the state man entered at last.

A master of understatement, this guy is, Press kept to himself.

"Let me talk to the guys in the criminal investigation office. I'll get back to you with a name so that you can be expecting the call," Kleinmeier finished. "It should be soon."

28

Blaine Peterson was the only other arrival so far when Press walked into Cruiser's for coffee on Thursday morning. The farmer emeritus uncrossed his legs and nudged a chair out from the table with his boot as if he were clearing a milk stool for Press to sit on.

"How come you haven't been badgering the police chief lately?" Blaine asked wryly. "He managed to confiscate your computer for slander or something?"

The publisher spun the chair around and straddled onto it, hanging his elbows over the back as he leaned forward. Press wanted desperately to spill the whole story about the thieving top cop, but he swallowed hard and managed to keep it securely in him.

"I'm sure he'll step in it enough to get whatever he's got coming eventually," was all he said.

"You best leave the old boy alone," Peterson teased. "He's my neighbor, you know."

"Your *neighbor?* How do you mean?"

"He owns the old Gunderson place right next to mine," Blaine shrugged. "Well, it's in his wife's name the way I hear it, but *he* owns it as far as I'm concerned."

Had the older man just peed in the middle of the restaurant, Press wouldn't have been more surprised.

"Since when is all of this?" Press asked in astonishment.

"Bout six months ago I guess. I tried to buy the place from Old Lady Gunderson for a couple of years after her husband died. Figured my son could farm it along with our place, but she wouldn't sell," Peterson explained. "From what I hear, she just about *gave* it to Nordstrom."

"*GAVE* it to him!" Press exclaimed as his head lurched forward in a way that invited further explanation.

"Left it to him in her will or something the rumor goes," was all Peterson added.

"But she's not dead yet, is she?"

"Not the last I heard," the once farmer said with a tilt of his head. "She moved into them apartments for seniors over on the west side of town."

"Then Nordstrom doesn't actually *have* the place yet? I mean, things could change before she dies?" Press questioned.

"I dunno, I suppose. But they have been doing some surveying out at the place. Plans are for a subdivision, the grapevine has it," Blaine surmised.

"Interesting. How big a farm is it?" inquired Press.

"Couple hundred acres. My son leases the land, but just for this summer. Payments go directly to Nordstroms. And some young, funny-weed-smoking couple's renting the house," Blaine offered, crossing his right boot over his left knee again. "Shacked up, you know? Ain't married."

Press fingered the coffee cup and tugged it in tight circles on the tabletop as he mulled the situation.

"How far out of town do you live, Blaine? I mean from the city limits?"

"Half a mile, maybe. The city starts just the other side of the Gunderson place."

Press' mouth kinked as if a chain had just been yanked there to turn on a light.

Wayne Boginoski and Lyman Dunnington doubled the number at the coffee gathering now, and Press let the subject drop.

Barry followed Press' beckoning into the publisher's office and the two sat down.

"A new wrinkle in the Nordstrom situation," Press announced. "Did you know that he, or rather, his wife owns a farm outside of town?"

Barry hummmphfed through his nose. "That's news to me! About all I could see him handy at on a farm is scaring crows."

Press told the other about his conversation that morning with Blaine Peterson. "Blaine says he thinks Wilma Gunderson practically *gave* the place to Nordstrom. At first he said she left it to him in her will, but she's still alive the last he heard. Blaine's son is renting the farmland this year and pays the Nordstroms."

Barry rattled his head from side to side in disbelief.

"That must have been a frog in the pants of her kids or relatives," he supposed.

"I'm not sure she has any," Press tried recollecting. "Didn't the Gundersons have a couple of sons killed in Vietnam?"

"Now that you mention it," Barry conceded. "Any idea where Mrs. Gunderson lives now?"

"For some reason I'm thinking she's in Valleyview Retirement Apartments and Nursing Home," Press said with a sideways tic of his head. "I can't remember if Blaine actually mentioned that during our conversation or if I just made my own assumption." There was a pause while he drummed a medley of thoughts on his desk with his pen.

"When you make your courthouse run to Parsons, check the land records in the register of deeds office and see if you can find out how the transaction was recorded, if it has been yet," Press suggested as a boss would. "Also, spend some time and see if Nordstrom or his wife own any other property in the county. You may end up having to get somebody at Countywide Title Company to do a computer search for you. Their office is a couple of blocks down from the courthouse on the same side of the street. If you do, just have them send us the bill."

"Hey, Dad." With a smile that Press detected as all too motivated, Jeremy greeted his father from behind a can of Pepsi.

"Hey, Bud," Press greeted back as he tossed a "what's he up to now" glance at Abby, who was drying her hands on her apron as she turned from the kitchen sink. She merely winked as she pecked him on the lips and returned to shucking the husks off the ears of sweet corn.

"I've saved you and Mom the trouble of trying to decide what to get me for graduation," Jeremy advised as he straddled a chair at the table. Press pulled out another chair and sat down around the corner from his son.

"I can hardly wait," he said, returning an expectant grin of his own.

"You know, I really should have a better car if I'm going to drive back and forth all the way between here and the University of Missouri for breaks and weekends and stuff," Jeremy began with unabashed enthusiasm. "And I might get a job in Columbia to help pay for college and I could use a good car for that. Caravello Cars has a really nice, black Dodge Intrepid on the lot. It's only two years old and has less than thirty thousand miles on it."

Press didn't flinch. "Actually, I was thinking of something more practical, like socks and underwear." Abby couldn't stifle her giggle.

"D-a-a-a-d." Jeremy's balloon was deflating. "Just think about it. Then Kate could have the Cavalier."

"Or, we could just get Kate a car."

"Yeah, but, Dad, this is a *graduation* present. It would be really special."

"Hey, Mom could stitch your name into the underwear. You'd probably be the only guy on campus with monogrammed jockey shorts."

Jeremy rolled his eyes.

"So how much under the mileage is the sticker price for this 'really nice' and probably very sporty car?" Press asked, drum rolling his fingers on the tabletop.

"Less than ten thousand dollars," the son offered with something between a wince and a question hooked in the corner of his eye and mouth.

"Well, I guess I was thinking more along the lines of an Apple laptop that you could use at college," Press came back, stilling the finger drum. "For that kind of money we could outfit the whole family in new computers."

Press nudged his chair away from the table so that he could see both his wife and his son.

"Shall we take a vote?" he suggested, a silver sparkle reflecting off his hazel eyes. "All hands for the car?"

Jeremy hoisted his hand weakly with a wave of defeat.

"Computer?"

"That gets my vote," Abby said as she dropped the ears of corn into the pan of boiling water on the range top.

"I'd still vote for the socks and underwear," Press said grinning, "but on tie-breaking votes, your mom usually wins."

"You really didn't think you had much of a chance on that one did you?" the boy's mother tweaked as she dispatched five dinner plates onto the table.

"No, but it was worth a try," Jeremy laughed as he unstraddled the chair. "How long till supper?"

"By the time you wash up and call your sisters, we can sit down to eat."

Press got up and gave his son a couple of pats on the shoulder before getting the silverware out of the drawer to finish setting the table while his wife took the ribs out of the oven.

"Kate said Becky Hartley has been back in school for several weeks now," she reported.

"Hmm," was her husband's response.

"I guess her folks have reconciled."

"PRESSING MATTERS"
May 4

Perhaps deserving of our admiration as much as our support are those among us who have fought and are overcoming their personal demons, whether it's people who've given up smoking cigarettes or those recovering alcoholics and drug users. I know from my personal battle with obesity just how hard it is to deny yourself something you enjoy; to defeat those cravings that have overwhelmed your body and spirit. The nagging desire is always there, whether you give in to it or not, no matter how long you've resisted the temptation. You have to respect those who have faced their weakness and persevered in their determination to overcome it. If we could just energize that same tenacity and determination to conquer our moral and ethical weaknesses, things like lust and greed....

29 "I've found some interesting stuff," Barry said as he dropped his note pad on Press' desk and pulled a chair under himself. "I'm not sure what it all means or if it will lead to anything, but it's definitely punching the buttons on my curiosity mode."

The editor reported that the Gunderson farm had been deeded over but apparently no money had changed hands that Barry could find a record of.

"It's now in the name of 'ADN Properties, Incorporated' and guess who the officers are in the corporation?" Barry said, offering an open palm towards his boss.

"Well, how wild a guess would it be to say Derek and Alma Nordstrom?" he replied, swivelling his chair a couple of quarter turns, his eyebrows narrowing in consideration.

"Derek's the president and Alma's the vice president. And *Susan Parker* is the treasurer." Barry arched his eyebrows for emphasis and sat back in the chair. "I called the secretary of state's office and had them look up the articles of incorporation."

"Susan Parker!" was the startled response. Press laced his fingers behind his head and surveyed the ceiling as if inspecting it for cracks in the plaster.

"That puts an interesting twist in the Hartley affair. I wonder what her role in all of this is?" he mused. "I just heard that Wes and Sharon are back together. Was it just coincidence that Hartley was screwing Nordstrom's business partner? Or is there a more significant string that ties them all together? More than Hartley's sob story to us?"

"I don't know, but it's more complicated still," Barry added. "ADN Properties, *Inc.* owns four more farms in the county and seven commercial properties in Fremont."

Press whewed and shook his head slowly.

"This is starting to sound like something from Hollywood," he posed.

"The angles sure seem to be coming from everywhere, just like in the movies," Barry agreed. "We've got all the elements in the making – sex, money, and intrigue."

"Yeah, I just hope we don't run into a smoking gun somewhere along the way," Press said. Speculating aloud, he continued. "You almost have to wonder whether Hartley's involvement with the Parker woman wasn't business as much as bedroom? I'd also like to know if Sharon Hartley isn't involved in some way, or at least how much she knows? If there's a business dealing that involves Mrs. Parker, don't you wonder if she didn't know about it? And was Parker's tiff with Hartley really a jilted lover's spat or was it over some financial shenanigan?"

"It sure would be hard to believe that a guy who looks like he's wearing a shoe-polished wig could be so good in the sack that he can keep two women coming back to him," Barry asserted as a grin of the devil shimmered across his face.

Press gave the notion a concurring laugh.

"Where are all of these places that ADN owns? Is there any pattern to them?" he asked.

"In all honesty, I didn't think to look until I was halfway back to Fremont," Barry admitted. "I'll check it out when I go back to Parsons next week."

It was ten minutes before their appointed time when Press finally managed to ease the car into an empty stall at the far end of the public parking lot across the street from the state office building in Avery. It was one of those uninteresting, four-story limestone brick buildings, municipal in nature, that housed regional offices for an assemblage of state bureaucrats.

Past the ground floor offices of the transportation and social services agencies, Press found his way to be elevatored up to the fourth level where the state's attorney general had assistant space two doors down. A small office foyered the facility where a receptionist was seated with barely room for two visitor chairs. The hallway behind her led anonymously to legal operations elsewhere in the interior of the building.

The woman looked up but not seemingly at him when Press announced who he was to see. He sat down while she punched a number on the large telephone panel and announced the publisher's presence.

Mr. Kleinmeier will be with you in a moment," she announced flatly.

The receptionist had offered little more than another clackity-clack to her keyboard when a long, split rail of a figure, bespeckled and mostly hairless at the top, angled all elbows and knees out of the hall.

"Mr. Williams, Jarred Kleinmeier. Nice to meet you at last," he offered with a trace of a smile and an extended hand. He aimed his head toward the hall and said, "Come on back."

Kleinmeier escorted Press into his corner suite and closed the door behind them. Stuffed into a chair opposite the working side of the desk was a man Kleinmeier introduced as Joe Granger. Older than the other two, Granger smiled a formal smile as he hoisted himself half out of the seat and offered Press his hand.

The other man looked to Press to be anywhere between forty-five and seventy years old. His face said middle age but the shine of his completely bald head, the pure white in the Van Gogh on his chin and the mustache above, and the belly that bagged over his belt buckle suggested he could be much older.

"Does he look grandfatherly enough to you?" Kleinmeier asked as he put himself into the chair behind his desk and Press filled the other visitor seat. Granger's face broadened into a toothy grin at that and Press chuckled into the knuckles pursed against his lips.

"Pliable is the term that comes to mind," Press ventured tactfully. "He has the kind of look that suggests he could be whoever you want him to be."

"That's exactly what we say about him," the state attorney said. "If Joe had been in Hollywood, he'd have gotten dozens of Oscars for the roles he's played for us over the years. He's a top undercover man. Would you believe he's only forty-seven?"

Press hmmphfed and nodded in wonder.

"Rheumatic fever took most of my hair when I was eighteen," Granger said as he passed a hand over the shiny skin on top of his head. "Other than a few more wrinkles, I haven't changed a bit since then, except now I only have to dye the beard if I need a younger look."

Kleinmeier informed Press that Joe was being set up in Fremont with a profile fitting the seniors that Nordstrom seemed to be preying on.

"He's taking early retirement due to a heart condition and moving to Fremont in order to be nearer his sister, who does, in fact, live there. The two of you will be the only ones in town who know what he's really there for, but *you're* not to say anything about him to anyone. If you see him on the street, you don't know him or acknowledge him in any way. You say nothing to your wife or anyone else. Is that clear?"

Press shrugged his acknowledgement.

"Joe's sister works at the cannery and doesn't know Nordstrom or anyone on the police force, so no one's suspicions should be aroused."

Kleinmeier went on to say that the state criminal investigations unit would attempt to set up a sting operation to try to catch Nordstrom in the act of stealing from Granger's house. A Fremont EMT would be working with them when the time came to fake Granger's death at home, but the man didn't know what the operation was all about.

"We'll also have the house fully wired with cameras and sound," Kleinmeier noted.

"Do you have a place to live yet?" Press asked, looking at Joe.

"Not yet, but we'll arrange something suitable within a week or two."

"I'd suggest you pull Wes Hartley into the picture," Press said, turning to Kleinmeier. "Tell him your character's background and what you're looking for. I have a hunch word will get to Nordstrom without you having to go looking for him."

Kleinmeier's look suggested a need for more information.

"We just found out that Nordstrom owns quite a bit of real estate in and around town through a corporation called ADN Properties," Press explained. "Nordstrom and his wife are listed as officers in the corporation along with a woman named Susan Parker. We don't know how it all ties together yet, or even if it does, but Susan Parker is the woman Hartley told us he'd been having an affair with. He said she went ballistic on him when he tried to break off the affair and Nordstrom took care of the matter for him."

Kleinmeier and Granger passed Charlie Chan, "Ah, so" looks.

"Yes, that certainly is worth noting," Jarred replied. "Maybe nothing will come of it but, all else considered, it just gives us some more to look at."

The trio finished up the details and Press got up to leave.

"Can I at least tell my editor what's going on?" he asked. "Barry's been involved in this from the start."

"Best not," Granger said. "The fewer people who know, the better. This could take several months to a year."

"Just tell him the state's investigating," Kleinmeier confirmed with an indifferent motion in his shoulders.

Barry's memo noted that two of the ADN farms were just northwest of Fremont and the other two on the southwest outskirts of town. The seven properties that the corporation held in the city were in a lightly developed part of town: an old warehouse that was leased for storage, some vacant lots, and a couple of older houses that were rented out. Nothing that jumped out at him, according to the note. Nothing ignited in Press, either.

30 “You know, in spite of all the nagging about your grades over the years, I’m still proud of you, Son,” Press said as he hugged the tall, blue-robed youth outside the Fremont High School auditorium.

“Thanks, Dad, for all you’ve done for me,” Jeremy returned. His grin turned almost shy. “You know, Dad, I’ve never really said it, I guess, but of all the people we studied in history and of all the big names in the news today, you’re the one I admire most. I’ve never really wanted to be like anyone else but you.”

Press yanked the boy to him again in another monstrous hug, choking on a wad of tears. Tears also streaked Abby’s mascara as she put one hand on Jeremy’s shoulder and stifled a sob of delight with the other.

A lifetime flashed through Press’ mind. He hugged Jeremy long and hard as if to cement the moment in history. He had always thought his life had been short-changed in not being able to make his own father proud of him. To make up for it, all he had ever dreamed of was to make his wife and children proud, to admire the man he was. In that moment, Jeremy had fulfilled so many dreams for his father.

"It's hard to believe that we have a high school graduate," Abby said as she pulled up the covers and nestled into the crook of her husband's shoulder.

"Yeah, I can remember bringing the two of you home from the hospital like it was this morning."

"It seems like this morning was a long time ago now, though," Abby sighed. "Between getting everything ready and then the ceremony, and then the party. We must have fed half the county today."

Indeed, Jeremy's graduation celebration had drawn significant numbers, not just classmates but friends of his parents. Parking was at a premium for two blocks in either direction from the house for much of the day. Throughout the afternoon and evening visitors and partygoers had trooped through the house for a bite and a beverage as they offered congratulations and asked about Jeremy's choice of college before heading to the next graduate's fete.

"I thought it was kind of interesting that the Hartleys showed up," Press admitted. "To look at them, you would have never known there was ever a problem between them."

"Lots of people have problems and work them out," Abby suggested, a bit of surprise filtering out of her tone. "Don't you think most problems can be overcome if two people work at it?"

"Depends on the size of the problems and whether both are in the forgiving or willing mood, I guess. Sometimes I wonder just how many families have some deep, dark secret to hide." His thoughts flashed briefly to his father's Naval past, a story untold in his son's lifetime.

"What secrets do we have to hide from everybody?" Abby asked with a playful poke at her husband's ribs.

A twinge of guilt pricked at Press' conscience and he gave a brief notion to telling Abby about his conversation with his Aunt Eleanor. He quickly passed on the thought, however, not wanting to darken the mood or happiness of the day.

"None, I suppose, unless you're hiding something from me." Press pecked his wife's forehead. "But suppose it was me. Would you be willing to work it out with me if I had another woman on the side?"

"That might get your coffee laced with arsenic," she came back, digging a knuckle into his ribs. "Anything else I could probably work out."

Press rolled toward his wife and began kissing her gently as he slid his hand under her pajama top, caressing her breast and toying lightly with the stiffening nipple.

"Press, my parents are in the next bedroom," Abby protested through a quiet giggle.

"How long have we been married?" he countered as he continued kissing her neck, intent on romantic arson, and started disengaging the buttons on the front of her pajamas.

"Besides," he said, coming up for air, "what's the difference between having your parents or Kate in the next room?"

"It's just the idea of it," she replied, a huskiness entering her whisper as she tugged his T-shirt over his shoulders. Abby's parents had arrived from Minnesota the night before and were afforded Kate's room for the weekend. Kate, whenever she returned from her tour of graduation parties with Casey Delaney, would sleep on the hide-a-bed downstairs in the rec room.

The years had not diminished the passion of Press' and Abby's lovemaking, although it was now more relaxed and deliberate. No longer was there the urgency that accompanied their early exploits in the back of Press' Plymouth, or in his tiny apartment when he could coax his college roommate off the premises for the night or at least a couple of hours. Those were the times when sex was attacked rather than experienced, for fear the world might end before there would be another occasion.

Now they took time to explore each other's senses and relish in every detail, anticipating the other's delights. He massaged her moistness until she had twice peaked in soft gasps and muffled moans, arching her back and pumping her pelvis to the rhythm of his plying fingers. Then it was his mate's turn. Abby rolled onto her knees astride her husband and quickly mounted his stiffness, rocking feverishly as he continued to caress her hardened nipples. Three times, as he neared his bursting heat, she sat back and held his erection tight within her, delaying his eruption. At last she felt her own urge peaking again and they pumped hard together as they exploded in one, united burst of passion.

When they had finished, Abby slumped back to his side and exhaustion completed the cycle from the height of arousal to the depth of sleep.

"PRESSING MATTERS"
June 1

My son, Jeremy, was among the two hundred seven graduating seniors who participated in last Saturday's ceremonies at Fremont High School. Obviously, I'm proud, though no more so, I'm sure, than any other parent of a graduating child. While it is

> difficult to watch a child move on toward adulthood, each new stage is as exciting as the past has been satisfying. We want to hold on to those moments of their youth and cherish them forever, yet each new year brings promise and satisfaction of a different sort. I look forward with enthusiasm to his years in college and his career. He's chosen journalism and will attend the University of Missouri in the fall. Who knows, maybe he'll follow in his dad's footsteps and some day take over the *Gazette* and bring it to new heights. While I don't really want the time to pass any faster than it is already whistling by, I am eager to see where life leads him. I hope it leads him to a woman as wonderful as his mother and to some children – my grandchildren – who will provide him with all the joys and fulfillment that he and his sisters have brought to Abby and me. There are many admonitions delivered by commencement speakers to young people to go out and change the world. Rather I would offer the hope that the world does not change my son. He has so much to offer the future. I am so proud of him….

The sound of knuckles rapping on his door Monday afternoon caused Press to jerk his head up from the computer on his credenza. He had just finished typing his column and sent it to the printer in the composing room.

"Got a minute?" Barry asked as he moved to one of the chairs opposite Press. "Big weekend, huh?"

Press nodded. "As much as I hate to see Jeremy get older, I'm glad to have the ceremony and party stuff over with."

"Well, Angie and I are about to embark on that family journey," Barry said with an even wider than usual wrap-around grin. "We found out Friday that she's pregnant."

"That's wonderful," Press cried as he stood and moved around the desk to pump his editor's hand. "Why didn't you two say something when you were at the house Saturday?"

"Well, that was your big day. We thought it might be sort of like imposing."

"Imposing, hell! That's great news any time." Press occupied the chair next to Barry and the two discussed a range of subjects relating to the entry into parenthood, one from experience, the other from anticipation.

"Back to business," Barry entered at last, "I've got a feature story ready for this week on residential security for senior citizens. It's pretty basic stuff. We really don't have much crime in town for them to worry about, but old folks don't seem to know that. They see all that stuff on TV and think the Mafia is rampant in Fremont." He waved his pen and tucked it behind his ear.

"In tracking down some information for the piece, I did find out some interesting things about Nordstrom." The editor told his boss that the police chief had a hand printed poster in the senior citizens center offering 'free security inspections' by the Fremont Police Department. The center's manager, Grace Kolinsky, had told Barry that Chief Nordstrom had put up the poster about three years ago. She provided the names of several people she knew who had taken advantage of the offer. Barry said he called them just to see what services the department rendered during the inspection and found that Nordstrom was the only one who apparently did the checks.

"How long the inspections took apparently depended on whether the older person lived alone," Barry noted with a curl to the side of his mouth. "Arlyn and Jane Wymore told me that

Nordstrom didn't spend more than ten minutes at their place, but Hattie Cummings said he was at her place for more than two hours. Spent a lot of time going through every room in the house."

Press leaned back in the chair and steepled his index fingers under his jaw. He wondered if Granger was settled in town yet. God, it's hard to keep from spilling that business to Barry, he thought as a touch of frustration tugged at him.

"I am using some of the tips he provided to them in the story, but I also did confirm those ideas first with the department. Most of the stuff that I got from the P.D., though, came from Anson Bonner or Sergeant Belter," Barry continued with a snort. "Derek's not speaking to me at all anymore, although I haven't really tried to confront him on anything."

"I bet that breaks your heart," Press interjected.

"Actually, it does rankle me a little. It's the principle of the thing."

Later that day Press called Jarred Kleinmeier out of curiosity to see if Granger had moved to Fremont yet. Yes, the state attorney told him, Granger was living in a small bungalow near downtown that he obtained through the services of Wes Hartley's real estate office. But, Kleinmeier restated, don't expect anything to pop anytime soon.

On a lark that warbled in the back of his mind, Press dialed Dick Flater's office.

"Is this city council business or are you pedaling ads? Or can I sell *you* something for a change?" Flater teased from the other end of the line.

"Trying to satisfy my curiosity, actually," Press replied. "Have you ever had any dealings with ADN Properties?"

"You mean Nordstrom's company?" the realtor came back.

"That's the one."

"What, are you two out ringing each other's bell again?"

"Not really," Press answered. "I just keep trying to add one and one and it keeps coming up one-and-a-half. I'm trying to find the other fraction is all."

"Sure," Flater said with half a snort. "Actually, I have represented sellers two or three times when Nordstrom was the buyer. A farm outside of town and a couple of older places. One was a warehouse, as I recall. I guess I should say I 'co-represented' the sellers. Hartley actually sold the places, but I had the listings."

"Did the name, Susan Parker, ever come up in any of those dealings?"

"No...at least I don't recall it."

"Do you know her at all?"

"The name's not familiar. Why?"

"Just trying to add fractions," Press said again. He shifted the phone to his other ear and swiveled the chair so he could look out the office window. "Do you recall anything unusual or different about any of those transactions?"

Press could hear the other's breathing during the long pause that followed.

"Nothing really unusual," Flater offered tentatively. "I do know that Hartley had an interest in each of the deals."

"How so?" Press turned back to his desk and hunched forward in anticipation.

"I have no idea what it is," the man replied. "It's just that, under state codes that regulate real estate transactions, a broker has to file a statement with the closing documents disclosing that he has a personal interest in the sale besides just the commission. Hartley did that at each of the closings. The codes don't require that the interest has to be specified."

"A lot of good that does," Press entered with a tint of sarcasm. "Is there any way of finding out what that interest is?"

"Not that I know of. He might be a shareholder in Nordstrom's corporation, for example, but I don't think you can find that out without a lawsuit."

"Why would he want to hide it, if he was?" Press wondered aloud.

"Lots of reasons, I suppose," Flater suggested. "In real estate deals, sometimes a seller might not be willing to part with the property if he knew who he was really selling to or what the intended future use of the property might be. You'd be surprised at how many third party deals take place in the world."

"Probably not, just because not much surprises me any more," Press admitted. "Were any of these properties greatly under priced?"

"Oh, bargains, maybe. Nothing I'd call a steal in real estate terms."

Press thanked him for the information and the call ended.

"Somehow none of that surprises me," was Barry's only reply when Press later informed him of the conversation with Dick Flater.

The clock on the nightstand said two thirty-five in the morning when Press struggled the sleep from his eyes and threw back the bed covers.

"Who the hell could be at the door at this time of the morning?" He was fumbling into an old pair of jeans and at the same time stumbling toward the bedroom door. Abby hurried on her bathrobe and peeked from the hallway as Press went to the front door and flipped on the porch light.

"It's Barry and Anson Bonner," Press relayed to his wife has he opened the door.

Tears were streaming down Barry's face. He had a Fremont Pioneers baseball jacket thrown over an old T-shirt and was still wearing pajama bottoms. His sneaker laces weren't tied. Anson was a step behind Barry, looking dully at the patrolman's hat that he rotated slowly in his hands. Something told Press that trouble was about to grow a new meaning.

"What's the matter, Barry?" Press asked with a laugh that wasn't funny. "Did Nordstrom run you in on another trumped up charge?"

The editor shook his head slowly and hauled in a huge amount of air through a sob.

"Press, it's Jeremy....

"Oh, God, no!" Press slumped against the door frame and grabbed the open screen door for support.

"No, no! Press, tell him no! That can't be!" Abby was screaming behind him.

"Don't do this to us. Guys, please don't do this to us," Press was pleading to the two men standing helplessly before him.

At the sound of their parents wailing, Kate and Cassie had entered the living room. Seeing Barry and Deputy Bonner at the door, they were instantly shocked into the realization of what was taking place. Screaming hysterically, they latched onto their mother and the trio crumpled to the floor.

"I'm so sorry, Press," was all that Barry could tender in consolation. Even a wordsmith of the editor's significance suffered without means to report it thoroughly, though the tremble of his lips said he was trying.

Numbed with grief, Press pulled back and dumped himself into a swivel chair as both Barry and the deputy edged cautiously into the living room. The wails of Abby and her daughters hushed to muffled sobs as Barry began as best he could to explain the awful news he carried.

Jeremy and two classmates, Adam Kelso and Teri Moore, were killed in a one-car rollover between the Fremont city limits and the reservoir. Kelso had been driving his father's Dodge sedan. Another classmate, DeDe Daniels, was in critical condition in the intensive care unit at Parsons General Hospital.

The rest of the night was a hellishly long one in the Williams' house.

31

Even later in the week, DeDe Daniels would still be mostly comatose and doctors' expectations for her recovery were thin as a shadow.

Details of the accident were still sketchy at best. The families learned that the four had been seen at a beer party at the reservoir just before county lawmen arrived to break up the affair. Derek Nordstrom had reported the accident, saying the car was fleeing the scene of the party at a high rate of speed when it left the highway and flipped over several times. All four of the youths had been drinking but Coroner Bud Callahan told Press that none of them was drunk by legal definition. The problem was that all were under the legal drinking age. The three dead youngsters were eighteen; DeDe just seventeen.

The fact that none of the youths in the car had been wearing seat belts gnawed at Jeremy's father.

"Why hadn't the boy buckled himself in?" Press puzzled to himself again and again. He knew it was one of Jeremy's own first rules about driving. His son never let anyone in his car without everyone first securing seat belts. It was an awful "if" that would co-habit his beliefs with virtually every thought of Jeremy for the rest of Press' life. "*If* only he'd been wearing his seat belt, maybe he'd still be alive!"

It also angered and frustrated Press that Jeremy had even gone to the party at the reservoir.

"After all the trouble we've already had. The problems with Nordstrom. Why the hell did he go? Why was he even there? He *knew* better!" The questions kept skipping through his mind like a scratch in an old record.

Press and Abby had spoken briefly with the Kelsos and Moores. There was an entire language available to them and none of the words seemed to fit the moment, other than to assure themselves that the three youngsters were all such good kids. Their parents spoke of how each had been so looking forward to college in the fall; they had such bright futures ahead of them.

Ben Kelso was ravaged with guilt. "I just don't know what would have possessed him to do such a thing. I'm so sorry," he kept repeating. Press and Abby tried to assure him that they didn't hold him responsible, that no one would ever know what was going on in their children's minds. They left when they could offer nothing more. Ben was still blaming himself for the deaths of the three children.

A joint service was held for Adam Kelso and Teri Moore on Friday morning at Redeemer Lutheran Church in town. Both were members of the church and the two had been a couple since late in their sophomore year in high school. Attending the rite only multiplied the dread that Press and Abby faced that evening and the following day.

Jeremy's funeral was surely the biggest Fremont had ever seen, according to Patrick Coughlin, owner of Coughlin and Sons Funeral Home. Visitation had been scheduled at the funeral home for four until nine the evening before, but it was nearly eleven before Coughlin finally closed the door on the end of the procession of mourners. The slow-moving, melancholy line had been constant all evening, sometimes extending nearly a block from the entrance to the funeral parlor. Even floral arrangements were so numerous that many were placed along the front walkway, seeming to funnel the whole town into the room where Press, Abby, Kate and Cassie were huddled to receive condolences. It was a closed casket wake; an enlargement of Jeremy's senior photo poised on a small table next to the coffin.

The pastor at St. James Catholic Church had agreed to allow the funeral service to be conducted there, since it was the largest church in Fremont. Still, the capacity was stretched to near bursting as nearly every member of six high school classes, past and present, attended, along with parents, friends and acquaintances from throughout the community who were on hand to share the Williams family's grief. Snuffles, muffled sobs and wails thickened the heavy summer air throughout the service, as not a single eye went undabbed, fingered, knuckled or swiped.

It was a day Press wanted to end quickly and yet he didn't. He was tired, drained. He wanted the whole thing over with and still, he knew that when it was over, Jeremy would be truly gone. He didn't think he could bear that.

Sitting in the front pew, Press heard little, saw little of the ceremony. It was as if the blood had stopped moving within him. He heard Cassie's wails as he hugged her to his side. He felt the clench of their hands at his other side, his and Abby's; heard her sobbing, along with Kate's next to her.

He deciphered patches of the minister's remarks: "...life snuffed out too soon...no one knows why...in God's hands...."

But mostly, Press' eyes ached with the picture of Jeremy throbbing behind them. He saw his son's constant smile under a snatch of dark hair that dangled over his forehead. Jeremy's laughter echoed across all eighteen years recorded in his father's memory. He could still feel the boy's monstrous hug wrapped around his shoulders. Press' throat burned and his jaw quivered in a steady battle to contain a scream that was rumbling within the depths of him.

It was mid-afternoon by the time everything was finally over; the church service, the graveside ceremony, and the luncheon in the church basement. As they assembled at Press' car, Barry strode over and offered to drive them home.

"Thanks, Barry, but I can handle it," Press replied quietly.

In a moment it was just the four of them. Abby collapsed in her husband's arms.

"I don't think I can go back there...go home, Press," she cried hard. "I can't help but see Jeremy everywhere."

"That's exactly why I have to go home," Press said over the tremble of his jaw. "I don't want to turn him loose. I just can't let go of him yet. Ever!"

Press took the telephone off the hook as he followed Abby and the girls through the kitchen. Kate and Cassie went quietly to their rooms and Press went into the bathroom for some aspirin to quell the raging headache that had pounded in him for hours.

When he returned past Jeremy's room, he found Abby sitting on her son's bed, caressing the pillow and crying softly. Press sat down beside his wife and they fell together, tears flowing freely from both sets of eyes. A moment later Kate poked cautiously into the room. In minutes Cassie had joined them and the four huddled precariously on Jeremy's twin bed. They stayed there into the dark, telling stories and remembering their son and brother, laughing and crying alternately, until exhaustion pushed aside their broken hearts and they could go on no more.

The two girls went to bed and Press went to the kitchen. The refrigerator and counters were filled with casseroles and ready-to-eat dishes that had been brought by friends and neighbors. He put a couple of slices of cold meatloaf and a glass of milk into him and went back to Jeremy's room. Abby was lying on her son's bed, quietly crying again. Press asked her if she'd like something to eat and, when she simply shook her head, he touched her hand in a way to weld their emotions together and led her to their own bedroom.

When Press awoke the next morning the covers beside him were empty. He found Abby and the girls spread across the living room floor amid stacks of photo albums and shoe boxes of family pictures. Tears streaked all three faces as again they were buffeted between waves of laughter and sobbing.

"Look at this one," Abby said, lifting a photo to him like an agate she'd just discovered in the sand. "Remember that Christmas when we took the kids to Disney World?"

Press accepted the picture and slumped heavily onto the floor with the remains of his family. Photographs are supposed to be a way of preserving the present into the future, a way of defeating mortality, he thought as he shuffled through those remnants of his son's life. But he decided that photographs of those he cherished, this loved one now in the ground across town, also are reminders of the frailty of life. Pictures are doorways that open both ways, he thought, into the past and into a future that surely lies ahead for everyone. He felt his own life had begun its final approach that terrible night when Jeremy's ended.

The photos brought smiles and cries, mingled with puzzles and anger. Press found himself recalling every harsh word he'd ever had with Jeremy, along with reciting inside him all the myriad of things he should have said and didn't. The times he'd told Jeremy that he loved him weren't nearly enough. Not even a thousand times more would have been enough to fill his young son's abbreviated lifetime.

Press had seen people of his own generation die. That had never seemed quite right since death, he considered, was reserved for the old. His parents had been old in his mind, even though his mother had died younger than he was now. But she was of another age, not his. Even after that, considerations of mortality loomed distant from his usual thoughts. But this was the first time he had been confronted by the pall of death in someone so young and it was his own son. He found little to console himself. The notion that Jeremy had so many years to grow into, and now he wouldn't, kept badgering him like an ancient water torture.

Press had tried over and over in the harsh set of days since the accident to examine his beliefs and found that he had none. Though he had been brought up with a scattering of church, and later a regular coaxing to it from Abby, he found that now he was as irreligious as a block of stone. He had no coherent or profound way of thinking about death at all, much less the senseless death of his eighteen-year-old son. He had figured that whatever degree of goodness one could offer to one's tiny package of moments in the world was all the significance there was to life, but how could that even be, with the loss of one so young? How much of his son's goodness was never presented? The death of a child is a time without answers, just guesses. Press wished he were better at guesses.

"I can't do this now," was all he could announce without spilling the scream inside him as he slid the album from his lap to the floor and hurriedly got up. Abby and the girls glanced at each other and then three sets of damp eyes followed him down the hall where he disappeared into the bedroom.

When Press walked through the newsroom on Monday morning he was greeted with a startled hush and stare. At the door to his office he turned and, with a small wave, told his employees simply, "What else would I do?"

He placed himself tentatively in his chair, debating whether or not to run from the building, but finally began to wander through the foothills of sympathy cards and notes from newspaper colleagues and others from around the state that lay on his desk. When he finished, Press thumbed through the telephone book until he found the number for the Fremont Medical Clinic, dialed, and left a message for Dr. Benton Cassidy to call him as soon as he was free.

He spent the next series of moments staring out the window, his elbow on the arm of the chair and his fingers knuckled to his chin in an upper body pose akin to a Greek statue. At last he turned to the phone and hit the intercom button, asking Barry to come into his office.

"How are things going?" Barry asked grimly as he slipped into the chair across from his boss.

Press cinched a corner of his mouth and shrugged. "A bit less life to us but we have to go on." He bent forward on his desk and leaned his head into the angle of his thumb and fingers.

"Tell me what you have on the…uh, incident the other night. About the party and the, uh, the accident."

"Not much really, Press." Barry's eyes visited the carpet mostly, spending occasional moments on the publisher. "The reservoir's always been a favorite place for the kids to party. Sheriff's patrols check the park occasionally. It was a pretty routine beer bust."

"The other night you said Nordstrom had called in the accident report?"

Barry nodded.

"Where was he? When the accident happened, do you know?"

"I guess I don't," Barry replied softly as he checked out his shoes. "The accident report just says he saw the car leave the park at a high rate of speed."

"But the accident was over two miles away," Press wondered, massaging his temple trying to wipe away a fog that would make the picture clearer in his head. "Did he follow them, or did he find the car on the way back to town?"

"I'm sorry, Press," Barry said, a dread creeping into his expression like a child about to receive a thrashing. "I was so wrapped up in who it was in the accident. I never thought to ask for details like that at the time. Just thought I'd find out this week."

"Don't worry about it," Press offered with a dismissing wave. "I'd just like to know as much as I can. I need to know…."

He sucked his lips tight into his mouth and stared into the top of his desk.

"I'm on it," the editor said as he eased himself out of the chair. His throat pinched at the sight of the discomfort on his boss' face and he hurried himself from the office before either might launch another round of tears.

Half an hour later, Dr. Cassidy returned Press' call.

"I was wondering how you see the Daniels girl doing?" Press wanted to know. "The hospital won't give us any kind of a read other than an official 'no change'."

"Strictly as a friend, Press?" It was Benton's way of assuring anything he said was off the record.

"Mmmh," the publisher grunted.

"Looks like she's going to pull through. She's still in bad shape and there could still be setbacks. That's why they're keeping quiet. They don't want any surprises or disappointments."

"At least there's *some* good news lately," Press said with a gush of relief. "Listen, Benton, I need a favor, as a friend." He told the doctor that he wanted to see DeDe as soon as she was able to talk.

"It's not for the paper, it's for me. This one's personal."

There was a long silence at the other end of the line as a basketful of whys, what ifs, and maybes were sorted out.

"It may be awhile," Cassidy said at last. "She's only come to briefly a few times. It could be days or weeks before she's able to really talk much. Even then, if it's details about the accident you're wanting, she may not recall much or be able to talk about it. And it could only be with her parents' permission."

"I understand that. I still need to, have to try."

"PRESSING MATTERS"
June 22

Life truly has its balances, it seems. For example, my son, Jeremy was one of the great glories in my tenure on this planet. For eighteen years, even through the troubled times – the spankings, the harsh words, the crawling into our bed at three in the morning to escape the twin ogres of thunder and lightning, the throwing up in my lap while waiting at the doctor's office – even through all of that, there was nothing greater in the world to glorify my own existence. But now he's gone. Life balances out. As immense as life's gifts can be, like a precious son's life, the tragedies are the totter to the teeter. Surely we will go on, his family and me. But there will be a crack in our lives as big as his heart was huge. Since that awful night last week the past has met me wherever I turn. I find myself recalling every instant with my son. And I keep inserting all those things I wish I'd said and didn't. These days are not filled with hours and minutes of the moment. Rather they're filled with the times I've lived with the son I miss so terribly....

32

I suppose I'll have to do something with the car soon, Press thought as he pounded down the driveway at the start of his jog on Tuesday morning. The red Cavalier was still parked at the curb, idle as a monument. His eyes dampened as a portrait of Jeremy smiled from behind the steering wheel and Press hastened his pace with an extra gasp of air. He'd offered the car to Kate but, much as she wanted one of her own, she said she didn't think she could drive it. She'd always see her brother in it. That image of Jeremy behind the wheel, the one he'd just seen, was precisely why Press didn't want to...couldn't bear to let the car go. Not just yet. Still, he kept telling himself that he would eventually have to deal with it. Maybe he'd trade it for something for Kate.

"With all the other things going on lately, I forgot to tell you," Barry said as he inserted himself into Press' office later in the morning. "Susan Parker is on the city council agenda tonight."

Press' eyebrows hiked into the furrows on his forehead.

"What's she up to?"

"She's representing ADN Properties and petitioning the city to annex the Gunderson place." Barry held up a copy of the council agenda like an auction bid on the whole county's summer crop of corn. "They're planning a subdivision and want the city to provide sewer and water, even streets."

"Why doesn't that surprise me?" The remark was as dry as a cactus with a thirst. "Have you asked Hartley about it?"

"He sees no problem with it. Thinks it would be great for Fremont," Barry said as he slouched against the doorframe.

"Naturally. I'd bet your grandmother's last dime that he has more than just political interest in the deal." Press rotated the chair sideways and crossed his legs. "Remember what Flater told me about Hartley filing a disclosure of interest document with those other properties?"

Barry arched his eyebrows with a shrug.

"But this property was simply deeded over to ADN. There's no disclosure statement," the editor imposed.

"I'd still bet Hartley's part of it," Press said, slapping his palm on the desk as though it might tamp a pinch of certainty into the sentence.

"Let's go see Wilma Gunderson," he announced flatly.

Valleyview Retirement Apartments and Nursing Home sat on the west edge of Fremont and had a curious name in Press' estimation. There certainly was no valley around unless you take in that vast basin between the Rockies and the rumpled slopes of Midwestern hills on the opposite bank of the Missouri River. And the view offered less than a likely subject for a landscape artist. East looked into the back yards of a ranch-style subdivision. The flat line of the western horizon was broken only by an occasional picket fence of wind rowed trees and a few prairie skyscrapers known as Harvestores and other grain silos.

It was a newer, single level facility of mottled brick, garnished to be as homey as possible for a sterile residential complex housing mostly a generation waiting to be snatched by eternity. Lace curtains framed the windows, the walls galleried a variety of tasteful art, and the reception area was furnished with chairs and sofas inviting considerable comfort. The middle-aged woman who staffed the visitors' desk greeted the pair with a pleasant smile.

"We'd like to see Wilma Gunderson," Press stated.

The noticeable lift of the woman's eyebrows suggested mild surprise.

"Are you relatives of Wilma's?"

Press shook his head. "We'd just like to visit with her for a few minutes, if that's all right."

"It's no problem," she said as she reached for the phone. "I just don't recall Wilma having any visitors since she's been here. She's been moved to our nursing care center for several months, now."

The woman dialed the intercom and asked for an attendant to come to the reception area. Moments later a high schoolish-looking, rust-haired girl, nicely rounded in the right proportions, appeared from the hallway. Her smile stretched the ample supply of freckles between her ears when she saw the newspapermen. The name badge on her pink uniform top announced that she was "Laurel."

"These gentlemen are here to see Wilma Gunderson," the receptionist reported.

"Sure, this way," Laurel said with a half turn toward the hall she had just come from. "I'm so sorry to hear about Jeremy, Mr. Williams. I graduated two years ago and knew him a little. He was a really nice guy."

"Thank you," was returned by Press and nothing more was said as the squeak and soft tap of the trio's footsteps echoed down first one hallway, then another as they turned to the right. Only the sound of an occasional television program accompanied their walk as they passed the long rows of rooms until they neared the end of the corridor where the nasal pinch of a man's voice was protesting loudly through a closed door.

"Bugs, bugs, bugs, bugs, bugs, bugs, bugs. Goddam sonofabitching bugs. Bugs, bugs, bugs everywhere. Somebody get rid of these goddammed bugs. They're driving me crazy. Bugs, bugs, *bugs*, bugs, bugs. Bugs, fucking bugs everywhere. Get these goddammed bugs out of here!"

The girl turned to Press and Barry with the suggestion of an embarrassed grin and continued to the last room on the left, where she knocked softly and opened the door. When the two hesitated, she motioned them in with an unconcerned flip of her hand.

"You have visitors, Wilma."

Slouched in a wheelchair beside the twin bed, Wilma Gunderson pointed an unexpressioned stare at Bob Barker as he hosted *The Price is Right* on the TV set mounted atop the dresser. A matched pair of stuffed chairs surrounded the small table just inside the door. Those, along with a floor lamp in the corner, all too quickly added up to the room's furnishings. There was a bathroom and a closet along another wall and the large window looked out on a swing and large wooden playset in the back yard of a soft yellow ranch home.

Wilma was a thinly boned woman who had on a light green and white checked house dress and gray slippers that were probably cream colored when new. Except for the splotches on her face and arms the color of August-dried farm mud, her skin was as drained of radiance as the hair drawn into a bun atop her head. Her fingers were gnarly as sycamore branches and woven awkwardly in the crease of her less-than-ample lap.

Press eased himself tentatively onto the edge of one of the chairs next to Mrs. Gunderson as Barry stood just inside the door alongside Laurel.

"Mrs. Gunderson, this is Barry McGinn and I'm Preston Williams," he began. "If you don't mind, we'd like to ask you some questions."

Wilma shifted her stare from the TV to Barry and a smile blossomed across her face like a sunflower opening into the sun.

"Why, Ronnie, it's so nice of you to come."

"Uh...no, ma'am. I'm Barry McGinn." Barry's glance fidgeted from Wilma to Press to Wilma to the young girl beside him.

The smile drained slowly from Wilma's face like spilled corn syrup and her eyes lowered to the hands in her lap.

"Alzheimer's," was all the girl said when Press and Barry turned to her with question marks attached to their expressions.

Press pawed his knees, debating whether to leave or forge on.

"Mrs. Gunderson, we were wondering about your farm," he tried.

The woman looked at him as if the chair he occupied was vacant and then revisited Barry.

"Ronnie," she said with the sunflower smile of recognition illuminating her face once more. "I've missed you so much."

"No, Wilma, this is Mr. McGinn," Laurel tried gently.

Wilma's eyes dropped once more and so did the smile.

Press shrugged his surrender and stood up.

"Is Artie McShane in?" he asked when they were back at the visitors' desk. Press knew the nursing home manager as a fellow Rotarian. Moments later the manager's office door opened across the hall and McShane, a short, middle-aged man with hair the color of darkest night, waved them in.

"Gee, Press, I was sure sorry to hear about your son," Artie said as he guided the two to comfortable chairs across from his desk. "That's just an awful tragedy."

"Things like that happen. We just never expect them to happen to us. We'll deal with it somehow," Press said softly as he sat down.

There was a quick moment of uncomfortable silence before McShane tactfully traded subjects.

"Well, gentlemen, what brings you out here this afternoon?"

"What can you tell us about Wilma Gunderson?" Press asked with a left tilt of his head.

McShane picked up a Bic from his desk and began rotating it between his thumbs and forefingers, his glance echoing from one man to the other and back again.

"Well, uh, I can't give out a lot of details. We can't violate our patients' right to privacy. You understand that, don't you?" He looked from Press to Barry for affirmation and went on. "I can tell you that, between assisted living and nursing care, she's been with us about two years. I don't know what you're looking for, really."

"Her farm was disposed of, or surrendered, in kind of an unusual way, shall we say," Press began cautiously.

"Oh, I can assure you I wouldn't know anything about those kinds of matters," the nursing home manager interjected quickly.

Press raised his hand to note that it wasn't what he was looking for.

"It's our understanding that Mrs. Gunderson received nothing in return for deeding her property to another party. Those circumstances, along with some other things we're looking into, have jogged our curiosity." Press paused and deposited a brief look on Barry before turning back to McShane.

"She has no living relatives, is that right?"

"As far as I know," Artie replied over a small shrug.

"Can you tell us who's handling her affairs or how she's paying to live here?"

"No, no, I can't tell you anything about her financial arrangements," the man asserted, the knot of his paisley tie jigging in front of his pale blue collar. McShane swiveled slightly in his chair and glanced down like a poker player sneaking a peek at his hole card. "I suppose it would be okay for me to tell you, though, to talk to Derek Nordstrom if you need information about her affairs."

Not-so-surprised glances passed between Press and Barry.

"Does he pay her bills?" Press explored.

McShane dropped the Bic and raised his palms as furrows creased his forehead. "You'd have to talk to Mr. Nordstrom about matters like that."

Press thanked McShane briefly for his time and the two newspapermen exited.

"For not being able to tell us anything, I think he gave us enough," Barry registered as they got into Press' Buick.

"Enough to keep us going, anyway," the publisher concurred.

Abby was standing at the kitchen dinette table, her back to him when Press came in from the garage. Her shoulders quivered gently and he could hear his wife's quiet sniffling. There were five place settings at the table.

Press hugged his arms around her and clutched her tight. Still facing the table, a hard sob quick-gasped from deep inside her, followed by a low groan that sounded like a saw blade dragged slowly over old wood.

"Ahhhnnnnnngggggh," she wailed from somewhere in the well within. "I just did it. I didn't even think about it." Abby arched her head back on her husband's shoulder, letting her agony escape more freely from her throat. "Oh, God, I miss him so much!"

Tears tumbling off the tremble of his own cheeks, Press turned Abby to him and cinched her against his quaking chest. There they lingered a long time, merged in an anguish known only to parents who've had their flesh snatched from them.

"I see him everywhere, when I'm awake, when I dream at night," Press spoke at last, his chin resting on top of Abby's blonde head. "I see his smile. I hear his laugh. I can't imagine how it will ever stop. It's like I've suddenly got another shadow."

He let a long sigh shudder out of him as slowly he released his wife and began putting the extra plate and silverware away. Dinner was late that night, a somber gathering of four.

33 There were no words spent between them as Press drove his wife toward Parsons on Saturday afternoon. It was one of those hot, cellophane days with only an occasional wispy cloud that generated not even a ghost of a shadow as it whispered east on a breeze. The air hung heavy on everything and made breathing a labor, like sucking wind through a wool shirt. Though the wild daisies and black-eyed Susans smiled bravely along the roadside, their leaves sagged limply at their stems and there was a thickness to the air that presaged a storm bound from somewhere beyond the western horizon.

Benton Cassidy had called in the morning. The doctor reported that DeDe Daniels had recovered sufficiently that her parents had agreed to allow the Williamses a brief visit at the hospital.

There was a buzz between his ears as his mind rambled through the myriad of questions Press wanted to ask. He needed to know every instant of his son's last hours; the things he said; the things he smiled at. And that last, terrible moment. He needed to know it, feel it, see it if he could. He parleyed questions in his head, seeking delicate ways to broach the questions he was driven to ask.

I wonder how much she'll even recall, Press posed inside himself as he eased the Buick into the visitors lot at Parsons General Hospital. Sometimes the mind blocks remembrance of tragedies, he knew, until the person was sufficiently healed to cope with the mental anguish as well as the physical. Sometimes those visions were blocked forever.

The door to DeDe's private room was ajar and Press tentatively nudged it open wider. The girl's mother was seated on the edge of the bed and her father occupied a chair on the far side of the room. They both stood when they saw Press and Abby, and smiled as they invited the pair to enter. Press gave a solid wag to Mr. Daniels' hand and they clasped each other's shoulder as their wives shared an extended hug.

DeDe very closely resembled a mummy out of an old Vincent Price movie. Her head was mostly covered in gauze and tape. Only the green glint of her left eye showed through the bandages that covered the top of the head, the entire right side of the face, including the eye and ear, and the bridge of her nose. A stovepipe sort of neck brace seemed to secure her head as far above her shoulders as awkwardly possible.

The girl's upper torso was armor plated in a cast that included all of her right arm. The limb was elevated and supported by a system of cords and weights and pulleys dangling from the ceiling. The hand projecting from the cast was painted in pink and yellow disinfectant and so swollen it looked like a rubber glove that had been inflated for use as a makeshift balloon. Metal rods protruded from every finger except the thumb. The left arm was bare and she clutched the metal rail at the edge of the bed, perhaps to balance herself against a starboard list.

A hospital sheet draped across her lower body and upper legs. The right foot and leg was in a cast that extended somewhere under the sheet. Another cast covered the left ankle and leg as far as the knee.

"Hi," she very nearly whispered.

"How are you doing, Hon?" Abby asked gently as she nudged up beside her husband, who stood at the foot of the bed and shifted his weight from one foot to the other.

"Okay, I guess," was all that came back.

"It sounds like she'll be here for at least a couple of months longer," Mrs. Daniels entered. "She's had four surgeries already. We don't know how many more she'll need yet."

"Hope you're naturally a lefty," Press wished with a nervous laugh.

"I'll have to learn to be for awhile anyway," DeDe replied, a hint of a smile emerging from the barely noticeable curls in the corners of her mouth.

"She was thrown from the rear driver-side door," Mr. Daniels said, "after the car rolled the first time." He looked at Press, not sure what details he should offer or just how much the others wanted to hear.

"You were very lucky," Abby suggested.

"Sometimes I don't think so," the whisper of a smile vanished and the young girl whimpered now through the fingers pressed to her lips.

"No, no, please don't think that way," Abby cried as she moved around her husband to the side of the bed where she could put her hand on the girl's uncast arm. "We're so glad that you're going to be okay."

All of them were crying now and there was a long quiet, interrupted only by sniffles and the passing of a tissue box among them.

"I, uh, don't really know how to ask," Press began at last, his voice lowered and his eyes flickering from one face to another. "Do you, ummm...can you remember much about that night? The things that happened? Can you talk about any of it?"

"I'll try." DeDe raised her left hand and laid it on the pillow above her head. "I know I can never forget it."

Adam and Teri had dated for a couple of years. He had picked her up and then they'd gone to the Daniels' house to get her and Jeremy. It was only her third date with Jeremy, she noted. The four had talked about going to a movie in Parsons but Adam really wanted to go to a party at the reservoir.

"Jeremy said the police had been hitting the beer parties there pretty regularly," she noted. "I don't know if he really wanted to go."

Adam had said he knew that. He said he knew to park out on the road so they could get away if the police came and blocked the entrance to the park. The couples finally agreed to go to the party.

It hadn't been going on all that long when they got there, DeDe reported. It was early yet. The sun hadn't gone down. They had parked some distance from the picnic grounds and Adam had ushered them along a trail through the woods. One of the guys had a quarter-barrel of beer in the open trunk of his car and DeDe said she and Teri and Jeremy were still drinking their first plastic cups of it when the police arrived. Adam was on his second.

"We threw the beer down and ran through the woods," she said, slowly polishing the metal rail of the hospital bed with her hand now. "When we got to the car, one of the cops was standing next to a police car a little ways down the road. When we jumped in the car and Adam started to drive away, the cop got into his car and came after us. He had the lights and siren on and all."

A tremble came to DeDe's lips and she tucked a finger under the bandages beneath her left eye in an effort to dry the moisture accumulating there. She drew in a long breath and let it stagger out of her before continuing.

"We were all yelling at Adam, telling him that he'd better stop. I could tell that Teri was crying and I heard Jeremy beside me yelling at Adam to pull over. But he wouldn't. He just kept going faster and faster. I don't know why. I tried to get him to stop. We all did. He just wouldn't." She was sobbing now, the words spurting through wet gushes. Her mother moved to the edge of the bed and laid a hand on the girl's forehead.

"The policeman was right behind us. I don't know how fast we were going, but when Adam wouldn't stop, the guy pulled out around us. He cut in front of us real fast. Adam slammed on the brakes to keep from hitting him." The words were belching out of her in tear-soaked tremors by now. "The car started to swerve and I remember we were all screaming. All of a sudden the car was upside down. It's the last thing I remember until I woke up here."

"I think we should stop for now," DeDe's father said as he came to the bedside and motioned in a way that suggested Press and Abby head toward the door.

"We understand," Abby accepted as she tucked her hand around her husband's elbow. "We hope you continue to get better real fast, DeDe."

At the door Press hesitated.

"Can I ask just one more question?" The two gave back an expressionless look as their daughter's sobs began to soften. "Do you know who the police officer was?"

All of them looked expectantly at DeDe.

"Yeah…sure," she sniffled. "It was the police chief."

"Derek Nordstrom?" Press flailed the words with his tongue.

"Yeah."

"Press, please slow down." Abby's words were the first uttered between them since leaving the hospital room. Her face was blanched and her lower lip shuddered as she stared at her husband as though she was seeing something in him for the first time.

Through his rage, Press had not noticed the speedometer needle nudge past ninety as the car sped over the open blacktop back toward Fremont. Like a clock wound to the breaking point, every muscle in his body flexed to the verge of snapping. An anger Press had never known seethed through him from the clench of his jaw, to the fingers strangling the steering wheel, to the foot that drove the gas pedal nearly into the floorboard. At his wife's frightened words, he managed to back off the gas more nearly to the speed limit. The number of miles between the towns diminished by half before he spoke at last.

"That sonofabitch killed our son!" The words boiled around his clamped teeth like molten steel.

"I know! I know," Abby whimpered, tears washing down her face. Added to her grief over Jeremy's death were the hurt and anger of DeDe's revelation, and now fear lent its awful hand to the battery of emotions that were tearing at her insides. It was fear born of uncertainty over what Press' rage might unleash in him. In all their years together, she had never seen a fury in her husband so neighbored to violence.

"What are you going to do?" There was a hesitation to her question, seemingly uncertain over whether she really wanted to know the answer.

Press hadn't looked around his anger yet to give much thought to what he would do. For the moment he was too filled with rage to even consider the range between what he really wanted to do and what he likely might. There would be time for rational considerations later. Now he would just let the storm rage itself out inside him. When it subsided and he could think clearly, he would decide what steps might be in order. For now, he simply needed to vent his anger over the way Jeremy's life had been snuffed so senselessly.

"I don't know yet," was all he told his wife.

Press spent the night wrapped in darkness in a recliner chair in the basement. When Abby asked if he'd like some supper, he simply said he wasn't hungry. The anger and frustration left little room in him for anything else, even food. She didn't disturb him again.

Later, Cassie tiptoed down the stairs, dressed in her long summer nightgown. She stopped beside him, her finger pressed uncertainly to her chin. Press scrunched to the side of the cushiony chair to make room for her and she curled up next to him.

"What's wrong, Daddy?"

"I just need to think about some things, Sweetie," was all he could produce. He wasn't ready to spill his anger yet, especially to Cassie. Or Kate, for that matter. In his own mind he still didn't know how to explain the matter to himself. How could he now explain it to his daughter? They spent a long time in the quiet, Press stroking her hair and Cassie listening to her father's heart beat in the hollow of his chest.

"I hope you feel better soon," Cassie said at last as she tugged herself from the chair to go to her bedroom.

"Thanks, Hon. Sleep tight."

Well past midnight he kept pouring over all that had happened. He kept telling himself that nothing was going to bring his son back, yet that reality did little to quell his rage over the way Jeremy's death had come about. He thought of confronting Nordstrom.

I'd like to bash the little bastard's brains out, he told himself in more than one flurry of notions. Even more often, somewhat to his own surprise, his mind glimpsed the gun secreted in an unpanelled portion of the wall behind his workbench in the furnace room. He hadn't seen the gun since he stashed it there shortly after he and Abby had moved into the house. It was an old, .45 caliber Colt semi-automatic that had belonged to his father. When he was fourteen, Press had removed the gun from his father's dresser and hidden it. In a drunken stupor a few nights earlier, the old man had waved the gun around as easily as if his hand was empty. He had threatened to shoot nearly everyone from his wife, to members of the town council, to "the next sonofabitch who walks into my goddammed gas station and wants change so he can by cigarettes from Grady Slocum's machine across the goddammed street!"

Press didn't know where his dad had gotten the gun. He'd never seen it before and he never asked his father about it. If Mick was ever suspicious about the Colt's disappearance, he never let on. Press figured his mother suspected what had happened to it but she was as unlikely to give it any more mention than she would if she'd passed gas in church. Each of them was simply glad to have the weapon out of the house. If it was out of sight, it was out of mind.

Press had only fired the gun on one occasion. The summer he turned sixteen, he and J.D. Gonring had taken it out to a gravel pit east of Banning to shoot at some old beer cans they brought along. Between them they could only afford one box of shells and when the last round was fired they decided that neither had the makings to replace Audie Murphy in the war movies.

He didn't know why he'd kept the pistol all these years. There were rare occasions when he'd thought about selling it, but, for whatever reason, the effort always seemed like too much trouble. Press had made a point to never mention it or show the gun to Abby. It wasn't that he was opposed to guns or even people owning them. He just never felt the need for one. Until now.

Maybe it's just fate, Press thought. The notion chilled his spine and he shifted in the chair. Perhaps this is what the gun was meant for all along. For me to use to avenge my son's death. Maybe it's just the tool needed to complete my destiny.

Over and over Press thought about killing Nordstrom. He visualized himself in a dozen different scenarios. He could imagine the act itself. The easiest way would be to sneak up on the Chief of Police while he was sitting in his squad car and shoot him in the back of the head. Press knew he wouldn't do it that way, however. He wanted to see the fear in Derek's eyes the instant he knew the price was about to be paid for the death of Jeremy Williams. Press wanted to see the chief's pain and anguish, although it could never equal what he, himself, had already been through since Jeremy was killed. He pictured himself shooting Nordstrom several times before killing him. Shooting him in the knees, then the groin. He wanted the chief to suffer and suffer a lot before he died. Those notions, along with pictures of a smiling Jeremy tumbled in Press' mind and quirted his body in the chair throughout a painful night.

He'd argue later that killing the police chief would only be stooping to Derek's level, besides darkening his own future and putting his family through even more pain. Still, it was like a mental venting that somehow seemed to help. But was merely venting enough to get him through the rest of his life?

Periods of hopelessness flushed through his head as well. Maybe the gun was meant to use on himself. Perhaps that would be the only way to end his own pain. Or maybe he should just sell the *Gazette* and move away. Proceeds from the sale of the newspaper would probably support him and his family comfortably enough. Still, either of those choices would mean that Nordstrom had won. Press couldn't let him get away with that.

When at last sleep overtook him in the chair, it came in more like a series of fitful comas. It occurred to him in one of his periods of awake how much he needed sleep and yet how at odds with it he was this night. Morning came without rest and Press climbed wearily up the steps.

After a long, wordless hug from Abby, he changed into his jogging clothes and went for the longest run he'd taken in years. Somewhere outside of town, on some gravel road, the name of which Press didn't recall, he sat down in the dry, mid-summer grass at the side and cried for more than an hour. More than another hour later, when he was sure his tears were spent, he began the long trek back to town. This time he walked.

Late Sunday afternoon, Press called Galen Perry at home and arranged a meeting in the lawyer's office first thing the next morning. Then he called Barry and asked him to be at Perry's office also. Abby would complete the foursome.

Press and Abby were seated in Galen's office when the attorney's secretary ushered Barry into the room.

"Sorry I'm late," he offered as he seated himself next to his boss.

"No, you're on time. We were early," Press corrected. A trace of smile flickered across his face, then quickly extinguished itself. He rocked his head back and inhaled a reinforcement of air before letting it slowly escape from his mouth as he ran the fingers of his left hand down the front of his neck and loosened his tie a notch with a tug. He gazed evenly across the desk at Galen.

"The crash of the car that killed our son and two other children was no accident," he began coolly, the set of his jaw determining the tension as much as the words. "Derek Nordstrom as much as killed them!"

Barry and Galen exchanged gaping glances and shifted in their chairs. The attorney picked up a pen from his desk and began rotating it with his fingers. Barry was gnawing on the knuckles of one hand.

It took nearly a quarter of an hour for Press to relate their visit with DeDe Daniels at the hospital in Parsons and her revelations about the kids leaving the park when sheriff's deputies arrived to break up the beer party. His voice was cold as December gravestone as he told of the Fremont police chief forcing the car off the road, resulting in the deaths of Jeremy Williams and two other teenagers.

A heavy quiet filled the office when he finished. After a long pause, Press crossed his legs and continued.

"My first impulse Saturday afternoon was to find Nordstrom and beat him until his life was gone and I simply couldn't hit him any more. My second impulse was to take a gun and kill him." His voice was even and echoed no strain of emotion. He gave no hint that the weapon was already in his possession.

Abby fluttered back the tears as best she could and chewed on her lower lip as she reached across the chairs to touch his arm.

"As much personal satisfaction as either might have given me at the time, even through the peak of my anger, I knew those weren't realistic options. At least not now," Press admitted with only the slightest hesitancy in his conviction. "That's why we're here today. I…Abby and I…need some options."

Galen 'whewed' softly and leaned forward on his desk. Barry's head swayed slowly in disbelief, busily mulling everything and saying nothing.

"Without question, the facts being as you state them, you have undeniable grounds for lawsuits against Derek personally and the city, although, technically on this matter, he was helping the county so we may have to go there with it," Perry began. "Maybe all of them...." Press interrupted.

"Let me say first, Galen, that money is not our primary interest. Money will not bring Jeremy back to us!" He glanced at Abby for verification and saw the clinch of her jaw in agreement. "I want Derek Nordstrom hung by every body part available and stretched in every way possible!"

"Certainly, I understand, Press," Perry replied with a brief flip of a hand. "But we can't just go out and throw a noose over a tree limb. Lawsuits are part of the process. And we'll try to get him removed from his job. Besides, Press, if the city and county get sued because of the surly weasel, it'll make them so mad at him that they'll want to hang him, too. There has to be some sense of righteous indignation felt even among politicians. I don't know if he's actually broken a law, anything criminal, but we'll also look into that."

Press looked at his wife who returned a shrug and then jugged his head in concession.

"What, uh, kind of story do we want on this?" Barry asked after clearing the astonishment from his throat and leaning forward on his elbows.

"Nothing yet," Galen interjected quickly. "Legally, all we have is hearsay at the moment. The first thing we have to do is get a formal statement from the Daniels girl. I assume that since she talked to you, she's capable of giving one now."

"It was hard for her. I don't think the police have even talked to her yet. And you'll have to get by her parents," Press said. "I don't know how cooperative they'll be."

"I'd think that they would want Nordstrom's hide, too, considering what this has done to their daughter and what he's put them through," Barry suggested.

"Yes, but they're most concerned for DeDe at the moment." It was Abby's first ante into the conversation. "They might not be ready yet."

"You're probably right," Galen agreed. "You have to understand that nothing is going to happen fast, even if I got her statement tomorrow. You need to be prepared for a long, drawn out procedure."

Leaning forward, he pursed his lips and gazed from Press to Abby and back to Press.

"I can assure you, though," he vowed, "I will be on this matter the instant you're out the door this morning. But it could be a long time, a couple of years even, before anything is really settled."

"I don't know if I have that much wait in me," Press said as he shifted forward in the chair, readying to leave.

34

There were times when Press needed separation from ink and paper and news and neighbors. This was one of them. There was a pull in him that needed giving in to. Press had yanked back on the tug these weeks but he knew that ultimately he must yield to whatever force it was within him that was dragging toward that awful footage of blacktop and gravel; that terrible spot where Jeremy's last gasp had escaped him. He knew that seeing the place of his son's last moments could not fetch the boy back. Perhaps it was just another small step forward, a step toward letting go.

The trip was unscheduled. Jeremy had visited his father's memory no more often than usual today, which was nearly all the time. Press simply got up from his desk and left the office, giving the receptionist a terse notice that he was going out for awhile.

The day was lying varnished under a fresh coat of sunshine after a steady rain had washed the night. Heading north in the Buick, Press left the windows down and the air conditioner off, preferring to let the searing wind hurtle at him in billows. It was a hard wind, not cooling. It had blown the sky free of clouds and pushed the thermometer's red line just over the one hundred mark, but Press acknowledged it only enough to remove his tie. Instead his focus was on the lad whose smile kept beaming back at him in the window of his memory.

He turned east, those four miles on the county road toward the reservoir. With Jeremy's image visiting in the seat beside him, Press recalled those times – too few times, he thought now – when the pair headed to the water impoundment on days just like today for an afternoon of fishing. Jeremy's voice floating again from the backseat – younger then – his father remembering the times, Abby beside him, when the family went for picnics at the county park. They were smiling times; always Jeremy's times were smiling it seemed. The vision of the lad's never-ending smile etched forever in his father's remembrance.

The car slowed as it approached the slight lift in the horizon. Though he hadn't been here since the wreck – it was no accident, he now avowed – Press knew the exact spot. Two black lines, two ebony arrows of death aimed off the pavement into a shallow ditch. They crossed a pair of smaller screech marks, perhaps the pair with accompanying brake lights that had forced the youthful Adam Kelso to veer his car into the ditch. He eased the car onto the shoulder and left the engine idling as he stared across the road. Waves of black-eyed Susans and daisies and foxtails rippled in the wind between the brown grit of the roadside and the waist-high field of feed corn on the other side of three-stranded barbed wire fence.

Press turned off the ignition and stepped out of the car, standing for a long moment against the wind which tried to yank his shirt from the tuck of the brown belt around his middle. He sucked in an extra share of breath as a bracer to get himself through the coming ordeal. Slowly he walked across the road and followed the dark lines of skidding tires to the end of the blacktop and the canals that dredged through the gravel and dirt of the shoulder and vanished over the shallow ditch. In weaving, sometimes staggering steps, he followed the ruts and gouges and shards of glass and pieces of chrome and a headlight frame where the car had tumbled and rolled and, where it finally laid in mortal rest, now flowers remembered. In vases and jars and glasses and plastic cups, dozens and dozens of them, most dumped helter-skelter by the wind, flowers left in visits to that gentle slope away from the road. Placed there by friends and family who had come ahead of Press to ponder their missing friends and children; Jeremy and Adam and Teri.

Tears were streaming down his face as he slumped to his knees and, sitting on his heels, he threw back his head as if to challenge the sky.

"Why, goddammit? Why?" Press buckled forward, sobbing hard and pounding the ground with his fists. "Why Jeremy, goddammit? Oh, God, why Jeremy? Why? Why? Why?"

Turning to sit, elbows on his knees, he buried his face in his hands and cried. He cried until the sobs ran dry and still he cried. Even in the wondering of what Jeremy's last thoughts were in that last terrible moment as the car tumbled and bounced; that time knowing his son must have faced an awful terror and heard the screams and death rattles of his friends. Even still, it was that implacable smile of his son's that was relentless in his father's tormented memory. The smile was genuine, that of a young man who loved life and everyone in it. It was his mother's smile and Press was reminded of it every time he looked at Abby.

What fraction of the day had passed, Press didn't know when he stood at last and brushed the grass and moist dirt from his trousers. The sun had marched a bit farther toward the western rim of land but how far he could not be sure. If any cars had passed, he was unaware. None had stopped. His face felt dry and cracked, like mud some days after a puddle.

Back in the car, he eased onto the highway and continued east two more miles to where he turned left into the county park. The gravel road made an acorn-shaped circuit through the scattered sycamores and cottonwoods and soft maples and oaks to the reservoir and back out to the entrance. Press parked nearest the water. It was a cooler place, shaded and sprinkled with picnic tables and iron barbecue pits and occasional swings and slides and sandboxes.

With the ear of his imagination Press could hear the teenage laughter, the pounding bass of someone's boombox or car radio. He could see the flirting and sense the rush to the Braille method of loving in the back of cars or nearby bushes. And he could feel the mix of excitement and fear that must have exploded on the scene when the first squad car emerged through the trees on the narrow lane.

He sat there another long while, as though sharing a casual drink of memories with his friends, those friends of his son's. Amid the ache that tore at everything inside Press, there was still the rage. That slow, simmering kettle within him that wanted to boil out and scald the very bowels of Derek Nordstrom. However long it took, Press knew the fire in him would not be quickly tempered. He now knew the meaning of hate, a passion he had never felt before. But he hated Derek Nordstrom. Oh, how he loathed the man. He mulled the notion from every angle the wind might blow and some it couldn't and, though the rage didn't flag, Press knew he couldn't let it consume him. The day that happened, he decided, Nordstrom would win. He could not, *would not* allow that to happen. For Jeremy's sake, for the sake of Abby and Jeremy's sisters, Press would see that the police chief met his justice. If not justice at the hands of the law, then he vowed the hands would be his own. He still had the gun and, for the moment at least, he knew he could use it.

Back on the county highway the sun was lowered into Press' eyes as he headed back toward town. He slowed the car to a stop one last time to look at the spot where his son had died. Reaching across the seat, he opened the glove compartment and took out the digital camera he had brought along. Stepping out of the car, he crisscrossed the highway, shuttering pictures of the skid marks from every possible angle, always careful to include those two smaller sets, the ones he held accountable for his son's death. Somewhere in his consciousness, it occurred to Press that those dual short-lined strips of rubber scars might provide one more piece of the puzzle; complete the picture of Derek Nordstrom the killer. Just maybe provide the knot in the noose that would hang him.

Snugging the door of the Buick closed once more, Press shuddered another long series of breaths inside him and eased the car away.

"You've been awfully quiet tonight," Abby observed as she bunched under the covers and nuzzled up to her husband. Press told her about his visit to the site where Jeremy died. Abby was quiet for a long time until he wondered if she hadn't fallen asleep.

"I can't go now," she finally cried softly, "but when I decide to, I want you to come with me." Press said he would.

35

The soft rap of knuckles on his door caused Press to end his stare out the window and turn back to his desk.

"I've got some stuff you'll be interested in if you've got a minute," Barry announced as he pointed himself toward a chair in front of his boss' desk.

Press waved him to sit.

"Big confab at city hall yesterday morning," the editor said after he placed himself on the edge of the chair. "The mayor had me and the new guy from the radio station there, along with Butler Devane, the cannery manager, and Gary Burger. Burger represented the Fremont Development Commission." Barry paused to suck in an extra amount of breath.

"The reason for the meeting was to announce plans for a new industrial park involving almost twenty-six acres beginning at the north side of the existing cannery property and west of Division Street. Devane said the cannery is planning a major expansion on the site that would add almost a hundred new jobs. Burger said the development commission has a commitment from a Midwestern chain of medium-sized discount stores to locate one of its three new warehouses in the park. He also said the commission is working with some light manufacturing concern to locate here but he wouldn't give any details on that one yet."

"Sounds like it should be good for the city," Press confirmed.

"Yeah, it should," Barry agreed, "but it still perked my curiosity to do something I should have done awhile back and just never got around to it." He leaned heavily on the left arm of the chair as he continued.

"This morning I went over to the city treasurer's office and finally checked on the locations of those seven ADN properties in the city. And guess what?" A smug crinkle in his mouth pushed his cheekbone seemingly higher.

"Don't tell me," Press said as he rocked back in his chair, "they're in the proposed industrial district?"

"Every one of 'em," Barry confirmed. "And you can bet that property values will skyrocket as soon as word gets out about the proposal."

"Things just keep getting 'curiouser and curiouser,' as the saying goes," Press said with what was almost an added chuckle. "Any idea how long Nordstrom's group has had those places?"

"Between eight and twenty-two months. You know that plans for this industrial move had to have been going on for awhile. Somebody had to leak information to Nordstrom," Barry offered.

"Or had to have a personal hand in it from the beginning."

"Hartley?"

"Who else?" Press said, hunching forward and thumping his pen on the desktop. "We know he's had an unspecified interest in some of those real estate deals. He *has* to be in on it! Especially if you factor in the Gunderson deal. It's all just too coincidental."

"Do you think Devane and Burger are involved?" Barry asked as he scooted deeper into the chair.

"Probably not," Press replied with an offhand wave of his pen. "I don't think Devane's even been in town two years, has he? He came here from Kansas City after Fredman retired. And Burger's just too peas and cucumbers to plot anything bigger than a vegetable garden. I don't think he could begin to envision an industrial park without Hartley and Devane there to lay it out for him."

"So how do we find out about Hartley?" Barry posed.

Press dug a knuckle into his lips and gave a pondering head shake.

"What if we just confronted Susan Parker and asked her outright?" McGinn suggested.

"If she's at all smart, she'll know to keep her mouth shut," Press countered. "I doubt she's that lacking in smarts."

"What if we bluffed her? Said we knew all about her affair with Hartley and their involvement in ADN Properties. If she really did have a tiff with Hartley, maybe she's still mad enough to spill." Barry came back.

"Maybe," Press shrugged. "But let's keep that one up our sleeve for awhile. I'll think on it some. Maybe talk to Galen.

Might be our surest bet is just to go ahead with some lawsuit to force the issue of who has holdings in ADN."

Suddenly Press leaned forward, his eyes narrowing in order to perhaps squeeze out a new thought.

"Wait a minute," he said. "Remember when we were going through Nordstrom's juvenile log? One of the incidents listed was Butler Devane being hauled in for slapping his wife around!"

Furrows plowed in neat rows across Barry's forehead.

"You're right," the editor replied with a cornerwise nod. "But how could there be a tie between that and the industrial park project?"

There was a pause while the two measured possibilities.

"There might be no connection at all," Press said finally as he lightly scratched above his Adams apple. "On the other hand, if the industrial project was already underway, Nordstrom may have been doing Devane a favor to keep everything going smoothly."

"My guess would be at least that much," Barry wagered. "The cannery expansion gives me a reason to talk to Devane. I'll see what I can dig out of him."

"Just don't give him the notion that you're onto anything," Press cautioned.

The editor nodded his understanding.

The publisher's shifting to some papers on his desk told Barry the meeting was over.

"Keep digging," was all Press finished with. Barry gave a thumb up as he turned to leave.

The receptionist was about to lock the front door to the *Gazette* office when Jarred Kleinmeier returned Press' call. Press asked about any progress made by Joe Granger and was told that he had made contact with Derek Nordstrom and nothing more. Press then filled in the state's attorney on Nordstrom's involvement in his son's death and the curious fact of the ADN properties located within the proposed industrial district.

"You know, Nordstrom is some kind of turd," Kleinmeier declared after a prolonged pause, "but it might just be that it's your mayor's who's the real pile of shit!"

Press half snorted at the country eloquence of the description.

"I guess the thought has struck me but in not so colorful terms," he admitted.

"Pardon my lack of grace and tact. I've gotten the feeling that the chief is a crook, no doubt, but I think he's just small bang and no science to his rocket," the state lawyer continued. "It may just be that this Hartley's brains have gotten Nordstrom into fireworks more sophisticated than mere bottle rockets."

There was a thoughtful pause between them.

"Keep me informed of what you find," Kleinmeier said at last. "You may be getting close enough to Hartley for us to get involved."

"You mean I don't have to go to the DA first?"

"Nah, this call will be on our nickel."

Moments after hanging up, the phone announced itself again. Everyone else had gone home, so Press answered.

"It suddenly dawned on me," Kleinmeier said at the other end. "Have you told anyone else about Nordstrom's involvement in your son's death?"

"Just our editor and my lawyer, Galen Perry," Press related. "As you'd expect, we're gonna go after the guy."

"Listen, my advice is to do everything you have to do to get ready," Kleinmeier insisted. "But don't file any actions yet, and *don't go public!* Not in any way!"

"Why not?" Press had plentiful surprise in him.

"Look, I know you want to nail this sonofabitch and you have every right. But if you give us a chance to get him through Granger's cover, it's just one more hammer on his coffin lid."

"What about the other kids' parents?" Press wanted to know. "If they talk to DeDe, they'll likely find out. And we all ought to be involved in any action against Nordstrom."

"Can you trust them?" Kleinmeier asked.

"I don't know. We haven't talked."

"Well, talk if you have to, just make sure they wait until we're ready with this other charge, too. But for God's sake, don't let them know what it is or give Granger's cover away!"

Press said he understood.

36

It was another week before Galen Perry finally called Press.

"Listen," the attorney began, "if what the Daniels girl told you is true, we're going to extract so many pounds of flesh from Nordstrom that he wouldn't make a good Halloween skeleton!" He went on to say that, based on DeDe's story, the police chief had violated both the city and county policies governing high speed chases. And, he could likely be charged with homicide by the negligent use of a motor vehicle.

"But, like I said," Perry summarized, "it all depends on DeDe Daniels. I want to get a deposition from her and even a polygraph test but she's still in the hospital in Parsons and, so far, her parents won't let me near her."

"Why the heck not?" Press' surprise was announced in his tone.

"They say she's been through too much already. Her father says he just wants his daughter to get better and have the whole affair over with."

"But Nordstrom's responsible for her having to go through all of it! He virtually *killed* three kids!" The boil was bubbling into the publisher's words.

"I know that, and you know that," Galen allowed, "but we've got to find a way to convince Mr. and Mrs. Daniels that it is in both their interest and their daughter's to pursue the case."

"I'll work on it," Press declared through teeth not quite clenched. "I'll talk to the Kelsos and Moores. So far I don't think they even know the real circumstances of the wreck. I can't believe they won't be as outraged as Abby and I are. Between us we've got to be able to bring the Daniels people around."

Press hesitated a moment.

"There's just one more thing." He bartered options in his head for ways to announce what needed to follow. "We can't file any complaints or actions until I give the word."

"What the heck are you talking about?" Galen came back in the near vicinity of a bark.

"I can't tell you anything right now." The discomfort edged between Press' words as he selected them cautiously. "It's just that...there's a good chance we can get Nordstrom on a lot more...more than this. Things are in the works but I just can't say yet."

"Come on, Press. At least throw me a rope of *some* kind here!" Galen said, a near begging sort of whine to his voice.

"Sorry," Press returned, shaking his head a fraction. "You'll just have to trust me that it's absolutely vital that we keep it quiet at this point."

"All right." Galen let out a gush of air in uncertain concession. "You're the boss, but I hope you know what you're doing."

With a mist verging on rain dampening the evening, Ben and Marie Kelso were half trotting up the sidewalk as Lance and Bernadette Moore entered the living room. Press offered the couples their choice of seating while Abby collected beverage orders. The Moores chose coffee, Marie Kelso asked for a glass of water and her husband politely declined.

"This is a lovely house." Mrs. Moore forced a smile, darting a glance around the room as she edged herself onto the front of the couch beside her husband.

"Thank you," Abby replied as she hosted the coffee and a glass of water.

There was a formal quiet of anticipation until Abby was seated and Press began.

"Thank you all for coming," he started after ridding a nervous catch from his throat. "We were wondering if any of you have been to see DeDe Daniels...in the hospital?"

A quick moment of exchanged glances and fidgets followed.

"We, uh, stopped in, just for a few minutes. A couple of weeks ago. Just to say 'hi'," Bernadette offered, her eyes on Press and Abby briefly before escaping to her husband and then the Williams' carpet.

Ben Kelso fixed his look on his wife, his lip quivering to the beat of his pounding heart. "We just...just couldn't bring ourselves. I couldn't face her."

"Mr. Kelso...Ben," Press inserted grimly, "What happened to our children *was not* your fault. It was not Adam's fault. The fact that our kids are dead lies solely, squarely on the shoulders of Derek Nordstrom!"

The oxygen level in the room diminished measurably as the four visitors gasped in unison.

"Certainly it was wrong of those kids to run from that beer party. They shouldn't have tried to get away when the squad car's lights and siren came on. But Derek Nordstrom killed our children and put DeDe Daniels in the hospital as surely as if he'd used his gun!"

"How can you say that? I mean, how are you so sure?" Lance wondered, the amazement dripping from his face.

Press told them of the visit he and Abby had with DeDe and the girl's revelations about the night of the party at the reservoir. He related her story about the car chase.

"There was no accident," Press said, the words growling between his teeth. "Nordstrom purposely forced Adam off the road and into the ditch. I've talked to an attorney, Galen Perry, and everything Nordstrom did was a direct violation of both city and county policies for automobile chases. And besides that, he's probably guilty of homicide by reckless or negligent use of a motor vehicle!"

Room temperature was rising as nervousness turned to confusion and tumbled quickly toward rage. Murmurs rumbled back and forth among them.

"That's incredible!" Ben Kelso stammered, his disbelief exercised in the shake of his head. He unseated himself and stood gaping out the picture window as he pounded a fist into his opposite palm.

"That's just goddammed unbelievable!" He turned to face the others. "He's a cop, for chrissake!"

"Ben, your language," Marie reminded through her tears as she took his hand and pulled him gently back to the sofa beside her.

"I'm sorry, but I just can't believe that a cop – the chief, himself – could do something like that!"

"Are you sure, Mr. Williams?" Bernadette wondered again with an unblinking look at Press.

"All we have is DeDe's story right now," Press acknowledged. "But I did go out to the scene of the wreck. The skid marks are still there. Not just Adam's. There is a short set of tire marks, too. Like might have been made if Derek pulled in front of the kids and hit his brakes just hard enough to force Adam to swerve to avoid hitting him."

Heads were shaking as though choreographed.

"What can we do now?" Marie wanted to know as she gently knuckled the tears from under her eyes, unable to keep up with the flow.

"Well, you can talk to your own attorney or you can join with us. We've already got things underway with Galen Perry," Press said as he looked from face to face. "There are just a couple of things...."

No one seemed to exhale as the others waited for Press to add to his announcement.

"We can get everything ready to go but we can't go public with any of this. And we can't file any suits or complaints just yet."

Around the room eyes saucered back at him, including Abby's.

"What the hell do you mean?" Ben growled, his back stiffening. "First you drop this bomb on us and then you tell us we can't do anything yet?"

"No, no, I didn't mean that we can't do anything yet," Press defended with a wave of his hands. "Like I said, we can get everything ready to go, even at a moment's notice. It's just that there are other irons in the fire right now. I can't tell you what, but if we go public now, it'll ruin some things that...things that have been in the works for some time. All I can say is that we have a chance to really nail Nordstrom for even more things! You'll just have to trust me on that. It's just absolutely necessary that we have to keep all of this to ourselves for the time being."

A long sigh escaped from Press as he sat back and gave Abby a reassuring pat on the arm. The silence declared that thoughts were in progress with formal statements to follow.

Lance Moore was the first to venture his conclusions.

"I guess I've never had any reason not to trust you, Mr. Williams. Most folks around town respect you and that's enough for me," he said quietly as he checked his wife's look for concurrence. "I'm willing to go along with whatever you suggest."

The Moores and Williamses turned expectantly to Ben and Marie.

"I suppose we can go along, too. For now." Ben's reluctance grumbled out with the words.

37 "I talked to Butler Devane yesterday afternoon," Barry said as he settled into a chair across the desk from his boss. "He sounds all business." He told Press that one of the first directives the corporate office had given Devane was to find a place to expand the plant.

"Hartley sold a house to him when Devane moved to Fremont. Devane said it was just sort of natural then that he went to Hartley to look for an expansion site for the cannery. Especially since Hartley's the mayor and all. Figured Hartley would know about any incentives that might be available."

Barry paused to get a refill of air.

"I asked him when that meeting took place and it turns out to be just a month before ADN Properties made its first purchase in the proposed industrial park."

"Did he say when Hartley got back to him with any suggestions or proposal?" Press wondered as he mined wax from an ear with the cap from his Bic.

"Sounds like it took a few months but a lot less than a year," Barry explained.

"So it could be that Devane just provided the inspiration to Hartley without being a party to it all," Press speculated. "So why did Nordstrom give him favored treatment on the battery to his wife situation?"

Barry hitched a speculative twist to his mouth.

"Maybe the bad publicity would have put Devane in trouble with the corporate office? Could be Nordstrom – or more likely, Hartley – figured either the unfavorable PR or a possible management change might queer the deal. Drag it out, if nothing else."

"You're probably right," agreed Press with a back tilt of his head. "Devane may be a bad act at home but that doesn't necessarily equate to shady land deals. Besides, I doubt Hartley and Nordstrom want to cut anyone else in on their operation unless they have to."

Barry shrugged forward as he prepared to leave.

"By the way, what's happening with the Gunderson annexation?" Press amended the discussion slightly, stopping Barry at the door.

"It's on this month's council agenda. Flater says it'll likely pass unanimously."

"PRESSING MATTERS"
July 27

> Finding topics to fill this column over the past two decades has not always been easy. Sometimes I have simply struggled to have either opinions or ideas worth note. But particularly troublesome have been these recent weeks. It seems there is little to find either humor or depth of thought in of late, even in politics. I find it nearly impossible to remove my thoughts to anything but my son....

For more than a month the somber of an empty place at the table had dismissed the usual dinner banter in the Williams kitchen. Barely was there any energy, it seemed, to muster a response to "please pass the salt." With another quiet meal nearly concluded, Cassie sat with her head lodged into one hand while she pushed spaghetti around on her plate with the fork in her other.

"May I be excused?" she asked.

"Honey, you've hardly touched anything," Abby debated.

"I'm just not hungry."

"I suppose," her mother yielded with an uncertain look to Press.

"I'm worried about her," Abby admitted when the girl was gone. "She doesn't eat. The kids come by and ask her to play ball but she won't go. All she does is sit in Jeremy's room and play his video games."

"Yesterday when I was walking back from Dairy Queen, she had Jenny down in Darby's front yard and was threatening to beat her up," Kate injected.

"But Jenny Darby is Cassie's best friend," Abby cried, the soft lines in her forehead hardening into a frown.

"I have to admit, I don't feel like doing much either," Press said, "but I'll see if I can talk to her."

The door to Cassie's room was ajar and Press gently nudged it open the rest of the way with the soft rap, rap, rap of his knuckles. The girl was lying on her bed, head propped on one hand as she paged through a magazine with only half-hearted interest. Without looking up she tucked her knees to make room for her father as he settled onto a corner of the bed.

"I was thinking that you and I haven't done lunch for awhile," Press offered with a pat on Cassie's knee. "How about if I take off work tomorrow and we go to Parsons? You pick the place to eat."

"I suppose," was her reply. She still didn't lift her eyes to meet her father's.

Silence was the company in the car with them until they reached the outskirts of Parsons.

"Have you decided what kind of food we're treating ourselves to?" Press asked, intruding on the quiet at last.

"I don't care. A&W's fine, I guess."

"Root beer does sound awfully good right now. It's a nice day. We could go through the drive-up window and eat at the park."

The suggestion was met with a "sure" from his daughter.

Press bought a cheeseburger, order of onion rings, and a large root beer for each of them and drove another three blocks to a small park along the river. It was a quiet refuge surrounded on three sides by houses that had served three generations or more. Besides Press and Cassie, only a couple of youngsters claimed any of the park as their own this afternoon. They were penduluming on the only set of swings; a place where the high sun was able to wedge through the canopy of sycamores and oaks older than the town itself.

Ignoring a choice of the dozen or so picnic tables scattered around the park, Press chose instead to sit under a giant sycamore next to the unhurried river. Dragonflies hovered above the prairie mud-colored water, darting through the summer air when the sight of a gnat or mosquito presented a luncheon entrée.

Nothing was said as the pair ate with their backs against the tree. The quiet was broken only by the crinkle of burger wrappers, the occasional buzz of flies, and the nuzzle of the breeze through the leaves above them.

"You haven't been one to spend a lot on talk lately, Cass. That's not like you," Press directed at his daughter finally. "Anything up?"

Cassie answered with a single shrug, accompanied by a major pout. She continued to let her eyes drift along the slow-moving water.

"Thinking about your brother a lot?"

The girl's lips pursed tight against her teeth and she gave a double nod as water topped the levee of her lower eyelids. Cassie sniffed a soft, damp spurt of air into her.

Press reached for Cassie's hand that rested on the lap of her denim shorts and gave it a long squeeze.

"I know, Sweetie. We all miss him a lot."

"Nngggghhaaah" groaned out of Cassie like the mournful wail of a distant train whistle as she leaned forward onto her drawn up knees.

Press reached his arm around her and hugged her to him, biting his own lip to gate back the agony that wanted to scream out of him. The tears on his cheeks matched the flow of his daughter's.

"Why, Daddy? Wh…why did Jeremy have to die? I miss him so much!" The questions came gasping through her sobs.

"I don't know, Baby. I don't know," he whispered as he rocked her gently, holding her head snug to his chest. "I don't think anyone knows. I know. It just doesn't seem right."

Press didn’t know what else to say. Any other offer he could think of at consolation even he wouldn’t believe. Cassie would see through that.

Uncounted minutes passed until Cassie's hard sobs softened to snuffles. At last she leaned back against the tree once more and palmed a measure of the salty moisture from her eyes.

"He used to tease me all the time and I'd act like I was mad at him," she whimpered. "But I really didn't mind. Now I wish I hadn't acted so mad at him." The sobs came back a bit, softer now, then quickly turning again to quiet sniffles.

"He really was a nice kid, wasn't he?" Press allowed. "I see that huge smile of his everywhere I turn. I can't get that picture of him out of my mind either."

They sat in an extended quiet again while the breeze slowly dabbed their faces dry.

"You know, Hon, Jeremy wouldn't want us moping over him forever," Press said after gathering in a slow drink of air and letting it out even more slowly. "We can't forget him. We never will. But he'd want us to move on. We have to go on with our lives." It was a truth he had a hard time accepting himself.

Cassie offered a small shrug of acceptance.

"Did Mr. Nordstrom really run the car off the road?" she posed uncertainly, looking at her father now. "I heard you and Mom talking."

"It seems likely that he did," was all Press could answer.

"But he's a policeman. Why would he do that?"

"Honey, policemen are people just like the rest of us. Sometimes they do things...once in awhile a policeman turns out to really be a bad guy. I don't know what Chief Nordstrom was thinking or why he would do something like that."

Cassie turned her gaze to the spidery sweep of willows across the river.

"Are we going to sue him, Dad?"

"I suspect we will," Press replied, running a hand down the straight gray hair on the back of his head. "What he did was wrong. I want him to pay for that. But as much as I want that, we're going to have to keep it to ourselves for awhile, Hon."

"How come?"

"He may have done some other bad things, too. No punishment will ever be enough for him as far as I'm concerned," Press said, a grim shadow darkening his eyes. "So I want him to have to pay for anything and everything we can get him for. Does that make sense to you?"

Cassie nodded.

After a slow walk back to the car, Press drove them to a sporting goods store where Cassie looked at rollerblades and baseball mitts. In the end she wanted only a new batting glove which Press bought for her. The mood on the ride home was lighter, though not much was said that mattered. Press soon burrowed himself into his own thoughts once more. For the first time, it seemed, he realized just how deep the gash was that had been cut into his family. The anguish had sliced into the hearts of his two girls as much as it had his own and Abby's. And his hatred for Derek Nordstrom intensified.

38

"Look what came over the fax machine this morning!" Barry gushed as he practically threw the paper onto the desk in front of Press.

The publisher quickly scanned the page and gave a half quizzical look up at his editor.

"So the state's finally going ahead with the highway bypass around town. It's about time, I'd say."

"Yeah, but look at who the guy is at the Department of Transportation who sent the press release! The name in the upper right hand corner," McGinn urged with a beam that widened the space between his ears.

"Ray Parker?" Press said, a question mark hooked to the side of his mouth.

"Ray Parker, as in *Susan Parker's ex!*" Barry filled in the blank look on his boss' face.

"Oh, *that* Ray Parker," Press said as the light turned on behind his eyelids.

"And guess what else?" Barry was almost giggling with the boyish knowledge of a secret about to be spilled. "I checked on the location of those other four farms ADN owns. They're right in the path of the proposed route of the new highway! And not only that. They're on either end of it, right where it will connect up with the old road."

"And those will be prime locations for new development!" Press avowed with a slap of his hands on the desk.

"You bet," Barry agreed. "Gas stations, restaurants, hotels, the works!"

Press rocked back in his chair and swiveled his head in amazement, pondering his eyes into the wall behind Barry.

"This bypass thing has been in the works for several years. It's plain that Susan Parker had a pretty good line on the project before she and her husband split," Press wagered with the confidence of a sure bet. "And Hartley picked it up from her sometime between escapades in the sheets."

"This almost *has* to confirm that Hartley's involved in ADN Properties," Barry judged.

"It definitely adds an interesting spice to the ragout, doesn't it?" Press passed a hand down the side of his face and scratched vigorously under his chin.

"And what'll you bet that another proposal will come before the city council soon to annex those properties?" he posed with a snort. "All of that new development will need sewer and water, and that will increase the value of the land even more!"

Press wagered correctly. Mayor Hartley had just such a proposal on the city council agenda for the very next meeting. It was referred to committee where fast and favorable action was expected.

In a call placed the next morning, Press related the new information to Jarred Kleinmeier in the state attorney general's office.

"With what we already have, that ought to be plenty of information to get my boss to allow us to open a John Doe investigation," Kleinmeier said. "I'd bet my next paycheck that we'll find out that everything you suspect is true."

"When word of this gets out, what impact will it have on Granger's operation?" Press wanted to know.

"None," Kleinmeier assured him. "It'll all be kept secret until we're ready to file charges. Besides, the John Doe may not be ready by the time we nail Nordstrom. You know what they say about the wheels of justice grinding slowly. Around here sometimes, if the wheels were on a car, it wouldn't get around the block in a month." He told Press to be certain, however, that the matter would be pursued with all the vigor the state's attorney could muster.

"Is anything happening yet with Granger?" Press shifted the conversation to another track.

"I talked to Joe yesterday," Kleinmeier told the other. "Nordstrom's been over to his house twice, supposedly offering suggestions on how to safeguard himself from burglars. Apparently spent quite a bit of time. Joe said Nordstrom made particular note of his jug of coins and a couple of guns. Even told him specifically where he should put them out of sight. I'll be setting something up with an EMT, hopefully this week, so that we can make a move there soon."

It's funny how your shadow sometimes bears little resemblance to the body it so darkly mirrors, Press mused. The sun had just blinked its full appearance over the rooftop rim across the street and stretched the silhouette beside him entirely across the yards and driveways as he jogged past. It was one of the finest dawnings late summer could present, the sky empty of wind or clouds. The steady whump, whump, whump of his Nikes battering the sidewalk beneath him was the only disruption to the quiet. Not even a dog was barking in any distance around him. Nor was there any early morning grumble of a car headed toward some early venture at work. Only the even whump, whump, whump of his gait and the greetings of first risen cardinals and robins and wrens. Press could not even listen to his own breathing without making an effort.

Running had become more random than ritual over the last pair of months. The unspring in his legs was a major morning headline declaring the risk of open rebellion from his knees and shins and thighs. He was almost surprised that his lungs hadn't sided with those warriors below.

Like so much of other times in Press' aloneness of late, his thoughts were in the vicinity of Jeremy. Doubts spoke to him in full pages. Maybe his son would be alive if he hadn't pushed Derek Nordstrom so hard. Was it always worthwhile to point out that some public official wasn't being a proper servant; to make note that he was a sonofabitch, even if you're right? Had it cost Press his son?

The notions of doubt were thumping on the backside of his eyeballs ever more severely than was the reproach from his legs. One of the reasons Press had given less effort to his running was because the time it took left him alone to his thoughts, to those considerations of self-doubt. A lot had developed in the last year. In the depths of him he knew he was right; knew he had acted responsibly as a journalist. But had the price been Jeremy?

"PRESSING MATTERS"
August 24

School starts next week. It'll be the first day ever for so many youngsters. It was an emotional day for my wife and me more than a dozen years ago as we watched that big yellow bus engulf our first and hurry him off towards growing to adulthood. My wife managed to focus the camera through her tears and I had to choke back the heart that had removed itself to my throat. The ritual was no different each time our daughters proceeded in turn, although as parents we accepted the inevitable with a bit more dignity. Jeremy would have been off to the University of Missouri this week. Abby and I had even anticipated the difficulty of accepting another of our child's initial steps towards letting go. Instead we found ourselves having to let him go much too soon. A child's funeral is a rite no parent should ever have to endure....

39 Galen Perry's tug on Press' arm outside Cruiser's reined the publisher to a halt as the two were leaving the café after morning coffee.

"Listen, I was going to call you later anyway," the lawyer began. "I haven't been able to get anywhere with the Daniels folks. I think it's pretty clear that you and the other parents are going to have to talk to them. They're really adamant about protecting DeDe."

Press dragged in an extra dose of air and let it reluctantly escape through his puffed cheeks as he balled his fists into the pockets of his sport coat.

"Yeah, I suppose," he acknowledged. "I hate like heck to, though. I wonder if I might not feel the same way they do if the burdens were reversed."

"It's in DeDe's interest and her parents' too, though," Galen countered. "If it was my daughter, I'd sure want Nordstrom punished for what he did. And without the girl, we don't have much of a case to go on. We could subpoena her for the trial, but an unwilling witness is not likely to be much help. Who knows what she'd say under those circumstances?"

Perry was right, Press knew. He said he would get on it right away.

Wally Daniels ran a small engine repair shop in what had been one of Fremont's first gas stations a block west of the four-way stop. It was a tiny, used-to-be-white stucco building with a green-tiled archway supported by a pair of square stucco pillars. *Sinclair* could still be seen through the decades-thinned cover of paint on the archway façade. The pumps, long since relegated to some junkyard, had been replaced by a sandwich board bearing the hand painted announcement, 'Daniels Small Engine Repair'.

Press breathed in a batch of resolve and walked inside. Daniels was seated at a bench under a side window. Wearing jeans, a faded red T-shirt, and greased to his elbows, he was stripping parts from a small motor, the variety of which Press hadn't the foggiest notion.

"Unless you got a lawnmower needs fixin', I doubt we've got much to talk about," Daniels announced matter-of-factly.

The abrupt greeting lifted Press' eyebrows as if he'd been swatted with a rolled up newspaper.

"Is that so?" Press replied evenly as he looked about for something to sit on or lean against that wasn't coated with some measure of lubricant or grime. Finding nothing for support, he folded his arms across his chest and stood uncomfortably, gazing at the side of Wally Daniels as the man continued to wrench here and ratchet there on the motor.

"Yup," Daniels replied without altering his attention or expression. "That lawyer of yours has been calling me and my wife ever since we brought DeDe home from the hospital. Told him the same thing. DeDe don't want to talk about the accident any more."

"Is that your statement or hers?"

Daniels laid the wrench down and cocked a sideways look at Press.

"Amounts to the same thing, don't it?"

"Look, Wally," Press began as he shifted weight, "I know your daughter's had a traumatic experience and I can understand that you don't want to put her through anything painful again. But she's *alive!* My son and two other kids are dead. And your daughter spent how much time in the hospital? All because of Derek Nordstrom."

Daniels made a feeble attempt at wiping the grease from his hands with an even grimier rag and stood up.

"No, *you* look, Williams," he growled, aiming a lubricated finger at Press. "My girl nearly died, and three kids did, because the Kelso kid tried to outrun a cop! It's his old man's ass I oughta be suing!" He punched his fists to his hips and fixed an unfriendly stare on the other man.

"I don't deny that what the kids did was wrong," Press answered with no back down in his voice. "But all law enforcement agencies have well defined policies for high speed chases. Nordstrom violated all of them!"

"He wouldn'ta had to if they hadn't run!"

"Hell, man, the guy knew who every one of those kids was before they ever got into the car. He had their license plate number." The mercury was rising in the tone of Press' voice. "Nordstrom could have backed off and picked up each of the kids at their homes later. It wasn't like he would have had to go to Omaha or L.A. or someplace to find them!"

"That don't matter to me," Daniels said as he brushed past Press to the door and opened it to declare the meeting ended. "Now, like I said, we don't have anything to talk about."

Press stared a moment, shook his head, and left with a soft "hmmfph."

"What's up, Hon?" Abby nuzzled into her husband's ear as she began massaging his shoulders. Press was sitting hunched over the dining table and an open can of Diet Sprite.

"I tried to talk to Wally Daniels this afternoon and got nowhere." Press sipped some soda as Abby slid into a chair around the corner of the table from him. "He thinks the whole thing is Adam Kelso's fault for trying to get away."

"I suppose I can see his point," Abby allowed as she fingered the edges of her apron, her eyes lowered to avoid her husband's.

"Abby, for God's sake, Nordstrom *ran them off the road!* That should have never happened, even if the kids were trying to get away!" He slapped a hand on the table and Abby was startled. She reached over and took it.

"I know, I know," she cried. "I'm not arguing with you. It's just that I can see Mr. Daniels' point, too. The kids shouldn't have tried to run."

"Yes, but you have to think about the nature of the crime, too," Press pointed out, the exasperation filtering out of him. "They were leaving a beer party. They weren't shooting it out with the cops after a bank robbery. If Nordstrom wanted to bust Jeremy, all he had to do was wait for the kid to come home."

"I agree," his wife granted with a nod that shuffled the blond hair forward off her shoulders. "But what can we do now?"

"I guess all we can do is talk to the Kelsos and Moores." Press shrugged. "Maybe we can go as a group to talk to the Danielses. I just don't know what else we can do at this point."

Press had played telephone tag with the Kelsos and Moores and Galen Perry for two evenings before managing to arrange a meeting in Perry's office for the following Monday night after everyone finished work.

Press and Abby arrived first and Galen ushered them into a small conference room. A pot of fresh coffee was on the table, along with seven cups.

"Help yourselves," the young attorney said, aiming a hand at the coffee. "I'll go watch for the others so I can unlock the door for them."

When the seven surrounded the table minutes later, Press restated the main elements of his meeting with Wally Daniels.

"He was pretty adamant," Press said with a nod of his head at the others seated around the table. Then, resting a hesitant look on the Kelsos, he added, "I don't know how to tell this other than to say it right out. Ben, Daniels thinks the whole thing was...was Adam's fault."

"What?" Ben Kelso launched himself forward in the chair and pounded the table so hard that coffee splashed from the cup nearest his fist. The slap of his anger awakened audible gasps from his wife and the Moores as much as Press' announcement.

Press threw up his hands and shrugged.

"Daniels says nothing would have happened if the kids didn't try to run."

"But the sonofabitch didn't have to run 'em off the road!" Ben declared, the hard line of his jaw notched forward.

"Look, Mr. Kelso, we all know that." Galen inserted himself into the discussion, separating the others with the forward jab of an open hand like a referee at a boxing match. "I think we all know what the situation here is and it won't do any good to get mad at the Daniels family. What we have to do is to put together a plan to get them on our side."

Ben Kelso grudgingly sat back in his chair but the set of his jaw was still forward.

"You know all the legal things, the reasons why we're doing this." Bernadette Moore was aiming in Galen's direction. "Can't you talk to Mr. and Mrs. Daniels? Convince them that we need to do this?"

Perry shook his head and followed the spin of the pencil he was rotating between the thumbs and forefingers of his hands. "They know I'm just the hired gun here. I've tried and they're not going to talk to me at all. Attorneys get that reaction a lot. They think we're just in it for the money."

"So what do you propose?" It was Lance Moore this time.

Galen dropped the pencil on the table and scooted deeper into his chair.

"You folks are the ones with the case to be resolved," he said with a small turn of his open palm. "I'd suggest that you simply go, as a group, to the Daniels home and try to talk to them. Be honest. Tell them what this means to you. How you all feel."

There was a brief interlude while looks were passed and each of them bargained reasons for rejecting the notion against the likelihood that the cause of justice would stop here if they didn't plead their case to the Danielses.

"Who would make the appointment for us to meet with them?" Marie Kelso asked at last.

"Unh, uh." Press head-wagged himself forward to lean his elbows on the table. "If we try to set up a formal meeting, they'll simply decline or find some way to get out of it. I think we just have to pick a time and show up together at their house. If they're not home, we just go back another time and keep going back until we talk to them."

"I think you're right. They'd say no to a meeting," Galen agreed. "But as determined as they are – especially Mr. Daniels – I think it still might be hard for them to slam the door in your faces."

The discussion waged on for another half an hour before it was finally agreed that the Moores, who had a van, would pick up the other two couples near seven the next evening. They hoped to catch Wally and Veronica Daniels after supper that night.

The sun was only an hour from setting behind the Daniels' snuggly packaged, pastel green house when the Moores' van pulled to the curb in front. After a collective gather of courage, the six emptied the van and assembled on the sidewalk for a two-by-two march to the doorstep, Williamses, then Moores, followed by Kelsos.

Mrs. Daniels opened the door and stood wiping her hands on the apron that skirted her bluejeans. A smallish woman with dark eyes set under an ebony canopy of short-cropped curls, she wore the half-expectant look of a person about to be preached at by Jehovah's Witnesses.

"Mrs. Daniels, if we could," Press began with a quarter turn gesture toward Abby and the others, "we'd like a few minutes to talk to you and your husband."

"Oh, uh, sure. Please come in." She stepped back to politely usher her company into the small living room. Mrs. Daniels tried to smile but didn't quite, uncertain it seemed, as to whether a smile was appropriate. She stood a moment assessing the number of seats and the number of sitters.

"I'll get a couple more chairs. WALLY!"

She darted into the kitchen and gathered a vinyl covered dining chair under each arm. "Wally, we have company," was yelled to someplace through another door. Returning to the living room, she settled the chairs near the kitchen as the others settled into a tight circle facing her.

A screen door banged at the back of the kitchen and Wally Daniels came to the living room and stopped, a momentary surprise pasted to his face. The surprised look turned dark as he glanced around the room and verged nearly on outright anger when his eyes fell on Lance Moore who was sitting in the owner's favorite recliner. Wally handed an irritated glare down to his wife before dumping himself heavily onto the kitchen chair beside her.

"I guess I don't need to ask what this is all about," he said flatly, his hands perched on his wide-set knees.

The others turned to Press to lead them into whatever discussion would come.

"We don't want to take much of your time," Press opened. "We just want to impress upon you how very much we need your help – and DeDe's."

Veronica Daniels slid a nervous glance at her husband as the set of his jaw tightened another notch.

"Talk if you want, but we told you before, DeDe won't!" The words had the hardness of metal as they tumbled out of Wally's mouth.

Press nodded and continued, his eyes fixed on Mrs. Daniels rather than her husband.

"Our kids were very precious to us, as we know DeDe is to you." Veronica bent her head a fraction in agreement with Press. "What we want to do certainly isn't going to bring our children back or make your daughter heal any faster. We just want to see the man responsible get punished for what he did to them."

"Seems to me that's gonna be kinda hard to do since he's already dead!" Wally sneered directly at the Kelsos.

"Now wait just a damned minute!" Ben cried, springing off the sofa as if he'd been spiked by a cattle prod, his fists balled at his sides.

Wally Daniels rose and stepped sideways to brace himself for a challenge, while Press launched himself between the two. The men's wives were frantically tugging at belts and elbows and anything else they could grasp in an effort to get them returned to their seats.

"Come on, guys. Come on. Please. This isn't what this is all about." Press stood glancing back and forth between them until each was returned to sitting.

"Wally, we talked about this in your shop the other day," the publisher said as he eased backward into his chair. "It's like I said, we all know the kids shouldn't have tried to run."

He was pointing his words at Mrs. Daniels again.

"But the fact is, every law enforcement agency in the state, and probably the country, has a specific policy in place to dictate police actions in just such a circumstance. Derek Nordstrom not only violated the policies set by both the Fremont Police Department and the county sheriff's office, he intentionally ran the kids off the road. Mrs. Daniels, there is a law on the books that calls that murder, just as if he'd used his gun. It's homicide by negligent use of a motor vehicle."

The tremble to her lips as she stared up at her husband admitted that it was a notion as foreign to her as the Aztec language. Wally looked only at Press.

"All we want is justice for our kids. All four of them. We want to see Derek Nordstrom punished for what he did." Press settled his elbows onto his knees and clasped his hands.

"Let's be *really* honest," Wally Daniels interrupted. "What you really want is to make some bucks off the situation. I'm not puttin' DeDe through more hell just so you guys can get rich off it!"

A mix of sighs and gasps slumped through the collected couples.

"No, no, that's not it at all!" Bernadette Moore was shaking her head, directing herself also at Veronica. "As I understand it, there's just no other way to get at the police chief for what he did."

“Yeah, we’ll probably sue him later,” Lance Moore said. “But the negligent homicide is a criminal matter. That comes first. There’s no money in that and probably none later if we don’t make that case first.”

"We can't even go to the city to get him fired without your daughter's statement," Abby inserted. "We have two daughters. I understand that you don't want DeDe to endure any more pain. But without her help, Chief Nordstrom will have gotten away with killing our son and these folks' children." She directed her hands widely in the direction of the Moores and Kelsos.

"He will have gotten away with nearly killing your daughter," Abby finished, her gaze fixed on Veronica.

"Without DeDe, we have little or no case at all." It was Press once more. "All we have is a small set of tire tracks on the road where Nordstrom cut in front of the kids and hit the brakes."

"You've been trying to nail Nordstrom for a year, now," Wally bartered again with Press, his words still rigid but his tone softer. "You're just continuing your vendetta toward the police chief!"

Press slumped his head deeper into his neck and shoulders. “Maybe the whole thing’s my fault, then. Maybe our kids are dead because Nordstrom was getting back at me.”

"I don't think that's relevant, even if it were true," Lance entered on Press' behalf. "Whatever else Derek may or may not have done, it all pales in comparison to what he did to our children that night in June."

"Mr. and Mrs. Daniels, even if you don't care about our children, don't you want someone to answer for what DeDe's been put through?" Marie Kelso asked softly.

"We care…cer…certainly, we care," Veronica whimpered, tears starting to moisten her cheeks. "It's just that…that DeDe's been through so much…." She shook her head slowly and both she and her husband stared into the carpet.

"Mr. and Missus Daniels, have you really even *asked* your daughter what she would or wouldn't do?" Ben Kelso wanted to know. Wally and Veronica eyed each other and each fidgeted slightly. Their lack of other response was the answer to Ben's query.

There was a contemplative quit in the conversation, thoughts seemingly frozen in some glacier of time while everyone passed uncertain looks around the room except the Daniels couple. They simply stared at the floor.

"Wally, Veronica," Press broke the hush. "I haven't talked at all to Abby about this, and I don't know what the others will do, but…would it help at all if we said we'd give whatever settlement we might get to some charity? You pick it."

Abby gave an approving nod at her husband and the other guests considered the new thought among themselves.

"I…I don't think you need to do that," Veronica offered as she passed a hand under each eye to clear the dampness. She looked up at Wally. "We'll talk."

"We're not trying to get rich. Like I said, we know that going after the chief won't return our kids to us or make us feel the loss any less," Press continued quietly. "It's all about justice and without DeDe's help, there won't be any for us or our children."

"We need to think about it," Veronica came back, rising as she laid a hand on her husband's shoulder for support. "We'll talk. I suppose we should see what DeDe wants, too…."

As the visitors gathered themselves out of their seats and readied to leave, Press stepped forward and offered a hand to Wally. The other looked at the extended hand, then upped his gaze to meet the newspaper publisher's eyes. Slowly, without softening the set in his jaw line, Wally raised himself off the chair and shook the hand.

In turn, Ben and Lance gripped the Daniels hand while the three wives exchanged hugs with Veronica.

"Thank you for coming," from Veronica Daniels was all that was said as the trio of couples walked slowly down the sidewalk to the van.

40 "There's a call for you on line one," the receptionist announced as Press entered the *Gazette* building.

"It's going down this afternoon," declared Jarred Kleinmeier from the other end when Press picked up the receiver in his office.

"I can hardly wait," Press replied, rounding the desk to put himself into his swivel chair.

"Anybody in your office got a scanner?" Kleinmeier wanted to know.

"Yeah," the publisher said. "Both my editor and my sports reporter who is also my best photographer. Why?"

"Because when the 911 call goes out, we can't have them showing up on the scene and screwing things up," the state attorney replied with an edge of surliness that surprised Press.

"I'll see that they're both doing something else. But they wouldn't respond to a call like that unless it was the mayor or some really prominent person in the community. Neither of my guys have ever heard of Granger," Press defended.

"Sorry." Kleinmeier's tone softened. "I just want everything to go right. If it happens like I think it's going to, tomorrow you'll be able to hit him with all the other lawsuits you want."

"No problem. While I have you on the line, have you gotten anywhere on the Hartley situation, yet?"

"I can't give you anything on that just yet. I still don't know how long it will be."

Kleinmeier told Press he would call him as soon as they had something from the sting operation on Nordstrom and the conversation ended.

With all the casualness he could produce through his excitement, Press checked with both Barry and Sport Henry to make certain no 911 call would spark their curiosity. Sport was covering a Fremont High School cross country meet in Avery and Barry was leaving in a few minutes for a regional planning commission meeting in Parsons. Neither would be near a police scanner all day.

Press smiled inside himself.

The morning dragged as if it were being hauled in the back of a county highway department truck. Press skipped coffee with the bunch at Cruisers for fear he might not be able to conceal the commotion inside him. Telling the receptionist simply that he would be back, he left the building and started walking.

At the Town and Country Convenience Centre Press stopped to buy a *USA Today*.

"Missed you at coffee this morning," Bernie Randazzo noted as he punched keys on the cash register and handed Press two bits change for his dollar.

"Yeah, I got tied up with some desk work," Press lied.

Outside, he folded the paper and tucked it under his arm as he stood on the corner debating over which way to go. Finally he headed for Water Tower Park, a distance of eight blocks.

It was a good day for a walk. The globe of sun was the only interruption in the cellophane sky and barely a sniff of a wind was ushered in off the plains. It would have been hot if not for the canopy of maples and sycamores and occasional oaks that shadowed most of the sidewalks along the way. The summer had been a mostly dry one and yards that weren't watered regularly were tan and brittle. Thirst-stressed leaves were already beginning to litter the lawns and line the street side of the curbs. Press recalled his childhood in Upper Michigan where dry summers meant duller hues to the normally spectacular fall colors.

Smugness packaged the assortment of thoughts inside him as he walked. All he could think about was the possibility that Derek Nordstrom would finally get a measure of the justice he was due. Press kept returning to his first conversation with Anna Mae Conroy; then skipping to the dual set of logs the chief had maintained in order to hide items from the public; back again to Nordstrom's questionable involvement in those land dealings. But most of all, Press was thinking of Jeremy. Nothing would bring the boy back, but Press vowed to make Nordstrom pay for taking his son from him. His only distraction before the park was a bright wave from Merrilee Skinner. Clad in shorts and a halter top, Merrilee was mowing her lawn as Press walked by. She was an attractive, yet not quite beautiful woman who carried herself in such a way that would jerk a parson's head to attention, even if she dressed like a nun.

At the park, Press picked a bench under a sycamore that had been seeded probably around the birth of the town and sat down. Unfolding his newspaper, he glanced quickly at the front page and then wandered his eyes around the green island between neighborhoods.

Aptly named, the park surrounded Fremont's first water tower. It was a pastel green canister, held forty feet in the air by a cone of limestone and concrete. Use of the structure had been replaced over the years by two giant bulbs, like onions grown upside down, one north and one south of town. For the last decade of its disuse, an ongoing debate had ensued among city officials as well as residents over whether to tear it down as a dangerous eyesore or to restore it as an historic landmark. The *Gazette* had editorialized on several occasions in favor of saving the old tower.

For the time being it was preserved, just as it had been when it served to slake Fremont's thirst, by an eight-foot-high, chain link fence that was topped by triple strands of barbed wire. Every couple of months park department employees would open the padlocked gate to allow neighborhood youths to reclaim the variety of balls, toys, caps and shoes that had somehow found their way onto the wrong side of the fence.

Before the recent economic and population booms, the two-block-square park had been the western boundary between old Fremont and what was then considered *new* Fremont. Houses west of Water Tower Park were post-World War II ranches that spawned a rotating crop of baby-boomers whose children, along with the newcomers and grandchildren of the older neighborhood to the east, gathered in twos and twenties in the open expanse around the water tower. While the few trees that had been planted had long since matured to match the original greenery, even now there was plenty of room for ball games, bicycles, juvenile bickering, and bumbling first romances.

Today, however, only a couple of mothers with their toddlers occupied the park. They were pushing the youngsters to squeals and a slow, pendulum rocking of the swing set on the other side of the water tower.

Press tried to read the newspaper but found himself concentrating on little more than a cursory scan of the headlines. Working the crossword puzzle drew little satisfaction. He was too absorbed in the details of the Nordstrom matter; details like a school full of kindergartners' dangling shoe laces that needed tying.

He wondered how Nordstrom and Susan Parker ever got tied together in the real estate market. It had to be through Hartley, he was certain, but how? And how did Hartley manage to keep his ties to both his wife and the Parker woman? Press figured pieces of the puzzle would soon be falling into place but his curiosity was eating at him like a batch of chiggers.

His watch told him only a fraction past an hour had elapsed. At this rate he would be a much older man before the day was behind him. Press folded the newspaper and, taking a deep drag of September air, lifted himself off the bench to head back to the office.

"I've got to get busy or I'll drive myself crazy," he lectured to no one around.

Press slogged through the rest of the day with uninventive paperwork, interrupted only by a longer-than-sixty-minute lunch hour.

It was with little depth of discovery that Abby noted his agitation through dinner and afterward.

"Just some things at the office that have me a little edgy," was all he disclosed. "I'll let you know if anything comes of it."

Night came as a small season of its own, noteworthy only in its restlessness for Press. Sleep, when snatches of it came, seemed almost to surprise him awake again.

He was in the office early, pacing through the composition room to read letters to the editor already in place on a layout page and see what the week's leading headlines would be, then to the front office to check for messages and yesterday's cash sheets.

Returning to his office he sat, back to the desk, pondering the outside beyond his window as the minutes trickled by on turtle legs. Another grain-gold day, the roof rims across the street providing the only seam in the turquoise sky. Press turned to his desk, swiveled back to the window, and back to his desk again. When the minute hand on his watch finally struggled one notch past eight o'clock, he picked up the telephone and started punching in digits. Before he could finish, the receptionist's voice entered through the speaker on his desk set.

"A Mr. Kleinmeier on line two for you, Press."

"We got him!" was Kleinmeier's first gush from the other end.

"Fantastic!" Press said, a smile pushing his ears broadly apart. "Tell me everything!"

The state attorney stated that everything had gone with the precision of a Swiss watch. Granger's sister had called 911 to report that she had been unable to reach him for two days. The EMTs, both of whom were in on the sting, got to Granger's house first, followed immediately by Nordstrom, just as expected. The chief quickly dismissed the two EMTs, saying he would call the coroner.

"Granger said the hardest part of the entire operation was lying on the bathroom floor for an hour and a half." Kleinmeier's words mingled with a chuckle. "He said Nordstrom never entered the bathroom once the whole time. He was too busy going from room to room and in and out of the house. We caught everything on hidden video cameras."

"When did you confront Nordstrom?" Press wanted to know, the information not coming fast enough to match his excitement.

Kleinmeier said a Department of Criminal Investigations agent and a deputy were in an unmarked car down the street. They followed the chief to his house and called in another agent and deputy, also in an unmarked squad parked a block from Nordstrom's house.

"Nordstrom never suspected a thing," Kleinmeier related smugly.

When the police chief started to back out of his driveway after unloading the goods from Granger's house, the two squads moved in. The DCI agents showed Nordstrom a search warrant and entered the garage. There they found a wide assortment of specially marked items from Granger's, along with a lot of other stuff that offered plenty of reason for legal curiosity.

"Could have had a hell of a rummage sale in that garage," Kleinmeier surmised. "The DCI boys told me Nordstrom wilted like a wet shirt when they showed him the warrant. They searched the house, too, but didn't find much that might lend itself to this case."

Kleinmeier told Press that the chief was taken to Parsons where he was charged initially with theft. According to the state attorney, Nordstrom clammed up after recovering a bit from the shock of being caught red-handed. He immediately called a lawyer in Parsons and wouldn't make any statements to investigators.

"I'm almost surprised that you got Schell to issue the charges," Press interjected. "We couldn't even get him to write a letter to Nordstrom telling him that he had to open his logs to us."

"The attorney general's office carries a bit more weight," Kleinmeier replied. "At this point I doubt Schell will be a problem. We've laid it all out in black and white for him and caught Nordstrom with his fingers in the pie. Not much gray area to muddle through."

"So when will Nordstrom get out? Will there be bail?"

"I pretty much expect that the circuit judge won't require any bail. Will probably let him out this morning on his own recognizance since he is the police chief and all. I doubt Schell will argue the issue much," Kleinmeier admitted. "If it goes to trial, it'll probably be moved to another county anyway. I'm sure Nordstrom won't want the trial here if it goes that far. I doubt the ornery old bastard'll plead guilty, that's for sure. We'll want to get Nordstrom for abusing his office as well."

He added that he was sure someone in Fremont, a point directed at the publisher, would want to pursue the matter with the local police and fire commission.

"You can bet on that," Press assured. He thanked the assistant attorney general for all his cooperation.

"Hey, it's *you* who has a lot of thanks coming from us, Mr. Williams," Kleinmeier replied with a surge of enthusiasm. "Without everything you provided us, we'd have never had a clue to get involved with this case. I don’t always like the press but you newspaper folks have done a helluva job with this. I have to congratulate you."

"Well, I'm sure we're not done yet," Press acknowledged. "We've still got some more pieces to squeeze into the picture."

Press called Barry into his office and spilled the story detail by detail through his excitement.

"That cranky old turd's finally going to get a measure of what's coming to him." The satisfaction oozed out of him as Press leaned forward, bracing an elbow on the desk and delivering his chin onto his knuckles.

"So this is why you didn't want any story out right away on what the Daniels girl told you, huh?" Barry said, his ears parted wide with an amazed grin. "You could have *told* me, you know."

"No I couldn't," Press came back. "You'll never know how much I wanted to tell you. Abby, too. But Kleinmeier was adamant about not letting anyone else in on it. I think you have something major for page one now, anyway."

"I'm on it," was Barry's end to the conversation.

Galen Perry received the next telephone call from Press. When the publisher was through filling the attorney's head with details, Galen's enthusiasm was tempered.

"If Nordstrom's been doing everything you say, he surely deserves what he's going to get," Perry allowed. "But unless we get some cooperation out of the Daniels family, we're still not going to get anywhere on the other matter. How did your meeting with them go?"

In his excitement, Press had forgotten to report anything on the session with Wally and Veronica Daniels.

"Abby and I, along with the Moores and Kelsos went to the Daniels house the night before last, just as we planned," Press relayed with less than enthusiasm. "Wally still thinks the whole thing was Adam Kelso's fault and that we're just trying to get rich off the situation or something. I think we may have gotten through to Mrs. Daniels, but I don't know. She said they'd see what DeDe wants, but I don't know how much influence she'll be able to swing, even if we reached her. I guess we'll just have to wait and see."

More than anything since the grain elevator explosion forty-seven years earlier, the *Gazette's* account of Police Chief Derek

Nordstrom's arrest rattled every cage and rocked windows and doors throughout Fremont. It sent tremors all around the county as well. When the newspaper had reported the chief's earlier dashes across legal borders, reaction was prompt and directed at the *Gazette*. This time, however, though it was the topic around every dinner table, water cooler and coffee shop, the response was one of shock. Those who weren't numbed by the revelation that Nordstrom was a thief were outraged that their top cop could be a crook.

Aside from Nordstrom himself, Mayor Wes Hartley was about the only other one in town without something to say on the matter. He said simply that it was a matter for the Fremont Police and Fire Commission and refused further comment. The Police and Fire Commission, in the meantime, scheduled a meeting for Monday night.

Press was confronted everywhere by opinions and badgering for details. It was the biggest news event in the two-plus decades he had owned the paper. He couldn't help but wonder how folks would react when, and *if*, the rest of the story about Nordstrom ever came out.

"PRESSING MATTERS"
September 14

There is an arrogance of power that afflicts not just heads of state – the Napoleons, the Tsars, the Nixons. Whenever authority is unchecked it can be abused at every level of our lives. Some people feel their sense of power – real or imagined – gives them the right to act without consideration for those around them or for the moral effects of their actions. I've seen its manifestations in Little League coaches, business executives, and minor elective office holders. As a college student, I worked for a catering manager who thought he was the god of accommodations dining. Ultimately, we are all accountable, however. We cannot disregard rightness in our actions, we cannot wantonly abuse our positions and those persons we deal with without answering ultimately to some higher authority. Derek Nordstrom has held his office so long that he apparently thought he could take advantage of people and circumstances for his personal gain and do so with impunity….

41 Galen Perry was the last to arrive at Cruiser's on Friday morning, a smug grin widely separating his nose and chin. The subject of Derek Nordstrom had already been hashed and rehashed among the six other regular coffee patrons more than the owner's sassy waitresses or bad food had in six months. In fact, coroner and restaurateur Bud Callahan was even on hand to add flavor to the story with details of his participation in nabbing Nordstrom.

"He calls me at home about four o'clock and tells me there's this stiff over on Oak Grove Terrace. Apparent heart attack victim," Callahan related with a flourish of both hands. "I get over there just as he's leaving. Tells me the guy's on the bathroom floor."

Eyebrows were arched and ears cocked in anticipation around the rectangle of tables.

"So Nordstrom leaves now and I go into the bathroom." Callahan threw both hands to his chest like he'd been shot. "Here's this guy, standing next to the tub with nothing on but a smile. I gotta tell ya, I damned near had the big one myself!"

After whewing substantially and chugging a slug of coffee into him, the man continued.

"He's holding a finger to his mouth and telling me to be quiet in case the chief is still around. After I put my wits back together a bit, he tells me the whole thing has been a sting to catch Nordstrom stealing. Well, you could have knocked me over with a string of cooked spaghetti."

It took no coaxing for Press to relate how Anna Mae Conroy's visit to the *Gazette* office had gotten Barry and himself to looking into the matter in the first place. By the time he finished, it was time to shake dice for the coffee tab. Blaine Peterson lost for the third day in a row and was becoming playfully less than gracious about the matter.

Galen, closest to the door, lingered long enough to escort Press to the sidewalk.

"You look like you've been bustin' to tell me something all morning," Press goaded. "I hope it's something good."

"It's *great!*" Galen beamed. "Wally Daniels called just before I left the office while ago."

Press sagged onto the hood of the Buick he had managed to park conveniently right in front of Cruiser's. There was only one question in the look his eyes fixed on Galen and the attorney's nod provided the answer.

"They're going to help us. I got the impression that his wife and DeDe both had been working on him, but the story of Nordstrom's arrest in yesterday's paper really turned the trick," Perry gushed. "He said he supposed the chief really was a bad actor."

Relief slumped through Press' shoulders.

"I'm so happy I could hug you right here on the sidewalk," the publisher cried.

"Please don't," Galen chuckled. "You know that's how ugly rumors get started in these small towns."

Press waved him off with a smile.

"So what's next?" he quizzed.

"My secretary and I are going to their house at four o'clock to take DeDe's statement. I'd rather do it at my office but Daniels is still insisting she's not real comfortable with it yet. Would rather do it at home after school." Perry added that he would try to arrange a polygraph test for the following week. Wally was really upset over that, he said.

"He thinks his daughter's statement ought to be enough," Galen continued. "I had a hard time convincing him that it was simply backup to make the case stronger. Nordstrom's lawyer would argue that she was making the whole thing up as the basis for a lawsuit."

"Well, keep me informed," Press said, slapping a hand on his friend's shoulder as he turned toward the driver side door, ending the discussion.

Press drove home instead of back to the office. Abby was vacuuming the living room floor and didn't see him come in through the kitchen. A wry grin crept onto his face as he reached down and unplugged the vacuum. Abby puzzled a look first at the canister, then her eyes followed the cord back to where Press held the plug devilishly in his hand.

"Oh, Lord!" she cried, clamping a hand above her bosom. "Don't *do* that to me, Press! You scared me half to death! What are you doing home now anyway?"

"Can't I come home and see my sweet wife if I get the urge?" Press teased.

"Yes, you can. But you *don't,* so what's the occasion?" Abby recovered as she wrapped her arms around her husband's neck and gave him a spousely peck.

Press squeezed her to him a moment before stepping back.

"I couldn't wait to give you some news and I didn't want to do it over the phone," he said less playfully. "The Danielses are going to let DeDe talk."

Abby covered her gasp with four fingers.

"Wally Daniels called Galen this morning," Press added as he anchored himself to the arm of the sofa.

"Oh, Press, that's such a relief!" Abby thumped her heels and clapped her hands to her thighs and chewed the corner of her lip. "I don't know whether to jump for joy or cry."

"I kind of had the same feeling when Galen told me outside of Cruiser's while ago," Press admitted as he passed a hand down the back of his neck.

There were notions in Press that wanted for himself and the other members of his family to get on with their lives; to let Jeremy rest in peace. And yet, there was also a lingering bite in his conscience that wanted payment exacted for the loss of his son. Press argued within himself for justice rather than vengeance but, because he had grown to hate the police chief so passionately, he was never quite sure which side was winning. In the end, he knew his own memory of Jeremy could never be less than fitful if Nordstrom did not face some form of retribution for what he had done. Abby, Press was as sure as their years together could determine, battled the same mix of notions.

"What's up, Boss?" Barry wondered as he huffed into the publisher's office right after lunch and began shucking himself out of his windbreaker.

"We'll probably have another major story for you to break after next week," Press replied, a smile not quite making it to his face.

Barry slapped a small note pad on the edge of the desk and edged onto the front of a chair.

"DeDe Daniels is going to give her statement to Galen this afternoon," Press told. "Galen's going to confirm it with a polygraph next week and then as soon as he gives the okay, you've got your story."

"God, I'm so happy for you and Abby," Barry said, settling back into the chair. "I'm sure you can't feel any real closure to the whole situation until the truth finally comes out about what Nordstrom pulled."

"Closure. I guess that's it," Press said, mulling the number two pencil he rolled idly between his fingers. "I knew something had to be settled before I could let it rest. I just couldn't think of what to call it. I'll never get Jeremy's memory out of my mind, but I guess I could never be at ease with it until something was done about Nordstrom."

He was gnawing on the insides of his cheeks now and moisture was rimming his eyelids, making Barry quite uncomfortable.

"Well, just give me the word and I'm on it," the editor said as he stood and turned to leave.

"Barry." The name caught him at the door.

"Thanks," was what Press finished with.

42 "Police and Fire Commission suspended Nordstrom, with pay, until there is a legal outcome on the charges he faces," Barry reported from the open doorway to the publisher's office on Tuesday morning.

"With pay?" Press wondered, his face darkened by the effects of a frown.

"Yeah, I checked with Chuck Glorioso over in the city attorney's office about that," Barry confirmed as he leaned a shoulder into the door frame. "I guess that's pretty much standard procedure in dealing with misconduct cases involving law enforcement types. Until the legal proceedings are determined, at least."

"Somehow that just doesn't seem right that the weasel can have so much time off and still get paid," Press said, irritating the stub of a whisker on his jaw that the razor had missed.

Barry blew a soft snort through the curl of his upper lip and nodded his head in agreement.

"It could be a year or more before the case even comes to trial unless Derek pleads guilty. Nice vacation, huh?" He half turned to leave and then, "Oh, while I think of it...."

The editor claimed a chair across from Press and leaned forward onto his knees.

"I did talk to Ray Parker down at the Department of Transportation late last week." Barry glanced down at the end of the Bic he had been gnawing and stuffed the pen back into his shirt pocket. "He told me that the engineering plan for the bypass proposal had been set for five or six years. In fact, Hartley had met with DOT engineers about it several times. Parker said the route wasn't any big secret, it just hadn't been formally announced until the state put the funding in the department budget. I didn't let on like anything was unusual. I just was following up on the bypass story. I don't know if he even has a clue that his 'ex' is involved in any real estate dealings. Or with Hartley either for that matter."

"I suppose," Press mused, scratching his jaw roughly now. "Since he's lived down state for awhile, he wouldn't necessarily know about her pushing to get the Gunderson place annexed unless he happened to be one of our subscribers."

"You know, something that really bugs me is how the heck Hartley has been able to keep this whole thing together with his wife and all. He's *got* to still have some involvement with Susan Parker," Barry asserted, his eyes narrowing. "How does Sharon let him get away with it?"

Press pinned his elbow to the desk and rested his chin into his open palm, drumming the fingers of his other hand on a dictionary.

"Unless there's some incentive for one of them to talk, I don't know that we'll ever know the answer to that one," he speculated. "I should give Kleinmeier a call and see if he's been able to dig up anything on ADN Properties yet."

"Hey, man, these aren't the only things I've got to work on, you know!" There was a touch of surly mingled in Kleinmeier's words. "Between working with Granger on this Nordstrom thing and all the other cases we've got going, I just haven't had time to get at it yet."

"Sorry, I didn't mean to sound pushy," Press apologized. "I know you've got the whole state to deal with and all I have is Fremont to think about. I was just curious."

"I understand," Kleinmeier offered with less grump now. "I have to tell you, though, just finding out whether Hartley's involved in that real estate corporation may be the easy part. The investigation to back up any charges in the matter may take quite awhile."

The state man paused for air.

"And I don't know *what* we'll come up with in terms of Nordstrom's involvement in that one. Unless we can find some way to prove that he used undue influence of some sort as police chief, he may be okay legally. Same goes for his wife and the Parker woman. Unethical, maybe, but I just don't know if we'll have the legal grounds to nail him further."

Press thanked Kleinmeier for his time and asked again to be kept informed. The state attorney agreed.

"Just don't expect things to happen tomorrow or the next day."

Without hanging up, Press punched a button for another line and dialed Galen Perry's office.

"Just wondering if you've arranged the polygraph for DeDe, yet?" he asked when Galen's secretary put the call through.

"This afternoon at three," Galen came back.

"When will you know the results?"

"Pretty much right away. Why?"

"I'd like to get the story in this week's paper," Press stated. "Keep as much pressure on as possible. Momentum kind of thing, you know? Can you call me as soon as you've got something definite?"

The attorney said "sure," and added that he'd been meaning to give Press a call.

"I'd like you to take a look at the statement DeDe gave me. See if there's anything she told you that might have been left out. It would also help if you pick up on any inconsistencies that we might need to work out. When can you come over?"

"Give me about fifteen minutes if that's okay with you."

Press gathered himself out of the chair and headed for the newsroom.

"Keep your pencil sharpened," he advised Barry, rapping his knuckles on the editor's desk. "Galen expects to confirm DeDe's story with a polygraph test this afternoon. He's going to call me as soon as he's got it."

"I've already got the headline stored in my head," Barry announced as he turned from the computer keyboard. "*Survivor accuses police chief in deaths of three teens.*"

"I can't think of a better one," Press said as he started toward the front door, then paused. "You might want to try to set up an interview with the girl this evening. The story would probably be better for you coming straight from her rather than from her deposition."

Barry nodded and reached for the telephone to make the effort.

Press walked the three and a half blocks to Galen's office. He hadn't run yet this week and he figured even the short walk would do him good. It was a fine day, the peek-a-boo sunshine filtering in and out through medicine ball puffs of cottony wads billowing across the sky ahead of some approaching weather change.

The skeptic in him had dogged Press with a bone of concern. What if DeDe's story had changed significantly? What if there were inconsistencies that might weaken the case? Would anything come of the case, even if her statements were solid? He kept telling himself as he walked that he shouldn't be concerned until he read the statement, but Press could sometimes be a notorious worrier. His college roommate had even teased him about it, saying that when he was in the womb, he probably debated to himself whether the opening could ever be big enough.

"He's waiting for you," the secretary said through a casual smile as Press walked through the front door and continued down the hall to the square of legal space Galen worked from.

"You're two minutes early," Perry cracked through a grin as he handed a document to the publisher.

"I suppose you'll add that to my bill," Press shot back as he grabbed the papers and took possession of a leather chair across from the lawyer.

Emotions bounced through him like a loose ball in a close basketball game as he flipped slowly through the pages. Anger exchanged with lip-trembling sadness that was finally tempered with relief by the time his eyes coursed through the final paragraph. It was almost word for word the same version DeDe had unfolded to him in the hospital.

"I can't find any noticeable variation from what she told us," Press said, posting his chin in a contemplative pose between his thumb and forefinger. The vision in his mind was replaying images of DeDe in her hospital bed, her body covered nearly head to toe by casts and bandages and iodine. It revisited skid marks on a lightly-traveled stretch of county pavement, and turned to the lean and square-jawed Derek Nordstrom, his lips set in their standard contemptuous sneer. And of course, there was Jeremy. Jeremy and his eternal smile. It was the only image of his son that ever came to Press these days. He knew that the memory of Jeremy was being pretty selective in its visits, but he didn't care. The good in the boy outweighed all else and that was all Press needed to recall. Jeremy was gone now because of Derek Nordstrom and that matter of how his son's death had come about was the ache that needed tending to.

"Good," Galen said, declining with both hands as Press stretched across the desk to hand back the deposition. "Keep that and let Abby go through it, too. Just in case she might pick up on something that was missed," he added.

Press rolled the papers into his left hand and settled again into the big leather wingback.

"Assuming everything goes as expected this afternoon, what happens next?" Press wanted to know.

Perry ran a set of fingers through his short-cropped hair, his head cocked in a three-quarter set and his eyebrows arched high into his forehead.

"Well, the first thing I'll do is set up a meeting with Del Schell. Give him a copy of the deposition and polygraph results and ask him to file formal charges."

"What if he won't do it? You know how spineless he can be." Cynical was worrying its way through Press' thoughts again.

"The charges the state boys fed him probably stiffened his backbone enough to get him going on this, too. Schell has to realize by now what a slime ball Nordstrom is," Galen surmised as he leaned back in his chair and rotated a pen in two sets of fingers. "I wouldn't worry about his response until we need to."

In the meantime, the attorney said he would file a formal complaint with the city's police and fire commission. It would take a bit longer to ready the lawsuits against Nordstrom, the City of Fremont, and the county.

Little more was said of consequence and the two shook hands before Press exited.

"I hope it's more good news you're bringing home for lunch." Abby's eyes were twinkling as her arms rounded her husband's waist and she tugged him to her.

"Pretty much," Press replied, twitching his nose. He kissed the top of her head and nuzzled through her soft hair, inhaling the memory of Breck Shampoo that still clung from the morning washing. He kissed her again and then guided her to the sofa.

"I've got a copy of DeDe's statement. It seems to me to be almost exactly as she told us, but Galen wants you to go over it to see if there's anything left out. Check to see if anything seems to be inconsistent, too."

Abby took the pages and folded her legs onto the couch as she leaned against him, Press' arm draped around her shoulder. There was only quiet between them as she read slowly through the girl's words. A couple of sniffles as she finished the last of the pages told Press that tears were very close.

When she had read the end of the statement, Abby palmed her nose and swiped a finger under one eye at the same time.

"I don't know how many times I can keep going through all of this. All of these terrible memories." She snuffed softly and buried her face into his shoulder.

"I know. It's hard. I had the same thoughts when I read it," Press soothed. "But we have to keep going. We have to do this, if nothing else, for Jeremy."

"Is it really for him or just to get back at Chief Nordstrom?" she questioned through an almost sob.

"Both, I guess. Can there be one without the other?"

Abby didn't answer and he secured his other arm around her and rested his chin on top of her head. Several minutes passed. At last she drew back and settled her feet again to the floor.

"I guess it's pretty much as I remember her saying to us at the hospital," she said, again passing a hand under her nose and dabbing a finger under each eye. Standing, she started toward the kitchen. "What would you like for lunch?"

Galen's call came shortly after four that afternoon. DeDe Daniels' story was solid.

When Press relayed the information to Barry, the editor pursed his lips forward and nodded positively. He'd arranged an interview at the Daniels' home for six-thirty.

The aftershock caused by the *Gazette's* revelation of the latest accusations leveled against Derek Nordstrom was seismically only the slightest measure less tumultuous than the first news quake to rock Fremont a week earlier. Phones at the newspaper office rang steadily and letters to the editor began filtering in demanding to know how the mayor and city council could have let a man like Nordstrom remain on the job so long and calling for the police chief's immediate resignation or dismissal.

"Quite a turnaround from when we were criticizing him for keeping two separate logs awhile back," Barry hmmfphed as Press read through a couple of the letters.

Press smiled.

"Yeah, I have to admit this is one of those times I'd like to run an editorial that says simply, *We told you so.*" He handed the letters back to Barry. "The funny part is, it's not even over yet."

"PRESSING MATTERS"
September 21

Heartbreak is the loss of a child under any circumstances. There is a horror that compounds the loss beyond the capability of words to express. That tragedy is the knowledge that a man who is sworn to uphold the law – a man respected and expected to be above corruption – that such a man could willfully force a car carrying four teenagers off the road, killing three of them and leaving a lifetime of scars on the fourth, is simply appalling beyond comprehension. There must be accountability for that most reprehensible action....

43 District Attorney Del Schell filed three counts of negligent homicide by use of a motor vehicle and one charge of reckless endangerment against Derek Nordstrom less than a week after the *Gazette's* news account of DeDe Daniels' accusation.

Although Nordstrom, himself, remained silent and secluded as a rare stone, his attorney, Elliott McCarver, was interviewed by Barry for a story in the following week's *Gazette,* and stated that not guilty pleas had been entered on each count. For the record, he said that Nordstrom had simply followed the Kelso car the entire way, never pulling in front of it. McCarver further asserted that the additional set of tire tracks could easily have been made by someone trying to avoid hitting a deer. He charged that the girl's accusations were financially motivated and made at the urging of her parents and the families of the three dead teens.

Schell, meanwhile, sent criminal investigators to the scene of the crash to take samples of the tire marks, which were still ample after more than three months. Samples were also taken of the tires on the police chief's squad car, which was now parked in the city garage since Nordstrom's suspension.

On behalf of the four families, Galen Perry had also filed a complaint with the city, charging that Nordstrom had violated the Fremont Police Department's written policy regarding high speed chases. The police and fire commission met the following Monday night to consider the matter.

The five commission members occupied folding chairs, one at each end and three along one side of a rectangular table in a small room on the second floor of city hall. The five were Georgia Brackett, who represented the city council; John French, a restaurant owner; Sylvester Gordon, a foreman for a major highway construction contractor; Roger Davis, who was employed by the county social services office; and Ed Delaney, an environmental engineer at the cannery, who chaired the commission.

Press, Barry, and Galen claimed seats along one wall of the small room. In the expected absence of the police chief, Elliott

McCarver sat opposite the trio. Except for being overdressed for the role, McCarver had a look about him that could more easily have passed for the village drunk. He wore a disheveled brown suit, obviously over-employed from the polished elbows, knees, and ample seating arrangement at the back of the slacks. The man's belly exploded over his belt, causing his off-white shirt to forever untuck and the cuffs of his pants to crumple around his ankles. His collar was unbuttoned with the loosened red paisley tie angled to one side beneath his suit coat. McCarver had longish hair the color of old ivory, which drooped in odd geometries about his head. He was regularly wiping it back over the top of his forehead with one hand or the other in order to provide himself with slightly better vision than that of a sheep dog.

Elliott McCarver's appearance, however, belied the fact that he was considered the best criminal defense attorney in four counties. He was particularly revered by anyone accused of drunk driving or spouse abuse.

The commissioners had in hand copies of DeDe Daniels' statement, the polygraph verification, and the police department's rule on vehicle pursuit, when Delaney gaveled the meeting to order. After cursory opening remarks, he asked Galen for comments on behalf of the families.

"I think Miss Daniels' statement speaks for itself," Perry suggested, leaning forward but not getting up. "As you can see from the written policy regarding high speed chases, Chief Nordstrom's actions on the night of the children's deaths clearly violated that policy. It is our contention that Mr. Nordstrom should be removed from his position permanently."

With that he settled back in the hard wooden chair as Press shifted slightly and Barry propped one knee up to offer better support for his note pad as he wrote.

Without being called on, McCarver came out of his seat as if being ejected from a saloon.

"Mr. Chairman, on behalf of my client I have to object to this entire proceeding." He shuffled the length of the commissioners' table, alternately attaching his right forefinger to his upper lip and pointing it slightly skyward as though it were a lightning rod to gather thoughts. " Gentleman…and *lady*…." The barrel-bellied barrister paused and pointed a gratuitous bow at Georgia Brackett. "With no other collaboration than one Miss DeDe Daniels' statement, this whole matter is simply hearsay."

"Mr. McCarver," Delaney interrupted from behind what was almost a smile and a gesture toward the chair next to the lawyer's coat and briefcase. "This isn't a Perry Mason courtroom. Please have a seat."

McCarver angled his upper torso to face the commission, again directed his finger upward like a cocked pistol but thought better of it and returned to his chair without firing.

"Mr., ah, Delaney, my point is quite simple. There is no case here and this matter should be immediately dismissed." The lawyer reached into the next chair and retrieved his coat and briefcase, expecting, it appeared, that the meeting was about to be ended.

"Excuse *me,*" Galen intervened. "But by the chief's own statements after the crash, there is every reason to believe that department policy was violated."

Clearing his throat and twisting left and right to inch himself forward as he spoke, Perry continued.

"In Mr. Nordstrom's report to the sheriff's department afterward, he stated that he saw four teenagers get into a car parked along the highway, *and gave chase!* We have to assume that the *chase* was not a Sunday afternoon drive."

"But the fact was, the kids *were* fleeing. Trying to get away." It was Georgia Brackett who interrupted this time to the plup, plup, plup of the eraser end of her pencil tapping on the table. "Doesn't that demand that any law enforcement officer should exercise whatever means necessary to make an apprehension?"

"Absolutely not!" Galen replied coolly through a three-quarter shake of his head. "This involved four teenagers leaving a beer party that got raided. The police chief was not chasing some bank robbers who had just killed a teller or something." He tossed a cold glance in McCarver's direction before returning a confident look to each of the commissioners.

"Derek Nordstrom knew at least one of those youngsters before he ever got into his squad car to give chase. There was more than enough daylight left and he was close enough that he could see all four of the teenagers clearly. At the very *most,* all he had to do was get close enough to get the license plate number. He could have easily picked the kids up at home later. They certainly weren't going to flee the state just to keep from getting busted for underage drinking."

"And that's precisely what Chief Nordstrom was doing. Following the car," McCarver burst in with a wave of dismissal, not looking at anyone in the room. "I doubt we'll ever know what made that young man swerve into the ditch."

"Then what are the extra set of skid marks from?" Press erupted, nearly launching himself from the chair. Galen reached out a hand to hold the publisher in place.

"Who knows?" McCarver shot back, a sneer parting his lips as he stared at Press. "Those marks could have been made anytime. Somebody trying not to hit an animal or something."

Ed Delaney gave a soft rap, rap of the gavel and asked that matters be discussed more civilly.

"Mr. Perry, how can you be sure the other tire tracks were made by Chief Nordstrom?" Georgia wanted to know.

"Well, Mr. McGinn and Sport Henry from the *Gazette* were out there the next day taking photographs. Mr. Williams took additional photos later. Those pictures clearly show two sets of tracks."

"Those marks could have been made weeks earlier," McCarver barked.

"Elliott, you'll have your chance," Delaney hushed with another rap of the gavel.

"We're also confident," Galen continued through an icy stare at his counterpart, "that rubber samples gathered by criminal investigators at the scene will match the tires on the chief's squad car."

Delaney casually directed his gavel at McCarver for a response.

"Seems to me, Mr. Chairman, that you ought to wait then until you have further evidence from the crime lab." McCarver flipped a wave from his fingers before leaning his head onto his hand, his arm resting on the back of the chair next to him.

The chairman aimed the gavel back to Galen.

"We still contend that the chief knew precisely who was in the car and that there was no need for a chase at all," Perry asserted. "Without the irrational rush to pursue those kids, they quite possibly would never have reached speeds that would have resulted in a crash with fatalities or injury. We believe that Derek Nordstrom's actions were reprehensible and indefensible."

"You've heard my arguments," McCarver shrugged. "They don't have a case."

Ed Delaney banked a glance in each direction at his colleagues and, gathering no indication of further questions, thanked the audience and announced that the commission would be going into closed session for the balance of the evening.

Outside the municipal building the three shuffled in an uneasy triangle as they waited silently for Elliott McCarver to pass.

"Gentlemen," he said with a formal smile as he hurried by.

Press with his hands stuffed in his pants pockets, Barry and Galen with arms folded across their chests, simply nodded and allowed their eyes to accompany Nordstrom's lawyer to his car.

"So, what do you think?" Press asked when McCarver was gone.

"Hard to say," Galen replied, hunching his shoulders in the cool night air, his breath wafting ghostly into the night away from the light above the city hall doors. "Delaney's with us, I'd bet. Probably French, too. Georgia's not. I can never figure where she's coming from. Gordon and Davis are simply hard for me to read. I can't pick up on their body language."

"I'd say they'll probably split," Barry offered. "Davis almost always votes on the side of employees in any kind of job complaint. He's heavy into the county employees' union. The only thing that might make his vote different this time is the fact that Nordstrom's position is administrative." He tucked his note pad into his pocket before zipping his jacket and jamming his hands into his pants pockets for warmth.

"Gordon almost always supports management. In this case, that would be the city, of course," McGinn finished with.

"In all honesty, I can't see them firing Nordstrom yet," Galen said, turning his upper body first to Press, then to Barry and back to straight forward. "I think the only real argument McCarver had was to wait until the trial gives them conclusive information."

"So what can they do to him?" Press wondered, question marks arching his eyebrows. "They've already suspended him."

"With pay," Barry inserted.

"That's probably the commission's most likely option at this point," Perry speculated. "Suspend him now *without* pay for some period. Maybe until the trials are over, assuming there's no plea bargaining in the meantime."

Abby had on the blue, medium flannel nightgown that she always retrieved from her lower dresser drawer around the first of October, regardless of whether the weather yet said fall or clung to late summer. She was in bed already when Press came in, braced on one elbow and reading the hard cover version of *The Bridges of Madison County.*

"Any good?" Press was only half curious. The other side of his brain was still back at city hall as he hung his tie in the closet and dropped his shirt and trousers to the floor.

"A lovely romance," Abby said through a smile as she tucked the paper cover flap to save her place and laid the book on the nightstand. "As usual, better than the movie. As much as I like Clint Eastwood, I kept seeing Sport Henry playing the photographer in the movie. The image was just too incongruous."

She giggled as she sat up, folding her arms across her knees as she watched her husband disrobe.

"So, did the police and fire commission do anything tonight?"

Press sat on the edge of the bed to pull his socks off and his undershirt.

"Nah, not while we were there, at least. They went into closed session after Galen stated our case. We waited around for almost an hour and decided they might go past midnight debating, so we left. We'll find out in the morning." Abby shut the bedstand light off as he slid under the covers. "We're not sure what they'll do, if anything. They might just suspend him from his pay as well as his job, Galen thinks. Maybe until the court cases are settled anyway."

Abby snuggled closer and draped her arm across his chest, lightly toying her fingers through the thin copse of hair that grew there as she stared at the shadowy figure of her mate. It was her signal that she was hungry for marital satisfaction. Though she was almost always an eager and willing partner, it was Press who most often initiated their sexual escapades. In more than two decades together, Abby had never ventured further than a playful finger romp through his chest hairs to invite sex between them. In those rare instances when he did not respond, she simply fell asleep in that position, usually long after he did.

This night, Press rolled to meet her and began gently massaging her already stiffened nipples. Abby squirmed closer to kiss his forehead and lips. In moments they were a pair tangled in passion and twisted bedcovers. When she had completed her norm of three modest eruptions and he exploded with his usual vigor, they lay quietly for long minutes to recapture a steadier breath cycle and heart rate.

Finally Abby got up and went into the bathroom. When she re-opened the bathroom door, in the light that filtered into the bedroom she could see that Press had put on a clean pair of briefs and was lying on top of the sheets, his head propped on the pillow against the headboard. She turned off the light and crawled across the covers to nuzzle her head into the crook of his neck and shoulder.

"Do you ever think about us having another baby?" she posed after a time, a touch of melancholy filtering through the words.

"*Think* about it? Yeah, I suppose." Press clapped a hand lightly over the hand she laid on his belly. "But I'd never give it any serious consideration. I don't think I could go through that…this…any of it again."

Abby cranked her head a notch off his shoulder and looked at the dark silhouette of her husband's face.

"Why not?" It was a curious question, not a disturbed one.

"Abby, I think about the girls all the time now and it scares the heck out of me. It terrifies me, worrying about what if something happens to them. Thoughts like that crossed my mind occasionally when Jeremy was alive. I just never lingered on them. Now I worry about every little thing that Kate and Cassie do. I don't want to go through another child's whole life with that kind of fear in me. Maybe it's irrational, but I can't help it.

Besides," he said, kissing the top of Abby's head, "I'm probably too old to be starting over now, anyway. And I don't really want to be staring into my seventies when one of our kids graduates from high school and college."

"I suppose I'd feel the same way in the end," she conceded. Then with an affectionate pat, pat on his stomach and kiss on the cheek, she added, "But you're *not* too old. You'd make a great daddy and someday you'll be a terrific grandpa."

"The latter I can still wait a bit for." His hmmfph came out more like a small chuckle.

There was no more conversation between them and they fell asleep awkwardly bundled around each other. The next morning Press had a stiff neck.

44

Press was more than two miles into his morning run when rain began to fall. It was misty at first but it quickly turned to a steady volley of small, pickle-colored water bombs that splattered widely when they burst about him. In barely a dozen sloggy strides he was thoroughly drenched, the splash down his face blurring the brilliant autumn hues into a puddle of pastels, like thin watercolors running off a canvas. He gave passing consideration to dashing through some alleys in order to shorten the distance home but decided he was already so wet that it would offer little benefit to quit early.

Behind him, a car slowed to match his pace as he neared an intersection, but Press didn't notice through the downpour. Then, a mere two strides from the curb, he heard the engine rev and through a sideways glimpse saw the car start to turn down the side street he was about to cross. He tried to stop.

Momentum carried Press into the street where he threw out his hands to keep his body from slamming into the side of the auto as it passed. The motion of the car speeding by when his hands hit the door panel spun him around and sent him sprawling backwards in its wake, the pavement scraping his soggy sweatpants off his buttocks.

"Sonofabitch," was all he could muster without time to give it more artistic consideration. Press jumped up immediately, yanking up his sweatpants as his eyes trailed after what he determined to be a gray Ford. Brake lights flashed and the car turned without signaling at the next corner. Through the blur of the rain he couldn't even tell how many people were in the car or the sex of its driver, much less make out the license plate.

Press turned and walked slowly across the street, checking himself out as he went. The only injuries he could find, other than the embarrassment of having his pants yanked nearly to his knees, were the red, skinless scrapes on his elbows and a mild case of road rash on the back of his lap. He didn't notice the ache until he began to rub them. The pain from the bruised and raw butt worked its way into his stride as he finished his run home.

"You look like a old barn cat that got caught in a storm at my grandfather's farm," Abby greeted with a laugh and a towel when Press stomped into the kitchen.

"I darned near became a cat of the road kill variety," he grumped as he grabbed the towel and mopped at the hair that hung limply about his head and then dabbed lightly at the skinned elbows.

"Oh, Honey, what happened?" The glow on Abby's face quickly extinguished when she saw that her husband was hurting. "Sit down. I'll get some iodine and some bandages and another towel."

"I'm not sure I want to sit, since I spent some time sliding on that end, too."

Her forehead furrowed deeper as she paused to look back at him a moment

Press dragged off his soggy running shoes without bothering to untie them. He left them and his socks on the kitchen floor and, still toweling, he proceeded after his wife toward their bedroom.

"What happened?" Abby wanted to know when she came out of the bathroom, her hands full of towel and body patching gear.

"I don't know," Press said, ducking himself out of his faded, gray, UW-Eau Claire sweatshirt. "Maybe I just wasn't paying attention. I nearly got hit by a car."

He tugged down his sweatpants and briefs and twisted half a turn to survey himself for posterior damage. Finding no visible dents or dings other than the red scrapes, he picked up his wet clothes and took them into the bathroom where he laid them across the side of the bathtub.

"It was almost like someone intentionally tried to run me over," Press told Abby when he went back into the bedroom.

She handed him some clean briefs and began tending to his scraped elbows.

"Could you see who it was?"

He shook his head and winced loudly when she applied the iodine.

"Oh, you big baby. It's not that bad," Abby scolded out of a smile.

"I might not have even seen it, only I'd swear he gunned his engine as he started around the corner. That's a unisex 'he'," Press added, giving the bandages a pat, pat as Abby finished. With an impish twinkle in his eyes, he finished, "Most likely it was a woman driver."

She gave him a playful swat on his bare bottom.

"Hey, that's right where I fell," he yowled half seriously.

"Any more smart remarks and I'll spank you harder next time, Big Boy." Abby poked a finger into the leftover round of his belly before heading back to the bathroom with the iodine and box of bandages.

"Wait till I'm not so bruised and I'll give you an hour to stop," he teased after her as he bounced one foot at a time into his briefs.

"Press, cut that out. The girls haven't left for school yet!" Abby said in a loud whisper from the bathroom door. She wore a frown but her eyes were smiling through it.

Cruiser's was unusually crowded for mid-morning and the waitresses had little time to parry insults with the six men who squeezed around the single table available to them.

"Boy, when you want a *little* service around here, that's all you get," Blaine Peterson said out of a sideways grin as the woman in a pink uniform set a mug of coffee in front of him. She replied only with a quick glare that would have knocked the green John Deere cap off the corner of his head if it had been a swat.

"You're lucky she didn't hand you that coffee in your lap, minus the mug," Wayne Boginoski quipped when she left.

"Would that be 'grounds' for a lawsuit, Galen?" Charlie Delaney, the local hardware store owner wanted to know.

Five sets of eyes rolled above a chorus of groans and Galen shook his head. "Not a case I'd want to take."

"Speaking of law cases, Ed tells me that Chief Nordstrom's been suspended *without* pay now," Charlie put in as he prepared to take a swig of coffee. It was Delaney's brother who chaired the Fremont Police and Fire Commission.

Press and Galen arched eyebrows at each other.

"What'd they get the little weasel for this time?" Gene Proctor wanted to know.

"Violatin' the city's high speed chase policy," Delaney replied as he darted a cautious look at Press and Galen.

"Result of the incident when Press' son was killed," Galen anted.

A quieter mood settled over the table like it had been suddenly isolated from the rest of the eating place.

"It's hard to believe the stuff they've got Nordstrom on would go on in a small place like Fremont." Lyman Dunnington gave a couple of wags of his head. "That kind of thing wouldn't surprise me if it happened in a big city."

"That's just it," Press countered. "It *is* small town stuff. He'd probably never have had the same opportunities in a big city."

"A guy like him would have been into something else, though," Delaney said, waving his empty coffee mug at the waitress across the room. "A turd's still a turd no matter where you dump it."

"I'm surprised Nordstrom's left you walkin' upright yet after everything you wrote about him in the last year," Blaine jabbed at Press with a grin following his words from under the bill of his cap.

"I'm not so sure he's not still out to get me," Press snorted, half a smile curling the corner of his lips as he held a hand over his coffee mug, signaling the waitress not to pour. Laughing at himself, he reported being nearly run down earlier in the morning and held out his bandaged elbows as proof for the others to see.

"Didn't get the license number?" Wayne asked.

"I take it you weren't up yet?" Press said, looking at Boginoski from under a furrowed brow. "It was raining cats and dogs. You couldn't have read Charlie's hardware store sign from half a block, much less a license plate. Besides, it happened so fast I was sitting on my butt in the middle of the street!"

"What kind of car was it? Derek's probably driving his wife's car now that he can't use the squad any more." Charlie was half joking.

"Gray, looked like a Ford," Press replied. "I couldn't tell you what year. Cars look so much alike these days that I have trouble telling them apart."

Charlie and Galen exchanged startled looks.

"I'm sure Nordstrom's wife's car is gray," Galen declared to a couple of nodding heads around the table. "I couldn't swear that it's a Ford, though."

"I think it is," Charlie said.

The others looked at Press, half expecting a distant rumble of thunder from the cloud that darkened his eyes in an instant.

"I really think we ought to file a complaint," Galen suggested.

Press sucked in air until his lungs could fill no more and let it out slowly through the puff of his cheeks. When he breathed next, the cloud on his face had lost its storm.

"Heck, I couldn't even swear that it wasn't my own fault," he said at last with a small turn of his hand and a shake of his head. Press scooted the chair back and dug both hands into his pants pockets as he pondered the half-empty coffee mug in front of him.

"Police and fire commission suspended Nordstrom without pay, now. Indefinitely," Barry said as he followed Press into his office.

"Yeah, I heard." Press hung his jacket on the peg behind the door and slumped into a chair in front of his desk. Barry occupied the other.

"They said they'd review the suspension when the outcome of the other charges against him are settled," Barry added.

"You don't happen to know for sure what kind of car Derek's wife has, do you?" Press asked as he leaned back in the chair, his fingers laced across the top of his head.

Barry exaggerated a shrug and widened his eyes. "I don't have the foggiest. Why?"

"Just curious." Press related his jogging incident once more.

"Why would Nordstrom try to pull something like that on you now?" Barry wondered when his boss finished. "He's facing criminal charges, not editorials. And I'm sure he couldn't possibly know that you're the one who turned the state boys loose on him for stealing from dead people."

"But now he's not getting paid," Press noted pensively. "I'm the one who filed the complaint with the police and fire commission, remember?"

"Yeah, but he's made good money all these years, not just from his police chief salary, but those properties he owns and whatever he stole," Barry said doubtfully as he turned his head a quarter. "He can't be hurting that bad. At least not yet."

"Depends on his lifestyle, I guess. More likely he's just really pissed now and would use any way he could to take it out on me." Press unlaced his fingers and let his arms drop to the sides of the chair. "After all, if you think about it, we did start his whole downfall."

"So what are you going to do about it?"

"Not much I *can* do, really." He stood up and rounded to the business side of his desk. "Besides, in all honesty I can't say that I shouldn't have looked closer before jogging into the street. All I was thinking about at the moment was the rain. It does seem awfully coincidental, though."

Evening after dinner found Press in the furnace room fumbling in the open panel behind his workbench. It was still there. He eased the package out of the wood frame and laid it on the bench where he stared at it a moment before unwrapping the cheesecloth. The gun was a little dusty but bore no signs of rust. He hefted it in his right hand and picked out a dial on the clothes dryer in the pistol's iron sights. Press laid the .45 back on the cheesecloth and placed a new box of cartridges next to it. He'd purchased them at the hardware store while in Parsons that afternoon. He wasn't sure which button to push in his mind that might tell him why he bought the shells. Protection in case Nordstrom came after him again? An option in case Nordstrom's trial went awry? Whatever the reason, Press had given in to an impulse. He let the questions drop. He wrapped the box of cartridges and the .45 together in the cheesecloth and replaced the package behind the workbench.

45 Winter had brawled itself out in Fremont. March winds came scrubbing in from the plains to scour the town, then the rains of April had rinsed new life into the small community and the rolling hills bounding it on three sides. The sycamores, maples and oaks were caped in green again, tulips and daffodils trimmed lawns twice-mowed already, and country roadsides were ablaze with paintbrush, black-eyed Susans, wild daisies and dandelions. The sights and sounds of birds wafted on the warm breezes, lifting spirits as new energy flowed through the streets of the community like an injection of caffeine.

But Press was restless. His pattern of sleep followed a schedule no more regular than the weather. It was most often interrupted by stormy fits and sometimes it seemed not at all inclined to submit to any nighttime accommodation. Days at the *Gazette* office left him often frustrated and irritable. He was prone to long afternoons at Water Tower Park when it wasn't raining and the common spark of imagination had abandoned his weekly columns.

The vision of Jeremy still haunted his father at almost every turn, but it was different now. In the first weeks and months Press was saddened and then angered over his son's death. Gloom, however, had since become an unspoken companion, like the drag of a heavy chain. It drained his energy and motivation as surely as a vacuum of the spirit. Press simply walked from one day into the next without elaboration. He took more interest in Abby and his daughters, trying to draw them closer, but it was a joyless endeavor. He regularly suffered from a conscious dread that some new tragedy might remove them from him as well. Press harbored only one anticipation with any kinship to enthusiasm.

Derek Nordstrom faced three separate court dates, but the earliest was still two months away. If the wheels of justice grind slowly, Press figured Nordstrom's train had been parked at a siding. It irritated him that the first two trials would be held in the Whelan County Courthouse in Avery. Galen assured him that moving the pair of trials to another county was to be expected. Still, Avery was eighty-five miles away. That meant getting motel rooms during each of them. Not many people from Fremont would likely attend. Press wanted people to see for themselves what a sleaze the suspended police chief really was.

Nordstrom faced the theft charges first. Barry would cover that trial by himself. Press and Abby, along with the Kelsos and Moores, planned to attend the negligent homicide trial which was to follow a week later.

A civil trial was slated for August in Parsons. Galen had filed lawsuits against Nordstrom personally, the City of Fremont, and the county on behalf of the families of the three young people killed in the car crash as well as DeDe Daniels. The suits asked for a million and a half dollars from Nordstrom and from each of the municipalities. If successful, each of the parties would receive four and a half million dollars in damages.

After taking some time to heel his aches and bruises, Press was running again, daily now but always on the alert for a gray Ford. He'd seen a similar car around town on occasion but he could never be sure it was the one that had nearly ground him into pavement texture the previous fall.

He also had seen Alma Nordstrom on a couple of occasions; once in Kmart and once while picking up some groceries for Abby. Like her husband, Alma was smallish. But where Derek was angular and bony, she was frail and slightly stooped. Her iron-gray hair was cropped short and drooped loosely over her ears, and she had a flatish nose that struggled to hold up her rimless glasses. Press thought she looked worn out for as long as he had been aware of who she was. In a pair of decades they had never spoken.

Even before she spotted Press, her eyes were downcast, her movements edgy and hurried. Their glances encountered by chance both times and hers was gone in an instant. If she had other purchases to make, she forgot them. Alma Nordstrom had gone directly to a checkout counter, paid for her purchases and left immediately. Press found himself somewhere between bemused at her reaction to him and sad for her. He simply could not imagine the woman having the character or motivation to either confront Derek or involve herself in any of her husband's activities. She was probably terribly ashamed and embarrassed.

Neither Press nor anyone he spoke with had seen Derek Nordstrom since being relieved, temporarily at least, of his duties at the police department. No one seemed to know whether he had holed up in his house or taken up temporary quarters elsewhere.

Four days before the Memorial Weekend Press received a call from Jarred Kleinmeier.

"Just thought you'd want to know that we're requesting that misconduct in office charges be brought against Wes Hartley," he told Press. "I expect that the formal request will go to your district attorney in the next week or two."

Kleinmeier went on to note that Hartley was one of only four shareholders in ADN Properties. In the state attorney's words, Hartley had clearly used his position to gather information that would both enhance his real estate business and amass considerable wealth through his corporate venture with the Nordstroms and Susan Parker.

"What's the price he'll pay if he's convicted?" Press asked.

"The max is five years in prison and a ten thousand dollar fine on each count." The state attorney indicated that he wouldn't expect major jail time, however. He said he'd seen maximum fines in some cases but jail time was limited to a year or two, often with early parole.

"At this point, though, I'd say that Hartley's definitely the one in deepest pig shit in this particular situation," Kleinmeier noted. "Not only is he facing misconduct charges, but he'll likely lose his realtors license as well. *And,* if some smart lawyer catches onto it, he might encourage the previous owners of the properties involved to file lawsuits against him for the difference in the real value of their holdings and what Hartley and ADN bought them for."

"Can't the previous owners go after the other shareholders, too?" Press was curious.

"No, just the realtor who misrepresented the value or withheld information that might affect future values," Kleinmeier declared. "Speaking of the other shareholders, unless one of them will break down – and no one's come close yet in our interviews with them – none of them will likely face any legal recrimination in these particular cases. In fact, we may never know all or any of the details about how ADN got hold of the Gunderson property. We can't find any record of money changing hands. Wilma Gunderson, as you know, is incapable of giving us any information and she has no living relatives. All we could get out of the ADN group is that she *gave* 'em the farm. Unless we can find a way to prove that Hartley or the chief used undue influence on her by power of their positions, we can't get them for anything on that one."

He said the Gunderson deal would be part of the misconduct charge against Mayor Hartley, however, since he used his office to get city sewer and water to the property so it could be developed by ADN as a subdivision.

"Is there any reason why we can't do a story about the expected charges now, or interview Hartley?" Press asked.

"Not that I can think of. Go for it," Kleinmeier answered. "Oh, and before I forget it, there is another little twist that might interest you."

He paused for effect.

"Hartley's wife, Sharon, and Susan Parker are sisters!"

As soon as the conversation ended, Press called Barry into his office.

"Major news break in the offing," he announced when the editor was seated across from him. Press had one of those 'have-I-got-a-story-for-you' looks tattooed on his face that triggered the curiosity key in Barry.

It took nearly a quarter of an hour to lay out the details of his conversation with the man from the attorney general's office. Barry held an open-mouthed grin somewhere between smug confirmation and amused surprise throughout his boss' revelations.

"Most of this stuff we had a pretty good idea of," Press summed up with. "But there is an interesting twist that puts a few things in a new light." As Kleinmeier had done to him, he kept Barry waiting a moment. McGinn's head chucked forward in anticipation.

"Sharon Hartley and Susan Parker are *sisters*!"

Barry's eyes went from teacups to saucers. His surprise was followed by a snickering sort of laugh.

"I guess that explains why Mrs. Hartley apparently forgave the mayor and came back from Minneapolis," he exclaimed. "It's probably hard enough to break up a family by marriage, but even harder when it also means breaking up a family by blood."

Press leaned back and meshed his fingers across the back of his head.

"Yeah, and you throw a business bond in there, too, and things can really get messy."

"Is this stuff for the paper, yet?"

Press nodded. "You bet. Kleinmeier says we can state that charges are expected to be filed in the next week or so. I say invite Hartley in for an interview." With a smug grin he added, "Assuming he'll agree to the interview, I'd like to sit in on it when you talk to him."

"I'll get on it right away." Barry stood and tapped four fingers on the publisher's desk as he turned to leave.

Mayor Hartley arrived at the newspaper promptly at eight o'clock the next morning. Barry ushered him into the publisher's office and closed the door behind them. There were handshakes and an exceptionally brief exchange of pleasantries as seating took place.

"So, what do you fellas want to talk about this morning?" Hartley asked. His smile echoed on and off again several times as he fingered the end of his necktie.

"We'd like to ask you about your dealings with ADN Properties," Barry opened with a plain face.

Hartley straightened immediately.

"I've…uh…represented them a few times, I guess. Through my real estate office. Why?"

"We understand that you're also a shareholder in the company," Barry said.

"Who told you that?" Now the mayor was shifting the knot of his tie and glancing from editor to publisher and back.

"We're just trying to find out," the editor dodged.

"Well, I don't think that's any of your damned business!" Hartley's ears shaded crimson under his sprayed-in-place black hair.

"We think it's very much the public's business to know if the mayor is using his office to line his pockets," Barry said evenly.

"Listen, I don't know who the hell you've been talking to, and I sure as hell don't know what you're talking about!" His fingers were squeezed around the arms of the chair as he spoke. "Apparently, you've been hearing some goddammed lies!"

"Has anyone from the attorney general's office talked to you about your involvement with ADN Properties?" McGinn pursued.

Trying to look surprised, Hartley denied talking to anyone about any involvement in the property investment company.

"Let's cut to the chase here," Press inserted. "Wes, we've been in contact with the attorney general's office. We know that you're probably facing misconduct in office charges within a week or so. We're offering you a chance to give us your side of the story before we print it."

Hartley wilted like two-day-old lettuce. He said nothing for a long moment, two fingers pursed to his lips and staring sideways into the wall, perhaps hoping to find some secret passage for escape there.

"I think it's best if you talk to my attorney from now on." The mayor pushed himself out of the chair to leave.

"Who would that be?" Barry inquired.

"I don't have one yet."

"Wes, we can see how you got involved with your sister-in-law in this," Press probed, "but how did you manage to tie up with the Nordstroms?"

Hartley looked down at Press like a man expecting the next punch might surely send him to the floor. He walked to the door and rested a hand on the knob.

"The chief and I…uh…I guess we've been friends for a long time. Anything else," he said with a quick turn to face Press, then Barry, "you can find out from my lawyer." With that he opened the door and disappeared quickly out the front of the office.

"Well, did we learn anything new?" Press asked when the mayor was gone.

"Not anything more than we could have expected, I guess," Barry replied, his head tilted left a bit.

Press puffed a long exhale through the amen gather of his hands. Dropping one set of fingers over the knuckles of the other, he rested his chin on the fold and surmised, "I guess you have all you need for a story. I don't think it's worth trying to talk to any of the other three."

"Probably not," Barry concurred, lifting himself out of the chair. "I doubt they'll talk to us at all anyway, but I'll try, just for the record." At the door, he turned back with a parting idea. "I think I'll call Dick Flater, too. See if he has any thoughts or reaction."

Half an hour later, Barry was back at the publisher's door.

"Flater says he's surprised and yet he isn't," McGinn reported. "Says he was always kind of curious about some of the deals but thought Hartley was too smart to get himself into anything illegal."

"Did Dick give you any idea of how the city council will respond?" Press wondered.

"There probably won't be any formal action before the trial, assuming there is one," Barry replied. "They can probably ask for his resignation but they don't really have grounds until the matter's legally settled. The old 'innocent until proven guilty' concept."

"I kind of wonder if Hartley won't resign on his own, whether or not it goes to trial," Press speculated.

"Hard to say," Barry offered with a shrug. "He doesn't have a lawyer, yet. He might even end up pleading guilty or no contest."

When the *Gazette* broke the story about the mayor's self-dealing in real estate through his business involvements, the reaction whirled darkly through Fremont like a spring twister. Calls and letters flooded the newspaper office expressing shock that such activity would take place in a small community like Fremont, many adding a demand for the mayor's immediate ouster or resignation.

Before the round of dice for the coffee tab it was the only topic of conversation among the large coffee crowd at Cruiser's on Thursday morning.

"I always thought Fremont was kind of a sleepy place," Bernie Randazzo commented. "Until the Nordstrom matter, and now Hartley, I don't think we ever had more than some minor burglaries and a few marijuana busts."

"Hartley probably felt the same way," Lyman Dunnington offered. "Figured nobody would ever notice."

"How'd he ever get caught? I mean, how did anybody ever have a reason to start digging into the matter?" asked Gene Proctor.

"I guess I'd have to say that we started it. Our interest was based on something you told me awhile back," Press offered with a nod toward the retired farmer. "When we started trying to find out how the Gunderson farm changed hands, we started coming up with more questions than answers. After we uncovered more purchases by ADN Properties, all involving Hartley as the realtor, we became suspicious of his part in the scheme. Then when municipal projects started showing up around those properties, we put two and two together and called the attorney general's office with the information. They took it from there."

"Regardless of how this turns out, I'll bet Hartley's out come November," Randazzo said with a self-assured nod.

"Wonder who'll run for mayor then?" It was Dunnington wondering.

"Flater for sure," Galen asserted.

"How about Ed?" Bernie asked Charlie, referring to the Delaney brother who chaired the police and fire commission.

"I honestly don't know if he has that kind of ambition," Charlie said over a shrug.

"Whoever it is, I bet they'll be watched closely for a long time after this mess," Dunnington observed.

"Wonder if you'll have a new police chief by then?" Blaine snorted.

Bernie set his empty coffee mug back on the table. "As far as I'm concerned they could throw a rope over a big sycamore limb and hang Hartley and Nordstrom from each end of it," he said scornfully.

There were nods and shrugs and grunts around as Blaine stood to retrieve the dice box. Charlie lost and paid the coffee tab for the second day in a row, grumbling all the way to the cash register and out the door.

The following week Wes Hartley was formally charged with twelve counts of criminal misconduct in office, carrying a maximum penalty of five years in prison and a ten thousand dollar fine on each count.

46

The family's second graduation party in a year, Kate's gathering again overflowed the house and the lawns, front and back. Still, the tone was more subdued as guests, particularly the adults, were cautious, uncertain of how the lingering presence of Jeremy's memory might weigh on the Williamses. They were careful not to broach the subject.

Jeremy was very much in the thoughts of Press and Abby. They were sure, too, that both Kate and Cassie were mindful of their brother's graduation a year earlier, but neither made mention of it as the weekend approached. Not until the ceremony on Saturday morning when Kate, as valedictorian, gave her speech.

As she approached the end of her remarks she paused, staring at the pages trembling in her hands as they rested on the podium. Then, raising her head to let her gaze travel slowly around the audience, her lips quivered and in a cracking voice she continued.

"As you know, this has been a very difficult year for me and for my family. It was…it was a little less than a year ago that I…lost my brother. I loved him so very much. Jeremy's unflinching cheerfulness…his kindness…in spite of our brother-sister squabbles…he was always my inspiration. I've personally dedicated this year, my scholarships and the honors I've received to his memory.

"We leave here today full of hope and anticipation. I ask you to please remember Jeremy Williams. He was with us such a short time. He can be an example to all of us. Lead our lives with daily cheer. Fill them with kindness. Live each day to the fullest. Because, despite all our best hopes and expectations, our time can be so short. Thank you." Her last words choked out as barely more than a hoarse whisper as Kate grabbed her notes and fled back to her seat.

Though the principal returned quickly to the podium, long moments elapsed before he could gather himself enough to continue the program.

Cassie was sobbing hard and Abby hugged her close. Press circled an arm around Abby and tears flooded both their faces. Around the auditorium not many eyes were dry.

When the ceremony ended, blue graduation caps were launched into the air like a squadron of square Frisbees as cries of joy and farewells and hugs were passed throughout the crowd.

When Casey Delaney brought Kate home so she could get ready for the afternoon party, Press met her in the hallway. He wrapped his arms around her tightly and held her in silence for a time. Leaning back finally, he gazed down at her, tears welling behind his eyelids, and whispered, "I'm so happy to have you as my daughter. I'm very, very proud of you."

"Thanks, Dad. I love you." She kissed his cheek and pulled away to her bedroom to change.

The party was still going strong at three in the afternoon. Press had just carried two more cases of Pepsi up from the basement and dumped them into tubs of ice before dumping his exhausted body into one of the lawn chairs on the patio. Benton Cassidy dragged a folding chair over and plopped it down beside Press.

"So what's Kate going to do this fall?" he asked cheerfully.

"Going to the University of Kansas to study architecture," Press replied with a satisfied smile.

“What happened to accounting?” the doctor posed.

“Decided she’d rather build things, I guess.”

"Full scholarship?" Benton asked.

Press nodded, his head and chest swelling with noticeable pride. The smile on his face changed to plain as he gazed at the two sets of fingers twined around one knee.

"What a sibling rivalry that could have been," he sighed. "One kid at Missouri, the other at KU."

An awkward quiet spilled between them as Benton put a hand on Press' shoulder and gave it a squeeze and a nudge.

"She already knows who her roommate will be. A girl named Vicki from Rifle, Colorado," Press turned the subject lighter, the corner of his mouth abutting another smile.

"Well, they ought to get a bang out of each other," Cassidy punned wryly and they shared a clumsy laugh.

"Becky Hartley was at Casey's party yesterday," Kate announced at dinner on Monday night. "She said she and her mom are moving to Minneapolis again. Leaving today."

"That's too bad," Abby said as she passed the casserole dish to her husband.

"Yeah, I guess her college plans are pretty much up in the air right now," Kate continued as she readied a fork full of beans to her mouth.

"Did she have plans to go any place in particular?" Press asked.

"Mmm," Kate grunted to allow time to swallow. "She'd been accepted at Creighton, but she doesn't have any scholarships. Now Becky doesn't know if her dad can pay that much. She's going to look into Mankato State and maybe Eau Claire."

"Why not the University of Minnesota? It's right there in the Twin Cities," Abby wondered.

"Too big," said Kate. "She's pretty much a small town girl at heart. Me, too." She grinned at her mother, her lips pursed to keep the next load of casserole from exploding out of her mouth.

"What about you, Cass?" Press queried. "The next four years are going to pass awfully fast. Any ideas on where you want to go to college yet?"

Cassie gave an almost vigorous shake of her straight blond hair and kept her silence.

"I think Cassie wants to be the first woman second baseman for the Kansas City Royals," Kate said with a teasing grin at her sibling.

Cassie squished her lightly freckled nose in return.

"There's nothing wrong with that that I can see," Press responded with a mild shrug and raised eyebrows.

Abby rolled her eyes at her husband and kinked a frown onto her face. Cassie continued to add nothing verbal to the dinner talk until she had finished eating.

"I have softball practice. May I be excused?"

Abby nodded.

"I wish you wouldn't encourage her so much," she grumped at Press when Cassie was gone. "All she's said about high school so far is how she wants to go out for basketball and softball and can't make up her mind between volleyball and cross country."

"What's so bad about that? As long as she keeps her grades up," Press scooted his chair back and stared in mild amusement at his wife.

"She needs to start thinking about being more lady-like sometime." Abby dabbed her mouth with her napkin and stuffed it back onto her lap.

"Don't worry, Mom. Cassie will do fine," Kate said with a broad smile and a pat, pat, pat on her mother's forearm as she shoved her chair back. "I'm going to Casey's. I'll be home before midnight."

"I certainly hope so. You have to be at work at eight in the morning," Abby reminded after her. Kate had gotten a summer job working as a checker at Casey's father's hardware store.

"I know, Mom," she called over her shoulder as she bounced out the front door.

"I get so scared any time either of those two is out of my sight," Abby cried softly.

"I think about that a lot, too." Press stood up and rounded the corner of the dining table to rub his wife's shoulders.

"Do you think getting her that car was the right thing to do?" she asked, reaching back to put a hand on his. Press had finally taken the Cavalier to Caravello's Used Cars shortly before Christmas. Just two weeks ago, he had taken Kate back to let her choose her own car to complete the trade. Kate picked a practical, two-year-old, burgundy, Dodge four-door. It cost Press an additional three thousand dollars but he had no qualms about the selection.

"Of course." He bent down and kissed the top of her head. "We have to turn her loose sometime."

Minutes before twelve that night they twice heard the gentle squeak of the front door as it opened and closed before Kate quietly padded to her room. It was their unspoken ritual for nearly a year. No soft kck, kck, kck's from Press or settled quiet breathing from Abby until both girls were safely home.

A week later, Wes Hartley and Barry McGinn were sitting in front of Press' desk shortly after lunch. Hartley sagged in the chair like a man who had just been thoroughly beaten.

"I...uhm...just came in to let you know...I'm quitting," he said without looking up, pawing at the unpressed creases of his trousers. "I'm announcing my resignation at the start of the council meeting tomorrow night. Flater can run the meeting."

"I'm sorry things had to turn out this way," Press offered matter of factly, although he wasn't sure that was his true feeling. He found it hard to really feel sorry for the man. Hartley had fouled his opportunities and his life so completely.

"Have you found a lawyer yet?" Barry asked.

The mayor shook his head slowly. "I haven't had the energy." He rested his elbow on the chair arm and braced his head between his thumb and fingers. Something between a gasp and a sob burst from his mouth and his shoulders bounced up and down as he began to sob hard.

"God, I've fucked things up so bad," Hartley cried somewhat just short of wailing.

Press and Barry shifted in their seats and echoed glances from each other to Hartley and back again, not certain as to what to do or say. In the end they did neither, although Press did retrieve the box of tissues from a lower drawer once more and slide it across the desk toward the mayor.

Hartley ignored the gesture. After a time the sobbing subsided and he palmed his red eyes. He dragged a handkerchief from his hip pocket and wadded it into each eye. Sucking in a deep breath of resolve, he stood slowly and pushed the handkerchief back into the pocket.

"Do me one last favor," he said as he moved toward the door. Press and Barry checked each other's looks and glanced up at him in anticipation. "When you write the story, please just tell people how deeply sorry I am. My wife and daughter especially. I'm sorry for everything." And he left.

"Do you think he's okay?" Barry asked when they were alone.

"I don't know. He didn't sound good," Press said as he rotated his chair to look out the window to see if Hartley had parked on the side street. He wasn't there.

"What do you think we can do? Is there something we should do?" Barry was wondering.

"I don't know. Call somebody maybe. His wife is in Minneapolis." Press turned back to his desk. "Might call the police or a doctor. I just don't know. Maybe we could wait and see how he is at the council meeting tomorrow night."

In the end they did nothing.

Friday morning Barry came slowly into Press' office and closed the door behind him. His banana smile was turned upside down.

"Wes Hartley was found dead in his garage two hours ago," he reported as he slumped into a chair, his shoulders sagging like someone who carried heavy weights in each hand. "He'd been there awhile. Everything was closed up. The car had finally run out of gas."

"Awww shit." Press sagged with an anvil of guilt that suddenly dropped on his shoulders. "We should have called somebody. Dammit, we should have called somebody." His head was shaking slowly at an angle.

"Yeah, but who?" Barry returned with a sad shrug.

"Hell, anybody. The police! They would have at least known some way to respond."

They sat a long time without speaking. Barry stared at the hands folded into his lap. Press, elbow on the desk and his chin buried into the palm of his hand, gazed blankly straight ahead.

"I need to get out of here for awhile," Press decided finally. "Take the rest of the day off if you need to."

Barry simply shrugged and said nothing.

Press went home.

"Press, what's the matter?" The question worried on Abby's face as she came up from the basement and saw her husband slouched in the big armchair. "You're *never* home this early!"

"Wes Hartley killed himself." The inside of Press' mouth was so dry he couldn't have worked up even a small spit and the words tumbled out like loose gravel.

"Oh, my," she said as she sat down on the edge of the sofa and began to toy with the elastic on the front of her sweatshirt. "That's too bad."

"I should have done something."

Abby's face skewed in a small puzzle.

"When he came to my office Monday to tell us he was quitting as mayor, Barry and I both could see that he wasn't in good shape. We even talked about it afterward. Why the hell didn't I do something about it?" His head wavered slowly from side to side and he pounded his fist lightly on the arm of the chair.

"Honey, what could you do?" Abby asked, leaning forward, her elbows on her knees.

"I could have called *somebody*. I *should* have called somebody. I don't know." He wiped his hand down his face and looked sadly at Abby. "I didn't feel too sorry for him at the time. I mean, he did make his own nest. But nobody should go out like that. Not kill himself."

Neither could think of much else to say.

"I feel so badly for Becky," Abby said finally. "That poor girl."

Press pursed his lips and nodded a fraction.

He spent the rest of the day at home, moping, finding little to do. The weekend differed not much from Friday.

The mayor's funeral was held on Monday. Press and Abby and Barry and Angie McGinn occupied a pew near the back of the church. They were a sizeable portion of those in attendance.

Sharon Hartley sat together with her daughter and her parents in a front pew. Becky's shoulders jounced sharply to the uneven rhythm of her sobs. Sharon's tears had been spent some time back. If Mrs. Hartley had any emotions left, none leaked out. Her sister, Susan Parker, sniffled quietly and sat in a pew on the other side of the church, two rows behind Wes' mother and father. The elder Hartleys had driven up from their home in the Ozarks. Derek and Alma Nordstrom sat by themselves near the middle but far to the right. Derek fixed his gaze on some unspecified point at the front of the church and never wavered from it. It was the first time Press or Barry had seen the suspended police chief in several months. In the rest of the church were a scattering of city officials, the employees from Hartley's real estate office, and a few friends.

Press wondered at the scarce attendance. Though he had opened a large box of troubles for himself, still Hartley had been mayor for nearly a dozen years. Ultimately, Press decided that people stayed away, simply not knowing what else to do. It was, it seemed to him, almost as if folks thought that coming to the man's funeral might in some way convey acceptance of what he had done. Or somehow incriminate themselves as accomplices. Even Press had given passing consideration to skipping the funeral. But he had avoided Wes when Hartley all but screamed at him for help as surely as if he had been bobbing helplessly in a river. He could not bring himself to stay away from this. Though it was in no way any sort of redemption, Press could not keep away this time.

When the service ended, the congregation stood and funeral director Pat Coughlin ushered the six pallbearers and the casket back down the aisle. They were followed by Sharon and Becky Hartley; Becky still sobbing and hugged to her mother; Sharon somber, looking neither left nor right. The rest of the family came next. As those remaining began to file into the aisles, Press briefly caught Derek Nordstrom's look. Derek menaced a glower at the publisher as if to ignite him, then hurried his wife out a side door and was not seen again.

Barry had spied the look as well. He glanced at Press and each thought about smiling but stopped short. A smile didn't suit their emotions at the time.

Outside the couples stopped briefly in front of the church to chat with Dick Flater and his wife. Press involved himself with only half his brain. The other half focused his stare over Flater's shoulder at the playground beside the church, which served as a parking lot during services. There he could see the heads of the Nordstroms moving among the cars. Press watched as the two parted around a car top and then disappeared beneath it. In a moment the car backed up, then proceeded toward the street. When the car emerged fully into view at the sidewalk it stopped before turning left into the street. Derek was driving. At the side of his stare, Press caught Barry looking at him and he looked back.

"The gray Ford?" McGinn asked. His eyes said he knew the answer already.

"I just wish I could prove it." Press let the words escape quietly through the near clench of his teeth.

"PRESSING MATTERS"
June 24

There is an ache in all of us to in some way care for the world, or so we tell the image in the mirror that stares back at us each morning. So why do we have so much trouble reaching out to one another in the merest of ways? Why do we draw lines where there are none; try to paint black and white where there is only gray; see need as a matter of choice? The consequence we create is indifference. In failing to define our responsibilities of the heart, we muddle in confusion and sometimes lives are lost or overwhelmed in the muddling….

47 In a surprise move, five days before his trial on theft charges was to begin, Derek Nordstrom changed his plea from not guilty to no contest and was sentenced to two years in prison.

The police and fire commission held an emergency meeting the following day and dismissed Nordstrom permanently. Deputy Sheriff Wayne Carter was chosen over the acting chief, Sergeant Bob Anderson, to fill the position.

Commission Chairman Ed Delaney later told Press off the record that the group felt new blood was needed in the department, leading them to bypass Anderson in favor of Carter. Besides Carter was well known and likeable and would bring plenty of law enforcement experience to the job.

"He's a good choice," Press agreed. "He's well respected and shows a lot of common sense in dealing with people." In the back of his mind, Press wondered with some amusement how long it would be before Mavis quit or retired. Somehow, he couldn't imagine working in an atmosphere less curmudgeonly than her crankiness demanded.

"As stubborn as the old sonofabitch is, the no contest plea surprised me," Wayne Boginoski acknowledged at coffee a few days later.

"I'd think it would be kind of hard to plead otherwise," Dunnington smirked. "Video cameras don't lie."

"He could be out in six months if he behaves himself," Galen entered as if teaching a course in law. "Besides, he's got more to worry about when the negligent homicide trial begins next week."

"Six months could be like six years to old Derek," Blaine suggested with a sly sideways glance. "Liable to be some boys in there gonna remember him. Teach him a whole new use for that skinny ass of his."

Snickers chorused around the table.

"So what's going to happen to him next week?" Dunnington pointed the question at Galen.

Perry glanced in turn at Press and shrugged non-commitally. "Those charges will be a bit tougher to prove. Unfortunately, there weren't any video cameras at the scene. Technically, he could face life in prison."

"But don't you have a lie detector test that proves the girl's telling the truth?" Wayne pressed.

"Yes, but it can't be used in court," Galen replied, drumming four fingers from each hand on the table. "The polygraph only confirmed for us that we have a case. We wouldn't have gone to the DA with it, nor would we pursue a civil suit, obviously, if we had any reason to believe that DeDe had made it all up."

"Press, for your sake I hope they hang the sonofabitch," said Charlie Delaney.

"That won't bring back my son," Press replied solemnly as he wagged the handle of the coffee mug back and forth on the table top. "I only hope there's some justice for what he's put us through."

A summer storm had rumbled through Fremont from the southwest during the night like an armored division on military exercises. There was a lot of boom and flash but the only real damage inflicted was on the town's sleep. Tornado watches had been issued but no funnel clouds were sighted. At mid-morning a thick bank of dark clouds still hung low over the area like oil smoke and pressed moist, heavy air onto everything living on the crust of earth beneath. The threat of storms was again in the forecast for the afternoon and evening.

Rest had not accompanied nighttime for either Press or Abby in several tries of late and the storm only served to further ward it off like an armed guard. Both took turns tossing and turning, reading, and alternating between the couch in the living room and the couch in the basement recreation room.

His shower had not refreshed him and three hours later Press still felt damp and heavy. Even with the Buick's air conditioner doing its best, their clothes clung to them like moist static as he and his wife drove toward Avery. Little conversation passed between them. Press had even turned off the radio and they rode together separated by their own lanes of thought.

This was the day Nordstrom's trial would begin on the negligent homicide charges. The morning would be taken with jury selection for the proceedings, which were expected to take at least the week. Press and Abby, along with the Daniels family, the Moores, and the Kelsos, would arrive after lunch for opening statements from the attorneys and possibly a first witness or two. A bloc of rooms had been reserved for them at the Super 8 on the outskirts of Avery.

Clouds of dread had been building up inside Press for days; clouds as dark as those that darkened the ride up from Fremont. He desperately wanted not to go through the details of Jeremy's death again, or to be reminded of the other families' pain either. He just wanted the matter to be ended. He wished the arrows of justice could somehow wound Nordstrom appropriately without the anguish of any trial. Press knew in his own mind that Derek was guilty even before the facts might be presented. Still, it worried him that Nordstrom might somehow go free. The Elliott McCarver factor was an unknown; McCarver considered the best defense attorney in a wide area. Who would the jury believe? Press thought again of his father's gun, the one he had tucked under the driver's side front seat of the Buick the night before. He didn't know if he would, or could. But he could see it in himself. It gave him another option. If the trial went wrong.

"I really feel badly for DeDe in all of this," Press said into the silence as the open farm country began to bump up against the outskirts of Avery. Rousted from her own depths, Abby looked expectantly at her husband.

"Schell's going to try to be as easy as possible, but McCarver won't hesitate to get down and dirty with her. He'll try to break her down. I hope she's ready."

"Is that really necessary?" Abby was looking past Press.

"It's his job I guess. I suppose I'd want him to if I were on the other end of the stick."

They checked into the motel and grabbed a quick lunch at the restaurant next door before heading downtown to the Whelan County Courthouse.

Four blocks off Main Street, the centenarian courthouse was a stately three-story structure of huge limestone blocks and white wood trim. A dull green dome sat atop the center of the building,

Press thought as though waiting for heaven to squeeze giant oranges on it. It occurred to him that the givers of human law always seemed to try to cathedralize their houses like there was some almighty correlation.

The Moores and Kelsos were waiting quietly at the edge of the rotunda when Press and Abby walked in. Del Schell was approaching from the other side of the circular room at the same time. Press was glad to see the district attorney had abandoned the rumpled look, at least temporarily, for one more courtly. He wore a sharp black suit over a light blue shirt and blue tie thinly striped in red.

First time I've ever seen his shoes polished, Press jotted inside himself.

The two looked at each other curiously. It was the look of truce at best, neither friendly nor hostile.

"I think we'll be okay with the jury," Schell informed them. A wry smile shaped out of his beard. "Seven men and five women. McCarver would have had all men if he could have. That's not sexist really," he quickly added with a glance bounced from one woman to the next and then the other. "It's just that men tend to be more law and order types. I think we have a good mix, though."

Schell touched Marie Kelso's elbow lightly and pointed toward the stairs. "The courtroom is on the second floor."

"Aren't we going to wait for Mr. and Mrs. Daniels and their daughter?" Bernadette Moore looked puzzled.

"They're coming a bit later," the district attorney said. "I want to save DeDe's entrance for the jury to see."

The door was on the side of the room and Schell ushered the trio of couples along the rail that separated the participants from the audience to a front row on the right hand side of the courtroom. Barry nodded at them from several rows back. He was seated with half a dozen other news types, the only others in the room, except for a man standing at a small television camera that was mounted on a tripod along the far wall.

Shortly, Derek and Alma Nordstrom entered, followed by Elliott McCarver. Derek and Elliott proceeded to the defendant's table and Alma sat directly behind them in the first row. While Elliott shuttled an 'almost' sort of grin at the three couples across the room, neither Nordstrom wavered their eyes from the front of the courtroom. McCarver's rumpled suit was a lighter version of the rumpled one he'd worn at the police and fire commission hearing last fall. His blonde-gone-old ivory hair wandered in several directions around his head as if combed randomly as a prank.

Derek's look was cold and unchanging, sculpted coarsely, it seemed, from a block of lake ice. He wore a beige sport coat and brown slacks. The shirt collar was open, no tie. His iron scruff of hair was combed but still bore a horseshoe crease from one ear around to the other from years of sitting a hat.

In a few moments after one-thirty, everyone stood and the judge entered from behind the bench. She was a forty-ish woman, large in her black robe, with medium-length auburn hair curled lightly in at the ends. A band around her neck secured large-lensed glasses with plastic frames that matched the color of her hair. When she had sat down and told Schell to proceed with his opening remarks, she immediately lifted the glasses off her nose and began lightly chewing the tip of the right wing. It was a habit she would continue regularly throughout the trial.

Del Schell nudged his chair back and stood to deliver his message straightforwardly, at times aiming his pencil or drumming it on the table to emphasize his points. He said simply that the prosecution would prove that Derek Nordstrom was a spiteful and vindictive man whose motive was retaliation over news stories and editorials printed in the *Fremont Weekly Gazette.* In attempting to arrest Jeremy Williams during a beer bust, he willfully, at a high rate of speed, pursued and forced the Kelso vehicle into a ditch, resulting in the deaths of three teenagers and the terrible injury and mutilation of a fourth.

When he was finished, Elliott McCarver strode over to the rail in front of the jurors, his forefinger pressed to his lips, and paused long enough to allow a whole new set of thoughts to enlighten him. When he lifted the finger from his lips at last, he thrust his hands together at the back of his jacket and began to pace back and forth before the jury.

"Ladies and gentlemen, I believe the prosecutor is entirely right." He stopped and tilted his head at the twelve quizzically. "This case *is* about retaliation! But *not* retaliation by Police Chief

Derek Nordstrom over some alleged media abuse, but retaliation directed from the families of those kids. They're hurt and grieving at the loss of three young people and the awful injuries to another. And we grieve and hurt with them. The loss of a child is a terrible, terrible thing.

"But we're going to offer you some facts...*facts,* ladies and gentlemen...that the prosecutor and the plaintiffs don't want to admit to. *Fact* number one," McCarver declared, the wave of a single finger counting in the air, "the four young men and women in question were at a beer party at a county park when the party was raided by law enforcement officers. They *had* been drinking, *illegally,* I might add, since they were all under the lawful drinking age.

"*Fact* number two," and he counted with two fingers held high this time, "they attempted to flee, at a high rate of speed, from an officer of the law. That, too, is illegal.

"And, *fact* number three," three fingers now aimed at the courtroom ceiling, "Police Chief Derek Nordstrom was simply doing his job. The job the public expects of him. The job the public *demands* of him.

"Finally, I expect we'll expose this case for what it's really all about. And that, ladies and gentlemen, is about *money.* You're going to be introduced to a little lady who has piled up lots of medical bills for her family. That's what this case is all about." McCarver raked his fingers over the top of his head, causing a swatch of hair to stand straight up above his forehead.

"They've talked her into coming up with this cockamamie story with the idea that eventually this is going to civil court where they can get some money to pay off those doctors' bills. And, in the doing, make the other parents a little richer to ease their grief."

With that he again folded his hands behind his ample seat, gave an unfriendly smile to the front row of the audience, and returned to his chair.

The district attorney called DeDe Daniels as his first witness.

The bailiff opened the courtroom door and motioned into the hallway. Seconds later, DeDe entered the room slowly, followed by her parents. The court became very quiet except for the shifting of bodies on wooden seats and the shuffle of fingers to lips to stifle the collective urge to gasp.

Dressed in a medium-length, green plaid skirt and light yellow, pullover blouse, DeDe limped distinctly like she wore a spike-heeled shoe on one foot and a loafer on the other. Jagged as the previous night's lightning bolts, a scar rippled from beneath the hemline of her skirt down the outside of her right leg to nearly her ankle. Her right arm swung uselessly at her side, the fingers gnarled as the tendons that made them function had been drawn back up inside her hand. What struck everyone in the courtroom most, however, was her face. A deep, red scar serrated the right side from the top of her forehead along the edge of her eye to the juncture of her lips. It curled her upper lip slightly and yanked the corner of her mouth tightly toward her eye, giving the girl a permanently startled look.

The elderly bailiff extended his arm uncertainly in case she needed assistance as he escorted her to the witness stand. She never took it. Wally and Veronica crossed the room and seated themselves next to Press and Abby.

The Williamses had not seen DeDe since that day in the hospital nearly two months after the crash. At that time she had been largely smothered in bandages and casts. Press looked at his wife. Tears had trickled down each cheek. He looked at the jurors and found that Abby was not alone. Even the judge was leaning forward, resting an elbow on the bench with a knuckle held discreetly under one eye.

After she had been sworn in and gave her name, Schell asked her, in her own words, to tell what happened on the night of the accident.

Slowly, methodically, DeDe looked at the jury as she had been coached and related the events of the evening. Mostly she held her emotions, although her voice cracked noticeably when she retold the part about the car rolling over.

Press gave sideways glances first at Wally and Veronica Daniels and then at the other parents. Each presented the same pose, jaws set, eyes focused straight ahead, emotions smoldering just below the veneer.

When she finished, the district attorney asked if she knew why Adam wouldn't stop when the police car came after them.

She said she didn't. "We were all yelling at him to stop but he wouldn't. He didn't say anything. He was sort of laughing and he just kept going."

Schell asked DeDe if she knew who was driving the police car.

"Yes."

"Is that person in this room?"

"Yes, it was Chief Nordstrom." She pointed at the man sitting with Elliot McCarver at the defendant's table. Derek's expression was changeless.

"How do you know it was Chief Nordstrom?"

"Adam had parked the car out on the road. When the party got busted, we ran through the bushes back to the car. When we came out, Mr. Nordstrom was leaning against the police car, a little ways behind us."

"How far away from you would you say he was?"

"Maybe twice as far as that wall." DeDe pointed to the back of the courtroom.

"And what time of day was it?"

"It was evening, but the sun hadn't gone down yet. It was shining on him. We could see him real plain."

"Did he say anything to you? Yell to you? Tell you to stop?"

"No. He didn't say anything," she answered with a distinct shake of her head.

"Would Chief Nordstrom have any reason to recognize you? Would he know you by name?" Schell asked.

"Probably. As part of a school-to-work program, I worked in the police department after class for a semester. The first part of the school year. I did filing and typing mostly."

"In other words, he knew where to find you if he needed to?"

"Yes. I suppose so."

Schell asked DeDe about her injuries. She said she'd spent nearly three months in the hospital in Parsons, including a month in the intensive care unit. She'd had six operations and would have probably that many more. DeDe said her doctors told her she might not get back the use of her arm. Reconstructive surgery was planned for her face.

He asked about her school plans. Most of her senior year she'd missed and couldn't graduate. She hoped to finish next year but the surgeries might cause more delays in her education. She'd initially planned to enroll at the technical college in Parsons after high school but that would have to wait.

When he was finished with his questioning, Schell thanked her and sat down. It was Elliott McCarver's turn.

"Miss Daniels," he began, rolling a pencil between his thumbs and forefingers as he approached the witness stand, "you and your friends had been drinking at the party that night at the reservoir, right?"

"I'd finished most of one beer. Teri and Jeremy were still on their first. Adam had just started on his second drink."

"Now, you knew that none of you were legally old enough to drink beer, isn't that right?" McCarver was leaning on the rail beside her.

"Yes."

"So you *knew* you were breaking the law?"

"Yes, I guess so."

"You guess so. And when the sheriff's officers showed up, you tried to run away, too. You knew *that* was also illegal, didn't you?" McCarver laid his head back, waiting for her to answer. His lips pouted forward and he chewed on the insides of his cheeks.

"I never really thought about it at the time. We just didn't want to get caught. If we didn't have to."

The lawyer turned his back on her and walked slowly along the rail in front of the jury.

"Miss Daniels, why do you think Adam parked the car out on the highway instead of in the park with the rest of the young people?"

"Lots of beer parties at the reservoir get raided. The police always block the road going into the park. Adam said that the last time several kids had parked out on the highway. When the cops showed up they managed to get away." She shifted slightly in the chair.

“Were other cars parked on the road on that night as well?”

“Yes.”

"This time, though, Chief Nordstrom was waiting out on the road?"

"Yes," was again her answer.

"Why didn't Chief Nordstrom pursue any of the other cars? Didn't any of them try to flee?" McCarver pressed.

"We were the first ones out to the road. The first ones to leave."

McCarver wheeled around and looked at her sharply.

"Have you ever used illegal drugs, Miss Daniels?"

"No!" The kink in the other side of her mouth showed her contempt for what she viewed as a foolish question.

"You weren't doing any drugs the night of the party?"

"No, of course not! I told you I'd had part of one beer!" She looked quickly at Del Schell, then her parents, and back at McCarver.

"Did any of your three friends do any drugs that night? Did they have any drugs with them?" he pursued.

"Not that I was ever aware of. As far as I know, I don't think any of them ever used drugs. I don't hang out with kids who do."

Press was beginning to visibly bristle at the line of questioning. He could sense temperature changes on either side of him as well.

"Did you throw anything, or did you see anyone throw anything down as you were running away?" McCarver kept after her.

"No! We threw our beers down but that was all."

"Did you throw anything, or did you see anyone throw anything out of the car as you were driving away from the police officer?"

"No, nothing!"

McCarver changed his tack along with his direction, now pacing slowly in front of the judge's bench, his hand rubbing his forehead, perhaps trying to start another notion moving inside it.

"What does your father do for a living, Miss Daniels?"

"He owns a small engine repair shop."

"Got health insurance, does he?"

"Yes, some."

"Does your mother work, too?"

"Yes, part-time in the school cafeteria."

"Does she get insurance, too?"

"I don't think so. Just what my father has."

"I bet your hospital bills are pretty high, huh?"

"Yes."

"Do you know if your dad's insurance covers all of them?"

"I don't think so. I'm pretty sure it doesn't, actually."

"How are your folks gonna pay off all those bills, do you know?"

"I don't know. They don't talk to me about it much."

"When did they first talk to you about the accident? When did they talk to you the first time about what happened?"

"I don't know the exact date. It was sometime after I woke up in the hospital. They told me that my friends…that the others had died."

"Did they try to help you remember? Give you any details?"

"They asked me what had happened. What I could remember." She glanced at her parents directly for the first time. "They didn't push me much. They knew it hurt a lot to think about it, especially at first."

"Did they ever suggest any aspects of the accident? Maybe tell you that you should say the car was forced off the highway?" McCarver was staring at her with the semblance of a glare.

"Absolutely not!" she cried. "Everything I've said is exactly what I remember. It's what happened!" Her lips were trembling and tears were just behind her eyes.

"Miss Daniels, didn't your parents suggest that, if you said Chief Nordstrom forced the car off the road, you might be able to get some money to help pay off those awful hospital bills?"

Del Schell objected to the questioning, charging that McCarver was badgering DeDe and trying to put words in her mouth. The judge agreed.

"This is a criminal proceeding, Mr. McCarver, not a civil lawsuit."

"I'm simply trying to establish a motive for lying, Your Honor." McCarver returned to his chair, stretching out lazily and tossing the pencil onto the table. "No further questions at this time."

DeDe was dismissed and threw a tearful and angry stare at Nordstrom's lawyer as she walked slowly in her uneven steps toward her parents.

After admonishing the jury not to discuss the case or any of its details with anyone, the judge adjourned the trial until nine the next morning.

McCarver stood gathering papers into his briefcase as the courtroom emptied. Beside him, a polar glare from Nordstrom followed Press out of the room. The glare ignored the presence of any others, designating the newspaper publisher as solely responsible for all of the ex-police chief's troubles.

That night the Williamses, Moores and Kelsos had a quiet dinner at the restaurant next to the Super 8. Wally and Veronica Daniels chose to take their daughter elsewhere to eat. Press figured they didn't want to talk about the trial. Neither did anyone else.

"I thought DeDe did fine today," Marie Kelso said shortly after the trio of pairs was seated. There was a brief acknowledgement in the form of nods and grunts and the subject was changed. Discussion was light and of little consequence during the rest of the meal. The families had no strong social ties and little of mutual interest to discuss. There was only the accidental bond of tragedy that held them and dinner ended without desert or after dinner drinks. The couples went quietly back to their rooms.

"I'll be so glad when this whole blasted thing is over," Press sighed as he yanked his tie off and flung it over the back of his suitcase. He grabbed the TV remote and surfed through the cable channels while Abby called to check on the girls and report on the day's happenings.

"The girls are fine," she said as she replaced the receiver. "They're curious, of course, about what's going on." Abby went into the bathroom and closed the door, and Press tuned the TV to a news magazine program.

When she came out she had on a white terrycloth robe over her blue summer nightgown. Shoes off, Press was sitting against the headboard of one of the queen-sized beds, both pillows under his back. Abby grabbed a pillow off the other bed and curled up beside him, her head snugged against his chest. She draped an arm across his waist.

"I wonder what's going to happen tomorrow," she said through a yawn.

Press was gently massaging her back.

"I don't really know what order Schell is going to do things in. I know he's going to call on me sooner or later. Maybe Barry, too."

Forty-five minutes passed and the network feed switched to the local news on the Avery affiliate. Abby was asleep. First came reports on a house fire and funds needed from the city to continue providing lifeguards at Avery's three public swimming pools. Those were followed by a brief story about the former Fremont police chief going on trial for negligent homicide in the deaths of three teenagers who were fleeing from a drinking party that police had raided. The account showed video footage of DeDe testifying, as well as a panning view of the family members and a prolonged clip of a stoic Derek Nordstrom. The reporter's voice recapped DeDe's testimony over the video. He added a lot of emphasis on the underage drinking that took place, along with special note of the defense lawyer's attempt to bring the issue of money into the trial.

Something about the reporter's voice irked Press and he turned the TV off. Maybe he heard more vocal emphasis in places and maybe he didn't. Press knew he had biases and maybe he imagined more to the television account than was there. But to him, it was reported as though the matter lacked any meaning beyond inconsequential; that the parents had little cause to be upset over the deaths of their children. The guy, Press thought, treated it just like another Hollywood-type cops and robbers chase.

He eased Abby's hand back to her side and got out of bed. After outing himself from his trousers and shirt, Press sat down at the small writing table and quickly paged through the free copy of *USA Today* that the hotel had provided. Unable to concentrate on more news, he dropped the paper into the wastebasket and went into the bathroom. When he came out, Abby had curled herself and her pillow onto her own side of the bed.

He turned the lights off and crawled in beside her but, spent as he was, sleep did not visit him soon. Press could not keep his mind from again traveling around McCarver's suggestions and innuendoes as he had grilled DeDe Daniels that afternoon. It must take a real different sort of creature to do that, he decided sourly. It seemed like nasty came as naturally to McCarver as a morning bowel movement. Press knew there certainly were innocent people who needed defense lawyers. Yet he couldn't understand how the right to a fair trial could include trying to make truth elastic and stretch it so out of proportion till it was almost beyond recognition. Some of McCarver's comments hinting that DeDe was lying were, themselves, a very near neighbor to blatant prevarication in Press' view.

When sleep did come, it was not restful.

The trial reconvened the following morning with the cast of characters seeming to have assigned seating. The only noticeable difference was the change of clothes for all but Elliott McCarver, who either had on the same rumpled suit or all his suits were rumpled the same and the same color. DeDe Daniels and her mother were also on hand at the start, seated prominently in the first row for all the jury to see.

The proceedings opened with the district attorney calling on an expert from the state crime lab to reconstruct elements of the crash scene. The man, Emory Thompson, testified that rubber samples taken from the skid marks matched the tires of both the Kelso vehicle and the police chief's squad car.

"Can you tell which set of marks was made first?" Schell asked.

"The tracks from the squad car appear to have been made before those made by the other car. As best I can determine, the other car skidded over the marks left by the squad car."

When asked why the Kelso car didn't collide with the squad car from the rear, Thompson stated that, in his opinion, the chief's car's brakes were never fully engaged. He hit them hard briefly but then continued on. The brakes on the Kelso boy's car locked up to avoid rear-ending the squad car and the driver lost control, skidding into the ditch where the vehicle rolled over.

Schell finished with the man and it was the defense attorney's turn.

"Mr. Thompson, is it possible that those first skid marks, the ones you attribute to Police Chief Nordstrom's car, is it possible that those tire marks could have been made some time well in advance of that tragic car crash? Days? Even weeks?" McCarver intoned.

"That would be strangely coincidental given the circumstances."

"But that's not what I asked, is it, Mr. Thompson?" McCarver stood facing the witness stand with his arms folded atop his ample belly, a grin on his face that was not intended to be amiable.

"I asked if it were *possible* that those tracks could have been made on some other day?"

"Possible, yes. Probable, no."

"Thank you, Mr. Thompson. I only wanted to know if it was possible." McCarver unfolded his arms and returned to his chair. "No further questions, Your Honor."

The district attorney's next witness was Bud Callahan, the county coroner. Callahan testified that each of the three dead teenagers had consumed alcohol but the level in the blood stream was well below the state's standard for intoxication. He said that, in fact, it was well below even the most rigid legal limits imposed anywhere in the country. When Schell asked if he thought the alcohol level was enough to impair their judgment, Callahan replied, "Not in my opinion."

When McCarver's turn came to question the coroner, the defense lawyer hammered hard at the fact that the teenagers *had* indeed been drinking, regardless of the amount.

"Don't you think, Mr. Callahan, that considering the young age and inexperience of these three young people, that even the least bit of alcohol would affect them differently than, say, a forty-five-year-old man who drinks a martini or two every evening?" McCarver pressed.

"Possibly," Callahan conceded. "Still, the amount of alcohol in the bloodstreams didn't indicate that in my mind."

"But you do agree that it's possible. Isn't that right, Mr. Callahan?"

"Possible, yes but…."

"That's all I wanted to know, Mr. Callahan. Thank you." McCarver gave an end-of-the-discussion wave and sat down.

The direction of the testimony proceeded similarly when the prosecutor called on the physician who first treated DeDe Daniels at the hospital in Parsons. He also stated that he didn't think the alcohol levels in the girl's blood stream were sufficient to cause impairment but, under McCarver's prodding, agreed that her judgment might have been altered due to her youth and inexperience with beer.

Press had sat through the morning's session in a fog of his own, a mist of the sort created if someone had left a hot shower running somewhere in the room. There was an awareness in him but not a connection to what was happening. He couldn't determine whether his head had spilled its thoughts during the night or he just had too many of them to focus on any one or a few. He was startled to fully awake when the judge adjourned the trial for lunch and Del Schell leaned over the rail and told Press that he would be the first to take the stand when they reconvened at one-thirty.

"Anything we need to go over before then?" Schell wanted to know.

Press worried the notion around a bit and finally shook his head.

"I guess I can handle it."

Press and Abby had sandwiches and sodas with the Kelsos and Moores at a corner luncheonette a block from the courthouse. They chatted unoriginally until Elliott McCarver and the Nordstroms came in and took command of a booth nearby. No more words were uttered and six sets of eyes ceased to focus beyond each other and the table in front of them. Had anyone noticed, the same restrictions were self-imposed on Derek and Alma Nordstrom and their lawyer. The three couples finished eating quickly and went outside. The sun was high and uninterrupted and they were all sweating in seconds. A half-hearted wind buffed them face first, just enough to muss their hair but gave no comfort. The six walked slowly back to the courthouse and loitered in the air-conditioned rotunda until nearly one-thirty.

"The prosecution calls on Mr. Preston Williams," Schell declared when the court was back in session.

Press gave Abby's hand a squeeze and moved to the witness stand. As he sat down he gave a single glance at Derek Nordstrom. The chief's expression was changeless as marble except for a barely perceptible narrowing of the eyes when he looked back at Press.

When he was sworn in and had formally given his name and occupation for the record, the district attorney's questions began aiming at the newspaper's role with the Fremont Police Department.

"In those months prior to the crash that took your son's life, Mr. Williams, how would you describe your relationship with Mr. Nordstrom?" Schell asked.

Before Press could reply, McCarver bellowed an objection.

"This line of questioning has nothing to do with this case, Your Honor."

Schell issued a soft snort of irritation before offering his reply. "It leads to the real motive Mr. Nordstrom had for wanting to pursue the car with those teenagers in it."

"Overruled. Proceed, Mr. Schell," the judge determined as she continued to chew on the tip of her glasses frame.

"Mr. Williams, again, can you describe your relations with Mr. Nordstrom?"

Press leaned forward, his elbows on the armrests and his hands clasped in front of him.

"I'd say strained at best."

"Why was that, Mr. Williams?"

With little vary to his expression or show of emotion, Press related the difficulty he and Barry had had in getting the department's incident records and that it had taken court orders to induce the chief's compliance with the state's freedom of information law. And there was also the matter of the paper's reporting on the chief collecting triple wages for working Sundays and holidays. In both instances the newspaper had run stories and editorials critical of the way in which Nordstrom was running the department.

"The chief didn't like the kind of attention he was getting," was the conclusion Press put on the telling.

"Did he ever threaten you as a result of your dealings on these matters?"

"In my office once. He called me a carpetbagging sonofabitch because I'm not from Fremont originally, and told me that I'd better watch my step."

"Did anyone hear him make that comment to you?"

"Probably my whole staff," Press said calmly. "He was pretty mad at the time."

"Did Mr. Nordstrom ever make good on the threat? Did he harass you or anyone close to you in any way?"

Press explained that the chief had personally written a speeding ticket to his editor, who lives on a lightly-traveled, two-block-long cul-de-sac. He wrote another ticket to his sports reporter who parked too near a fire hydrant while on a photo assignment.

"On several mornings the police chief was parked in front of my house when I left for work. He quit that when I took photos of him."

Schell went back to his table and retrieved some pictures from his briefcase. Press identified them as the ones he had taken and, after they were entered as evidence, they were shown to the jury. When they were finished, Press continued.

"After that he started parking on a side street a couple of blocks away. When I'd drive by, he'd follow me to work. My editor and photographer waited down the street one morning, and when he pulled out from the side street, they took videos of him following me. After that he followed me another time while I was jogging but no more."

Schell retrieved some photos from his briefcase once more.

"Can you identify these pictures?" he asked, handing them to Press.

"Yes, those are still photos made from the digital video Barry McGinn and Sport Henry took on my behalf." Press handed them back to Schell who had them placed in evidence before again giving them to the jury to view.

"Were there any other instances involving Mr. Nordstrom that you might view as intimidation or harassment?"

His look alternating between Del Schell and the jury as he spoke, Press told of the ticket Kate had received from the chief for allegedly crossing a yellow center line. He noted that she had been forced to take tests for alcohol consumption. The tests proved negative. And there was the ticket Nordstrom had given Jeremy.

"Nordstrom also picked up my son at another party and charged him with underage drinking but he conveniently forgot to give him a Breathalyzer test. When the test was finally administered and proved that Jeremy had not been drinking, Nordstrom changed the charge to possession, claiming he'd seen my son holding a beer. That charge was later dropped also."

"So, in your view, Mr. Nordstrom knew your son by sight and would have easily recognized him on the evening of the party at the county park?"

"There's no question in my mind."

Press answered a small battery of other questions without major points being inflicted. When Schell was finished, Elliott McCarver stood and ambled slowly to the witness stand, one hand on his hip and the other massaging the back of his neck. He stopped in front of Press for a long moment suspended in thought.

"Mr. Williams, would you say there are a lot of teenage boys in Fremont?" he said at last from under a sideways look at Press. The lawyer had a smirky way of looking at people, like he'd seen them before they'd put their underwear on and knew their most naked secrets.

"Not as many as there are in Des Moines or Omaha, I'm sure." The man irritated Press like a case of chigger bites. How the heck else are you supposed to answer a question like that? he kept to himself.

McCarver gave back a surly sort of smile. "I'm sure we can all agree on that, Mr. Williams. But wouldn't you also agree that there might be enough boys in Fremont that Chief Nordstrom might not know every one of them personally?"

"I'm sure he doesn't, but I do know that he knew Jeremy."

"Now, how can you know that, Mr. Williams?" he said with a condescending little turn of his head. He waved a hand in Nordstrom's direction. "How can we ever say for certainty what's in another man's head?"

"I know that I was in Mr. Nordstrom's presence, with my son, long enough that it would be nearly impossible for him *not* to recognize Jeremy." Press shifted in the hard chair, an edge given to his tone by his darkening mood.

"So you think your boy might be the only one Chief Nordstrom had any reason to come in contact with? Like there were so few other young lads that the chief ever dealt with that he just couldn't help but remember your son? Is that what you think, Mr. Williams?"

"The witness has already answered the gist of the question, Your Honor," Schell objected. The judge agreed and McCarver smirked as he leaned across the rail in front of the witness stand and stared at Press.

"By your own admission your son had a history at beer parties, didn't he, Mr. Williams?"

"I wouldn't consider *two* a long history. And I've already stated that the Breathalyzer proved negative after the first one," Press replied, trying to smother the simmer that was smoldering inside him.

"Those are the only two instance that you're *aware* of, isn't that right?" McCarver backed off a step and stuffed a fist into his coat pocket.

"I have no reason to believe there were more," Press offered flatly.

"But there might have been more instances that you weren't aware of. Isn't that so?"

Press rolled his eyes and replied, "I suppose."

McCarver turned away another pace, then turned to face the jury.

"Mr. Williams, you recall that time when your son was brought in during the first drug…excuse me, *beer* bust. You said that Jeremy wasn't given the Breathalyzer test immediately."

"That's correct." The words fell out as Press nodded.

"Do you know how much time elapsed between the time your son was picked up at the party and the time he was administered the Breathalyzer?" Elliott was leaning on the rail in front of the jury.

"I really don't know."

"Was it an hour? Two hours? Three?"

"It could have been. Like I said, I really don't know." Press echoed his glance from Del Schell to Abby to the jury.

"But it could have been awhile. Long enough for some of the effects of any alcohol consumed to have worn off?" The lawyer's eyebrows speculated higher and he turned to the jury to look for agreement.

"Your Honor, the witness is certainly not an expert in the use and effects of Breathalyzer tests," Schell protested quickly.

McCarver withdrew the question but looked at Nordstrom and all but winked as though he'd succeeded in sowing another doubt in the minds of the jurors. He walked slowly back to his seat and pulled the chair up to sit down and then changed the direction of his mind.

"Your boy ever do drugs, Mr. Williams?" McCarver asked with a pretense that the notion had just come to him as an afterthought.

Press could feel the hairs suddenly stiffen on the back of his neck. He felt like the skin on his face was suddenly too tight and his ears and cheeks began to sense an upward shift in temperature when he glared back into the lawyer's eyes.

"To my knowledge, nothing stronger than aspirin or Tylenol cold medication." The words managed to slip evenly through the grind of his teeth when he finally was able to get his mouth to work. He looked at Abby who was industriously chewing her lower lip.

"To your knowledge," McCarver reiterated with a turn to face the jury as he leaned one fist down on the table in front of him. "But can you say with absolute certainty that there is no way your boy ever used illegal drugs?"

"My son and I were pretty close. I think I can say so with all the assurance that any father can ever say about his son."

"But you can't be positive, though, can you, Mr. Williams?" McCarver asked from a sideways glance, his head bowed.

"No," was the angry response Press gave back, hardly able to squeeze it around the lump of rage that was balling in his throat.

McCarver sat down and the questioning stopped.

As Press walked by the lawyer he had an awful urge to knock the man backwards over his chair, but he knew it was an impulse he didn't dare yield to. Instead Press glared, wanting to beat him senseless telepathically, but the look was lost on McCarver.

Abby patted his leg and reached for his hand when he was back beside her. She tried to smile, but a smile did not go well with what she was feeling at the moment. His lips pushed tight against his teeth, Press took a long drink of air through his nose and let it out slowly.

48 The remainder of the prosecution's portion of the trial was consumed in small matters it seemed to Press. He let little of it in, hearing not much more than the shifting of bodies on hard wooden seats and the scuffing of dress shoes across the floor. Words came and went in varied notes as if the whole world was talking behind its hand. He wore his anger mood like a flannel shirt and the extra layer of warmth kept his mind off the goings on around him. Abby could see it on him and kept her comments brief as long as his mood lasted. She knew what was roaming in the gloom behind his eyes and it was best to let it pass in its own time.

When Elliott McCarver called the defense's only witness, Derek Nordstrom, Press yanked his attention back into the present. He could barely imagine what contortions the pair could use to extricate the chief from the judgment Press was sure Nordstrom was due, but he also knew that the truth was bungee cord limber in McCarver's hands.

Nordstrom wore a dark blue sport coat over a light blue shirt that was open at the collar. He had on gray slacks and, when he sat down in the witness chair, he tugged the seams up a bit for comfort, the white athletic socks showing under the cuffs. His first glance was at Press – a quick, cold one, their eyes locking for a moment with some vile message passed between them – and then his eyes moved only between McCarver and the jurors. He smiled a little but it was a feigned softness betrayed by his posture.

After soliciting the lawman's oral biography in police work and stretching to uncover some semblance of community service and church involvement, McCarver asked Nordstrom about the Fremont Police Department's presence at a beer bust at a county park.

"Our department and the sheriff's office often offer each other mutual assistance when there is a need for additional law enforcement presence," Nordstrom said evenly, looking directly at members of the jury. "The sheriff often asks for our help when attempting to make drug and alcohol arrests involving large numbers of suspects. Whenever those activities are in the northern part of the county, at least. We work cooperatively in trying to stop illegal drug and alcohol use in our community."

McCarver was pacing slowly in front of the jury panel. "Tell me, Chief Nordstrom, why were you parked on the county highway that night? Why didn't you enter the park itself with the other officers?"

"On a couple of recent similar operations, some of the participants in the illegal activities in the park had left their vehicles out on the highway. When the officers entered the park, a few of the perpetrators were able to escape. When I drove to the scene, I noticed one car parked on the road and decided to make sure no one got away this time." Nordstrom's expression was changeless as a doorstop as he spoke directly at the jurors.

"When you saw the four young men and women run out of the woods toward the car parked alongside the road, did you recognize any of them?" McCarver asked from his lane of pacing.

"Not immediately. A couple looked kind of familiar but I couldn't put a name to any of the faces. When I looked further I did decide that one of them was probably the Williams boy." Derek was leaning forward, elbows on the arms of the chair and his thumbs fidgeting behind the weave of his fingers.

The teeth were grinding in Press' mouth as he wiped a hand down the lower part of his face and shook his head slowly in Abby's direction. There was a noticeably audible snort from Wally Daniels on the other side of him. Nordstrom never let his eyes wander in their direction.

"What did you do then?"

"I immediately yelled at them to stop and started walking toward them."

"And what did they do?"

"They ignored my command and got into their car. As they began driving away, I went back to my squad car and started pursuing them."

"Did you have the lights and siren going?"

"Yes."

"And were you able to determine how fast they were going?"

"I followed them at speeds in excess of one hundred miles per hour."

McCarver changed his line of pacing to a path in front of the judge's bench and the witness stand. "Did you ever pass the Kelso vehicle?"

"No, Sir."

"But Miss Daniels claims that you ran them off the road."

"She's simply mistaken."

"Do you have any opinion on why she might say that?" McCarver asked.

"I can only guess that, because she was unconscious so long, her memory might be playing tricks on her," Nordstrom said with a shrug of feigned amazement. "Unless someone else put the notion in her head."

"Then how did the driver happen to go into that ditch?" McCarver paused and put an index knuckle to his chin to contemplate the issue again.

"I don't know. I saw the brake lights come on all of a sudden. The boy just lost control and swerved to the right. It caused me to brake momentarily to keep from hitting the car when he slammed on the brakes." Nordstrom made a feeble try to fit sadness into the slow shake of his head.

"Chief Nordstrom, that man from the state crime lab, Mr. Thompson…he said that your skid marks were made first. That the Kelso boy's car slid over your tire marks in a manner that might indicate you were in front of him and he tried to avoid hitting you. Do you know how that could be?"

Nordstrom leaned back in the chair, tilting onto his right elbow and looking past the jury as a man might be if attempting to guess the exact measure of the courtroom in cubits. "No, I don't. I looked at those tire marks myself and from all my years in law enforcement, I don't imagine how he could make that claim."

McCarver returned to the table and shuffled through some papers. After glancing briefly at a yellow note pad, he turned to face Nordstrom once more and sat on the edge of the table.

"Tell me, Chief Nordstrom, why did you choose to make such a vigorous pursuit of some kids who were merely trying to get away from a police raid on a beer party? Isn't the stiffest penalty they would face most likely a small fine?"

"Law enforcement officers pursue speeders, too," Nordstrom replied casually. "They seldom face more than a fine either."

"But was there anything more to your decision in this case?" McCarver pushed.

"Yes. I'd been given information that led me to believe that one of the occupants of the car was dealing in illegal amphetamines."

A small gasp chorused from the row behind the plaintiff's table.

"Which of the four young people was that, Mr. Nordstrom?"

"It was Jeremy Williams. We'd been watching him for several months."

"You're lying!" Press yelled. He immediately regretted the outburst but the words had escaped before his mind could disengage his mouth.

The hollow whonk, whonk of the judge's gavel echoed between the plaster walls of the room.

"There will be no more of that in my courtroom!" she said with a frown aimed directly at the newspaper publisher. Del Schell had turned and was gaping at Press also, his expression pleading for the exercise of self-control. The startled members of the jury were staring with a measure of disbelief.

Press wasn't sure if the crimson ignited on the front of his face from embarrassment or anger or both. Tears awash on her face, Abby tucked her hand inside his elbow in an effort to anchor his body and his words to the bench beside her. He looked back at the jurors with apology written in his eyes but unflinching conviction in the set of his jaw. Press dug his fingers into the front of the hard wooden bench on either side of him. A picture of Jeremy filled his father's head, the face on the picture held a look of horror at the accusation.

His head deployed smugly into the crook of his thumb and forefinger, Nordstrom stared directly at Press a moment with a ghost of a smile, a retaliatory light glinting from the back of his eyes that whispered "gotcha." Press took it in the same vein as nothing more than a posturing taunt from a journeyman pug whose finish would soon be the canvas, but it rankled him no less. He wanted ever so badly to tell Nordstrom to enjoy it while he could, that final round was coming to the bell and the former chief would be getting his own due in legal leather by the end of the week.

McCarver stared at the floor, seemingly counting his steps as he paced back to the witness box. "How did you come by this information, Chief Nordstrom?"

"It was an informant. I can't say who for obvious reasons."

"Did you find any illegal drugs in the car?"

"No, I think they got rid of them before they crashed the car."

"Why do you say that, Chief?"

"Because I'm pretty sure I saw someone throw something from the car as they were driving away."

"Hmmm." Fingers locked behind his back and head cocked up at a quarter angle, Elliott had stopped his pacing and rocked back and forth on his toes and heels. After a time he nudged his head in Press' direction and continued.

"Mr. Williams there testified that you were harassing him and his family over some things his newspaper had published about you. He obviously feels that the accident never would have happened if you weren't out to get at him though his son. What do you say to that?"

"His son was at a beer party, that's all. I had no way of knowing who might be there when the sheriff called for mutual aid to make the bust. As far as any tickets that were issued before that, I never wrote one that wasn't justified."

"What about the times he says you were waiting outside or near his home?"

"We'd had reports of prowlers in the area. I was just keeping an eye on the neighborhood."

The rest of Nordstrom's testimony was consumed in small details and ate up much of the remainder of the day. When McCarver finished his questioning, the judge conferred with the attorneys and adjourned the session until the next morning.

It was another long and somber night for Press and Abby Williams.

49 The next morning Del Schell began his cross examination with, "Mr. Nordstrom, what were your normal working hours?"

"Pretty much a usual forty hour week, I suppose." Nordstrom wore a shadow of a smirk on the face that looked from above his dark gray suit and dark blue shirt.

"Mr. Nordstrom, I want to know what days of the week you usually worked and what shift you took on those days." Schell was leaning on the rail directly in front of the witness.

"Tuesday through Saturday I worked days mostly. Sometimes, especially on weekends, I'd work four to midnight."

"Would you say it was unusual for you to work any night shifts?"

"Not at all. The department often has people on vacation or out sick. I filled in whenever necessary."

"But as the head of the department, would you say that manning radar traps is not customary in your normal line of responsibility?"

"No, I don't do that often."

Schell went to his table and retrieved some papers from a file and gave copies to McCarver and to the court clerk. "You know, Mr. Nordstrom, I've found some interesting information in the Fremont Police Department files since you've been gone. I went through your time sheets for the last year and found that the only times you worked nights, someone in the Williams family got ticketed or hauled in from a beer party or run off the highway. And the only times you were on duty early, the editor of the *Fremont Weekly Gazette* got a ticket or Mr. Williams happened to note you lurking around his neighborhood following him. How do you explain that, Mr. Nordstrom?"

Derek shifted in his chair and cleared his throat lightly. "Coincidence, I guess."

"Tell me, Mr. Nordstrom, how many tickets do you normally issue in a year for traffic violations?"

The chief shrugged. "I don't know. Quite a few I suppose."

"Quite a few, you suppose. Would you consider *four* quite a few?"

Derek squirmed a quick glance at McCarver. "I guess not."

Schell again fetched some papers from his desk and gave copies to Elliott McCarver and the court clerk. He showed a copy to Nordstrom as well. "Mr. Nordstrom, I have here copies of all the traffic tickets you issued in your last year on the police force, all *four* of them. Would you say it's more than mere coincidence that they were issued to Kate Williams, Jeremy Williams, Reginald Henry, the sports reporter for the *Gazette,* and Barry McGinn, the editor of the Fremont newspaper?"

For the first time in days a smile was beginning to tweak the edges of Press' mouth and he turned his lean on the bench toward Abby.

Nordstrom sat back in the chair and folded his hands across his lap. The rising irritation was narrowing his eyes as he stared at the prosecutor. "No, I'd say that was coincidence. That's all it was."

"Funny how coincidence in your mind can look so much like harassment to other folks," Schell suggested as he moved back to the prosecutor's table, a wry smile sliding onto his face. He stood between his chair and the table, staring at some scribbling on a yellow legal pad as if irked by his own words written there. The smile slid back off his face.

"You claim you saw someone throw something from the Kelso vehicle as they tried to leave the party. Did you ever look to see what might have been thrown from the car?"

"Yes."

"When was that?"

"The next day."

"Did you find anything?"

"No."

"Why didn't you look or have someone look that same night?"

"Too much confusion I guess, with the accident and all."

"Mr. Nordstrom, you're a trained law enforcement officer. In fact, the head law enforcement officer in Fremont. Aren't you trained to make decisions like looking for evidence at a crime or accident scene immediately?"

"We all make mistakes sometimes. I was upset because of the accident." Nordstrom shifted sideways on the hard chair.

Schell paused, the knuckles of his left hand pressed to his lips. "Did you search the victim's car after the crash?"

"No."

"Why not?"

"I assumed the sheriff's deputies did that."

Schell stepped away from the table and walked slowly towards the jury box. "That's a lot to assume, isn't it? I mean, I would think this would be a pretty big deal, catching someone with drugs. I would think a veteran police officer like yourself would be right on top of any opportunity to gather vital evidence."

"Like I said, I was upset over the wreck." Nordstrom's irritation was beginning to elevate the tone of his voice.

"So, did anyone in the sheriff's department contact you about any drugs found on the victims or in the car?"

"No."

“Had you even *told* anyone in the sheriff’s department of your concern that illegal drugs might be involved in this case?”

“No, I don’t think so.”

"You don’t *think* so.” Schell folded his arms across his chest and stared at Nordstrom. “So you have absolutely no evidence that any of these young people might have had any illegal drugs, do you?"

"All I have is what I saw. They looked darned suspicious!"

"They *looked* suspicious." The prosecutor looked at the jury and shook his head slowly before returning to the once Fremont police chief. "No one ever suggested that any of these kids had any illegal drugs, did they, Mr. Nordstrom?"

"I received an anonymous tip!"

"I thought you said it was from an informant?"

"Same difference!" Nordstrom growled.

Del Schell walked to the witness stand and leaned both hands against the rail, staring at Nordstrom. "You pursued four young people at speeds you admit were over one hundred miles an hour, you ran their car off the road causing three of them to die, and only because you wanted to get even with the newspaper publisher through his son, isn't that right, Mr. Nordstrom?"

"No, that's not right! It's a damned lie!" He spat the words out like gravel and gripped the arms of the chair, readying himself, it seemed, to get up and fling it at the prosecuting attorney.

"Badgering the defendant," McCarver objected and the judge agreed.

Schell backed off.

"Mr. Nordstrom, does your department have a policy concerning high speed pursuit of vehicles?"

Nordstrom nodded.

"You'll have to speak up, Mr. Nordstrom."

"Yes, it does."

"Enlighten us, will you? What does that policy dictate?"

"Basically, it says pursue with reasonable caution, get the license plate number, and radio for assistance."

"And does the county sheriff's department have a similar policy?"

"We copied ours from theirs."

"And does it say anything about running vehicles off the road?"

"Objection," McCarver shouted, lurching to his feet.

"Withdrawn," Schell retreated with a wave and the judge admonished the jury to disregard the question.

"Did you get the license plate number?" Schell asked as he rubbed an eyebrow.

Nordstrom said he did not.

"Did you radio anyone for assistance?"

Again, Nordstrom said no, that he didn't have time.

"But you pursued the Kelso car for nearly two miles. Surely your squad car was capable of getting pretty close to a family sedan in that distance." Schell propped his elbow with one hand and rested his bearded chin in the cup of the other as he launched a quizzical stare at the fired police chief.

"I was watchin' out to see what the driver was gonna to do. I had to think about safety first." The former chief finger-brushed a bit of sweat from under his lower lip.

The grilling went on for another twenty minutes with Nordstrom's discomfort growing more obvious at each of Del Schell's paces back and forth in front of the jury. The color had drained from the lawman's hawkish face and the surly confidence had sagged from his shoulders by the time the questioning ended. As the man walked back to the defendant's table, he looked directly at his wife for the first time in the entire proceeding. She was seated in the first row behind him, wearing a thin yellow dress and black pumps, her cast-iron gray hair knotted in a tight bun. She did not look up but merely continued to stare at the tissue she slowly twisted and shredded on her lap.

The rival attorneys wagered nearly all the minutes of the next hour and a half summing their own versions of the truth found in the proceedings. When they were done, the judge sent the jury members out to make their decision.

Press and Abby went to lunch with Wally Daniels, the Kelsos, and the Moores for the last time.

50 He waited for Abby to finish adding her signature to the documents and then Press slid them across the desk to Galen. In return, Galen pushed three checks toward his clients. Press let his eyes drink in the numbers on the checks for a bit and then handed them to his wife. He thought about smiling but couldn't bring it to his face. Leaning away from the desk, he took an extra amount of breath and let it flow slowly back past his lips.

"It's a lot of money and yet it's not," he said quietly through two fingers as he rested his chin on his hand, his elbow braced on the arm of the chair. "There's just no way to fix a dollar value on a son's life."

"I understand," Galen replied, "I do. About all that's possible is to see that Nordstrom pays the maximum for what he did to you. With all the jail time he's got coming and your monetary awards, I don't think you could do much more."

Press looked at Abby. He could tell from the way her lips were packed almost into her teeth that she was crying on the inside, even if there were no tears on her face. They were both mostly beyond crying outwardly any more. The ache would probably always be inside, he figured. It had been a long ordeal. The public portion was over but there would always be the private pain. That constant ache from something missing, a dead son.

"I know it's none of my business but do you have any immediate plans for the money?" Galen wondered, his voice floating softly across the desk.

Press shrugged a little and glanced at Abby. "Put the girls through college. Probably pay for a couple of weddings some day. We want to set up a scholarship fund at the high school in Jeremy's name. After that we just don't know. Some other charities we're looking into."

"Somehow I can't help but feel a bit sorry for Alma Nordstrom," Abby said through the slow shake of her head. She was still staring at the checks that she held spread out in her fingers. "How's she going to get through all of this?"

Derek Nordstrom would be spending at least eight years and probably more in prison as a result of his convictions for theft and negligent homicide. The couple's shares in ADN Properties, along with their home and, as it turned out, substantial investments, had been sold to pay the $1.1-million out-of-court settlements each to the Williams, Kelso and Moore families. County and city insurance had each paid another quarter of a million dollars to each couple. Press didn't know what financial arrangements had been made on DeDe Daniels' behalf. His cynicism rampant where thoughts of Derek were concerned, Press figured the investment money came from the profits of the former chief's thieving from the homes of dead people. One of the hundreds of thoughts that flowed like sheep through his wakeful nights was an attempt to find some way to use some of the settlement money to reimburse the families of some of those whose dead relatives Nordstrom had stolen from. He'd been able to latch onto neither a reasonable solution nor much sleep in his wonderings.

"I imagine she'll be all right," Galen offered. "I hear she's moved in with a sister. Somewhere back in Indiana, I think. They still had a pretty good chunk left after they liquidated their assets to pay the settlements *and* Elliott McCarver."

"If I were her, I think I'd have whatever's left either spent or in a Swiss bank account long before Derek gets out of jail," Press said grimly.

From Abby came, "I wonder if she'll divorce him?"

"Somehow I doubt it," said Perry, his eyebrows arched nearer the recession of his hairline. "Even after all he's put her through, she seems almost too timid to take a step like that. I get the feeling she's never had much of a life except to do his bidding."

"You kind of have to wonder how much she knew all along?" Abby mused some more.

"My experience has been somewhat limited, I'll admit," Galen said, "but I suspect spouses have a pretty good idea of what's going on in almost every instance like this one. She was just too insecure to question him on any of it, even if she wanted to."

"Do you think that applies to Sharon Hartley, too?" Press was curious in a somber sort of way.

"Yeah, I do," the lawyer replied. He tried to nod. "But at least she had the gumption to leave Wes when things came to a head."

"Still, she and her sister are both sitting pretty good." Press was looking out the window at the gray November with notions of somewhere far away in back of his eyes. "They still have half of ADN Properties between them. Do you think the Parker woman will ever be prosecuted over any of the real estate dealings?"

Galen wrinkled his nose as his head turned sideways. "I seriously doubt it. How do you prove that she fed Hartley the bypass information from her ex before Wes would have learned about it as mayor anyway? As far as the Gunderson place and the industrial park deals? All she has to do is claim that she just relied on Hartley's advice for investment purposes. No, whatever justice she gets, I doubt it'll be from the law. But any closeness she and Sharon ever had as sisters I'm sure is gone for good now."

Press hmmfphed and shook his head. "God, I wish we could figure out how they pulled off the deal on the Gunderson place. Blaine Peterson wanted to add that place to his for his son to run but Mrs. Gunderson wouldn't sell to him. Then Nordstrom somehow ends up with it."

"That, my friend, is one I doubt anyone will ever figure out. Neither the Nordstroms nor Susan Parker will talk. Sharon Hartley may not know all the details herself and Mrs. Gunderson is incapable of saying. Sure, if I were a betting man, I'd wager that Alzheimer's was already taking its toll on Mrs. Gunderson when the deal was forged. Nordstrom did her some favors and used his influence to con her into giving him the property outright. That would explain why there's no record of money changing hands. It would be perfectly legal unless Nordstrom used some undue influence of some sort through his position as police chief."

Galen backed his chair away from the desk and twisted his head atilt. "Look, Press, you've turned Nordstrom's world upside down and pretty much dumped it on him. You'll probably never get him spanked for every sin he's committed in his lifetime but you've come down on him hard. I suggest you try to let the rest of it go now. Take Abby on a nice, long vacation. Take the girls, too. Get away from all of this for awhile. Put the money in the bank. Invest it and get on with your lives. I know that's a lot easier said than done. Heck, it's a lot easier for me to say. I didn't lose a son. But you've both still got each other and the girls and a long life ahead of you. Try to start enjoying yourselves again."

Press and Abby looked at each other, a smile whispering into each of their eyes for the briefest of moments.

"Thanks, Galen," Press said as they stood to leave. "For *everything*."

Later, alone, Press drove out to the reservoir. He stopped along the way at the site where Jeremy had died. The skid marks had long since faded and all that remained to mark the tragedy were three simple white crosses on the embankment. One tilted slightly to the right. Press pulled onto the shoulder and took a moment to walk up the small hill to straighten it. The ground was hard and he tamped a couple of stones into the dead weeds at the base it to keep the cross upright. A few vases and jars that once held flowers were scattered about.

Press stepped back and stared briefly at the trio of crosses. His face buried in his hands, he cried long and hard one more time for Jeremy before getting back into the Buick and continuing on to the county park.

In the parking lot he angled the car alongside the row of boulders that were positioned beside the water to keep people from driving into the impounded river. The park was empty in shades of gray and brown. Even the picnic tables had been cached in the county garage for the winter. He sat in the car for a long time, thinking about all that had happened. He thought about his son and for one of the times tallied only in the countless notions and nightmares since Jeremy's death, Press wondered what he could have done differently. What could have preserved the young man's life? How could a newspaperman's delving into something so simple as a man getting hauled in for driving drunk turn something so tragic? How do you know when something that seems so relatively minor can destroy your life and family?

Press looked at the cheesecloth package on the seat beside him. He'd been thinking about this moment ever since the trial ended. He got out of the car and, taking the bundle with him, walked to the water where he set it on one of the flatter boulders and unwrapped the cheesecloth. The gun lay cold and gray against the rumpled cloth, which was long cracked with age. Opening the box of cartridges, Press somberly fingered a row of untarnished brass shells. Then he hefted the .45 in his right hand and pointed it aimlessly across the reservoir before slumping against the cold stone. For several moments he tap, tap, tapped the barrel mindlessly above his temple.

Lowering the gun, he turned the gun side to side. He cocked the gun a final time, then gently lowered the hammer again. Reaching back, with every ounce of energy he could muster, Press gasped in an extra surge of air and flung the weapon into the muddy waters of the reservoir. It took two turns but he emptied the box of bullets into his hand and threw them into the lake as well.

Press stood for a time, watching the echo of splash rings disperse across the surface of the water. When nothing more could be seen but the scuffs caused by the breeze on the lake, he wadded the cheesecloth and slammed it into a trash barrel on his way back to the Buick.

"PRESSING MATTERS"
November 12

It's been a year and a half now since my son died when the car in which he was riding was run off the road by former Police Chief Derek Nordstrom. Whatever justice the law may impose has been dispensed as best it can. But the question of whether any punishment is ever enough for causing a young man's life to be snuffed and a family torn apart –

that question will always remain. I still find it difficult to believe that the future will be anything but intolerable without my boy in it. If it weren't for the sadness and anger that still reside in me, I have come to wonder if I will ever be anything else but empty. Still, I have a wonderful wife and two bright, lovely daughters who have endured as much or more than I have. They deserve more of me. There is much of life left and I must find some means to put aside the emotional chains of the past eighteen months. As Thanksgiving Day approaches, I am grateful for the ordinary motions of life that keep me going. I will try to spread the comfort from those small efforts to those around me. Beyond that, anything I can offer is hardly profound. It is simply a fact that life goes on....

The End